Mrs Shim Is a Killer

Kang Jiyoung

Translated from the Korean by Paige Morris

doubleday

TRANSWORLD PUBLISHERS

UK | USA | Canada | Ireland | Australia
India | New Zealand | South Africa

Transworld is part of the Penguin Random House group of companies
whose addresses can be found at global.penguinrandomhouse.com.

Penguin Random House UK, One Embassy Gardens,
8 Viaduct Gardens, London sw11 7bw

penguin.co.uk

Penguin
Random House
UK

First published in Great Britain in 2026 by Doubleday
an imprint of Transworld Publishers

001

Typeset in 11.5/15.5pt Dante MT Std by Six Red Marbles UK, Thetford, Norfolk
Printed and bound in Great Britain by Clays Ltd, Elcograf S.p.A.

The authorized representative in the EEA is Penguin Random House Ireland,
Morrison Chambers, 32 Nassau Street, Dublin D02 YH68.

A CIP catalogue record for this book is available from the British Library.

ISBN: 9781529957518

Penguin Random House is committed to a sustainable future
for our business, our readers and our planet. This book is made
from Forest Stewardship Council® certified paper.

MIX
Paper | Supporting
responsible forestry
FSC
www.fsc.org   FSC® C018179

Mrs Shim Is a Killer

PART ONE

PART ONE

I

Shim Eunok

I am sharpening a knife. When I slide it into my electric sharp-ener and press the button, water flows from a tray, soaking the dull blade. The machine runs. Sparks fly off like flakes of dandruff. The honed edge, a sharp steel blue, seems to thrash under the fluorescent lights like a silver cutlassfish.

Flesh is tougher than a knife. Even a chef's knife used to slice into the tenderest of tenderloins will dull after a few days, causing a stinging pain in the wielder's wrist. The edged metal speaks to me. *I want to rest*, it says. But we still have a long way to go. The carving knife I'm whetting belonged to Mr Lim of Majang-dong, who had used it to slice open the bellies of live-stock for thirty-two years. It was two-thirds of a finger long and, at a glance, could look like an awl. He hadn't gotten rid of it, this knife that had stabbed him eight times in the upper leg, severed a main artery and left a deep scar on the inside of his thigh that looked like a giant snake had raked over his skin. Like a man who valued honour above all and had boldly set off down the path of revenge, every day at dawn Mr Lim honed that worn carving knife with a look of sheer determination. Only after the blade was so dull it could have been one of the blades in a shaving razor would he toss the knife into the recycling bin. Until then, the carving knife would never escape this rank, gamey hell.

With the knife fully sharpened, I waited for the butcher shop's owner to clock in. But by the time the mart opened and customers clutching leaflets and pushing carts were milling around inside, she still hadn't shown up. The day before, she'd sold a necklace containing more than seventy-five grams of pure gold to the jeweller on the second floor. It was obvious where she was headed to – the Cuckoo House. I sometimes got phone calls asking me to bring some seed money over there to get a game going, which was how I knew about the gambling den. The Cuckoo House always smelled of cigarette smoke and the sour tang of tangsuyuk. There, the owner would chew on pieces of fried pork that had gone cold over games of hwatu. So many thousand won bills stuck to the sweaty backs of her thighs.

'Eunok, didn't you hear? The butcher shop unni got hauled out in handcuffs yesterday.' This was coming from the bakery owner who sometimes dropped by the Cuckoo House with the butcher shop owner. 'She was finally on a winning streak when I guess the police stormed in. I heard she has to clear out the shop today. What'll you do now?'

The butcher shop owner often pretended she'd given into her husband's pestering and quit gambling, but as soon as he lowered his guard, she was back to messaging the bakery owner, and the two of them would disappear somewhere together. She'd always return smelling faintly of cigarette smoke and tangsuyuk. It seemed like the bakery owner had made it out of yesterday's mess in one piece. I, on the other hand, wasn't as lucky.

'I don't know. What *will* I do now?'

The shop shutting down meant I was now out of a job.

I took off my apron, chained up the handles on the deep freezer doors, and returned the keys. I wrapped the three knives I had brought with me to the job nice and tight in newspaper and tucked them into a nylon shopping bag. If I had to find a silver lining in all this, it would be that yesterday had been pay day. I opened the cash drawer and took out enough for that day's transportation. I hated the thought of losing even a single cent. *This is Shim Eunok,* I wrote in a note to the owner. *I'm taking out 2,000 won for today's transportation costs. I hope you get out soon so we can meet up around the Lunar New Year.*

I am Shim Eunok. An ajumma who turned fifty-one this year. A widow. Unemployed. And a mother.

I have a son, my dearest Jinseob, who's getting ready to return to university now that he's finished his military service, and a daughter, Jina, who gets good grades and is solid as a stone. It's been five years since my husband took his own life. He'd been suffering from diabetes since he was thirty-four. Still, he would rather die than eat brown rice. He started out on an oral medication but was taking high-dose insulin shots around the end of his life at age fifty-three. As his illness worsened, he had to have his pinkie toes amputated one after the other, and he lost his eyesight to macular degeneration. Surprisingly, he managed to hide the fact that he'd gone blind for nearly a year. It couldn't have been easy to go on living in the world off memory alone, but he spoke and acted no differently than he had when he still had his vision. Then one day he suddenly got in the car and drove off the main road, slamming into a new pub and killing himself in the crash. There was no way to know for sure that he'd gotten behind the wheel with the intention of ending his life. But the police ruled his death a suicide, meaning our family couldn't collect a cent of insurance money and had to sell off our own butcher shop to pay the pub for damages.

My son was in middle school when my husband died. As soon as he started university, he left it for the military, and from then on Jina started studying like crazy. There was no other word to describe the intensity with which she threw herself into her studies. She spent all day solving problems, comparing answers, erasing and repeating. Her little mouth was constantly moving as she memorized English words, and she converted the lyrics of a song called '100 Great Figures Who Brought Light to Korea' into timelines that she carved into her brain. I found work as a planner at the insurance company that hadn't done a thing to help our family, but without anyone to dependably sell to, even that didn't improve our situation. After rolling around from place to place like a dry little barleycorn, I finally found work at the butcher's corner in the mart.

I folded the two thousand won nice and neat and tucked it into my wallet. Seeing as I was now unemployed, I decided to walk. Shielding my eyes from the scorching sunlight with my hands, I passed the bus stop. I picked up a newsletter full of classified job ads. The trash collector must've already passed through, as there was only one copy of the newsletter left. Sometimes I wondered if the trash collectors and newsletter distributors had some sort of agreement going. To leave behind at least one so that jobless folks like me could find it, and so that we could all continue to coexist without ever seeing each other's faces.

I didn't feel like heading home. I was too scared to face the bills stuffing the mailbox full. I chased off a dozing pigeon and sat down on a bench, brought the newsletter up to my face and pushed my glasses up to read. The 'Help Wanted' section was jam-packed with listings. Jobs waiting tables, prepping side dishes, *looking for someone as dependable as an older brother to help out – Bora*, recruitment for loan workers, mass recruitment for telemarketers ... Well, when it came to waiting tables, the owners not only preferred Korean-Chinese servers who would work for cheap, but also rarely wanted workers older than them-selves. As for the job cooking side dishes, I considered applying, but the location was too far away. I didn't have the heart to give the Bora woman a call and ask whether she could use an older sister instead. And I had no idea what loan work entailed, but I noted the age limit for that and the telemarketing job, which asked for applicants aged fifty or younger.

Seeking housewives 40 and older to work, 3 mil per month guaranteed, 500% confidentiality bonus, Smile.

I was suspicious, having never heard of a place that would pay women over forty such a large salary, but it was the name of the company listed at the end that drew my attention. *Smile*. It was the nickname Mr Lim of Majang-dong had given me when I was first learning to handle knives. When I made a mistake, when I sliced my hand, when I dismantled a six-hundred-kilogram cow by myself – I smiled through it all. In general, I was the kind of person who smiled when I ought to have cried.

I took out my cell phone. My bill was overdue, so I couldn't use the phone as much more than a watch. It was a quarter to noon – only a few minutes until lunch. I counted the coins in my pocket and found a payphone. Slowly, I dialled the eight digits of the number listed in the ad and waited. After five rings, I was about to hang up, figuring no one would answer.

'Hello, you've reached Smile.'

It was the cheery voice of a young man.

'I'm calling about your Help Wanted ad. Is there anything I need to prepare to apply?'

I could faintly hear the young man shouting to someone, the sound muffled by what must have been his hand over the receiver. 'Boss, did we take out an ad? Should I just tell this person to come on down?'

Then he was back. 'No need to prepare anything. Just come by. If you head towards the police station near the intersection with all the gingko trees, you'll see a grey five-storey building. We're on the third floor. Room 301.'

Before I could respond, he hung up. I'd heard greetings being exchanged in the background before the line went dead. The intersection with all the gingko trees – that was a twenty-minute walk from my house at my pace and the perfect distance to consider the trek as exercise. Not knowing whether my ratty clothes would cut it for an interview, I stopped to look in the display window of a women's apparel store. My reflection in the glass showed me to be a textbook example of a country woman who'd just ventured up to Seoul from the boondocks. My green blouse with its worn seams, my lightweight 'refrigerator' pants. My nylon shopping bag with the mart's name crudely printed on the front. I was none too pleased to see that my hair, which

I'd just had permed last week, was too curly. I smoothed down the especially stubborn coils on the crown of my head and then went into the nearest stationery shop. Even though the man on the phone had said to just come by, it wasn't good manners to show up with nothing, not even a résumé, in hand. I bought a template and an envelope for three hundred won, borrowed a pen, and sat outside the shop under one of the outdoor parasols and wrote out my résumé by hand.

All I had for the Educational Background section was: Graduated from Yebong Middle School.

And for Work Experience: Ran the Saeng Saeng Butcher Shop, 2002–2013.

I considered adding some of my part-time jobs, but I wasn't sure whether to count how I'd floated from odd job to odd job like duckweed in a pond as work experience. In the end, my résumé came out to two lines. I thought about filling in the empty space with some of the brush pen drawings of orchids and bamboo that I used to do for fun in my school days, but I stopped myself, afraid that such doodles might be mistaken for a sign of dementia.

I bought a castella and some milk at the supermarket and, once I'd finished eating, slowly began my walk. With my hunger satiated, a sense of confidence I had never felt before had room to grow inside me. What work could possibly be harder than slicing open a huge animal's stomach? I tucked in my chin, determined. With every step I took, I could hear the knives in my shopping bag clanging against each other. I'd worried that if people heard them, I might draw suspicion, but everyone around me just kept right on. I gripped my shopping bag handle tight and decided not to worry so much about my surroundings. I was an ajumma, after all. Not a poor little girl or a young woman seeking opportunity or a cast-off old lady. The only person who was going to help me was me.

A little before one o'clock, I stood outside the grey five-storey building. An old security guard was nodding off when he saw me and saluted. I had never seen him before in my life, but he looked at me with fondness and swallowed a knowing laugh. It was better than mistaking me for a peddler and chasing me off, but I couldn't help but wonder whether he was also the sort of person who smiled when he wanted to cry.

I got on the elevator, but it didn't service the second and third floors. I pressed the button for the fourth floor, then waited. I looked in the mirror behind me and saw that white psoriasis was spreading at the corners of my mouth. I wet my finger with spit and wiped at it.

The building had two offices facing each other on each floor and thus felt cramped and filthy. Pebbles of gum and dried globs of spit had congealed and stuck to the stairs, and cigarette butts and dust bunnies rolled around like bales of hay. I did all kinds of gymnastics to dodge them as I went down to the third floor, where I found Room 301 right off the landing.

'Smile Private Detective Agency,' read the sign. A private detective agency – weren't they the same as those so-called errand centres? In movies and dramas, these were places that went digging into people's pasts and relied on muscle to carry out their unsavoury business. Not only did I feel like I'd wasted the three hundred won to write that résumé, but I also got the feeling that I'd signed my weak knees up for much more than they could handle. What reason exactly did a private detective agency have for hiring an ajumma like me? I was inclined to turn back and had even taken a step towards the stairs again when I heard a voice call out from behind me.

'Ajumma, starting tomorrow, throw in another yoghurt and probiotic drink.'

The door to the Smile Private Detective Agency office stood open and a man holding out an empty jjamppong bowl was shouting at the back of my head. He sounded like the young man who'd answered my call earlier.

'Oh, I – it's me, the one who called . . . I came by for the job interview.'

Why on earth did those words spring out of me? I could have just kept my back turned and pretended not to have heard. No need to reveal that I wasn't the yoghurt ajumma.

'Oh, right, from earlier. Please, come in.'

He dipped his head in greeting. Faint orange stains from the jjamppong broth coloured the corners of his shy mouth. As he'd instructed, I stepped into the office. The fusty smell of poor ventilation mingled with the smell of food. Instead of curtains, the windows were tinted black. I took in the decor – four desks and a leather sofa.

'The boss stepped out for a moment to brush his teeth. Would you like some coffee?'

I nodded, and the young man guided me to the sofa and disappeared. I would have expected big men to be sitting around playing hwatu or guzzling alcohol during the day at a place like this, but it was quite different from what I'd imagined. Each desk had a computer, and even though it was messy, the thick stacks of documents and plastic file folders made the space look like an ordinary office. Seeing as the young man had that close-cropped chestnut haircut and spoke in such a friendly tone, he didn't seem to be a gangster. I tucked the shopping bag behind me and began to look around the office. I heard footsteps approaching from the hallway. Then the door opened, and a short, middle-aged man in a light mix-and-match suit walked in. He was plump in the face and all around, and while he seemed magnanimous at first, looking past his glasses and into his eyes, he struck me instead as being cold.

'Boss, she says she's here for an interview.'

The young guy returned with two cups of coffee on a tray, passing by the older guy to set the tray down in front of me. The coffee wasn't in paper cups but sturdy mugs. The older guy dabbed at the wet corners of his mouth with a handkerchief. He picked up one of the mugs, and I saw that his knuckles were prettier than mine. Maybe a private detective agency wasn't as menacing a place as I'd imagined.

'A pleasure to meet you. My name is Park Taesang.'

Mr Park reached out for a handshake. I couldn't ignore his pale, slim hand and saw no choice but to awkwardly clasp it in my own.

'I'm Shim Eunok,' I said, handing him my résumé.

Mr Park blinked his heavy-lidded, deep-set eyes and scanned the paper. One minute, two minutes. He spent an awfully long time studying a résumé that only had two lines. Thinking he might be readying to lash out at me for submitting such a poor excuse for a résumé so shamelessly, my thoughts spiralled like the ridges on a walnut kernel.

'So you ran a butcher shop.'

For some reason, instead of replying, I feigned a smile. I could see the unassuming look on my face in the round mirror behind Mr Park. The freckles dusting my cheeks like sesame seeds seemed to give away the fact that I was dirt-poor and rather dull.

'You must know how to handle knives and other things rather well.'

I nodded. I wasn't as good as Mr Lim of Majang-dong, but I could slice and dice and was confident in my meat-cutting skills.

'Hey, Joongi, we still have the plastic knife from when we cut the cake, right? Would you bring it here?'

So the young guy's name was Joongi. He went over to the sink and seemed to be rummaging through a drawer for something when he pulled out a white plastic bread knife and handed it to Mr Park.

'If it's no trouble, would you mind holding this? Imagine you're cutting into a cow's ribs. Though, of course, I'm sure it would be better if we had a real knife.'

'Ah . . . actually, I have some!'

Even as I was wondering what on earth knives had to do with anything, I opened the shopping bag behind me and pulled out one of the big chef's knives. With the blade still sheathed, I imagined there was a commercial-grade cutting board in front of me and began sawing into the air, the tip of the knife pointed down slightly as though slicing into a ruddy, well-aged rack of beef.

'Raise the tip a little more. No, bring your arm up a bit. Yes, yes. That's right.'

Mr Park seemed entranced. I closed my eyes. In the thick darkness behind my lids, I tore tufts of fur from a huge black beast. Then I peeled back its pink flesh, the pungent odour of blood briefly grazing my nose before vanishing. The blade cut through the meat, pushed it aside, and dug right into the next piece. It was exciting, swinging the knife back and forth to a rhythm and beat. It gave me such strange pleasure to think that there was an audience willing to watch in awe as I did the work I'd always done on my own.

'That's enough. You may have a seat.'

My eyes snapped open, and I was back in that unfamiliar office. I returned the knife, now clammy with sweat, to the shopping bag.

Mr Park's face was flushed red. 'Thank you for honouring my request. It can't have been easy, considering we've only just met.'

He explained that, at first, the Help Wanted ad I'd seen in the newsletter was meant to recruit investigative researchers. There had been many applicants, but they were all housewives with no interest in running background checks on others, only concerned with earning some money to cover the costs of their own extramarital affairs.

'I'll make you an offer, point-blank. I'd like you to become a killer. Doesn't everybody have one person they hate enough to kill? If you decide to accept, Mrs Shim, you'd be able to help so many wronged people by fulfilling their most desperate wishes.'

The moment that strange word, *killer*, had sprung from his lips, I felt my underwear dampen as my bladder failed me for the first time in a while. My legs were trembling so much I didn't think I could stand. A killer. I couldn't believe such a job existed in real life. I knew he was serious. What his offer meant – what the people in this place must do – began to sink in, and I was fearful.

'I'll pretend I didn't hear that. My lips are sealed, so don't you worry. I'm really, really good at keeping secrets.'

I grabbed the shopping bag with quivering hands. I was scared that if I hesitated for even a moment, I'd become the next target for these people whose job it was to kill. I still had two kids to raise. I had to go home, turn off all the lights, draw the curtains, lie flat on my stomach and wait with bated breath. There was no way they would leave me alone, not when I knew the truth about them, what they did.

'Mrs Shim?'

Mr Park called out from behind me, stopping me in my tracks. The courteous 'Mrs' he used to address me didn't seem so sweet any more. Now and then, some of the employees from the mart's headquarters called me that. *Mrs Shim, I've told you so many times to make sure no water spills on the floor.* Or, *Mrs Shim, no matter how badly you have to go, you should use the restroom at lunchtime.* In my world, *Mrs* was even worse than *ajumma.*

'As I said before, we would like to offer you the position, Mrs Shim. We need some new blood around here.'

My feet were stuck to the floor. A single tear – or was it a drop of cold sweat? – dripped on to my shoe, leaving a lone speckle. Mr Park's tone when he said the word *Mrs* was unlike the tone of those full-timers from headquarters, which had always felt admonishing and pointed. When I turned to him, Mr Park was holding out a gold bar. I hadn't expected this little office to be home to high-value gold. Then again, in a world where paid killers existed, was a bit of gold really so hard to imagine?

'If you trade this in for cash, it's worth a little under seventy million won. There are two more of them in this safe. Handle this job well, and I'll give you one of these as your cut of the pay.'

Seventy million won. To earn that amount I would have had to work nearly ten hours a day every day for three years and not spend a cent. With that money, I could say goodbye to the days of not being able to pay the monthly rent – I could even *buy* a new apartment for my family. I could send my Jinseob back to university, pay off all the bills and taxes I had been putting off, and hire tutors for Jina. A seventy million won blessing – this was money that could make everyone happy if only I didn't have this petty sense of pride that was driven by guilt.

'You'll really give me that gold?'

Mr Park nodded.

I imagined my children, whom I'd barely managed to raise on my part-time earnings, going to lacklustre universities and working for lacklustre companies, roaming around from one city to the next and growing old as part-timers like me.

'Then I'll become a murderer,' I said. 'For seventy million won.'

Mr Park laughed. The young man next to him chuckled awkwardly.

'Mrs Shim, we prefer the term "problem-solver".'

I followed their leads and let out an uneasy chuckle. Birds of a feather and all that.

'Then we'll consider you hired. It'd be best to just use the knives you're most familiar with. As for your uniform, wear what's comfortable, just like you are now. Tomorrow morning at seven a.m. we'll come to pick you up at the address you listed on your résumé. We're thinking of having an all-day offsite training session. Oh, and there's a small per diem for taking part.'

Mr Park opened the safe and stuffed several fifty thousand won bills into an envelope. I didn't even have time to think about declining it before he was shoving the envelope into my shopping bag. The knives clanged quietly. It felt like the money weighed as much as a human life. On my way out, I acknowledged the security guard's sly smile and salute with a nod, then turned away from him with as blank an expression as I could manage.

The sun was still blazing. As soon as I opened the door to my apartment, I fell to my knees. As the sun began to set, I didn't even bother changing out of my clothes and went to lie down on the floor. I could hear the faint sound of the evening news coming from the television – it rang in my ears like tinnitus.

A little after ten o'clock, Jina came home. Her face was pinched with exhaustion.

'Mum, dinner.'

Without a word, I wiped down and set the kitchen table. Maybe it was because I hadn't fed her enough back when she was still growing, but Jina's shoulders were really narrow. I felt bad seeing the bone, smaller than a walnut, that protruded from the back of her neck.

'Jina-ya, I don't think I'll be home tomorrow night. Will you be all right?'

Jina ate without lifting her eyes from her vocabulary book. 'Why?'

I put some fish meat on her spoon. 'It'll be busy at the mart.'

'No matter how busy it is, a mart is a mart – why would you have to spend the night? Are you seeing someone?'

Jina was a clever girl. The mart closed at eleven, which meant it wasn't a great excuse for needing to stay out overnight.

'Seeing someone?' I scoffed. 'That's ridiculous! I got another part-time job, that's why. Serving food at a funeral hall. I'll iron three blouses and hang them up in your closet for you, so make sure you wear a clean one when you go out.'

I watched Jina's expression for any signs of doubt. She nodded. Right then, Jinseob came in and took a seat at the table.

'Mum, I'm going straight to bed, so just half a bowl for me, please.'

'They're working you hard, huh?'

Jinseob had started working part-time doing late-night deliveries and staffing a convenience store to pay for university. He looked rough.

'I'm tired from getting up so early.'

Jinseob took after his father, with his amiable eyes, slender build, and picky appetite. At the dinner table, his chopsticks kept finding the same one or two side dishes and nothing else.

'If it's too hard on you, quit. I'll work something out.'

'There's still time left to re-enrol, so don't worry. When I get paid, I'll handle it.'

The corners of Jinseob's mouth were rough and chapped. His hair, which went from sweat-soaked to dry to sweat-soaked again and again, hadn't been cut in so long that it completely covered the nape of his neck. My eyes stung from the smell of his pain relief patches.

Once the kids were asleep, I packed my bag. One old training outfit, absorbent underwear for incontinence, socks, a wide long-toothed comb, a skincare sampler, toothpaste and a toothbrush, some hardtack biscuits for when I was craving a snack, a glasses cloth, a cell phone charger, my cholesterol medicine, and the list went on. While I normally passed out the moment my head hit the pillow, that night I only managed to drift off briefly right around the time Jinseob was heading to work. I saw Jina off to school and checked the gas valve several times before finally leaving. I was standing outside the apartment holding my bag when an idling silver sedan gave a short honk of its horn.

'Oh goodness, were you waiting long?'

I had come out at seven o'clock on the dot, but they also seemed to have rushed over.

'We just got here, too.'

Mr Park was in the driver's seat. In the backseat, the young guy from yesterday was lying down, completely knocked out. I stowed my bag underneath the dashboard and climbed into the passenger seat. It was my first time in a car since my husband had died. With the ease of a veteran driver, Mr Park brought us out of the city. He kept to a single lane and didn't slam on the horn or try to pass anyone. I wondered whether maybe a long time ago Mr Park, like my husband, might have gotten into a horrible accident. Maybe he had survived by some miracle and now lived his life in this firm, unyielding way to prove something.

At some point, we pulled up to the spacious yard of a vacation home in Yangpyeong.

'Mrs Shim, you can get out here. I'll bring in your bag.'

Though they were a lot younger than me, I was uncomfortable with the fact that I would be sharing a house with men. But they treated me like their mother or a much older sister, with a familiarity to their actions and words.

Once he unloaded the bags, Mr Park grabbed a cushion the size of a person from the trunk and propped it up against the wall inside. He showed me how to slice its belly in a single stroke.

'Mrs Shim, a person is different from a cow or a pig. You might think only ignorant guys with gangster backgrounds become killers, but that's not true at all. A killer is a doctor minus the licence. When I was first learning to wield a knife, I started by studying anatomy. You already have the basics down, so I'm a bit more comfortable starting you out with this.'

Judging from his build, Mr Park looked like he would be a bit slow in his actions, but he caught his breath and fashioned his face into an expression of pure calm before nimbly grabbing the knife and, in the blink of an eye, tearing a slit in the big cushion's belly. The well-honed blade easily tore through the polyester material. It was like dipping a hand in water, like soap bubbles floating away on the wind. The cushion remained standing for a moment. But as soon as Mr Park turned around and disappeared into the kitchen, it fell forward, white cotton spilling everywhere. Joongi told me that Mr Park's skills were so refined that he'd even gotten recruitment offers from Japan.

'This is different from Sabaki.'

Sabaki was what we butchers used to call the act of deboning. Mr Park's skills were of a different nature than Mr Lim of Majang-dong's. Dismantling a dead animal according to its usefulness was nothing more than following a formula like a skilled factory worker. Depending on the situation, I might switch knives, and if I hit a wall, I might work together with a junior assistant to remove the fascia around the muscles or organs and scrape out the tendons. But as a killer, I would be alone from start to end. I couldn't swap knives midway through or bring in colleagues for backup if I found myself short-handed.

I watched in awe and fear. As if he'd picked up on it, Mr Park flashed me a smile.

'I bought some groceries, so let's eat before we continue.'

We cooked our meal together. Joongi washed the rice, and

Mr Park blanched the soybean sprouts. I boiled doenjang broth with spinach leaves and seasoned the sprouts with just a dash of salt. I made kimchi stew with pork shoulder, seasoned some big chunks of onion and cucumber, then stir-fried some beef brisket with mung bean sprouts. With three spoons reaching in for more and more of the kimchi stew, the pot was emptied in a flash. Since none of us drank or smoked, we downed five bottles of orange juice while listening to Mr Park's rambling tales of heroism.

That night, I had a dream I was standing in the butcher shop without a knife, at a loss for what to do as customers teemed around me. Three kilos of front hock, twelve hundred grams of ground meat, five kilos of boneless ribs. I had to sell the meat, but I couldn't, and as I stood there, flustered, the door to the shop quietly opened and in walked my dead husband. He didn't look emaciated like he had in his later years, but was instead his young, healthy self. He bore a striking resemblance to Jinseob as he elbowed past the other people in the shop and made his way to me. Dazed, I reached out my hand to him. I wanted to call him by his old nickname, Jina appa, but the words wouldn't leave my mouth. He smiled gently as though he already knew what I wanted to say, then reached into his jacket pocket and handed me something. It was a tiny knife, no longer than a segment of my finger, so small it wouldn't have been able to slice into a choco-pie, let alone meat. I accepted the knife, and even in my dreams, I shouted cruel accusations at him. The knife grew bigger then, and suddenly it was the length of two finger segments. I shouted at him again. This time, the knife grew as tall as my palm. Thinking that now it might be large enough to slice meat, I was going to scream at him again when my husband said: *Eunok. Let's slice some fruit with that instead. I hate the smell of meat. What will the kids learn seeing you do this? Let's stop with the knives.*

I bolted up in bed, a seething rage welling up inside me. My husband was picking a fight with me, looking down on me for trying to make a living when he'd never once in his life helped me to do so. I didn't deserve to hear him blaming me for how I was raising my children when he'd shirked all responsibility and abandoned me for the other side. Him telling me not to do something made me want to do it all the more.

I spent the entire training session learning from Mr Park how to stab people, how to sneak up on them, how to tell a person I should kill from a person I shouldn't. I diligently took notes in the memo pad I'd gotten when I worked at the life insurance company. I made slight, subtle changes to the terms as I wrote: *client* became *customer*, *target* became *meat*, *murders* became *cuts*, *murders-for-hire* became *sales*, and *investigative research* became *purchases*. I had to be careful to avoid any unfortunate incidents that might draw suspicion or tip off my kids.

My first client was a man with one eye. He was in his early sixties and wore a ring with a huge amber stone on a thick gold chain around his neck. As soon as he came into the office, he told Joongi to fetch him some green tea instead of coffee and a pack of Esse Change cigarettes. He ignored me and sat down on the sofa, spreading his legs wide. The eye he still had was cloudy, just like my husband's had been.

Mr Park remained standing and introduced me. 'This is Mrs Shim Eunok. She'll be handling your case.'

The one-eyed man looked disappointed to learn that the

killer he was hiring was not only a woman but also a sluggish old ajumma at that. Just then, Joongi returned with the bottle of green tea and the cigarettes.

'But why waste this young one's talents and hire *her* of all people?' the one-eyed man murmured, gesturing at Joongi and lighting a cigarette. Joongi hurried to turn on the air purifier.

'Please entrust this task to her this once,' said Mr Park. 'With the Smile Agency's life on the line, we'll find a smooth solution to your problem.'

The one-eyed man sipped his tea, then shook his head.

'This is the sort of thing there's no going back from. If she were to slip up, who would end up in jail?'

Mr Park took out a sheet of paper and wrote something on it, then handed it to the one-eyed man.

'Look,' said Mr Park. 'We pride ourselves on being the best at keeping secrets. Joongi – that kid isn't ready to kill anyone yet. Mrs Shim has been in the field for a long time. She's a real pro. Mrs Shim, grab a knife, would you?'

I stood and grabbed one of the knives on the table. Just as Mr Park had taught me, I raised the knife slightly and found my balance, getting lower as though I were about to stab a person right between the ribs.

'Most importantly, Mrs Shim won't stand out to anyone. She'll be able to slip in undetected. I mean, how is a man supposed to kill a jjimjilbang owner, a woman who spends the whole day in the women's bathing areas?'

He had a point. The one-eyed man had ordered the hit on a woman who owned a bathhouse. She was apparently his ex-wife. They'd lived together under the same roof for thirty-three years, but now she was getting ready to emigrate with her new husband and was encouraging their son to slowly eat away at the one-eyed man's fortune. I couldn't honestly say that this alone was an offence punishable by death, but it was hard for me to turn down my first-ever client.

The man closed his eye, thick brows knit in concentration. Suddenly, he made an OK sign and stood up.

'Well, as long as justice is served, I guess it makes no difference whether an ajumma is the one serving it. Let's do this.'

The rest of us let out sighs of relief.

After the one-eyed man was gone and we could all breathe easy again, I asked, 'What was that paper you gave him earlier?'

Joongi hurried over to me and whispered, 'It's what we call a suicide pledge. It's a promise that if we're ever found out, all of our company's employees will take our own lives on the spot . . . as a way to destroy evidence.'

My eyes went wide, and I turned to Mr Park. He'd been staring blankly out the window for a while, watching as the one-eyed man disappeared.

'That gold bar includes a life insurance bonus,' Mr Park said. 'If anything goes wrong, it will be sent to your children.'

'You're telling me this *now*?' I shouted, swallowing the tears that were threatening to spill over. 'I would never take my own life and leave my children behind!'

'Only company executives and full-time staff are included in the pledge. You're a freelancer, Mrs Shim. We couldn't possibly include a suicide pledge in your contract when you don't even receive employment insurance benefits.'

With that, Mr Park squeezed some paste on to his toothbrush and headed to the bathroom.

This was the first time I had ever benefited from being a

contract worker. I avoided Joongi's eyes – the eyes of a full-time employee – and went to hide in the office pantry.

I got straight to work. Every day I dropped by the jjimjilbang run by the one-eyed man's ex-wife. The place was described as a jjimjilbang, but it was more on the scale of a hot springs resort. There was an outdoor swimming pool on the rooftop, a room where it snowed, an amethyst sauna room, a germanium hot bath, and several other kinds of baths and saunas, a dozen areas in total, each the size of a sports field. I recognized the woman sitting behind the counter for the women's baths right away. Her face matched the one in the photo the one-eyed man had shown me. She was Yoon Heeja, the ex-wife.

'Oh goodness, I'd thought your brows were tattooed on, but I don't think they are?' I said, approaching the counter. 'Those are real million-dollar eyebrows you've got there.'

The plump woman, who was doing her nails, looked delighted at the compliment.

'This is actually semi-permanent makeup, but no one ever seems to notice. Why don't you give it a try? The unni over there doing threading learned how to do it properly over in Nonhyeon-dong.'

Studying her own brows in a hand mirror, Yoon Heeja smiled, satisfied. I praised her almond-shaped nails, the taut skin on her neck, and her amazing business acumen, then bemoaned my own lowly circumstances and shabby appearance. Heeja's eyes lit up with a sense of superiority.

'I should get going now,' I said then. 'It's around the time my daughter gets home from school. I'd like to try that permanent makeup or whatever it's called, too. Please introduce me when I come by tomorrow, would you?'

After chatting up Heeja, who seemed disappointed to see me go, I left the jjimjilbang. The next day, Heeja took my hand and led me grudgingly over to have my eyeliner tattooed on, and afterwards, she gave me some pumpkin sikhye to drink on the house. We chatted endlessly about Hyun Bin and Gang Dong-won, BTS and Na Hoon-a – all the sexiest men of this generation. Then we went into the amethyst sauna room and napped. The day after, I scrubbed her back for her, and the day after that, I lugged over some of the mul kimchi I had made at home for her to try. After about a month, Heeja started calling me her younger sister.

'Unni, do you ever have a day off?' I asked her.

I needed to seize on a moment when Heeja was alone, but she never seemed to rest.

'I take exactly one day off a year,' she said.

'When is that?'

Rubbing yoghurt on her face, she grinned. 'Tomorrow.'

'What's happening tomorrow that you'd close up shop when business is booming?'

'It's my birthday. I'm going to call up my family and friends and throw a little party on the rooftop. You want to come?'

At last, D-Day was nigh.

'Sounds like a day for only your closest friends – is it really OK if I'm there?'

'Of course – you're my BFF nowadays. Come by and have fun. We'll even get the grill going.'

I waved goodbye to Heeja with a warm smile and left the jjimjilbang. A cold sweat shone on my forehead, and my legs were trembling too much for me to take the subway. I caught a cab to the office and held myself together until I stepped inside, at which point all the tension suddenly left my body and I collapsed into my seat.

'Mrs Shim, what's wrong?' Mr Park rushed over to help.

Only after I'd had a sip of water and Joongi had given my arms and legs a massage did I finally manage to speak and tell them of my worries.

'Stay calm,' Mr Park assured me. 'As long as everything goes according to plan, you'll be fine.'

The plan he mapped out went as follows: I would attend Heeja's birthday party and act natural. Afterwards, as the guests began to trickle out, I would pretend I was leaving, too, but instead hide in the empty jjimjilbang. Once Heeja was alone or headed to the bathroom, I would come out of hiding. Then, using the knife I would have at the ready, I would stab her. On the off chance that there were witnesses or that she didn't die immediately and managed to scream for help, I was to call Mr Park right away. He said he would handle things from there.

When I got home, I didn't dare look my kids in the eyes and made an excuse about body aches to head to bed early. I dreamed I was dodging knives flying at me from all directions. In the morning when I woke up, I had the strange, unsettling feeling that the dream had been a premonition, and my hands trembled non-stop as I brewed myself some coffee.

'Mum, I feel like you've been going to the bathhouse every day lately. You even got your eyeliner tattooed on. Very suspicious.'

Jina had been on break since a few days earlier, but she still went to her campus every day. I was thinking I should buy her some ribeye once I sold off that gold bar, dissolving my anxiety in the hot coffee water.

'I started working at the jjimjilbang, that's why. I'll be home a little late today.'

I found the old ivory two-piece dress I had worn for each of my kids' graduations. Then on second thought – what if blood splattered on me? – I changed into a black sundress and slipped my newly sharpened knife into a fake alligator-skin handbag.

When I got on the town shuttle bus headed for the jjimjilbang, the driver, a familiar face by now, greeted me with a nod. I gave him a light nod in return, then found a seat and turned to stare out the window. Mr Park was driving in his car alongside the bus. The reminder that I wasn't alone quieted my nerves.

When I got to the jjimjilbang rooftop, a crowd of people were cutting up grilled meat. I approached Heeja and stuffed an envelope containing one hundred thousand won into her pocket.

'What's this for?' Heeja said. 'You didn't have to bring anything.'

'I didn't know what you'd like, and anyway, it's no more than the price of a cheap bottle of essence.'

Heeja made a big show of proudly waving the envelope around. Just then a greasy-looking man in his forties appeared from out of nowhere and wrapped his arm around her shoulders.

'Say hello, honey,' Heeja urged him. 'This is Shim Eunok – she's one of my regulars. We even share a hometown. She's a lovely lady.'

The man nodded at me flatly and said hello.

'This is my husband. He may look like a player, but he runs an IT company in the Philippines. Seems like he's making quite a bit of dough these days.'

Heeja had leaned in close to whisper in my ear, then cackled at herself, clearly tipsy.

IT, my foot. He probably ran an illegal gambling site. I swallowed this thought and slowly scanned the rest of the rooftop, searching for Heeja's son. A guy in his early twenties leaning on the railing caught my eye. His eyes were nearly identical to Heeja's, and he was smoking an e-cigarette with a bored look on his face. He didn't look like the opportunist he'd been made out to be, a schemer who had taken advantage of his father's worsening vision to syphon off his shares in a bid to take over his company. It was always the parents who had problems in cases like this. What fault could possibly lie with the kids?

People gleefully partook in the barbecue, then grabbed a microphone with the echo effect dialled up and sang old songs they knew so well that they didn't even need the lyrics and afterwards splashed around a bit in the swimming pool. While all this was happening, a few guests who had gotten completely plastered left and headed home. Once about half of the twenty or so guests were gone, I stood up quietly and pretended to make my exit.

'Unni, I really enjoyed the food. I'll get going now.'

Heeja's face had grown red as a tomato. She pulled me into a hug and planted a kiss on my cheek.

'Of course, I'll see you tomorrow,' she said. 'Let's sober up over some malatang.'

I grabbed my heels from the shoe rack and made like I was heading out, then went one floor down to hide in the amethyst sauna next to the bathroom. I closed the door, but the roaring voices and thudding music from upstairs resounded in my body like a heartbeat. I just had to wait for their noisy celebration to end. In the dark, my phone buzzed, making my whole body tremble. It was a Telegram message from Mr Park:

'All clear?'

'Clear!' I replied.

It was well after eleven o'clock when all the guests finally left. I tried to make out what was happening on the other side of the frosted glass.

Heeja was coming down the stairs.

'Honey, I need to use the bathroom, so could you clear away some of those dishes?'

Her sleepy voice hummed through the walls. The slap of her slippers drew closer to the bathroom. I opened my handbag and took out the knife. Even in the dark, the blade emanated a deep blue aura. I swallowed hard and carefully opened the door. The creaking of the hinge rang out. Heeja had just grabbed the handle on the bathroom door when she turned around.

'Who's there?'

She moved towards me. I wanted to close my eyes, but it was too late for that. Heeja's gaze fell on the knife in my hand.

'Eunok, dear? Why are you . . .?'

There was no straying from the plan now. I approached her, slowly, and pulled Heeja into a hug. Then I bit down on my lip and thrust the knife into her.

'Unni . . . If only you'd tried living like a decent human being.'

The butcher knife I had painstakingly honed just that morning dug into the tight, snug space between the ribs. The handle was the only thing between us, joining me to her. Just as I'd learned from Mr Park, I gripped the knife and slightly turned the hilt clockwise, then slid the blade right out. Her knees bent,

Heeja fell backwards. I didn't need to double-check – she was dead. A slaughterer could sense these things. The same way a clock whose battery had run its course would suddenly stop ticking one day, Heeja's heart had ceased its beating. I put the knife back in my handbag. Then I took the stairs that led outside. Across the street, I spotted Mr Park's car sitting with its hazard lights on.

'Mrs Shim!'

I gave them a nod, my eyes shining with tears. Mr Park and Joongi also wiped at the corners of their eyes.

A couple of days later, a bare-bones article about Heeja's death and an update on the status of the investigation made it into the newspaper, but I wasn't all that worried. Heeja hadn't known so much as my cell phone number, and we hadn't been that close, nor did we have the sort of relationship where we would have harboured grudges against each other. The police had to call in her ex-husband, the one-eyed man, for a brief questioning, but he told them he'd been at a hostess bar the day the killing occurred, and the staff there vouched for him. The afternoon he was cleared of the charges, I tucked a heavy gold bar into my handbag and went home early.

Years ago, the day I got home from the cemetery after my husband's funeral, I dozed off briefly and woke up again at dawn. When I absently turned on the television, a foreign film called *Interview with the Vampire* was airing. It was the scene where a beautiful man becomes a vampire and sees the world through his new, non-human eyes. All the shrubbery in the park, which had once seemed sound asleep, was suddenly quivering, and the eyes of a once-still bronze statue were now darting around. My eyes had brimmed with tears the whole time I watched. It wasn't that sad or frightening, but it made me afraid of my own reality, the one in which I'd been left all alone with my children and had to start looking at the world through brand-new eyes.

I was no ordinary ajumma, not any more. I was a killer. The world as seen through a killer's eyes was no longer a quiet, peaceful park. It was a jungle where scorching sunlight and torrential rains were forever alternating, a vast ocean with no lighthouse.

I am sharpening a knife again today. When the blade gets so dull it could be one of the blades in a shaving razor, would I be able to chuck it in the recycling bin without a second thought like Mr Lim of Majang-dong had? I don't know. But what I do know is that my knife still has a long way to go before it can ever escape this rank, gamey hell.

2

The Boss

I always wanted to be a CEO. My childhood dream was to sit in a swivel chair with good neck and back support behind a desk made of gleaming mahogany wood. Wanting to be a CEO was much more realistic than the kids who wrote down *president* or *scientist* as their dream jobs, after all, and if I did well enough, I could end up earning way more than them anyway, sated from all my success. Long story short, that feeling of being sated and full was one of the basic factors that drove people to do good. A fair number of criminals were people who were starving, and that sense of defeat allowed the seed of evil to sprout. While the seed of evil occasionally led them into the pockets of the rich, putting down roots was never easy. Rich people usually owned several overcoats, and they sent clothes to the dry cleaner's after having worn them just once, which meant the seed of evil naturally sought out and had no choice but to sprout in the damp pockets of poorer, hungrier people.

I hated the have-nots. And among them, the ones I hated most were those who lived their whole lives like fools. People like Byeongsu, the downstairs neighbour who was swindled out of his money by a trusted friend and, with no one to complain to, packed his things and ran off to some slum town; or Okhee from next door whose reputation was ruined by her boss at the factory where she worked to the point that she was eventually forced to marry and move in with him, then went on to pop out babies every year like a rabbit until she died at a young age – they were so unbearably pathetic. If you can't get revenge using your strength alone, you had to be willing to go to the ends of the earth to find someone who would make that revenge possible and never let them go. To do that, you needed money. No one knew how far the ends of the earth were, because it was obviously not a distance a person could cover on foot. If you wanted to slit some lowlife's throat or kick somebody's ass, you needed money to pay the proverbial ferryman and money for the poison and the knife. That was why I dreamed of being a CEO.

And so I became one.

A single glance at my business card would leave no room for doubt. Smile Detective Agency, the company I had named and set up the sign for on the third floor of a run-down building at an intersection that pulsed with the stench of maturing gingko trees come autumn, had made me a CEO at last. My desk wasn't made from mahogany, only Formica, but every morning I showed up at the office humming a cheery tune. The first thing I did when I stepped inside was to open the bottom drawer of that desk. Then I would run my hand along the inside of the drawer, which felt cool to the touch. A knife. I had stuck the handle and dull blade to the wall of the drawer with green masking tape, yet the knife still yearned to see the outside world, soothing and tickling my heart and my fingertips. The knife had dulled and rusted so much that it couldn't even serve as a can opener, but not a day went by where I didn't run a hand over it before I got to work.

Before I became a CEO, I was a killer.

When I first moved to Seoul, I was a rookie with no talents whatsoever except for the knife skills I'd inherited from my father, who ran a sashimi restaurant by the sea. Even so, since I'd never formally trained or worked in a kitchen, I just barely managed to get a job at a sashimi centre in Seoul. I had to learn everything from how to hold a knife to how to stun a fish from scratch all over again. The whole time I spent diligently filleting raw fish, I believed the best path for me in life was to become a sashimi restaurant owner, and since a restaurant owner was basically a CEO, that was how I'd finally achieve my dream.

Then I met Soondeok.

Soondeok was the only daughter of the sashimi centre owner. She was an ugly woman known to everyone in the neighbourhood by name. The cleft lip and palate surgery she'd undergone as soon as she was born had left her with a little scar above her lip, and when she was in first grade, she'd come down with such a violent case of chickenpox that her entire face was left as pockmarked as a rice strainer. As if the harelip weren't bad enough, the craters all over her face made her parents determined to become filthy rich. They seemed to believe that was the only way to ensure that Soondeok wouldn't be treated like dirt.

Her parents started out as fishmongers in a shop on the outskirts of the city and soon took over a sashimi restaurant downtown, and by the time Soondeok started high school they had built a three-storey sashimi centre and become known locally as a very wealthy family. That restaurant, the East Sea Sashimi Centre, was my first job. But Soondeok was not the meek, virtuous girl that her innocent-sounding name implied. She had a nose so sharp it could have pierced a fishing net, and that nose gave her the uncanny gift of being able to sniff out food by even the faintest whiff. She was a glutton who hated to see a single piece of salted radish go into her parents' mouths if she hadn't gotten the first bite. That was her only talent. She made terrible marks in school and couldn't cook or clean worth a damn. To me, it seemed like her entire life was comprised of eating and throwing fits.

As soon as Soondeok graduated from high school, when her parents realized that university was but a pipe dream, they put her to work behind the counter at the sashimi centre. But Soondeok, who always had a chocolate bar in her hands and her eyes glued to the TV opposite the front desk, had no interest in sales or sums. Even when enraged customers screamed at her and shouted for the manager after Soondeok miscalculated their bill, she would just carry on watching TV, shoving more chocolate into her mouth. By the time her mother realized what was going on and rushed over, wiping her hands on her apron, the customers would have already deducted their own compensation for emotional damages from the total bill, placed a smaller amount of money on the counter in front of Soondeok and strolled off towards the parking lot.

Soondeok started slimming down around the time I moved up from slicing radish to filleting fish. She threw out the chocolate bars she used to buy by the box and stopped eating one bar every ten minutes, and she cut down from six meals a day to three. The same girl who used to refuse to bend over and pick up money that had fallen on the floor, huffing that she couldn't be bothered, started tying up her hair and going for runs along the riverside and the sports field in the mornings and evenings. This all happened when I was twenty-one years old, around eight months after I'd started working at the sashimi place.

Soondeok shed so much weight that even if you weren't paying especially close attention, you'd notice. She still couldn't quite be called thin, but even so, her confidence skyrocketed. One day she stopped wearing those sacks she called pants and started wearing skirts, and from there the skirts she wore grew shorter and shorter. According to Ms Choi, an employee who liked to gossip, Soondeok had badgered her parents to pay for plastic surgery and gotten her eyes and nose done. The other employees flocked around Soondeok, who seemed to be changing by the day. They showered her with contempt disguised as compliments, but I tried my best not to get mixed up with that crowd. Whenever I locked eyes with her through the swarm of people – her eyes still swollen from surgery – I looked away first. I'd long known that she had a thing for me, but I didn't dare accept her feelings. As much of a country bumpkin as I was, having come to Seoul not even a year ago, even I knew better than to date the hands-down ugliest girl in the neighbourhood.

I did end up falling in love around then. Not with a woman, but with poetry. I was the youngest worker in the kitchen, but I was into something as old-fashioned as poems. After work I would go up to my room on the restaurant's rooftop and re-read my beat-up copy of Kim Namjoo's collection until I fell asleep. I dreamed of being a CEO who wrote poems. I spent the days imagining myself donning a double-breasted jacket, taking out a fountain pen and signing some documents, and on the weekends I would hold poetry readings and recite my own poems to my beautiful wife. But when I woke from those sweet dreams, all that awaited me was a sashimi knife with a fishy smell. My knife skills had improved the fastest out of anyone at the restaurant. According to the head chef, I had cold fingertips, small hands and thick wrists, which made me good at handling knives. I got better and better until at last I could fillet an entire flatfish in under five minutes.

When no one else was around as I was filleting fish, I would compose poems. I would lay the still-thrashing fish on the cutting board and pierce the crown of its head with a needle. *I wonder what you dreamed of*, I murmured aloud as the fish lost consciousness. *With a single stitch I've stolen away your tomorrows*, as I slowly peeled back its skin and drew out the white and perfectly fatty meat around the spine. *How many slices of that dream did I seize*, as I gently pressed down on its moist, springy skin with one hand and with the other slowly laid the knife down flat and sliced the fish into thick pieces. *The distant sky is reflected in this sweet sliver*, as the flatfish slept with no idea that its flesh was being stripped from its body. *Yet you remain dreaming*, as I tossed the bones with thin bits of flesh still clinging to them into a soup pot, yanked out the needle that I'd used to stun the fish, and watched as the fish came back to life. *I grab at a strand of the rainbow at the end of the world*, as I placed the docile fish meat atop a mound of pickled radish, arranged slices of carrot around that in the shape of a flower, embroidered orange peels shaped like fins, and then – for the grand finale – topped it off with the head of the fish, its gills still flaring. *And prepare myself for the long journey ahead.*

'Sounds pretty good.'

I turned towards the voice and found Soondeok standing behind me, holding a tray. She'd recently taken it upon herself to help with waiting tables. There were eight of us chefs in the kitchen, but of course my dishes were the ones Soondeok always served. The other staff members also got into the habit of calling her over once they saw that I'd finished plating. If Soondeok so much as saw me talking with one of the women on the staff, she would spend the whole rest of that day bawling her eyes out, so everyone had to watch what they said and did when she was around. Now, she smiled faintly as she took the plated dish, swaying her hips on her way back out to the dining area. I was embarrassed and livid, displeased with her sneaking up and eavesdropping on the poetry I recited only when I thought everyone else had gone off to lunch and the kitchen was empty.

That night, I chucked my tattered Kim Namjoo collection in the rubbish bin and read the current events section in the weekly newspaper until I fell asleep instead.

Soondeok grew more overt in expressing her affections. Even when our coworkers or customers were around, she would wink at me with abandon, and pick up the underwear I'd discarded in the rooftop room, wash it, and hang it on the clothesline to dry. But despite having succeeded at her diet, she was still the same girl, ugly enough to turn heads. The prosthesis on the tip of her nose was glaringly obvious, and her cosmetically altered eyelid creases were wider than her eyes to the point where she had to line them thickly or else she would look like she'd just cried her heart out. The way she smeared her face with the too-light foundation she'd bought at a department store to cover up her darker skin, she could have been mistaken for a kabuki actor.

'She's truly lost it,' remarked my coworker Lee Daeho. He was a show-off who bragged non-stop about the two convictions he'd managed to get on his record as a juvenile. The first was for snapping this arrogant neighbourhood kid's legs in two with a fireplace poker back in his hometown, and the other was for sexual intercourse under the pretence of marriage, a charge he'd picked up for taking advantage of a naive girl he'd met after moving to Seoul.

'It's not all about looks when it comes to women,' he said now. 'Anyone can see that every time Soondeok looks at you, her heart melts. Be nice to her. Aren't you eyeing the CEO spot?'

'I'd rather grow old and grey all alone before I picked up a girl with a pockmarked face and a harelip.'

'What a punk. Look – you either wield a knife for the rest of your life or take her out with a single slice when you get the chance. One is all it takes.'

Looking back on it, this was an extremely crass thing to say, but being the youngest, I was happy to dance to the tune the older Daeho was singing.

'For a guarantee that I would inherit the restaurant, sell Soondeok off to some deep-sea fishing boat crew, and then shack up with a real beauty afterwards? There's nothing I wouldn't do,' I said.

Soondeok was the owners' only flesh-and-blood family. If I could just stomach her for a little while, the CEO position at this massive sashimi centre that brought in more than ten million won in sales per day could be mine. The thought of it lingered long after the conversation with Daeho. But there was something I was overlooking at the time – the fact that no one in the world was more vicious than a) those who'd quit smoking, and b) those who'd succeeded at their diets.

Like a mischievous little kid, I found my curiosity and the temptation to get rich quick piqued, and I began dating Soondeok. When work ended, we would go for walks in the park together, and I would recite poems for her and take her to see new movies while holding her hand. I told her that her newly creased eyelids were pretty and even felt her up, hands fumbling over her thighs at the end of a dark alley with my eyes squeezed shut. I thought she would like that sort of thing. Knowing she had likely never gotten much of a reaction from a guy, I had no doubt she would probably be moved by my bold hands. But in that alleyway – more precisely, near the front gate of her house under a broken mercury-vapour lamp – Soondeok struck me clear across the face. So hard that I saw stars and my ears rang.

'Do I look that easy to you?'

I saw it then. The way her lips had trembled briefly with joy and exhilaration she couldn't hide quickly enough before lashing out.

'Sorry,' I said. 'It's because you're so beautiful.'

I scratched my head, swallowing another laugh that was threatening to burst out at how badly I'd misjudged the situation.

'From now on, please control yourself. Hands off until marriage.'

I was so grateful to hear those words. Soondeok's parents loved me, hardworking and polite as I was. I had just gotten a fast-track promotion to sous chef that winter. Soon it would be a whole year since I'd started working at the restaurant, and in that time, I'd grown surprisingly fond of Soondeok.

Late Sunday afternoon, just as Daeho and I were about to shake out the musty-smelling wool blanket outside my room, Soondeok's father came up to the rooftop.

'Come spring, I'll bring up your meals, so until then, use the guest room on the fifth floor. At mealtimes, come on down to our house and eat.'

Now I was really getting the son-in-law treatment. When my future father-in-law left, Daeho squatted down in the doorway, a cigarette between his teeth. 'Jerk. You sure have a strong stomach. Seems like you're putting up with that girl pretty well.'

The very same Daeho who'd told me to be good to Soondeok in the first place had completely changed his attitude after I got promoted. Granted, I *had* approached Soondeok with less-than-savoury intentions, but once marriage was on the table, my feelings towards her really started to blossom.

'Don't say that,' I said. 'It's not like I'm just getting married for the money. I see something in her.'

Daeho rubbed out his cigarette on the ground and stood up.

'You see something in her? What do you see exactly? The hell did you just say to me? You should be worshipping the ground I walk on, punk. Should we have beef tartare with the sashimi today? Should I beat your ass and serve it up?'

He rushed off to the kitchen and came back holding a thirty-centimetre sashimi knife.

'Come on, what's all this about? What are you getting so worked up over?' I said quietly, avoiding the murderous look in Daeho's eyes.

'I've been biding my time. What was it you told me? You'd

rather grow old and grey all alone before you picked up a girl with a pockmarked face and a harelip? Did you or did you not say that?'

Of course I'd said it. But I'd been mostly joking – there was only one per cent of truth behind that comment. Besides, I felt differently now. At some point Soondeok had started to transform from someone crabby and ugly to someone warm and tender.

'Yes, I said that. But now . . .'

A searing hot pain shot through my back. I felt a numbing pain in my chest, like something was tearing me apart from the inside, and I was gasping so hard for breath that I couldn't speak.

'Asshole.'

I heard Soondeok's voice behind me.

'See? What'd I say? You should've listened when I told you this jerk was coming at you with ulterior motives.'

I slumped against the doorframe to the rooftop room. I sank down slowly, the knife lodged in my back, thick blood staining the corners of my mouth and my eyes wild with resentment. I could hear Soondeok's panting breaths behind me. Like she was crying. Daeho lit a new cigarette. As it became harder to breathe, my vision rapidly narrowed.

Just when my body sagged and my head dipped down, someone grabbed hold of me and pulled me back. Soondeok must have yanked out the knife. I could feel my clothes growing soaked with the rush of warm blood spreading from the wound. If any other woman had overheard that conversation, she might have only *imagined* stabbing her fiancé in the back. But Soondeok had actually done it. I admired her for it. With the same exacting patience that had seen her through losing all that weight, she had aimed the blade of her revenge at me, the man who'd infiltrated her heart with dark intentions. I wanted to tell her it wasn't what she thought, but the coughing spasms and crushing pain made it hard for me to even open my eyes. The knife hit the ground with a clatter.

Bad guys had to be punished, even if it meant chasing them to the ends of the earth. I bent to pick up the sashimi knife. My wrist went limp, and the knife fell again to the ground.

'Oh? This asshole's still putting up a fight. Look at him trying to come at me while he's about to crap himself. You think you can take me out?' Daeho goaded.

I tried to stand upright. Soondeok passed me and approached Daeho squatting in the doorway. She took his knife from him.

'Gonna finish the job with that? Man, you really do go above and beyond. Truly commendable, Ms Lee.'

Daeho tucked his cigarette between his fingers to mockingly applaud her. Soondeok walked back towards me. I could see the fleshy tops of her feet where they were squeezed into her high heels. She reached out and slipped her hands under my arms, hoisting my skinny body up by the armpits with enough strength to stand me upright. She all but dragged me over to stand in front of Daeho. She snatched the broken knife from me, tossed it far away, and placed Daeho's knife in my hand instead. Then she covered my hand with her own around the handle of the blade.

'What the hell?' said Daeho. 'What are you doing?'

For the first time in my life, I was stabbing someone. I hardly had the energy to stand, yet the sensation in the tips of my fingers was more alive than ever. The blade cut through flesh and muscle and fat, briefly halting when it struck solid bone. I thrust the knife in again and again. Daeho took four stab wounds to the neck, chest, and stomach before he crumpled in the doorway like a torn sock.

'At first, he wanted money in exchange for helping me win your heart,' Soondeok said. 'Then he wanted double in return for finding out your true feelings for me. Despicable scum. He deserves to die. Of course, there's hell for you to pay too, Park Taesang. I'm going to punish you so brutally for the rest of your life that you'll wish you'd died like him.'

The rooftop door creaked open. I was still clinging to Soondeok, hardly able to catch my breath. I had underestimated her at every turn.

A middle-aged man wearing new shoes stood in front of us.

Soondeok turned me over to him. 'He should have blood on his hands for the rest of his days,' she said. 'Don't let him live a decent life. And until I tell you to kill him, you're responsible for keeping him alive.'

She handed the man a sheet of wrapping cloth. He had a massive build and was able to easily sling me over his shoulder and move quickly down the stairs before tossing me into an old, beat-up sedan.

'Listen up. You're a criminal now, wanted for the murder of Lee Daeho. The knife is covered in your fingerprints. Starting today, you're alive, but you're not living. That woman has paid the price of your life and signed a contract. As long as I'm alive, that contract will never be terminated.'

The man did not once tell me his name. I kept drifting in and out of consciousness. As I was being hauled off somewhere, someone who clearly didn't know what they were doing tended to my back, shoddily stitching up the wound over the half of the broken knife that was still lodged inside my body. Only later did I learn that they'd found the corpse of a young man who was roughly similar to me in height and looks, bashed his face in, and flung him from the rooftop to make it look like I'd taken my own life. Then after my poor parents were informed that I'd gotten into a fight with my coworker over a girl and killed myself after killing him, they left town and hid away in a hermitage somewhere.

Now I was legally dead. Wherever I was, whatever I did, it was the work of a ghost. Just like that man had told me, I was alive, but I wasn't living.

He taught me new ways to use knives. Over the next few weeks, I watched as he bought up corpses for me to practise on from a seller, known as Crocodile, who rounded up the bodies of people who'd thrown themselves into the river and sold them. He drew on the corpses with a marker pen to show me different ways to kill.

'Instant death, instantaneous death, and immediate death all mean the same thing. Snuffing out a life in the blink of an eye. You know how sometimes, you just barely touch glass or porcelain, and it cracks? Think of this the same way. Killing someone with the touch of your hand. Knives are mostly used to sever veins or puncture organs to incapacitate a person. The simplest way is to target the neck. If the vertebral artery and the veins are bleeding out at the same time and oxygen is blocked off, the brain won't be able to survive for more than one or two minutes. When you slit someone's throat, don't slice from the front. Most times, attacking from behind is the way to go. And don't cut a straight line across the neck. You have to trace a gentle arc. Like this. Just like a smile.'

The man used the marker to trace a grinning mouth on the neck of the corpse, one side of its face crumbled away like bloated tofu. I copied him, my lips moving slightly around the word *smile* as I swallowed down nausea.

Because I no longer belonged to the world, I had no one to turn to except for that man. Even if I had somewhere to run, I knew he would soon find me. He spent his days in a riverside office assembled from two shipping containers, and sometimes he would pick up his knife and set off on a long journey when he found some work through the grapevine. He would return in a day or two, wolf down a meal, and then proceed to sleep for the next several days straight.

The man knew a lot about the human body. He would even pick up and handle with his bare hands the corpses that had started to decay, full of reddish water and covered in black fly shit, with no reaction.

'Dead people aren't people,' he said. 'They're cuts of meat. No different than animals. When they were alive, they mattered. Once they die, they're just lumps of flesh that reek so bad not even dogs will eat them.'

He started bringing me to his workroom. He made me put my hand inside the knife wound he'd made in someone's body.

'I purposely went for the liver. You can usually estimate the time of death based on its temperature. It'd be hard to tell anything, though, if there's just an empty hole left where it should be.'

If you reached into the body of a person whose liver still hadn't lost its heat, the corpse's muscles would suddenly constrict. Like something trying to strangle you.

Aargh. I yanked out my hand, startled. But when the man

trained his intimidating glare on me, I reached inside again and felt around to determine the route the blade had travelled through this body. On those kinds of days, the man would go out and come back with a few pounds of beef, lightly cook just the outside and chew and eat the mostly raw meat like some kind of beast. His mouth glistening with oil and red juices, an unbearable stench on his lips, he would clean his plate with a perfectly indifferent look on his face.

I saw the man cry exactly once.

It was a swelteringly hot Sunday. Relying on a single fan to chase off the heat, we had eaten dinner together and retired to our beds. I had just started to drift off listening to the distant cries of crickets and the footsteps of people out on a walk when someone knocked on the door. Outside stood a woman in her early forties; she was weeping. The man slammed the door in her face. Then, as if nothing had happened, he lay down again on his back and started snoring. I got up around dawn as usual to pee, and when I pulled down my trousers and knelt by the plastic bottle I kept near my bed, I noticed that the moonlight was shining on the man's face, revealing thin tracks of dried tears.

'Listen up,' he said. 'My name is Oh Gilsoo. And I'm going to kill the woman who came to see me earlier.'

At the sound of his voice, it was like the pee had frozen solid. Not a single drop came out.

'That woman was my patient,' he said quietly, and proceeded to tell me about his past.

He had grown up in a family of doctors – his father, his mother, and both his older brothers. Naturally, he followed his family's wishes and became a doctor himself. That woman first came to him when he was still in residency. She had attempted suicide. A shocking eight times. She would be found unresponsive by her family and rushed to the emergency room, where every time, the man would perform CPR and administer the drugs that would save her life. Every time she opened her eyes, she gave the man – her doctor – a verbal lashing, her eyes seething. She said he'd snatched away her right to die. Each time, the man would retort that he had an obligation as a doctor to save his patients' lives, and if she didn't want to see him, she should go to another hospital the next time. And the eighth time she was brought in to see him, he struck her across the face. His anger flared up. He couldn't understand why she treated her own life, which other people worked so hard to save, with so little regard. That was when the woman, one hand on her reddening cheek, confided in him the reason she wanted to die.

Her father was a con artist, her mother was a gambler, and her older brother was a murderer. The same way the man had grown up surrounded by doctors, she had been born into a family of criminals. She had inherited all their talents. When she found that she couldn't control her base instincts, she would drive down quiet countryside roads and mow down anyone walking alone with her car, killing them. Afterwards, she would return home and attempt to take her own life.

She confessed to the man that for her, saving her own life meant someone else's life being taken.

Some days after that, the man quit his residency at the hospital. He was terrified of that woman turning up in the emergency room again. But somehow, she managed to find him again, even after he'd left. Whenever she couldn't control her killer instincts, she sought him out, and the man would choose some piece of shit excuse for a human to murder in front of her in her stead. But there came a time the woman sought him out late at night and not because of her urges to kill. She begged him to put a stop to this fountain of evil that was gushing to the point of overflowing.

Oh Gilsoo stopped his story there and went to get some water.

Later that night, he disappeared somewhere and didn't return for a week. This time he didn't binge eat and pass out like he usually did; instead, he came back looking wide awake.

Then one morning a few days later, the contract between him, me, and Soondeok was terminated. Oh Gilsoo had died. The Crocodile guy came round with his bloated corpse. His neat facial hair, the long hair on his head that had been tied up into a ponytail, his tall height, and his unusually stubby and gnarled little toes. It was him, no doubt about it. Crocodile asked me if it was OK for him to take the man's body. I nodded. That was probably what the man would have wanted. I packed the money pouch he had left behind, some clothes that were more or less scraps, and some knives. I had been a ghost for so long, and I was finally able to leave.

I re-entered the world without casting so much as a shadow.

Today I interviewed a new killer.

Last summer, someone new had come on board at the Smile Detective Agency. A woman. An ajumma, at that. We called her Mrs Shim. Wrinkles had started coming in early around her eyes and mouth, which sometimes made her look like she was nearing sixty, but when she smiled, she could have passed for eighteen.

Mrs Shim reminded me of myself. She loved knives, and

knives loved her. When she held one, her eyes would flash, glinting like a carnivore's. And not because of a simple desire to kill or because of a cruel heart. No, she had the pride of someone with a purpose. She had lost her husband and was still shouldering the futures of her two children. Of course, money wasn't the only thing fuelling her. Sometimes when clients with heart-wrenching stories came to us, Mrs Shim would clasp their hands in hers, listening closely and nodding hard all the way until the end, her eyes brimming with tears.

'Your tie looks nice today, Mr Park,' she said now, coming into the office carrying her shopping bag. Inside, I knew, were three well-sharpened knives.

'Would you like a cup of coffee?' Joongi greeted her, friendly as always. The two of us were already sitting down to drink.

'Seven people in total applied,' Joongi went on. 'So many, right? Especially since we posted that call specifically for people with prior experience working at detective agencies. But there were also ones who rang us up about the job but all started by asking

about the pay. As soon as they mentioned bonuses, I'd just hang up. I told the applicants to come by at ten o'clock, so it's about time people started showing up.'

Joongi had barely finished talking when someone came in through the front door. He was a young-looking kid who couldn't have been long out of high school.

'Excuse me,' he said. 'I'm here for an interview.'

Behind him walked another young man who looked a few years older and wore his baseball cap low over his face.

'I'm here for an interview, too.'

We hadn't put out a call for part-timers at a burger place, yet we'd managed to draw in dopey kids like these two. I had them sit on the sofa across from me and Mrs Shim.

'I'm not a high schooler,' the younger-looking one began. 'I dropped out last year and work at a petrol station now. I've never worked at a detective agency, but I'm damned good with the petrol guns. Here's a recommendation letter from the station owner. See?'

Han Dongsoo has not only contributed his outstanding talent and aptitude to our station, he has greatly enhanced consumer trust and the reputation of our business with his patience and sheer determination to locate the gas tank of any car, even foreign models he has never seen before. For this reason, I recommend him for the position of a killer. Sincerely, his boss.

Mrs Shim burst out laughing. The handwriting on his cover letter was the same as the handwriting on the so-called recommendation letter, and yet the boy looked so earnest about it all.

'We only hire adults,' I said politely. 'And besides, we're not recruiting killers.' With these words, I hoped the kid would get the message and go back to the petrol station he had come from.

'I know that's a lie,' the young man in the baseball cap cut in. 'Your eyes say it all. They say, *"I'm a killer. And I'll make you one, too."* '

This one had pale skin and bloodshot eyes. He reminded me of a shade plant that hadn't seen the sun in ages.

'I'm a tactician who's spent nineteen hours a day every day for the last three years brain training using online games. Don't try to fool me. I may not have the petrol gun-handling skills that this kid has, but I'm the best strategist in East Asia, guaranteed. I was considering becoming a pro gamer, but this place is closer to where I live, so I applied.'

After assuring the two of them that we would be in touch soon and sending them off, more candidates began to arrive. A woman in her late forties in a miniskirt with her bangs teased out like antennae; a middle-aged man who could do uncanny impressions of a siren wailing, a dog barking, and a newborn baby crying; an old man who came by because after he'd retired from the army as a sergeant, he'd been itching to find a use for his old baton.

Once all the applicants had left, Mrs Shim moved to water the plants around the office, frowning. 'I guess we'll need to scout people ourselves if we want anyone with actual experience, won't we?' she said.

'This place is like a townhouse,' I said. 'Everyone lives together under the same roof. Even if we didn't know what everyone looked like and only saw their skills, we would know right away who used knives and who didn't. Do you know why I wasn't satisfied with running a detective agency alone and decided to employ killers? Because I hated seeing the people around me murder even babies and women without an ounce of remorse. That just didn't happen back in our day; we had a code. Granted, hardly anybody wanted to kill back then. Perhaps it was silly to put out an advertisement – anyone with the skill for killing wouldn't be able to change jobs so easily anyway. They'd be too scared of revenge-seekers or rumours going around.'

Mrs Shim nodded. She had been my best hire. Thanks to her, the Smile Detective Agency's income had soared to number one in our industry. And still no one had suspected that our incredibly talented killer was an ajumma. More work was steadily coming in, requiring us to hire more employees, but I would rather sacrifice some income than put my people at risk.

'The woman earlier with the antennae hair who insisted she was unmarried even though anyone could tell she's had children looked pretty strong, didn't she?'

'Not strong enough to be a killer, but she might make for a good investigative researcher.'

Antennae Bangs seemed to have the sharpest sense of the bunch, and she was one of the most articulate candidates we had seen. We needed someone who had an ear to the ground.

'Well, at least we still have hope. If someone as clumsy as me can make a living as a killer, then as long as you train them well, they should be able to earn their keep.'

Mrs Shim looked at me as she squeezed the zit on Joongi's forehead. 'How about we set up an internship like the big companies do?'

Maybe she had a point. Sure, we needed killers, but hunting people down wasn't the only work a detective agency did. We also dealt out and collected money loans, dug up the dirt on affairs being carried out behind one spouse's back, reunited long lost relatives, and all sorts of other tasks. Joongi suggested that we assign every candidate – aside from the one woman we were eyeing to be a researcher – a certain case and then hire the person who produced the best results.

'What, do you want to see their TOEIC scores, too?'

Joongi laughed shyly. Right then, the office door opened and the security guard ajusshi stepped inside.

'Is Mr Park around?'

The security guard removed his cap and mussed his hair, looking around sheepishly at the Smile Detective Agency family.

Joongi bowed deeply, greeting him. 'Oh, sir, you must have come to unclog the toilet. I actually bought a plunger earlier, so I should be able to unclog it myself.'

'No, that's not why I'm here,' said the ajusshi. 'I came to apply to join the Smile Detective Agency, too. I was tempted by the lack of an age limit. I earn nine hundred thousand won a month working security here, but what good is that beyond a few trips to the colatec? So I decided to give moonlighting a try.'

The security guard – Kim Seokbong, if his name tag was to be believed – was a full seventy years old this year. Of course, he was hale and hearty as ever, but it was hard to believe that he was here applying to be a killer instead of signing up at the senior centre for their lunchtime hwatu matches.

'I'm so sorry,' said Mrs Shim, reacting quickly. She stepped towards the security guard with a sympathetic frown on her face. 'We've already chosen a candidate.'

'Why the long face, Mrs Shim? I heard everything from right outside the door.'

How much *had* he heard? Surely not the part about Mrs Shim being a killer . . .

'Have a seat,' I said, ushering him towards the sofa with trembling hands. Beads of sweat had formed on Mrs Shim's forehead.

'I knew Mrs Shim's shopping bag looked too heavy to be full

of napa cabbage,' said Mr Kim with a smirk that revealed a gold tooth.

Mrs Shim took a sip of cold water to calm herself down. 'Sir, how much did you happen to hear?'

'I'm not some blabbermouth old man. You're all like family to me. You think I would run my mouth about your business? Besides, I already knew about Mrs Shim.'

I wondered if he was just fishing for information, pretending to know more than he really did.

'Sir, our ears are ten times bigger than other people's,' I told him. 'Give us half a day and we could easily trace a rumour back to its source. Do you get what I'm saying?'

Mr Kim chuckled slyly. 'Of course, Mr Park. At this point, wouldn't it be easiest for everybody if you just hired me as a special employee? Look at it this way – you're getting a former mercenary who's done every kind of sport and been to every corner of the country in his youth. There are plenty of down-and-outs who used up all their good fortune when they were young and have nothing to show for it all these years later, but there are still some of us who are in good shape. If you don't believe me, why don't we all venture down to the basement sauna?'

Mrs Shim pressed her fingers to her temples as though a headache was coming on.

I had no choice but to double Mr Kim's security guard pay and set up a special task force in the security office. As the sole member and head of the task force, his most important mission was to call and inform us in the Smile Detective Agency office if any suspicious people came by. It was no different from his usual job, except that now he had the new title and an inflated salary. Mr Kim gave a hearty salute.

'Mr Park, you are indeed a good man,' he said. 'I hear Smile is the only office in this building that isn't behind on rent. And Mrs Shim, I enjoyed the fresh kimchi you made that time. It was a little salty, though. I have high blood pressure, so it would be nice if you could make it blander next time. As for Joongi, you ought to take that plunger to the bathroom on the second floor, too.'

Once the special task force leader left, we all deflated.

Joongi put on a pair of rubber gloves and grabbed the toilet plunger.

As I went downstairs and walked along the hallway, I could hear the trot medley Mr Kim was playing.

I felt the lyrics deeply and painfully in my heart: 'It'll be because of my feelings, my lingering, lingering feelings.' It was as though Soondeok's broken knife blade had scraped up against something inside my chest.

My lingering, lingering feelings would be to blame for everything.

3

The Shaman

I was in big trouble. In a few days, I would have to climb atop the jakdu blades and stand before my fate. I'd have to stick a pitchfork into the flank of a decently fattened pig and prop it up, ringing my little shaman's bell and spewing out nonsensical fortunes. Then the apprentice shamans, like fairies of lore in their fluttering hanbok, would hoist me up, the bright whites of my eyes showing, and set me down on the sharpened blades in the back of a sculpted dragon. Before I could even scream, the moment the blades cut into the soft, tender flesh on the soles of my feet, my dark blood would stain the steel as well as the apprentices' peach-coloured garments. Mrs Geum would faint, clutching the back of her neck, and with the soles of my feet split open like blood ark clams, I'd be hauled off to the hospital in an ambulance.

Even if by some miracle I survived, I could already see spiteful Mrs Geum showing up accompanied by detectives. She had already spent nearly thirty million won in fortune-telling fees to bogus shamans, ten million won on talismans to put a stop to her husband's cheating, and twenty million won to have an exorcism done on her son, who took after his mother and made piss-poor marks in school. Given that she would be shelling out a whopping one billion won for this latest kut ritual, I knew she wouldn't just let it slide. Besides, she'd already paid half the cost upfront and told me she would be coming by to pay off the rest soon, so I didn't have much time to find a way out of this mess.

It was fine. As long as I maintained my balance and had the apprentices to help with holding it steady, holding up the pig on the pitchfork could be done without too much of a struggle. But there was no fooling anybody when it came to the blades. I'd seen a documentary programme once that showed a shaman walking on the jakdu blades. First, a ripe watermelon was placed atop the blades to test their sharpness, and the fruit was instantly cleaved in two. Then the blades were oiled to a shine, and the solemn-faced apprentices swiftly hoisted up the head shaman – who'd been dancing and waving around her twin sacred swords – on to the twelve-step staircase of blades. Surprisingly, the shaman hopped from blade to blade even more vigorously than before, and the mouths of all the people who had come to watch the ritual fell open.

I let out a quiet gasp, too, as I watched the scene unfold on the TV. While marvelling at the fact that the world was full of incredible occurrences, I also felt a sliver of doubt about whether what I was seeing was real. Maybe the shaman had worn stockings made from a special material. Maybe the whole thing was the result of skilful editing. Or maybe all the so-called spectators in the crowd were actually the shaman's relatives. It was rare to find someone trustworthy in this world.

After all, wasn't I myself a fraud?

I hadn't set out to become a bogus shaman. Once upon a time, as a matter of fact, I was a CEO. A decade or so earlier, while running a tiny cigarette shop – all six and a half square metres of which I had inherited from my mother – I began reading books like *The Principles of the Saju* and *The Secrets of Heaven* to pass the time. To be honest, it was partially because of my own anxiety about possibly never getting married and never having my name added to someone else's family register. Rather than waste my days paying visits to fortune-tellers, I decided I might as well do something useful with my life. More than anything, it turned out to be pretty interesting and made the boring hours in the cigarette shop fly by. It was around that time when one of my regulars, Mr Park, came by, as drunk as a skunk.

He tottered into the cramped shop and took a seat on the squat red plastic stool next to me. 'Noona,' he slurred. 'I guess there really is such a thing as fate.'

'Is something bothering you?' I asked.

'I was fired from my eighth job today. In the five years since I was discharged from the army and started working, I've never once collected unemployment. It's not like I'm slacking off. I've been nothing but an obedient dog who's never late and always willing to work overtime, which makes it even more unfair. Suddenly my salary is a couple of months late and they're saying they have to cut staff. What does it matter how loyal you are? This is my fate. I just wish I could last more than a year at any given job.'

Mr Park reeked of rotting persimmons.

'Do you know your birthday down to the time of birth?'

His red eyes narrowed with suspicion. 'Why do you ask?'

'Since you keep lamenting your fate, I'm going to see if I can read it.'

He told me his date and time of birth.

'Looking at your fortune, you're facing a block at the moment. You'll have good luck with money from the ages of thirty-five to forty-five, but you'll have to struggle for the next four or five years before that pans out. Your type clings on to money, you see. But that's not to say you'll come into wealth by being greedy. Don't even think about starting a business, and try to focus on your studies. You have strong bigeop in your saju, meaning you're fairly quick-witted, so whatever you do, it'll turn out well as long as you stick to it.'

Mr Park stared at me, eyes widened.

'My studies . . . I was *just* wondering whether I should take the civil service exam before I got any older. Now I'm definitely leaning in that direction.'

He bought some cigarettes and left, and sure enough, he passed the ninth-rank civil service exam the following year.

From then on, all the neighbourhood ajummas started flocking to the cigarette shop. There was a constant stream of visitors asking about things, like their son who was sitting for the college entrance exam for the third time; the ten million won they had been scammed out of; or when their father-in-law who'd had a stroke would die. Because the ladies were always crowding the place, their sons and husbands naturally stayed away.

What men would have wanted to hear that nagging? 'I thought you were going to quit smoking.' Or, 'Kijoon-ah, you damned fool. You reek of cigarettes.' When my regulars started taking their business to the convenience store across the street, I decided to start charging a fee for telling fortunes. My mum, who spent her days making hundred won bets on games of hwatu at the senior centre, caught a whiff of the money coming in and showed up with an Aronamin Gold vitamin tin she'd converted into a cash box to set up shop. I would read someone's fortune for five thousand won and add people to a reading for an additional three thousand won each. Once word got around that we also offered a complimentary cup of cheap coffee brewed by my mum, the number of customers we saw coming in from the neighbouring areas steadily increased.

At first, I read fortunes the way I'd learned, however fumblingly. But I soon realized that what the customers wanted wasn't a reading full of hocus-pocus words like *myeong-gwan-gwa-ma* or *deuk-bi-yi-jae*. The secret to the shop's success ended up being my bluntness, which allowed us to grab this awful bull called life by the horns and wrestle with it together. My mum's commitment to the cause was a big help, too.

When customers came in, my mum would lower her head, pretending to brew coffee beside me, as she made her face into one of the coded expressions we had agreed on. I would steal a glance at her reflection in the desk mirror I kept placed in front of me so I could gather some information in advance. For example, the eyes were code for husbands, the nose referred to children, and the lips meant a bad case of arthritis. If my mum narrowed both eyes, that meant the customer's husband had cheated, and if she squinted only one eye, that meant the husband was losing his virility and failing to fulfil his manly duties. My mum had gathered this intel from the other elderly people who visited the senior centre and the public bathhouses nearly every day for years to gossip about their daughters-in-law, most of which turned out to be true.

Of course, the reason it wasn't one hundred per cent guaranteed was because some elders with mild dementia ran their mouths and spread false information from time to time. But even if some of the details weren't accurate, there was no need to panic. I could chalk it up to being an amateur whose main occupation was running a cigarette shop. If someone picked a fight, I could just go back to selling cigarettes and be done with it.

About a year went by like that, and I ended up making quite a lot of money. Without even advertising myself as such, I came to be called the Cigarette Shaman, and more and more customers from far-flung towns found their way to me by word of mouth. Once I earned enough, I sold the cigarette shop in the suburbs and found an office downtown to start up my fortune-telling business in earnest. Just like that, I had transformed from an amateur to a pro. However, I was still a complete and utter hack. Just someone who'd shoddily studied divination and had been lucky enough to inherit my fairly quick wit from my mother, who'd been appointed the neighbourhood chief so many times I couldn't keep track. I wasn't a real shaman who'd been given the title after having been possessed by a spirit or ritually inducted into the practice. In fact, I'd never once referred to myself as a shaman. That was just what other people believed and chose to call me. All I did was add a bit of flair and showiness to my actions, my garments, and my makeup to meet their expectations – the least I could do to repay them for all their support and give them a show.

So when Mrs Geum offered me one hundred million won to perform a ritual for her son who was retaking the college entrance exam, I didn't have the guts to turn down such a bold offer. By some twist of fate, it just so happened that the deposit I had agreed to put down this month for a place in one of the new planned developments was exactly one hundred million won. And now I was in no position to say I couldn't go through with the ritual and run away. Even if my feet had to be encased in saran wrap, I needed to stand on those blades. With one hundred million won, I could bring my little stint as a fake shaman to an end. With that money, I could put up a building on some property and live out the rest of my days in leisure off all the rent I would collect.

'Mrs Geum is here.'

At the sound of my assistant's voice, my heart dropped to the floor.

'Yes, of course,' I said. 'Come right in, Mrs Geum. I trust you've been well.'

Mrs Geum, a woman as stout as the money toad, took a seat across from me. Her eyes were smiling slyly behind her glasses.

'I'm here to pay the rest,' she said. 'I've been worried sick as of late, knowing my husband's business could go bankrupt at any moment and my son may not be able to go to uni. So it would be great if you could perform the ritual as soon as possible.'

It wasn't as though I hadn't been trying. Fearing the rumours, I went around to rituals performed only by shamans outside of Seoul who were known to be highly effective, but it was hard to figure out the trick to standing on the jakdu blades. I went to see a stuntman and tried to find ways to avoid my impending doom with nothing but my sense of balance. But that skill was impossible to master in a single day. The sight I captured on the camcorder I'd smuggled in was akin to acrobatics, the sorts of astonishing acts I didn't dare try to emulate, a display of the incredible talents of a real shaman.

'I'll call upon the great Jang-gun, God of War, for the date.'

I pulled out my brass hand bell and shook it, rolling my eyes up into my head. I trembled all over, murmuring a fake prayer I had all but memorized over the years.

'Aigo, dear Jang-gun. Come to me and grant me your divine words.'

Mrs Geum rubbed her hands together and bowed her head. I was about to lose my mind. No way did I have the courage to stand atop the jakdu blades. I needed a different plan.

'This year won't do,' I thundered, feigning the voice of the god. 'Anything you attempt now will end in disaster.'

Let's try to stall.

'Oh dear,' Mrs Geum replied. 'What can we do? Dear Jang-gun, please take pity on a poor woman like me and guide us towards an opportune date for the ritual. My poor husband will end up a beggar at this rate.'

A talisman. Let's get out of this bind with a talisman, one I can draw up with a snap of my fingers.

I adopted the god's voice again. 'Go forth and catch a male dog, three years of age, raised on a diet of nothing but white sticky rice, and write a talisman in its blood. This will be more effective than performing ten kut rituals. Have I made myself clear?'

Even to my ears, getting hold of a three-year-old male dog who'd only ever eaten white sticky rice sounded quite ridiculous. Still, it was important to keep a straight face. I had to make my mouth as solemn as I could to suit the god Jang-gun.

'If you say it will be more effective than ten kut rituals, I will trust your word unconditionally and do as you command,' Mrs Geum pleaded. 'Please look after my dear husband, whose bills are to be collected in a week. I believe in you, only you, O Great One.'

Mrs Geum paid me fifty million won in cash and disappeared. Instead of the blood of the three-year-old male dog raised solely on sticky rice, I used a brush dipped in the red cinnabar ink I always used for talismans and let my hand draw a random pattern. I had put off the danger for now, but I hadn't yet thought of what to do to prevent Mrs Geum's husband from going bankrupt in a week. I handed the talisman to my assistant, my head pounding and overrun with complicated thoughts.

My assistant opened the door slightly and poked her head in, looking uneasy.

'Ma'am, you have a customer.'

'Let's call it a day. I feel like my skull is about to split open.'

'She says she's not here to make use of your services,' she added. 'She just told me to tell you that Eunok had come to see you. Then you'd know.'

Eunok. Eunok. The name sounded familiar. So many women my age had 'Ok' in their names. I wondered whether she was some pesky solicitor, but I couldn't exactly think of a good excuse to turn her away.

'Let her in,' I said. 'And if there are no more customers with appointments, turn away any others who show up.'

A moment later, a tiny woman in a cheap blouse and Spandex pants who looked to be about my age walked in. Her features were as familiar as her name. She smiled the moment she saw me. Her skin was flushed the colour of fresh red garlic, and her expression appeared gentle and pure despite the many lines creasing her face. Once I pictured her without the wrinkles and with two straight pigtails instead of her short and curly helmet hair, I immediately remembered who she was.

'Eunok? The same Eunok who was really good at playing gong-gi?'

She smiled again. It was a smile so bright that it made her eyes crinkle up and disappear. For some reason, I couldn't remember her full name, but she was without a doubt the Eunok I remembered from elementary school. The girl with steady hands who would snatch up so many gong-gi marbles without missing that no one else's turn ever came. The girl whose cheeks were always red and the backs of whose hands were always chafed. Here she was as a middle-aged woman, standing in front of me now.

'That's right. It's that same Eunok. I heard you'd become a master shaman, so I searched all over to find you. You've gotten even prettier. You look like a celebrity now.'

Eunok's clothes spoke volumes about the rough life she must have led. The skin on her fingers was rough, freckles were scattered under her eyes like grains of sand, and even though it wasn't yet winter, white flaky dead skin had formed around her mouth.

'Hey, I was also wondering what you were up to,' I said. 'I even tried calling our school's alumni association to get in touch with you, but they told me your phone number had changed.'

Now and then I'd thought about Eunok. It warmed my heart to remember the girl who, every time I saw her, would slip something new into my hands. A chestnut, a baby chick, a tangerine, woollen gloves.

'But how could a shaman as powerful as you not be able to track little old me down?' Eunok said, pulling over a floor cushion and taking a seat close to me. The shopping bag she set down must have been awfully heavy, as it left a red impression on the palm of her hand.

'I heard through the grapevine that you'd gotten married. How have you been? How many children do you have? What does your husband do for work?' All the questions I'd had for her came spilling out at once.

'He got into an accident a few years ago and passed away. I have a son and a daughter.'

Looking at the dark expression on Eunok's face, even a novice shaman like me could see the life of hardship she had led flashing before my eyes.

'I never got married,' I said. 'I don't have a lazy husband dragging his feet around, but I also don't have clever little children of my own, so I feel lonely from time to time.'

As I was talking, Eunok stole glances at the myeongdu brass mirror and the taenghwa scroll featuring a painting of the Buddha hanging on the wall.

'Let's not do this here – we should go somewhere for dinner and talk over a meal. I'm not seeing any more customers today, and I was just itching to have a conversation with someone.'

There was so much I wanted to say to my old hometown friend after all this time. I had just stood up to change out of my work clothes when Eunok reached out and grabbed the bottom of my skirt.

'Listen, Shinja,' she said, pursing her chapped lips. 'I actually have a favour to ask of you.'

'As long as it's not to lend you money, you can ask me anything.'

As soon as I said it, I realized that I'd soured the mood. But no matter how far back I went with a friend, I thought it was best to nip the money issue in the bud. When a friend you haven't seen in forty years shows up looking a mess, nine times out of ten, they're having money problems.

'Please read my fortune,' said Eunok.

Huh – so she didn't want money? But it was still too soon to rule that out. How could I know she wasn't going to use the fortune-telling as a chance to whine about her woes and naturally segue into her money troubles?

'I don't really read fortunes for people I know,' I said. 'The predictions never seem to match up, weirdly enough.'

I went behind the folding screen and changed out of my clothes. I took off my jeogori skirt, the deep colour of red bean, and slipped into a white linen sundress.

'That's fine. I have my own reasons for asking. I know you'll understand, no matter how bizarre my fortune is. Because you're my friend. The two of us – we're friends.'

Eunok's desperate voice floated over the top of the folding screen and landed in my ears. She had come all this way to see me. I couldn't just callously turn her away. I could concoct a fortune for her, some assurance that no matter how hard life had been up to now, everything would turn out fine. I removed the binyeo holding up my hair, straightened out my locks with my fingers, then came around the folding screen and took my seat again.

'I usually don't do this sort of favour for anyone, but I'll make an exception for you,' I said. 'Tell me your date and time of birth.'

'I was born at nine a.m. on the twenty-seventh day of the sixth lunar month. Same year as you.'

I had to pretend I was being possessed by spirits whenever I performed kut rituals or did any divination, but for someone who offered up their date of birth like this, just writing out the details as I'd studied them on a piece of paper would suffice. Anyone could tell that she'd always had it rough, so there was no need for me to say it in as many words.

'Since we both know about your early years, we'll leave those out. It seems you were indeed fated to be a solitary wild goose, seeing as you lost your husband and are raising your children alone. Yet your great fortune has changed, starting from last year. Your great fortune doesn't necessarily mean good fortune, but more so that the tides of your life have shifted, and you're now living a totally different life than you were before. There's a strong presence of both fire and water in your innate fortune, and so you've experienced a lot of ups and downs, but now this new element of gold has entered through your Heavenly Stems and Earthly Branches in a powerful way. Because the fire in your fortune is strong enough to melt down the gold into something useful, this can mean both money coming into your hands and a chance to demonstrate your skills.'

With a fortune like this, she had not had any luck regarding her husband or her parents, but the arrival of a favourable great fortune meant that a small window of opportunity, however fleeting, could open up in her life. But there was one uneasy element in her fate. Gold was originally supposed to strengthen water. Hers was a fortune where the water was every bit as strong as the fire, and if the water were to overflow due to the energy from the gold, things could get dangerous. If Eunok were a man, I would have predicted something like a dishonourable dismissal from a job or else getting slammed with an unexpected lawsuit awaited her in the future.

'Then what sort of work would I be suited for?'

'Like I said, it would be best if your work could govern the gold in your fortune. Gold is a metal, right? You have a lot of needle energy, so you would do well to work with a sewing machine, or with knives as a chef – any sort of work involving metal, you would thrive in.'

Eunok's startled eyes followed the tip of the pen as I wrote down the details of her fortune. 'I guess the rumours of your talent really were true,' she said. 'I'm working with metal right now. The job pays well, and my work is going smoothly, but I get more afraid the longer this lasts. I feel like the fear is suffocating me. Will I be able to keep this up? How far will my luck stretch? Tell me that much. Please?'

Even when Eunok was younger, she was skilled with her hands. She knew how to tie the neatest butterfly knots, and she was better than the younger kids' mums at braiding their hair nice and neat. With those hands, I always thought she would do well working in a restaurant. But now, for some reason, I had this unsettling feeling that wouldn't go away.

'I mean, if it's going well, that's good, no?' I said. 'For now, work will keep coming your way. You'll have no problem making a living. But don't expect your good luck to extend to your children. What good are kids anyway? As you get older, money's all that matters. Just saving your money and living as elegantly as a noblewoman is the best, isn't it?'

I knew that Eunok would be disappointed if I were to list all the ill-fated energies enshrouding her fortune, so I kept quiet.

'You don't need to tell me about that. If I can get my kids married off, I'll be able to live an untroubled life. I wonder if my

weak heart can keep up this work until then.' Eunok clasped
her hands and held them to her chest.

'Just what are you doing that's got you worried about being
too weakhearted? What else could working with metal entail
besides working with knives?'

Every now and then I had customers like Eunok, single
mothers who had devoted themselves to raising their children
and whose hearts had hardened into lumps of coal. Most of
them came to me because they couldn't see how they would
manage to make ends meet, and they would ask me, with the
same looks on their faces as Eunok was wearing now, when they
could hope to get out of the muck. And every time I replied
without hesitation: you can wash your hands clean when you're
dead. I had to refrain from saying anything too hopeful. That
way, these women with their hollow expressions would be back
to see me again in just a few days' time, asking if I could at least
make them a talisman.

'So you know I work with knives.'

Eunok, who had been staring at me without a word, dropped
her head. All of a sudden, she quietly started to cry. I could see
the pain relief patches pathetically stuck on her knees, peeking
out from her skirt. I'd just said all that imagining she was working in a tiny restaurant or something somewhere, but it seemed
I'd hit the nail on the head.

'You've still got a long way to go before you're out of the
mire. But if that work makes it so you can put food on the table,
what's there to worry about?'

'Shinja, you're a real pro,' she said. 'How can you be so calm
knowing all this? Aren't you scared, finding out your friend is a
human butcher?'

A human butcher? What was she talking about now? As Eunok had said, I was a professional – a professional liar. I was the queen of quick wit, the master mollifier. I decided to try feeling this out.

'Of course not. I sometimes have people in your line of work come to see me. Hey, now, stop crying. No matter what work you do, is earning money ever easy? I know how you feel. Anyone who can do that job without guilt weighing on their conscience isn't human. I understand. But . . . how did someone as pure-hearted as you end up with this job?'

Eunok wiped at her reddened eyes with her sleeve, sobbing so hard her shoulders shook.

'I had to make a living, so I just jumped in,' she said. 'I had to put my children through school, but all I had as far as talent went were the chopping skills I'd learned from being a butcher. But at my age, without anything to my name, I couldn't set up my own shop. That's how I got started in this business. Still, I only kill people who deserve it. Yesterday, I dealt with a loan shark who lent money to poor women, only to charge them hundreds of times the cost of the loan in interest.'

Chopping skills . . . kill . . . dealt with—

These words struck my ears, one after the other. Here was Eunok, someone who wouldn't brush the nits off her head because she pitied the poor things, telling me that she chopped people up and killed them for a living. I felt a sudden twinge of pain somewhere in my head, like the time when, as a child, I was stung by a bumblebee in an orchard and dropped the basket of food I had been carrying on my head when I fell flat on my face from the shock.

'Shinja,' Eunok pleaded. 'I came to see you, knowing you

might call the police on me, but I didn't care. I heard how skilled a shaman you were and thought you might already know before I even said a word. But you treated me so calmly all the same – I can't help but cry. Now that I've told you all this, I feel like I can breathe again.'

Her voice kept swelling and breaking like the cries of cicadas at the end of the summer.

'So, simply put, you're a killer,' I said. 'I'm . . . glad you could get everything off your chest. But aren't you busy? No one to deal with today?'

'Nope, I'm all done for the day, and I have one more place to go in a couple of days. I hear he's a rapist. I ought to hack that bastard into pieces. We women can at least do that much to look out for other women, right? Anyway, I should pay you for the fortune-telling.' Eunok smiled wryly.

'Hey. Don't . . . don't say that. We're friends. I won't take your money.'

I was fumbling for the words. The cold sweat that had broken out on my forehead ran down into my eyes, blurring my vision. I wanted to grab an empty crock and shout into it, *My friend Eunok is a killer!* But if the old crock happened to shatter and my voice leaked out, if silver cuffs were to be slapped on Eunok's rough-skinned wrists, I knew her associates would hunt me down.

'Come on, work is work. Take this,' she said, thrusting a thin white envelope towards me. She had dabbed the corners of her eyes dry and was beaming, showing her teeth. Her smile was as bright as it had been when we were young, splashing around in the water in a little stream nearby, but behind it was a master swordsman swinging a sharp blade. The thought suddenly occurred to me that while it didn't feel right to charge her as my friend and a guest, there was something I could ask of Eunok the killer instead.

'Eunok, forget about the fee. Could you take care of someone for me instead?'

Eunok didn't accept my request right away. Probably because it went against her principles. She said it didn't sit right with her to take a life unless the person had directly harmed others or was enough of a villain to be considered a public enemy. But I wasn't one to back down. If Mrs Geum's husband went bankrupt, no doubt she would come for me, grab me by the hair, drag me to the police station and accuse me of fraud. I would lose everything – all the money and fame I had amassed, all the lovers I'd been seeing in secret all these years. Maybe I was the real villain in all this, but there was no need to tell Eunok that. I didn't believe in an afterlife. Nor in karma. All I could do was enjoy my life while I still had it to live.

'She's awful,' I went on. 'Probably because her family's filthy rich. Her husband owns two bus companies and a bunch of properties. She has a stepchild, her husband's from a previous marriage, but I hear she's abused the poor kid so badly he'll be walking with a limp for the rest of his life. For that alone, she deserves to die. It's only right.'

I pieced together the rumours I'd heard about Mrs Geum into the very picture of guilt. I hoped this would be enough for Eunok to reconsider.

'Child abuse? That's where I draw the line! Give me her address. I have to get home early today to pickle some cucumbers, but I'll head there tomorrow.'

I leafed through my address book and gave her Mrs Geum's home address and phone number.

'Oh, she lives near me,' Eunok remarked. 'That's perfect. Your phone could end up being tracked later on, so if I have any questions, I'll stop by to ask.'

She hoisted herself up with an *aigo, my knees* and headed out. Only after she had left did I start to worry that I might be accused of conspiracy to murder or even murder outright and spend the rest of my days in prison. But no matter how big a phony I was, I had accurately seen that Eunok's fortune was special.

A day, then two, then three, then four went by after Eunok came to see me. Time flowed on. Every morning when I opened the newspaper to the local news section, my chest seized up. Still no word from her. I wondered if something had gone wrong, but I didn't have so much as a phone number for her or any way to get in touch.

'Eunok is here to see you.'

It had been a week when she finally showed up again. My assistant opened the door, and in walked Eunok. I studied her face, but I couldn't get a read on her expression at all.

'Hey, is everything all right?'

I hadn't heard from Mrs Geum in all that time. That could mean she was alive and everything had worked out with her husband's business, or it could mean she was dead but no one suspected me.

'Shinja,' said Eunok. 'About Mrs Geum. She's going to pay you a visit soon.'

I choked on my sigh of relief. Not only was Mrs Geum alive, but she was coming to see me?

'So what are you saying?' I asked. 'Did you fail?'

Eunok looked at me with a blank expression.

'The day after I came by to see you, I went to the address you gave me,' she said. 'That woman lives in a really grand home. I waited outside for a while before I saw her – a plump woman coming out of the house carrying a grocery basket.'

She said she trailed the woman to a big discount mart. Mrs Geum filled her cart with high-quality fruits and organic vegetables, bought a few kilograms of expensive hanwoo beef and wandered around in search of other things to purchase. Eunok worried all her efforts might end up being in vain at that rate, so she decided to approach the woman.

'Oh my, aren't you Mrs Geum?' Eunok said, pretending to know her.

The woman stared back at Eunok in surprise. 'Who are you?'

'You came in for a meridian massage,' said Eunok. 'I was the one who took care of you, but I guess you don't remember.' She'd figured a wealthy woman like Mrs Geum would frequent the skincare shop the way regular people frequented the bathroom.

'You must have mistaken me for someone else,' said Mrs Geum. 'How could a lowly housekeeper afford something as luxurious as a meridian massage?'

With that, Mrs Geum pushed past Eunok and hurried away. But Eunok followed her and tried to find another opening.

'Mrs Geum, I know it's you. I worked as a foot massager before. Maybe that's when we met?'

Mrs Geum stopped her cart in its tracks and glared at Eunok, eyes flashing with rage. 'Now you're just rubbing salt in the wound. Yes, I am Mrs Geum. But I'm not the missus of the house as you seem to think.'

As I listened to the story, Eunok's voice pierced straight through to my inner depths.

'One of your lovers is a high-rolling old man, right? That man is Mrs Geum's husband. She knew you were a con artist from the start.'

Eunok heaped the facts on me like the master shaman I was rumoured to be. My mouth hung open – I could neither shut it nor say a word in answer.

'Right now, Mrs Geum works as a live-in housekeeper. She gets exactly one day a week to go out freely, and that day is today.'

Let me explain. I have two lovers. One is a young trainer I met while learning to play golf, and another who's an old but soft-hearted businessman, always quick to open his wallet. The latter, Mr Han, must have been Mrs Geum's husband. He'd left home and set up an office in Japan so that he could get away from his stubborn wife who refused to grant him a divorce, and he made trips to Korea only once or twice a month. I'd even patted him on the back for this and told him I found his bad boy charm attractive.

'Eunok, what am I going to do? You told me you'd take care of her! Do something!'

Eunok didn't say a word.

'Mrs Geum is here to see you.'

As soon as my assistant announced her, the door opened. Dressed to the nines as always, Mrs Geum entered the room and sat down beside Eunok.

My heart raced. 'I'm sorry. Mrs Geum, clearly I'm a crazy bitch. I won't see Mr Han ever again, I swear. And I'll return all the money, too.'

I couldn't look her in the eye. It felt like her gaze was burning through my forehead, my chest. I crawled over to the safe behind the folding screen and took out all the cash and gold bars to bring out to her.

'My husband disappeared and left me with only one house to my name,' Mrs Geum explained. 'I sold it. And I decided to use that money to catch a scammer shaman. I went to the Smile Detective Agency. That's where I met Eunok here. I pooled together the last of my savings and put all my money on you. Then I waited for my chance. The moment you were on top of the world and had gotten everything you wanted. What woman our age doesn't have a friend named Eunok? This Eunok is Shim Eunok. I don't know if her surname's the same as the Eunok you knew. Anyway, Mrs Shim, the money from the safe should be enough to cover your fee, right?'

Eunok – but not the Eunok I knew – nodded and stuffed the bundles of money and gold bars into her shopping bag. Then she took something shiny out of the now bulging bag. Just then, as I stood facing death, I remembered my assistant waiting outside the door.

'Miss Han! Miss Han! Han Eungyeong!' I cried.

Yet there was no answer.

'Think about it,' said Mrs Geum. 'The first time I came here, it was around the time you hired Han Eungyeong as your assistant. I'm glad to be getting my revenge now, but sad that my daughter will soon be out of a job. Unfortunate, but I suppose it can't be helped. When you can't kill two birds with one stone, you've got to aim for the bigger bird.'

As I watched Shim Eunok rummage through the grocery

basket and pull out a gleaming knife, I finally remembered. My childhood friend, Eunok. Short, tan-skinned Eunok. Her surname was Nam. Nam Eunok. Where was she, and what was she doing now? *Ah* – I should have just run the damned cigarette shop.

4

The Secret Agent

I'm a secret agent.

My job is to sneak into the enemy's fortress and observe their every move, to ferret out their true motives. I don't even need to mention that I possess both the killer body of an Angelina Jolie- or Charlize Theron-type as well as a cool, calm intellect.

I did my makeup as if polishing a diamond hidden deep inside a jewellery box. In the vanity mirror, I could see behind me a man who looked only vaguely Asian sprawled out on his side, drool running from his mouth. Last night – a little past two in the morning, to be exact – he had snuck inside the house. I really can't describe it any way other than sneaking in, the way he'd opened a window in the hallway and crawled in like some petty thief. But I decided not to hold a grudge. He was my husband, and at the same time, he was my boss. He'd hired me under the pretence that I ought to sit at home, do some online shopping, and try to live like a decent human being. I accepted his bold offer, saying that if he paid me enough to shop at the department store rather than online, I'd weave straw shoes for him out of my own hair. Of course, being a secret agent wasn't the sort of job that came with great wealth or fame. He made it a condition that I donate a part of my salary – which he had also been secretly embezzling from me – but I accepted the position as a secret agent for the public good more than anything.

I was the wife of a police officer, after all.

I drew on my eyeliner. Though I had called upon the power of modern medicine to obtain them, my alluring double eyelids were rather Western in appearance, so I had to line them as thinly as possible to avoid coming across as overly sexy. The foundation I had bought with my VIP coupon at an online shopping mall made my already lovely skin glow. I put on my lipstick, a soft Indi Pink, and rubbed my lips together, then ran a hair dryer near my forehead to add some volume to my bangs.

'Have you lost your mind? Do you know what time it is? What on God's green earth has you up at dawn powdering your goddamn face?'

My husband and I were from the same hometown. But it had been years since I'd corrected my accent and stopped mixing 'country talk' into my speech. I wondered what would happen if I did as I thought Angelina would do, point a gun at my enemy's head and say, *Hey, listen up. You all had better make like the wind and blow this joint. If you don't, you're screwed.*

'Your makeup is already done. What are you playing with your bangs for now? Boy, you're as gaudy as all get out. Don't you dare think about going outside looking like that.'

My husband scrubbed his hand over his face and got out of bed, grabbing a sports drink he'd brought home while drunk and taking a sip. He looked displeased as he kept his eyes fixed on me in the mirror.

'You must only be saying that because hearing everyone tell me how pretty and young I look when we go out triggers your inferiority complex.'

He laughed out loud as he shuffled towards the bathroom. Every time I exposed his true feelings, he laughed like that out of habit. He also used to do it whenever I came home from the beauty salon asking if I looked pretty.

'Listen good to what I'm about to say. Two phone calls a day, morning and night. Don't get all carried away and excited just because you're on a secret undercover mission. Keep your eyes peeled for killing, stomping, stabbing, piercing. You see or hear anything like that, you find out when, where, and who and then call and report it to me right away. Got it?'

He downed his hot potato soup straight from the bowl and then fixed his eyes on me.

'I guess it's better that way, since you can't text on account of your fat fingers.'

From now on, my new identity would be a young woman with both brains and beauty. Honestly, I had wanted to hide the fact that I was married at all, but yesterday I'd gotten a call from some ajumma demanding certified copies of my paperwork. I wondered if it was the woman who'd introduced herself as Shim Eunok when I went in for the interview. I knew her type incredibly well. They loved nothing more than meddling, except for stirring up rumours and gossip. They always looked tacky and unsightly, as if they'd given up on being women, all but demanding sympathy from others wherever they went. Just one look at Shim Eunok was all I needed to see that she was clearly in charge of odd jobs and chores around the Smile Detective Agency's office. But there was no need to make her my enemy. Maybe being decently nice to her would pay off somehow.

The whole reason my husband had appointed me a secret agent was because of the Smile Detective Agency. As of late, violent incidents had started cropping up more frequently in their jurisdiction. Corpses hacked up by someone with excellent knife skills were turning up all over. Knife skills that had been honed to slit throats, stab through the small of the back and aim for the heart with startling accuracy. My husband got all worked up over this, calling it 'the resurrection of Park Taesang the Butcher'.

This Mr Park had retired and opened up the Smile Detective Agency as an errand centre on the outskirts of the city and was living a worry-free life now, but he had at one time been a killer who had ruled that shadowy realm. Everywhere he went reeked of blood and was cordoned off by police tape. But my husband, and even his predecessor, could never get the man in cuffs. There was never so much as a strand of hair or a fragment of a fingerprint at the crime scene, and anyone who witnessed the killings would only click their tongues and say that the person who'd died had it coming, then refuse to testify. But the knife skills used in the string of murders that had happened recently were subtly different from his; they were a little more delicate, while also a little bolder. If I had to try to put it into words, it was as if we were seeing the return of a more refined Park Taesang – a post-Park Taesang, if you will. My husband believed he'd taught his skills to a new killer, and it was my job to find out who that new killer was.

'Lee Seongran, do you think that miniskirt looks good on

you? You're practically begging people to make radish kimchi out of your calf muscles.'

He could babble as much as he wanted, but I lived by my own style. Who knows? I could end up being the next one chosen to inherit the title of Park Taesang's protégé killer. Maybe then my husband would regret blowing all that hot air at me.

Though it didn't quite match my looks or my job, to disguise myself thoroughly, I took the village bus. Some students and old people were nodding off in their seats. Their faces made me think they had lived ordinary lives up to now and would spend the rest of their days never straying too far from what was familiar.

Unlike them, my face glowed with confidence and life in my compact mirror.

As soon as I entered the Smile Detective Agency, I spotted Shim Eunok wiping down Mr Park's desk with a rag, looking as matronly as I'd anticipated. Who would wear one of those red World Cup T-shirts these days? Not to mention the unflattering accordion skirt she had on underneath it. She looked at me and smiled as she made her way over.

'You can use the last desk. No traffic on the way?'

Look at her, acting all familiar with me on the sly, same as she'd done when we first met. Because of women like her, even respectable women like me were lumped in with every other uncultured lady of a certain age in this godawful world. I clicked my tongue and took a seat at the desk I'd been assigned. The high heels I was wearing for the first time in a while had made the soles of my feet numb.

A young man came in, a mop over his shoulder that was drip, drip, dripping water on the floor. He bowed his head in greeting.

'Mrs Shim, you're here early. And I see our other Mrs has clocked in early, too.'

It was one thing for him to refer to Shim Eunok as a Mrs, but me? Sure, I was technically middle-aged. But I knew for a fact that I wasn't so far gone as to be referred to as a Mrs like some common ajumma. The kid looked me up and down, gasped and covered his mouth, then disappeared behind the half-wall that divided the room.

'Mrs . . . bangs . . . eyeliner . . . don't know what to say . . .'

I could hear his voice sporadically from behind the room divider.

'Anyone who hasn't had breakfast yet, gather round,' called out Mrs Shim.

At the sound of her voice, the kid came around the divider again and shuffled over.

'You should gather round, too, ma'am,' he said to me. 'Mrs Shim brings us breakfast boxes every morning.'

So now I was a 'ma'am', while their odd-jobs lady Shim Eunok was a 'Mrs'? I couldn't accept that, but in the end, I was here to do a job. I couldn't reveal my true self by acting rashly; I needed my coworkers to like me if I was going to catch them out. On the table in the conference room, a small feast was spread out: rice with peas and seasoned bean sprouts, braised mackerel, sliced radish, summer squash fritters, stir-fried anchovies, and more.

'I have a brief announcement to make,' I said. I thought it would be best to set things straight from the start. If I just let it slide, I knew it'd become a habit and soon everyone would be calling me 'ma'am'. I was a secret agent – I couldn't possibly be treated like an ajumma.

The two of them split their wooden chopsticks apart and stared at me blankly, waiting.

'My name is Lee Seongran,' I said. 'Words like *ma'am* or *ajumma* or *older lady* – they're rude, you know. I'm about the same age as Eunok, whom you all call Mrs Shim, but even that seems like too much. Please call me Ms Lee. You may not be familiar with the term, but it's a more equitable English title than Miss or Mrs. You can do that for me, can't you? Ms Lee.'

As soon as I said it, I felt better, but then—

'What? A mizuwari?'

In walked Park Taesang, with his husky voice, long strides, and the faint scent of cologne emanating from him. He came to stand beside me. He had thick facial hair – he had given himself a close shave, yet there was a bluishness around his chin that gave this away. I'd never given him a proper look when I interviewed him, but now I could see that he was fairly handsome in a rugged sort of way. Rather than a legendary killer, he reminded me of a kind-hearted university professor. But when it came to eloquence, his skills left much to be desired. A mizuwari? Was he saying I was like watered-down alcohol?

'Boss, you're here,' said the kid who'd been grating on my nerves already. He handed Mr Park a set of chopsticks, smiling.

'Speaking of mizuwaris, should we all go out for a drink after work?'

'It's Ms Lee, not mizuwari,' I snapped.

Mr Park stuffed food into his mouth, perhaps to hide his grin.

'This kid's Choi Joongi, the youngest on our staff. If you have any questions, you can ask him. And here we have Mrs Shim Eunok. She's the eldest of us and helps with managing our operations here at the office.'

As Mr Park introduced them, I scanned each of their faces. There was no way this half-wit kid could be a killer. And seeing as she helped with managing operations, Eunok must have been an accountant or a general manager. In that case, it seemed the post-Park Taesang protégé had yet to clock in. Then again, I doubted that a killer would be dawdling away in the office. With wrinkled hands, Eunok was placing chunks of fish meat on top of Joongi's and Mr Park's rice. They looked pathetic in their shabby outfits. I couldn't help but frown, remembering how my family used to sit gathered under 60-watt light bulbs, pouring spoonfuls of soup into pots that had already been soldered with lead sheets countless times. Ceilings stained with rat urine, oil bottles grazed by rat tails, soap fragments gnawed to bits by rat teeth – as these images floated before my eyes like ghosts, I shuddered.

'Joongi, you have a meeting at five p.m. with a potential client who was swindled by a blackmail ring. Go investigate the situation and report back. Mizuwari – I mean, Ms Lee, you'll receive some documents from Joongi – read through them thoroughly and then we'll discuss. And Mrs Shim, you'll meet with me separately this morning.'

The meal boxes Mrs Shim had set on the table had been

emptied out in the blink of an eye. Everyone went to their own stations, either to do some stretching or to riffle through file folders. As Mr Park and Eunok disappeared into a small room on the other side of the office, Joongi set a stack of documents on my desk.

'These are family counselling cases,' he said, launching into an explanation about the files labelled with half-assed scribbles that were apparently his handwriting. 'There are a lot of investigations of spouses who had affairs, but also some requests from siblings or between parents and their children regarding inheritance issues. Here's a list of clients who have requested protection, and these files summarize fraud cases – not just instances of blackmail and intimidation, but cases of gold-diggers and gigolos, too. You'll see when you flip through. Oh, and this file has information on debt collection. If you have any questions, you can ask me or Mrs Shim anytime.'

'Do you all ever receive any requests for contract killings, things like that?'

My question must have hit the nail on the head because Joongi's face flushed. If I managed to coax something out of this small fry, I'd probably be able to sniff out the big fish.

'We are a properly licensed business,' he said. 'You should be careful that anything you just said doesn't reach the boss's ears. And I'll inform you about the matters of compliance for employees. We don't reveal our clients' information with any third parties. We don't include any false information or speculation when reporting the results of an investigation. We don't engage in any unethical or unlawful behaviour. If you ever come across a case that seems to have no leads and is beyond your capacity, you are to report it directly to the company and we'll assign an employee suitable for the task. You must also report any on-the-job slip-ups as soon as possible and prepare to take countermeasures. Ms Lee, is all of that understood? As long as you comply with these rules going forward, you shouldn't have too hard a time.'

After rattling off the guidelines, Joongi returned to his desk. I was disappointed I hadn't gotten the answer I was looking for, but no one ever felt full after only the first bite. I sent a message to my husband-boss.

Mr Park having private chat with ajumma. Strong denial re contract killings.

The most suspicious thing was that Mr Park was having a closed-door meeting with Eunok, but there was a chance that the meeting was to chide her about the awful state of uncleanliness around the office or to warn her about bringing in food from home. Still, as the classic saying goes, even the sauce tastes bitter in the house that's full of talk, and excluding Joongi who simply liked to meddle, it also seemed possible that Mrs Shim could be a person to keep an eye on. If only my desk were slightly closer to their meeting room, I might be able to eavesdrop. I wished then that I had some wiretapping equipment. At that moment, I got a reply. My husband must have been exerting himself all that while to type it out.

thts nnsnse

I set my phone to silent mode and put it away, then opened up one of the file folders. There was an overview of each client's information and case details, and the investigation process and results had been organized accordingly.

'I'm going to work outside the office.'

At some point, Mr Park had come out of the meeting room.

Now he was moving around hurriedly, brushing some dirt off his collar. I briefly met his eyes. I felt a short but obvious spark. His gaze drove a blade into your heart and pierced straight through it. Afraid I would be found out, I was the first to turn away. Once he'd left, I felt a jolt in my chest and a gasp leave my mouth as saliva pooled beneath my tongue.

'Ms Lee, you're drooling.'

Eunok tore some tissue from a roll and held it under my chin.

I sucked my spit back in and sat up straighter in my seat. My face heated up from embarrassment.

'I'm sorry, but we all have another task to work on this morning. Could you please just answer the office phone? All you'd need to do is jot down each caller's contact info.'

After Eunok bombarded me with orders, she exchanged a look with Joongi, who stood up and went towards the meeting room. He looked nervous.

'What kind of task?' I asked Eunok. 'Am I not allowed to know?'

She had already made to leave, but turned back, clearly flustered by my question.

'We don't want to burden you with all the nitty gritty work from the start,' she said. 'If Mr Park calls, tell him we're out of the office on business. We have something to finish up by tomorrow, so please cover for us, just for an hour or two. Sound good?'

Before I could even reply, the two of them shut the door to the meeting room. Not long after, the security guard from the first floor came up and just waltzed right in. I could hear some chatter on the other side of the door for a moment before the room fell completely silent. Just what could they all be scheming about while I was left in the dark? Could they be plotting to carry out a contract killing? Just earlier, Mr Park had given them all tasks to be completed by this evening or tomorrow. Were his instructions perhaps some kind of code? I decided all of this wasn't to be reported via text message. I tiptoed out to the end of the hallway and hid in the bathroom there. Then I called my husband.

'Yeah?' he answered, sounding annoyed.

'I'm in the bathroom,' I whispered.

'Since when do you need my permission for that?'

'Mr Park left the office, and the rest of the staff is in the meeting room.'

'And?'

'I need wiretapping equipment. For the phone and inside that conference room.'

'Don't you think you're missing the mark here? What could they all be discussing without their boss there? Hm? Just hold your damn horses, I'll be right there. I'm a busy man, Lee Seongran!'

I could hear shouts in the background on his end, then the wails of phones ringing.

'Look, Go Jungshik – if you don't want to regret it later, you'd better listen real good to what I'm about to say. Keep looking down on these guys and you'll end up with your neck wrung, you got that? When you hear they're meeting up all hush-hush without Mr Park, you don't smell a rat? Clearly, they're the big shots here, or they're trying to take him out. I'm telling you, forget about Mr Park – we need to focus on these guys first.'

I was so worked up that the country talk I thought I'd forgotten came pouring out. If my hunch was right, those three in the meeting room were plotting together and could end up stabbing Mr Park in the back. I thought again of the depth of his gaze from earlier.

'All right, I hear you,' said my husband, softening his tone like a dog with its tail between its legs. 'Let's finish up our workdays, and I'll see you at home, yeah?'

He hung up. Back at my desk, I flipped through file folders with trembling hands. All was still silent in the meeting room. Only at lunchtime did the three of them emerge to decide on their lunch orders and ask me to eat with them. I ordered kalguksu, and as I slurped my noodles I listened in on their conversation.

'Mrs Shim, my shoulder hurts,' Joongi pouted, swinging his arm.

'That's because your posture's bad,' Eunok replied. 'You have to straighten your back and push down from above like Mr Kim does. You've got a bit of a hunchback and tend to lift from below, so you strain your shoulders more.'

As Joongi ate his dumpling soup, he studied me, then sent Eunok a look. Clearly something serious had happened in the meeting room. Instead of simply convening to plot a murder, it was almost as if they'd already carried one out.

After clearing the table, Eunok cleaned up a bit around the office, and the security guard came with a cup of coffee to chat with Joongi for a while before he went back downstairs. In the afternoon, Joongi left the office to work outside, and Eunok went back into the meeting room alone. The whole time I kept watch over the empty office by myself.

When it was almost time to clock out, Mr Park called. He informed me that he'd be heading straight home from wherever he was offsite and hung up the call without asking any questions. Only after six o'clock did Eunok come out of the meeting room looking pinched. I wanted to take a look around that meeting room, but because Eunok had already cleaned up behind, I had to head home with nothing to show for the day's efforts. My husband got home only after midnight.

'Doesn't look like I can get wiretapping gear without a warrant,' he said.

'Then are you saying we should toss all the fish we caught back out to sea? I'm telling you, I've put my trust in scum like these guys before and ended up being played for a fool for ten years.'

My husband scratched his head for a while, deep in thought. Then he looked up again.

'It's not like there's no way to get the warrant,' he said. 'When we're dealing with suspects in a homicide case, we can do emergency wiretapping. But we can only bug them for up to thirty-six hours. If we can't get definitive evidence within that window, it'll hurt the prosecution, and the police department's reputation will go to shit.'

I had thirty-six hours to close the case. If the plot they'd been cooking up in the meeting room was set to have been carried out by tomorrow, I'd foolishly already missed my chance. I pressed my husband to go back to the police station. Then I waited anxiously for him to call as it neared dawn.

The call came well into the morning, around the time I needed to head to work.

'Hey, listen up,' he said. 'We got the wiretaps. One of our guys'll bring them to you. Stash one of them somewhere it won't be seen, and the other, my guy will set up directly in the terminal box on the first floor. If anyone asks, say he's from the phone company. If you do anything to screw this up, though, you're on your own.'

I hurriedly did my secret agent makeup and took a cab to the office. My lips were dry, and there was a prickling in the pit of my stomach as though it were full of chestnut burs.

When I got to the office, no one else was there yet. I kept checking the bathroom just in case, and then I took the elevator down to the first floor. A man in work clothes walked right past the security guard, dozing off at his post.

'Ms Lee Seongran?' the man asked.

When I nodded, he handed me a wiretap that looked like a pen. Looking around cautiously, I returned to the office to hide it inside the meeting room. There was an old Formica table and five chairs crowded uncomfortably around it. A pair of scissors, an awl, a handheld game console, an MP3 player, some shoddy plastic dolls and other junk were lying about. And last but not least, a rucksack as big as a person in the corner of the room caught my eye. It was about 160 or 170 centimetres in length, about as tall as a man on the shorter side or the average woman. Where the zipper that went across the rucksack stopped, a tuft of dark brown hair was sticking out. I felt goosebumps spring up all over my skin.

On the table were marks where it seemed like something had been chopped with a sharp object, and I could smell a faint chemical scent in the air. I desperately wanted to search that rucksack, but I couldn't muster the courage. I stashed the wiretapping device in the rubbish bin under the table and hurried out of the room. Not long after, Eunok and Joongi showed up, greeted me, and ate their breakfast, same as yesterday. So as not to arouse their suspicions, I joined them in eating the cooked beans and stir-fried fishcakes.

At last, Eunok convened the group.

'Mr Park said he'll be coming in late, so we should just see to our own work,' she told me. I returned to my desk.

The security guard, Mr Kim, flashed me a wink as he went inside the meeting room. I sat in my seat and gave them all my most dazzling smile, but I could feel several beads of cold sweat running down my face, cutting tracks through my foundation.

Several hours later, Eunok was the first one to come out of the meeting room, followed by Mr Kim and Joongi hauling the rucksack out and groaning from the effort. I noticed what appeared to be flecks of fresh blood staining the bottom of Joongi's clothes. They disappeared for a while with the rucksack and came back empty handed. Joongi took a white envelope out of his pocket and carefully handed it to Eunok.

'Mr Choi said to thank you for handling this so quickly. He put a little something extra in there for you, too.'

Eunok readily accepted the envelope and stashed it away in a drawer. Then she turned and locked eyes with me. I quickly turned my attention to the file folder on my desk, pretending to be leafing through it.

'I'll call Mr Park and tell him I have something to discuss with him. Play innocent for a bit, and then when I call, you come over with what we prepared. You can't afford to miss the timing, got it?'

Joongi gave a determined nod.

'And Ms Lee. Please forget you heard any of this.'

I nodded. I was a secret agent who had now uncovered their dangerous secret – that they killed people for money. I had misjudged them after all. Eunok was cunning, fooling Mr Park with her shabby appearance, all the while eyeing his position.

I skipped lunch, citing an upset stomach as my excuse, and waited for everyone to disperse. Eunok left with her shopping bag, saying she was going to work outside the office, and soon after Joongi left his desk as well. Once I was alone, I went into the meeting room and fished the wiretapping device out of the rubbish bin. When I returned to my desk, I considered listening to whatever the device had recorded, but my heart was seizing up in my chest and my knees were shaking, so I didn't dare. Just then the office door swung open.

'Is everyone working offsite?'

It was Mr Park. He walked soundlessly into the office, smelling faintly of cologne as always, and set a can of coffee down in front of me.

'I got it at the petrol station,' he said. 'Has your workload been manageable?'

'I still haven't had much of what you'd call a workload . . . But anyway, thank you for the coffee.'

Mr Park returned to his own seat, humming a familiar melody, then rummaged through his briefcase and pulled out a slim book.

'Do you enjoy poetry?' he asked. 'Everyone in our office is so friendly and hardworking, but our pastimes are worlds apart. They all hate reading. This here is a collection by the poet Ham Minbok.'

His voice was as clear and resonant as the woodblock that Buddhist monks struck as they recited their chants. The pace of his speaking was refreshing, with slowness and urgency in harmony. As he read the book, I was transported back thirty years to a time long before I was a secret agent, when I was a student shuddering as I read the essays of Jeon Hyerim. From the side, Mr Park resembled my literature teacher. My first love. I closed my eyes. Before I knew it, I was in my tight-fitting school uniform again. The shack infested with mice and thousand leggers where us five siblings huddled together, wishing we could grow up fast – it manifested in my mind's eye in a flash. My literature teacher came to class with a set of the major works of Korean contemporary poets he'd bought at a used bookshop. Sweet Seongran, always taking such good care of her little siblings, he said. His voice, so warm and hazy that it made me feel as if I were drifting off to sleep, reminded me of Park Taesang's.

'Oh, Mrs Shim. Yes, I just got back. Six o'clock? Of course. Everything's fine, right?' He had answered the phone while I was lost in my memories. He hung it up just as quickly.

It must have been Eunok calling him. I gripped the wiretapping device with a trembling hand and went over to Mr Park.

'Sir,' I said. 'You're being deceived.'

Mr Park shut his book and looked up at me in surprise.

'Pardon?'

'Mrs Shim and Choi Joongi are deceiving you. This is proof of that.'

I handed him the wiretapping device. It looked like a ballpoint pen, but as was fitting for the CEO of a detective agency, Mr Park immediately found the 'play' button and pressed it. I heard footsteps and some odd noises. Then came a familiar voice – Shim Eunok's.

'*Watch me carefully. Raise the pointed end high up and then bring it down. Why does a bright-eyed and bushy-tailed young one like you keep making mistakes? Mr Kim, you're no better – you just worry about cleaning up the mess. Don't just stab any which way but hold it in your hand like a bobbin of thread, roll it up, and push it in neatly. Yes, like that. Easier than you thought, right? Oh, blood! Watch your hands!'*

As he listened to Eunok's voice, frown lines appeared on Mr Park's face.

'How are we going to fool Mr Park?'

That was probably Joongi.

'I'm sure if we suggest meeting, he won't suspect anything and will come. If he says he can't make it, I'll have to go to him.'

'And what about Ms Lee?'

'When I call later, come by the office and get her.'

I felt a chill run down the back of my neck. Mr Park pressed fast-forward on the recording device. There was some scuffling before the voices returned.

'All done. Geez, my arms are killing me. I don't want to do this kind of stuff ever again.'

'Thanks to this kind of stuff, we can make good money. Oh dear, there's strands of hair everywhere.'

Mr Park turned off the device. To my surprise, he was grinning.

'So they're plotting something,' he said. 'Please pretend you know nothing about this.'

I returned to my desk, hands shaking, and sent my husband a text message.

6 p.m., trail Mr Park's car. And get a SWAT team or something ready. This is huge.

He didn't reply. I was anxiously eyeing the wall clock as Mr Park casually hummed. At five-forty, he stood up.

'I'll get going first,' he said. 'If you hear from anyone on the team, just give in and go along with them. Who knows? You might see something very interesting.'

Once he was gone, not even five minutes later, the office phone rang. It was Joongi.

'Ms Lee, come down to the first floor right away. I'm in a silver Sonata. Lock the doors and leave the key in the security booth.'

I slipped my handbag on to my shoulder. If this conversation had been bugged, my husband would have known I was in danger. I grabbed the key off Eunok's desk and locked the doors. I left the key with the security guard who was dozing off in the booth and turned around to find a car letting out three short honks. It was a silver Sonata. I climbed into the passenger seat with a total poker face intact. The whole time he drove, Joongi didn't say a word.

About ten minutes later, we arrived at a galbi restaurant on the outskirts of the city. A waitress led us to a special guest room on the second floor. Joongi and the waitress exchanged an indecipherable look. He accepted five sets of cutlery from the waitress and nodded his head vigorously. It seemed like a secret code of some sort. In his hand, Joongi held a black plastic bag that contained something boxy. Joongi slid open the door to the separate room and came face to face with Eunok and Mr Park.

'You all said you had something important to discuss. What's going on here?'

Mr Park grinned. It was hard to believe this man had come up against so many countless monsters, perhaps even been a monster himself, given how flawless his face was. As soon as I entered the guest room, the waitress slid the door shut. My heart sank. I clutched my handbag tight, hunched over, and found an empty seat.

Three pistol shots rang out – *Bang, bang, bang!*

I squeezed my eyes shut and put my head down on the table. I didn't hear any screams, though, nor did I smell any blood.

'Looks like even the special forces police chief has decided to join us,' Mr Park greeted someone warmly. The special forces police chief? Had my husband managed to round up some trustworthy guys from the SWAT team? I kept my head down. At that moment, something touched my shoulder. A warm, gentle hand. I raised my head the tiniest bit to peek at that hand. Fingernails cut down to the quick, fine wrinkles in the skin like the strands of a cobweb.

'Nice. Thanks to Mr Park, we'll get to eat our fill and then some today.'

The hand belonged to the security guard. A broad smile spread across his wrinkled face. Did these guys all refer to the security guard as the police chief of the special forces for some reason? I smelled gunpowder, but no one was bleeding or unconscious.

'Joongi, where's the knife?'

Joongi rummaged through a shopping bag. A knife! My final moments were surely drawing near. And still not a peep from my husband, who'd never once been helpful in his entire life. I was determined to search for the right moment to save myself, to haul ass and run. That was when the door slid open again.

In strode my husband, my greatest nemesis and regret on this earth, haughtily pointing his gun. Behind him were three guys who seemed to be the actual special forces, all decked out in their gear, standing low to the ground.

'It seems there's been a misunderstanding,' said Mr Park, as he got to his feet, hands in the air.

At long last, my duties for the day as a secret agent were complete.

As relief washed over me, my vision began to waver as I came down from the adrenaline spike. On the edge of consciousness, looking across the table at Eunok as she tried to hide her look of surprise, I saw something shiny like a cutlassfish fall to the floor from her waist. Like a dream.

When I came to, I was lying on my bed at home.

'You're up?'

My husband was watching a cable entertainment programme rerun with a bored look on his face and the volume up high.

'Did you take care of those guys?' I asked. Thanks to me, he might now be up for a promotion to lieutenant this year.

'Take care of them? You idiot! The hell am I supposed to do with you? How could you think those guys were killers? They had a light workload, so they got together to start a side hustle sticking the heads on those ugly little Moody Dolls. That's how they made enough money to take Mr Park out for a birthday meal. Did you listen to the bug all the way to the end? They said they get paid fifty won a head. Damn it, what could be more embarrassing than this?'

My husband had gotten himself so worked up that he went to the bathroom to rinse his face. I couldn't believe what he was saying.

'Does that mean I'm fired? Do they know I was undercover?'

He half-heartedly patted his face and around his bloodshot eyes with a hand towel before cutting me down with a vicious glare.

'What does it matter? You want to go back there?'

'Just answer me! Did you blow my cover or what?'

'No matter how big a sucker I am, I'd have to be out of my damn mind to let them find out that I know you. Would *you* even claim yourself if you were in my shoes? *"Yeah, I'm close with that dummy over there."* Ha. Never again will I fall for your nonsense. And don't you forget it!'

That was when I realized. That my husband's laughter had never been meant to disguise his true feelings. His laugh was an expression of a sense of futility. Like my laughter at this very moment. It held the hollowness of that snack they called 'empty bread', and the emptiness of slicing your hand on the cap after you had so been looking forward to that 'one more bottle' to drink.

I looked at the time. It was seven-thirty, and if I got ready now I could probably make it to work on time. I truly believed that the shiny, cutlassfish-like thing that Eunok had dropped before I lost consciousness was a sharpened knife. And I had a hunch.

A hunch that at some point that knife would end up buried in the body of the cheery, smiling Mr Park.

Feeling even more anxious than I had on my first day of work, I applied my eyeliner. A bit more thickly than I had the day before. As I swept the brush around my eyes, I created skilled smudges like a costume to cover up my inner feelings.

5

The Neighbour

Let's say you took somebody blond and blue-eyed who'd never stepped foot outside their home continent and you dropped them off in a cave along with a ten-year food supply. Then imagine you threw a Korean-English dictionary and a complete set of Pak Kyongni's *Land* novels at them. What would happen? Imagine that every day you fed them just enough food and administered just enough medicine to sustain them, then after fifteen years, you brought them out of the cave. What sort of person would they be then? Once they were finally able to see daylight again, they might find that they knew more about the narrator of *Land*, the only thing they had read in ages, than they knew about themselves. They might see the dazzling world laid out before their unaccustomed eyes and falteringly remark to the rescue team how much it resembled the vast fields of Pyeongsa-ri from the books.

If you had left them not with books but with a wire saw and a carving knife, they may have become a master sculptor, and if you had given them a violin or a trumpet, they could have honed decent performance skills. Even if you had left them with nothing, there's no question that after such a long period of meditation, they would have moved at least one step closer to knowing all of creation.

In order not to go mad in a confined space with nothing else to do, people tended to root out some task or other to keep themselves occupied. That was human nature.

In my case, I had been confined to this house with my husband for fifteen years. We passed the time doing nothing. Thus we became meditators. We did not know who imprisoned us here. To keep us trapped, they disguised an elderly man in a navy-blue cap with a whistle round his neck as a security guard to stand watch at the entrance of the building. He had such a sharp gaze and a rough way of speaking that it was hard to look him in the eyes. I was so scared of the gun and anaesthetics I knew were hidden somewhere in the waistband of his trousers that it had been a long time since I'd even dared to think about leaving the house.

Every morning, our captors left rice and kimchi, along with several side dishes, outside our door. The portions were laughably meagre for two people, and the food wasn't all that appetizing, but we would open the door just wide enough to stick a hand out and snatch the bag containing the food we needed to survive, cautiously bringing it inside. Every month, our captors would deposit just enough money into our account to pay our utility bills. We weren't sure when it had happened, but at some point, a freeze had been put on all the money my husband had been planning to use to escape, leaving him unable to spend a penny of it. I wondered if that bank account was accruing a ton of interest now that we couldn't go outside and spend the money in it. I took the bank book out of the drawer and turned towards the telephone that hadn't been functional in ages. Even now I was afraid the strange machine would roar back to life any second to pass along a threat from our mystery captors.

With no consumption, there was no waste. Trapped in our square of an apartment, we stared dully out the window all day. We watched birds fly past, heard children laughing, and caught a whiff of the burnt smell of potatoes roasting. My husband stood on the balcony and rummaged around in his pockets like he was looking for a cigarette. But ten years ago, he'd quit smoking. As if he could feel my worried eyes on the back of his head, he mumbled to himself, 'I didn't quit. I'm just enduring the wait.'

We weren't always this powerless. Seven years ago, my husband and I had racked our brains day and night to think up an excuse to go out. This was back when we had no idea about the surveillance cameras installed throughout the apartment. Compared to my husband, I was less shy around other people. Back then, I was just barely thirty years old, still new to having a married home. I clutched the letter my husband had written stating that we were being monitored by someone and went out in search of our neighbours in Apartment 608.

When I pressed the doorbell, a woman in a flowy, Hawaiian-style sundress opened the door. 'Can I help you?' she said, nodding slightly in greeting as she kept her hand on the door handle and eyed me warily.

I lowered my voice and hoped to quiet the pounding in my chest.

'My husband needs a screwdriver. A crosshead. Could we please borrow one?'

The woman's dark eyes quickly scanned my face, then all of me. It wasn't so late that it would be too rude to pay a neighbour a visit, and I was being nothing but polite. I wondered if it was because of my high heels with the pointed toes, but those shouldn't have disqualified me from being able to borrow a screwdriver. As the woman stared blankly at me, her lips pursed, I pressed the note I had brought with me into her hand. Then I waited, my body humming with anxiety, for her to unfold it. But the woman took her sweet time. Her expression creased into a concerted frown as she read the contents of the note aloud, one word at a time.

'Please. Help. We. Are. Under. Surveillance?'

The woman glared at me, fully suspicious now, then whipped around and marched towards her living room. Before I could say anything, she picked up the interphone.

'Yes, hello. I'm calling about the neighbour in 607,' she said into the receiver.

She proceeded to tell the man posing as the building's security guard everything. I hurriedly shut the door, then ran back to our apartment. My gaze fell on the number on the elevator display. The elevator, which had been sitting on the ground floor, began to climb. I had no doubt the fake guard would come storming into our apartment wielding a 300,000-volt taser the size of a cudgel, knock me and my husband unconscious and drag us off somewhere. I raced into the apartment, panting, and shut and locked the door behind me, but it was no use. I knew in just a few minutes, the door would swing open. My husband and I hid inside a closet and prayed for the moment to pass and leave us unscathed, but the guard found us right away, yanking the closet door wide open.

I was hidden among all the winter clothes I no longer had any reason to wear, but there was no point. There was nowhere I could run to escape the glowing eyes of the guard. As if I had been tossed into a deep body of water, I let out my last, futile breath and slumped over, my arms and legs going limp. I felt an intense vertigo, as if I was being sucked into a drain, as I lost consciousness.

When I came to, my husband and I were lying sprawled out beside each other on a bed. He was breathing so evenly, I thought he must have still been asleep. I sat up. But it turned out he had woken up before me. He rubbed his dry eyes and stared at me blankly.

'Are you OK?'

He nodded, mouth pressed shut. He sat up and looked down at the foot of the bed, where a filthy footprint, as dark as faeces, stained the sheets. Outside, rain was pouring. Even unconscious, we must have put up a fight. Our clothes and even our calves still had smears of mud on them. I went into the bathroom, turned on the shower hose and scrubbed the dirt off my legs. My lower body was stiff. Just what had happened while I'd been out cold? My husband came in silently, placing a hand on my shoulder where I sat crouched in the doorway. When I looked up at him, there were tears in the corners of his eyes. His face was pale, his hands cold. I wondered whether something even worse had happened to him.

He handed me the letter he had scribbled on a piece of paper.

Our every move is being watched. There must be cameras throughout the apartment capturing and sending footage of us to them. When we try to go out the front door, the automatic

sensor triggers the lights, so we shouldn't make any sudden
movements. If you have something to say, write it down.

I nodded. From that day on, we didn't dare try to leave the apartment, and we only conversed in writing. Mostly we talked about needing to find someone who would help us escape. We thought that, like in the movies, if we could open up the vents, there would be enough space to crawl through them, so we turned the bathroom lights off and took the covers off the vents, but there was hardly enough room to stick half an arm in before we hit an unending maze of PVC pipes.

My husband's Plan B was to write messages on sheets of paper asking for help, fold them into planes, and send them soaring towards the playground outside. He folded dozens of them tirelessly every day. I would take the finished ones he handed me and, keeping low to the ground, send them flying from the balcony, but they would only get caught in the trees lining the streets below or else fall into flowerbeds and get soaked in the rain. Not a single person seemed to be keeping enough of an eye out to notice any of them.

Then one year, right around the time children were getting out of school for the summer, it happened. One of our paper airplanes landed in front of two elementary school-aged girls. The girls opened up the plane and studied it together for a long time before they took off running towards a payphone. For a moment, we had hope. Not long after, a single police car pulled up in front of the apartment building, and afraid that the fake security guard would get to us before the police did, we threw the blankets over ourselves and crouched down. The bell rang. Whoever had pressed the button must have realized that the door was unlocked, as it soon opened. Through a gap in the blankets, I could see a line of sunlight seeping in through the front door and over the wood floors inside the apartment for the first time in a while.

'Is anyone here?'

Our hero – a real police officer.

I swallowed down the surge of tears welling up inside me and rushed to the entrance where the police officer stood. I had been stuck inside the house for so long that the muscles in my legs had begun to atrophy, and now I couldn't run as fast as I'd thought I could. Once I managed to stand up as straight as possible on ruined knees and reach the officer, I spotted the fake security guard behind him.

'Are you alone?' the police officer asked me, and the fake guard tensed.

'I'm here with my husband,' I said.

The fake guard whispered something in the officer's ear.

'Is it true that this paper plane came from this apartment?' asked the officer, holding up the folded paper plane.

'That's right. It's not a lie. That man is monitoring us. Please help.'

At some point my voice rose into something like a cry. The fake guard stepped towards me as I pointed at him, and the police officer briefly turned to him, tilting his head in confusion. Afraid the fake guard would try to harm me, I threw myself into the officer's arms and begged for help.

'Pack your things. I'll get you to a safe place.'

The officer sounded so trustworthy that I burst into tears.

'Our bags are already packed,' I told him. 'If you could just help us carry them, that would be more than enough. Honey, bring our bags.' I turned to my husband and waved him over, but he was still anxiously huddled under the blankets. With the fake guard's unhappy glare burning holes in my back, I went over to my husband.

'It's going to be OK,' I assured him. 'The officer said he'll take us someplace safe.'

But my husband stood firm.

'The police will be in cahoots with them. Just now, the two of them were whispering to each other. I'm telling you, something's up. Don't go with him. If they're the ones monitoring us, then there's nowhere to run. There's no such thing as someplace safe.'

Sure enough, when I turned back, the fake guard and the police officer were conversing in low voices. As always, my husband was right. When they were distracted for a brief moment, I rushed forward and shut and locked the door. The fake guard and the police officer knocked and kept pressing on the doorbell. If they really were the ones monitoring us, I knew that, just like last time, they would easily be able to get inside, so I began to move furniture to barricade the entrance. My husband and I had only grown weaker since then, and this time, we had only moved five wooden chairs and a dresser over to the door before we were completely exhausted. Our bodies were drenched in sweat, and we were panting for breath.

We listened to them banging and bumping against the door for a while before it burst open. The fake guard looked absolutely livid, and more strangers had joined him. They came charging into the apartment with their mud-caked trainers on and roughly grabbed me by the wrists. I struggled, twisting my entire body in their grip. But years of surviving on only the bare minimum rations meant it wasn't long before I was completely overpowered.

My husband and I were placed in separate rooms. They hooked me up to an IV and filled the drip with all sorts of drugs. Some of them put me soundly to sleep, and others made me rage like a storm. Just as it had been in our apartment, I couldn't come and go from this place as I pleased. The fake security guard and the woman from 608 each came in once, peered down at me with hard expressions, and then disappeared, and there was a pair – a man and a woman I didn't know – who came by to ask me things. Most of their questions were personal ones. They wrote in a notebook, then left.

Those people came by several times a day to refill the medicine that made me sleepy and told me to forget about how much I missed my husband. I had long, drawn-out dreams that felt like swimming through sludge water, in which my husband and I went shopping around for a newlywed home. We picked out new furniture and bought dishware and appliances. My husband in the dreams was fit and ruddy-faced, very different from my husband as he was now.

He and I had worked at the same publishing company. I did proofreading and copy-editing, and he was the supplier to the bookshops. We were so hard at work in our respective areas that we rarely saw each other around. It was only after we'd been working at the same place for three months that we ended up across the table from each other at a company dinner. Sat in front of the sizzling meat on the grill, he began to sing. Our boss had requested that I sing a tune, and it was my future husband who offered to do it in my stead. He held a bottle like it was a microphone and sang a sorrowful song. That was the last

time I ever heard him sing. He and I weren't especially exciting people, and we much preferred to listen to others rather
than perform ourselves. In my dreams, I relived the countless
days we had spent together, like a soap opera that never ended.
Sometimes I woke up crying or laughing, my head seeming to
grow lighter the more I replayed those memories.

They decided to release me. I only ever answered 'Yes' to
their questions, and they turned out to be kinder than I thought
and gave me permission to return home. They handed me a
paper with print as tiny as sesame seeds on it and told me to
sign. It didn't matter to me what it said. I desperately missed
my husband, and so I quickly scribbled my name on the line.
The next day, I was led home by the man and woman who had
visited me from time to time.

'There will be side effects. You may continue to experience
them for a while, but over time it'll get better. Be sure to take
your medicine three times a day.'

The man and woman turned me over to the fake security
guard, who gripped my shoulders and walked me to the front
door of my apartment. There was a plastic bag hanging from
the door handle. Even without looking inside, I knew there
would be rice and two or three side dishes. I removed the bag
and slid it on to my wrist, then opened the door. The inside of
the apartment appeared frozen in time, exactly as it had been
the day we were taken. Fallen pieces of furniture and appliances were strewn all over. If anything was different, it was the
fact that my husband wasn't there. I straightened out a couple
of pieces of furniture, then lay down on the empty bed. It still
smelled of my husband.

The next day and the day after that, my husband didn't come

home. So many times I picked up the phone receiver only to set it back down. After worrying for a while, I paged the fake security guard on the interphone.

'My husband still isn't here.'

The guard hesitated for a moment. Then he said, 'Your husband isn't coming back.'

'Why not?' I asked. 'Why wouldn't he?'

'Ma'am, please. Stop this. You know he passed away.'

The guard hung up. After telling me that my husband was dead.

My husband had always been a soft-hearted man. He didn't have it in him to say a rude word to anyone, and he didn't dare watch scary movies or dramas, knowing he couldn't handle them. He worried so much about his devotion possibly wavering someday that he never had children. What had those people done to my husband? Had he falsely confessed to something? I felt utterly drained. If those strangers had indeed belonged to some secret state agency, there was no way he could have avoided death at their hands, all because of what had happened that day so long ago.

My husband's only hobby in life was fishing. After we married, he found a proper river on the outskirts of Seoul and would spend one night camped out there every month before returning home in the morning. There were certain tricks that he alone knew about that spot, and though it was rare, he would sometimes even hook stingrays or big, hearty fish like croakers. That day, too, my husband said he had been eating some eggs he had boiled in a camping pot and staring out at the river.

Around an hour before sunrise, when the darkness was at its peak, he heard the low rumble of the engine from a nice car in the distance. My husband shrugged off the cold and his own sleepiness and watched what looked like the twin glowing eyes of a wild animal approach him. When the car was about a hundred metres away, it came to a stop at a spot upstream. Two men in white dress shirts and fancy black suits stepped out of the car and hauled something out of the trunk with some effort. The men didn't notice my husband there as they tossed something like a sack into the water. The river was narrow and deep, so no one ever swam in it, and there wasn't even a hamlet nearby where any people might live. There were also patches of unpaved road here and there, so the only people who might manage to find this spot were the handful of people like my husband, desperate to avoid company for a while and fish for hours on end like the Duke Tai of Qi in his exile. The men looked around, dusted their hands, then climbed back into the car and disappeared.

My husband waited, crouched low, until their car was out of sight. He watched the spot where they had tossed that sack. The currents were mild, just as they would have been any other day, and figuring that he stood a chance at catching something like a carp that would have otherwise been hard to hook, he cast his line out again. But his unease wouldn't die down, and soon after, he decided to reel in his line. Just then, something caught on it, the line cutting across the water as whatever it was pulled on the hook. He thought it might be a carp as big as his arm. My husband wrestled with whatever it was until the day began to break and the sky began to brighten, and only after seven a.m. did he finally manage, his entire body drenched in sweat, to reel in not a carp but that heavy sack. Seized with fear, he was debating how to toss it back when he felt himself taking in the refreshing morning sunlight and the gentle breeze, the flitting sounds of birds, to muster a sense of bravery he hadn't known he was capable of and untie the string that had been wound around the sack.

Inside was a dummy made of straw. With a round head and sprawling limbs. It smelled faintly fishy and also like dried grass, and there were large knitting needles stuck in its body here and there with dark bloodstains seeping out. My husband was as startled as if he had discovered a corpse, and he promptly tossed the dummy back into the river and went home.

After that day, he quit smoking. He also quit his job. He would burrow into the blankets and curl into himself, plagued by awful, intense fevers that made his teeth chatter. Pus spilled from his nose and ears, and his lips were covered in blisters. After spewing nonsense for several days straight, he would come back to his senses and stare at me with blank, unfocused eyes. Not long after he got out of his sickbed, the president was murdered. Through clenched teeth, he swore that the place where the bullet had pierced through the president's body was the exact spot where a knitting needle had been stabbed into

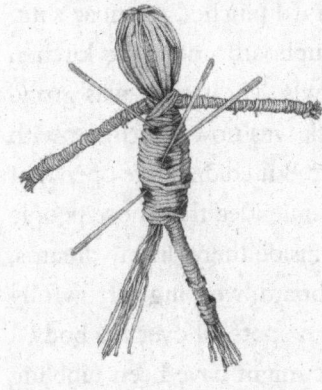

the chest of the straw dummy. He told me that if he'd pulled the needle out, he could have saved the president's life. That was when my husband started rambling about being the one who'd killed the president himself, and because he would frighten people when we were outside, I had to shut him up inside the house. Then soon enough, we were being surveilled by strangers in black, all but shackled to this house.

My husband wasn't the only thing that disappeared. After he quit smoking, the ashtray that had sat collecting dust in a corner of the balcony vanished into thin air. His mirror and tooth-brush, his shoes and shaving razor – one thing after another went missing without a trace. It was as if someone was slipping in like a wisp of smoke while I was sleeping and making off with his belongings. If my husband was truly dead, then his killer was probably someone I couldn't win against. I was afraid that, like the ashtray or the toothbrush, I too would evaporate, leaving not even a shadow behind.

I kept falling into deep slumbers and wondered if it was because of the medication they had given me.

I started skipping the pills. Suspecting that there was a camera installed somewhere, I would pretend to take them, all the while hiding the sleeping pills under my tongue. Then as I was brush-ing my teeth, I would spit them into the sink along with the foam from the toothpaste and rinse them down the drain. A foul stench was emanating from somewhere in the house, so strong that I could still smell it even if I pinched my nose shut. The source of the smell was the cupboard under the kitchen sink crowded with big pots and bowls. The stench was grow-ing stronger by the day, and the sink was now swarming with winged insects drawn in by the odour. But I didn't dare open that cupboard door, because I had the vague idea that those people had crammed my missing husband inside there. In my dreams, my husband emerged from the cupboard, weeping sorrowfully with several knitting needles stuck in spots all over his body. I couldn't bear to kill the insects that might have been nibbling away at his flesh. I would cover my ears to block out the ferocious whine of their wings, and just like my husband in my dreams, I would sob as quietly as I could, my chin trembling.

I stopped taking my medication, and I could feel my head starting to clear up. Then one or two of the vanished items began reappearing by the day. But my husband was dead. Escaping this place without him seemed meaningless. I wondered if it wouldn't be long before I, too, disappeared or died at their hands and ended up tossed into the river. It seemed inevitable, and there was only one way to avoid that fate. By disappearing myself first. I could slit my wrists or hang myself from the ceiling. But I couldn't remain trapped in this house until I died. It would take only a few seconds to open the balcony window, climb on to the railing, and shift my centre of gravity outwards, bending and straightening my knees. Once I steeled my heart, I began to feel restless. I washed a load of laundry, let the clothes dry in the sun, and stacked them up neatly in my wardrobe. I swept and mopped the floors until they shone. I scrubbed the dirt and dead skin off my body and neatly combed out my hair. I took out the silk skirt and jeogori I had worn at my wedding from the trunk I had stored them in and put them on. The garments smelled strongly of mothballs.

Having never eaten my fill or laughed with all my heart, I was much thinner than I had been as a new bride. If I'd had a mirror, I would have done my makeup nice and pretty, but I didn't have one. Lastly, I looked around the house that had been suffocating me for the last fifteen years and realized I felt no lingering attachment to this place whatsoever.

Without hesitation, I opened the door to the balcony. The plastic chair where I used to trim my husband's hair was propped up beneath the railing. Using the chair as a stepping stone, I began to climb up.

'Hello?'

The doorbell rang. I knew they would be closely monitoring my every move on the cameras, so I wasn't surprised that someone was coming for me. They wouldn't have been able to sit still, seeing me do something of my own volition. Because even if it was to die, they couldn't sit back and let me make a choice for myself without rushing to interfere.

'It's Jinseob's mum, from Apartment 608. Please open the door.'

Apartment 608 – that was where the woman I'd shown the note asking for help lived.

'Please, I feel like I'm going to pass out. Open the door, will you?'

Now she was coming to ask for *my* help. If that woman hadn't ratted us out, my husband might still be alive. I put one foot up on the railing.

'Honey, open the door. I think she's really having a hard time.'

It was my husband's voice that had spoken, I could have sworn. I turned around and there he was, standing in the doorway – like a miracle. He looked as sharply dressed as he had before we had been dragged out of the house, and as he looked at me, a smile slowly spread across his face. He pointed to the front door. What that fake guard had told me, that my husband was dead, had been a lie. Like the hero in a movie, he had fought off those strangers and made his way home to me through the darkness and the rain.

'When did you get here? Do you have any idea how worried I was?'

My husband was still pointing to the door.

'She's waiting,' he said. 'Hurry and open it. She's a nice lady.'

I stepped down from the railing on to the chair, then again on to the ground and hurried towards the front door. My husband smelled faintly of dried grass.

When I opened the door, the woman glanced furtively around the house as she stepped inside. 'I thought you weren't home,' she said. With her small stature and plump build, she looked to be a little older than fifty.

'What's the matter?' I asked.

The woman's face darkened, and her embarrassment was obvious.

'It's me, Shim Eunok,' she said. 'The one who leaves you the rice and side dishes every day.'

I'd known since long ago that she was in cahoots with the others. There was no need for the reminder.

'Please leave,' I said. 'I have nothing to say to you.'

At some point, though, she had entered the apartment and closed the door behind her. Now she stood before me, unmoving as a rock.

'Have you not been taking your medicine lately?'

This so-called Shim Eunok had taken off her shoes and walked right into my apartment without permission. I took a few steps back and looked over at my husband. He was sitting like a little child by the table in the main room, silently watching the scene unfolding before his eyes.

'Honey, run!' I shouted. 'This woman's here to take you away! You have to leave. Open the window and fly away like a bird! Quick!'

My husband paid me no attention.

'Here you go, starting up with this again. Granny Oksoon! Your husband passed away thirty years ago.'

Hearing this Eunok woman call me 'Granny', the backs of my hands grew marred by wrinkles and liver spots. She must have injected me with some sort of hallucinogen while I wasn't paying attention.

'Who are you calling "Granny"?' I snapped. I turned back to my husband. 'Honey, say something!'

My husband, who had been sitting like a wooden doll at the table just a few seconds earlier, now lay on the bed.

'You remember. Ever since that day seven years ago when you came to our apartment in those stilettos, we decided to be friends.'

'Ma'am, why are you doing this?'

Eunok took out several vegetables from her shopping bag, turned on the tap and began rinsing them.

'Until you come back to your senses, Granny Oksoon, I'll stay here with you. Why did you pretend to be fine and let them release you from the hospital? Here, first things first, have your medicine.'

She opened one of the TV cabinet drawers and took out a packet of medicine, then held it out with a glass of cold water.

'Do as you've been told, dear.'

My husband, who had at some point moved to a spot on the floor again and was thumbing through a photo album, told me to listen and take the medicine. As if possessed, I took the several pills rolling around in Shim Eunok's palm and swallowed them down.

'You can't pass away,' she said. 'You're the only one in the world who listens to me, Granny.'

Once I had swallowed the pills, it seemed as though my racing heartbeat slowed. Eunok chopped up some squash and peeled some potatoes.

'I did something bad again today,' she said. 'There was this guy who abandoned his parents overseas, then came back and spent up what was left of their assets. But it wasn't his parents who ordered the hit. It was his business partner. Anyway, I bought some marsh clams. I thought they'd be good for a soup.'

I sat perched on the edge of the bed, clutching my husband's sleeve. But all I was holding when I looked down was the faded bedsheet. My husband was nowhere to be found. The album he had been looking through was neatly slipped into a row on the bookshelf. The ashtray, the mirror, everything else, too, gleamed in its usual place.

'What's this smell? Granny, what's all this in the sink drawer? All the rice and side dishes have spoiled in here. If you skip meals like this, you'll have no strength. You shouldn't keep throwing all this stuff away. By the way, I hear there's a serial killer around here. There's really no need to worry since you never leave the house, but make sure not to open the door for anyone.'

Eunok opened the sink cupboard and chucked the leftover food, now covered in white mould, into a plastic bag. From behind, she began to look more and more familiar. Her friendly way of speaking, her short, permed hair, and her occasional habit of swallowing nothing. I suddenly came to my senses, as if an icicle had pierced its way inside my head.

'So you killed your target. Well done.'

'Granny Oksoon, you're back!' exclaimed Eunok with delight. 'Oh, this looks good. I'll just wash the rice, and then what do you say to a game of hwatu?' She shimmied with excitement.

'What fun is playing hwatu with a ten won bet?' I said. 'Why are you here instead of at home taking care of your kids?'

'They were my kids once, attached to my bosom, but they're all grown up now and find everything, including their old mum, to be a bother. Granny, you'll probably have the best lot in life since you don't have any kids.'

'A woman who throws caution to the wind. Isn't that what they say?'

'If you promise to take your medicine as prescribed, I'll find you a foster son.'

'Find me a new husband instead.'

I couldn't tell whether the fishy stench I smelled now was the smell of the clams Eunok had bought, the smell of the blood staining her hands, or the smell of the straw dummy that had been pulled from the water and had haunted my husband for all those decades after. I held up a hand mirror and examined my face. The new bride disappeared, and I watched an old woman with a face as shrivelled as a dried persimmon continue to move her empty mouth. Then my husband, who had become see-through, rummaged through his pockets for a cigarette, just as he had when he was young. The lying bastard!

6

The Killer

Auntie, my aunt who was only seventeen years older than me. My aunt who had said to me early one morning when I was eight, 'You need a real mum to feed you three times a day and take you to the hospital when you're sick. You must be tired of living trapped in this tiny place, too, huh?' My poor aunt. My aunt who held me by the wrist as she led me out of the house wearing a white lace dress and a red beret. My lovely aunt. My aunt who sat in the lobby of the crowded intercity bus terminal in the heart of downtown chewing on dumplings, her cheeks round and ruddy like fresh peaches. My aunt who was even more like a child than I was. My aunt who raised a hand to slap me for snivelling before she quietly looked around and stuffed a cold meat dumpling in my mouth instead. My twenty-five-year-old aunt. My aunt who, while I was chewing that dumpling the same way she chewed, disappeared forever into a sea of shoes, her accordion skirt fluttering. My aunt who was prettier than a flower.

I was craning my neck to see where she had gone and on

the verge of tears when he approached me. I was too young to tell how old a grown-up was, and he was either too young or too old to tell how old a child was, so he patted the beret on my head and asked me my age. My voice was hoarse from stifling sobs as I told him I was eight years old. His arms were solid like ancient trees as he scooped me up and held me to his chest. From that height, I could see the tops of people's heads, my vision streaky with tears.

His car was filled with all sorts of junk. I curled up between a pair of old hiking boots and a badminton racket and fell asleep. I remained submerged in the bogs of a dream even as he hoisted me up and carried me into a similarly cramped apartment. When I opened my eyes to the flickering fluorescent lights, I could see pedestrians in a hurry outside the man's semi-basement apartment window kicking up muddy water as they stomped past.

'You like milk?' the man asked, sitting me up. I was still half-asleep. He handed me one of the dozens of plastic pouches of coffee milk he kept all throughout the apartment. As I sipped, he made me rice with green beans and steamed eggs flavoured with salted shrimp. He brought out the food on a small table.

'Mister, if I don't feel so good, would you take me to the hospital?' I asked. It occurred to me that he might be the mum my aunt had wanted me to find, the one who would feed me three meals a day and take me to the hospital when I was sick.

'Do you know your aunt's phone number?' he asked.

My aunt changed her number often, and she hadn't told me the newest one. She looked so serious during the long conversations she sometimes had on the phone. Then she would set a bowl of ramen and a plate of sliced radish on the table, tell me to make it last for two meals, and disappear somewhere, only to return several days later. 'Don't open the door for anyone,' she always warned me. 'There's an old pervert who lives up the street and only has eyes for little kids. If he tries to come inside, stab him in the eyes with chopsticks. And it's no use being sloppy about it. Use all your strength to really dig them in there until you can't go any deeper. Got it, you little wart?' And every time I wondered if I could really defeat an old pervert with not a knife, not an axe, not a hammer, but a pair of chopsticks.

'I would tell you, but I can't think of the number,' I said to the man.

It was a small bluff. I didn't want to tell him that I lived alone with my aunt in a shanty on the same street as a creep.

'If you don't tell me, you can't get back home,' he said.

Honestly, I didn't want to go back. I was certain my aunt wouldn't be waiting for me. If I didn't tell him her number, maybe I could stay with him forever, my real mum who would make me food and place a cool, wet towel on my forehead when I was hot with fever.

'How come the egg is so salty?' I asked.

He poured me a cup of lukewarm barley tea and ran a hand through his hair.

On the second day, he asked for my address, and even though I complained that the seasoned bean sprouts were bland, I polished off the entire bowl. He washed my hair with warm water, then turned on the fan so that it would dry thoroughly. He cleaned my ears with a pick and loaded strawberry-flavoured toothpaste on my toothbrush for me to use.

'Mister, are you my mum?' I asked him.

Instead of making me put my stained lace dress back on, he

pulled out a lovely pink velour dress from his wardrobe for me to wear. It was tight and barely fit, but I loved the soft feel of the material and how it smelled faintly of soap. I liked my new clothes so much that I started humming as I sat on the floor beside him where he was lying down and began folding little paper boats.

He sat up and looked at me. 'You don't have a mum?'

'Nope, but it's OK. Because now I have you, Mister.'

His eyes searched my face.

'Then was it a lie when you said you couldn't remember your aunt's phone number?'

'Actually, Mister, I was abandoned. So I don't have any parents who would come and pay you money to get me back.'

He took the paper boat that had just opened up like a flower bud in my hands and crushed it. I felt a profound sadness well up at his sudden change in behaviour. Thick tears that felt like they would never end spilled down my cheeks. He said he wasn't going to make me any more fried eggs or stir-fried rice. He didn't comfort me or wash my hair. Hot, blue sparks danced in his eyes.

'So you knew what kind of guy I was all along, hm? I was abandoned, too. At the same bus terminal where I found you, twenty-five years earlier. For the first time in my life, I was wearing snow-white trainers, a new shirt, and new shorts. My know-nothing parents left me at the bus terminal in a rich neighbourhood. Hoping I'd catch the eye of some new money who'd struck it big in the city and was headed home with their riches. But what rich person takes the bus back to their hometown? I learned from a beggar who was basically no different from the parents who'd abandoned me and knelt on the floor of that terminal for ten years panhandling. But looking back on it now, I must have inherited my parents' stupidity. In a filthy bus terminal crawling with beggars, I believed I might find a princess in a fancy dress.'

I started crying, croaking like a bullfrog, and he gagged me with a long sock to quiet me. Then he went into his wardrobe, which was more like a cheap cloth tent. Inside were a shirt and a pair of long trousers that looked like they were for a young boy as well as two pairs of loafers. I couldn't make out what else was there.

'See this? It means you're not the first. My first kid was an eight-year-old boy. He told me his parents' phone number, and I managed to get a hold of them, but as soon as they got the police involved, I gave up. My second kid was a nine-year-old girl, a little twit who cried all day just like you. She wouldn't stop with all that wailing, so I had to give up on her, too. I hate noise. So you'd better cut it out right now. If you don't, I'll—'

But I couldn't stop crying, and he grabbed me by the collar and dragged me to the kitchen. A crock that came up to his waist took up nearly half of the already crowded space. He took the lid off and began wildly scooping out kimchi and dumping it on the floor. Then he picked me up and made me look inside. Something dark red was filling the crock beneath the thick plastic bag still damp with kimchi juice, and that other thing emitted a stench that was nothing like that of kimchi.

'I filled this thing with salt. That would stop them from rotting too fast, but I'll have to move it somewhere else soon. You want to go in there, too? Are you going to keep it up with the crying?'

If I could be the rich kid who didn't cry like he wanted, would he go back to being my mum? I could stop crying, but I couldn't become rich. I balled up my fists and wiped away my tears. I managed not to cry again so that when evening came, he carefully removed the gag from my mouth.

'How come you need money, Mister?' I asked him.

The poor man hadn't had lunch or dinner, so neither had I. I missed when he would pat my head gently as he asked for a phone number or address. Instead, he'd been lying there in silence all evening, frowning up at the ceiling.

'None of your business,' he muttered.

'Are you going to kill me?'

'Maybe. I *am* a person. Any person can kill another person.'

'But if you kill a person, you'll go to prison. You could even get the death penalty.'

'They give the death penalty a fancy name, but it's just killing people in the name of the law. And people made the law, so it's the same as people killing people in the end.'

I couldn't understand what he meant then, but I nodded anyway. He talked about all kinds of things until it was well into the night, but he never explained why he needed money or why he had to kill me. Only after dawn did I manage to drift off, and when I woke up in the morning, I saw him coming back from wherever he had disappeared to at some point in the night. He was holding a big travel bag. He scooped me up with one hand and opened the crock with the other, then peered inside it for a long time. There were two children tangled up together inside the plastic bag, their eyes wide and bulging. Both of them were naked, and the girl's long hair was twined around the boy's ankles. Even as I stared at that sight, I pressed my mouth shut and held back my tears, determined to be the child he wanted.

'You're a special one,' he said.

I perked up at the compliment.

'The bag's too small to fit you inside, too.'

As he swiped a wet towel over my cheeks and lips, I felt my vision blurring as though I had been struck in the head with a hammer.

'Mum.'

Before I lost consciousness, I called him 'Mum'. I couldn't be sure whether he had really grunted in response, but I let myself go limp, slung over his broad shoulder, and felt as peaceful and at ease as if I were swimming in warm amniotic fluid.

I tasted soil in my mouth, slightly bitter. I was sure I had opened my eyes, but it was so dark all around me that I couldn't see a thing. I could sense the man's rough breathing somewhere close by. Every time I breathed, the smell of grass and earth dampened by a recent rain shower combined to overpower me. I rolled over and realized both my hands and legs were bound.

'I should have been done by the time you woke up.'

Suddenly the man's face appeared over my head, moonlight seeping in around him and brightening some of the darkness. I realized I was huddled inside the same crock those other two kids had been in.

He was about to put the lid on again when I said, 'I have a secret.'

His face glowed pale in the moonlight.

'All right. You tell me your secret, and I'll tell you one of mine.'

He leaned back against a heap of dirt, tossed a cigarette up and caught it in his teeth like a gangster.

'My aunt told me I basically don't exist. Nobody wanted me

to be born, including my aunt, and she was the one who gave birth to me. But she forbade me from calling her my mum. She said men hate women with kids. She didn't tell anyone that I'd been born. I never got my shots or went to daycare or school. Instead of giving me a name, she called me a little wart. She said I was like a smelly lump that's fat and round with pus and oil. That's my secret. I'm not my mum's child, but my aunt's wart. That's why she got rid of me.'

He played with the unlit cigarette between his lips, twirling it around.

'You asked me why I needed money, right?' he said. 'I was a wart, too. One that had to be removed. There was an old man who lived his life staring at the loose change that fell from other people's pockets and drinking the days away until he became terminally ill. I was so excited to finally be out of that old man's clutches, thinking maybe I could actually live a decent life from that point on, when he hunted me down and asked me to remove the lump of cancer from his body. After I performed the operation on him, he kept pestering me to buy him all sorts of things that were supposed to be good for his health. He bought chaga mushrooms and wrung the water from them, scraped and boiled down elm tree branches, ground unbloomed dandelions into a powder that he would shove into his mouth at odd moments, and ended up living for exactly two more years. After all that, he randomly died in early summer from a cold. And right before he died, that old man told me he'd been sending half of my monthly earnings to my crafty parents. He said now that he'd told me the truth, he felt so much better. And then he went straight to hell. After that, I started looking for the parents who'd been playing dumb all while stealing the money their own kid had begged on his knees to earn. Once I managed to find those shameless punks, though, I had no way of going about getting revenge. So instead of doing it myself, I had to find someone to get revenge for me. I was bankrupt, though, and to get revenge, I needed money. But now, I'm planning to stop. I'm going to bury you here, then head to the police station and confess. I'm so curious to see the looks on my parents' faces when they find out their son is a murderer who's killed three little kids.'

He tossed the plastic bag containing the other two kids in the crock and put the lid back on. I was soon blanketed in heavy darkness, but my senses slowly grew sharper. I missed my aunt who called me a little wart. I wanted to act like a baby, use her arms as my pillows as I lay there, howling with laughter. I heard a gentle rustling sound over my head that reminded me of the sound of a soft hailstorm on a winter's day.

I was hungry. I felt like I could eat anything if it meant I would live. But people couldn't live on food alone. Air, I needed air. I didn't want to fall asleep, but in the darkness, a drowsiness came over me that I couldn't fight against.

'Oh? She's alive. There's one kid still alive. Stop photographing for a second and come help me get her out.'

It looked like the moon was long gone and the sun had risen. Light so bright I couldn't open my eyes in the face of it flooded the crock. Two men scooped me up and into the world once again.

'You all right, kid?'

I couldn't see what they looked like. One of the men must have opened the bag with the other kids in it, because the air suddenly filled with a pungent stench.

'Do you think you could tell us your parents' phone number?'

These men wanted to know the same thing he had. I couldn't answer. I drew in a deep breath, inhaling the cold early morning air, and got into the police car. As though they were waiting for someone, the men paced around that area. Meanwhile, I sneakily got back out of the car. If the world found out about me, I knew it would make things hard for my aunt.

I ran. I ran so hard I didn't realize my legs were being scratched up by hops and nettles as I gasped for breath and heaved from gulping down the air I hadn't been able to breathe all night. The men belatedly noticed I had vanished and started running around and shouting. I hid in the thickets and tried as hard as I could not to be caught. A child without a phone number wouldn't be welcomed anywhere. I wished I had a bunch of phone numbers then. But in order for that to happen, I had to be an adult. As I made my way through the shrubbery, I repeated what my aunt always said. *These fuckin' shitheads.* I felt better. Like I had become a little bit more of a grown-up.

From that day on, I lived with those two dead rich kids. It was like they were clinging to the ends of my skirt, refusing to let me escape. I didn't turn on the lights, even at night. Sometimes I missed that crock, where I had fallen into a slumber as deep as death. In the dark, it was like I could still hear his low, low voice. I began to live under the name Lee Soonyoung. It was the name given to me by a man who lived in a container box near the Han River. He was built like an athlete and wore his long hair tied up like a ponytail. He approached me, his face serious as though he didn't know how to smile, as I was standing by a public restroom taking shelter from the rain. He didn't ask me anything. He took me to his container box, looked at the cuts from the grass on my legs, put some ointment on them and blew gently on the wounds, fed me, then disappeared somewhere only to come back much later. In the end, I had no choice but to tell him about my aunt and the man who'd kidnapped me. He listened, his expression never changing. After four seasons had gone by, the man handed me several books.

'You have to live on your own from now on,' he said. 'So you'll have to study.'

What good would it do me to study when on paper I didn't even exist? But while I lived in his house, I had no choice but to do as he said. I didn't want to be thrown away yet again. If I had to leave, I wanted to do so of my own free will.

After several more seasons had passed, the man said to me, 'Starting today, your name is Lee Soonyoung. You're not some non-person any more. Take this.' He handed me a piece of paper with a twelve-digit number written on it. I noticed that there were still bloodstains on his hand that he hadn't cleaned. He must have killed a girl with that name.

The twelve digits were a resident registration number. Lee Soonyoung had been two years older than me, a girl too young to have committed any sin in the world. I understood the man who had killed her. He was a person, and people could kill other people. This was how I gained my third mum. The aunt who had given birth to me, the man who had forced me to grow up, and this man who had given me an identity, a sense of presence in this world.

After I passed my GED exam, he put me up in a small apartment on the edge of Seoul. The place was only about thirty-three square metres in size, but it came furnished with everything I needed. A vanity and mirror, a wardrobe and a bed, brand-new dishware and kitchen utensils. I didn't believe the man had picked out all this and decorated the apartment himself. When I imagined him using his thick, scarred hands, the same hands he used to stab and kill people, to pick out wallpaper and lino-leum tiling or to purchase furniture and dishware, it felt like a forced comedy.

'Get a job. As a web designer, a teacher, a bank teller. But nothing where you kill anybody. And no cats or pigeons. Even when I'm not with you, I'll know what you're up to. If you dis-obey me, I won't forgive you, and I will find you. Got that?'

This was the most he had ever spoken to me at one time. But people could kill other people. If I were going to kill someone, I needed practice. It seemed unfair that the man could leave the house, do someone harm, and come back, but I couldn't. Before I could even object, though, he left me in the new apart-ment with the sour smell of wallpaper glue and a dead girl's pilfered identity.

After he left, I didn't turn on the lights, not once. I didn't rush to look for a job like he'd told me to, either. I lived as Lee Soonyoung for twenty years, and not once did the man come looking for me. He'd left me a lot of money in my bank account, and once every few months or so, another large sum was depos-ited. I spent the money little by little and grew old that way. Those two children who were always with me, watching over me, didn't want me to leave the house. So I shut myself in, sang children's songs with the kids, and drew pictures on the walls. In all that time, the man still hadn't come back, and for a while the only indication I had that he was even still alive were those occasional bank deposits.

'I guess that man abandoned you, too,' said the little boy.

'But I know a way to get him to come back,' the little girl said.

I still desperately needed a mum to feed me three meals a day and take me to the hospital when I was sick.

'You have to do what he told you not to do,' the little girl went on. 'Then he'll have to come back to yell at you. What do you think?'

She was right. Both of the children, tangled together like a strange sort of pretzel, were watching me closely.

'How do you kill a person?' I asked the boy, who had one eye that looked like it was about to pop out of its socket.

'Your aunt taught you,' they both said. ' "*Stab him in the eyes with chopsticks. And it's no use being sloppy about it. Use all your strength to really dig them in there until you can't go any deeper. Got it, you little wart?*" '

They burst out laughing after doing a perfect imitation of my aunt's voice. I knew they were right. If I wanted to summon that man, I had to kill. I opened the sink drawer and took out a chopstick. Then I went to the entrance of the building and searched carefully for a target. It was nearly three in the morning, and there were hardly any traces of life. I heard a hacking cough coming from the playground. I made my footsteps light as I went towards the sound. When I got to the sandbox, I saw a drunk man lying on a bench sleeping. His hair was dishevelled, he was quite short, and he was wearing a sloppy suit and worn shoes. Aside from the occasional cough, he seemed to be sound asleep. I gripped the stainless-steel chopstick in one hand and approached him, peering down at his face. He had a dark beard and looked to be in his forties. His dress shirt was stained with spilled food.

Like my aunt had taught me, I stabbed him in the eye with the chopstick. The man, still drunk and sleepy, sucked in a deep breath, unable to stop this attack. I used all my strength to drive in the chopstick as deep as I could. As I mashed his eye and the alcohol-addled brain behind it, I couldn't contain the little shout of joy that shot up from deep inside me like a firecracker. Only after I wiped the bloodied chopstick clean on the man's shirt did I begin to cry, as I came to the dramatic realization that I had found a job to dedicate my life to.

Two days later, the drunk man's body was discovered by the security guard. But the man I wanted to see didn't come looking for me.

'Do you think he'll forgive me?' I asked.

The little girl's long hair was sticking into the little boy's ear.

'You only killed one person,' she said. 'If you really want him to be angry, you've got a long way to go.'

'If I go to prison, I'll get the death penalty. Then I might never be able to see him again.'

The boy curled into himself as though he were ticklish and replied, 'If you don't want to go to prison, you have to go somewhere bigger. It's too cramped in here.'

'But you two hate the light.'

'Exactly. You have to travel the world and find work you can do in the dark.'

The two children tickled each other until they dissolved into sludge that scattered through the air.

To find work that could be done in the dark, I decided to become a chicken sexer. I trained at a cram school for a year with the money the man had left me and got a job. As the round trailer rotated in the darkness, the individual lights came on, and sexers in masks and white gowns stood scattered around. Then you picked up one of the bright yellow chicks, shone a light on it, and determined its sex. How you did that wasn't by looking at its genitals. You could put them in the chicken sexing machine, but that took too long and could hurt the chicks, so it wasn't used much. The method that the human sexers used most often involved raising the birds' wings and looking at the patterning on their feathers. Then they tossed them down a little slide into separate bins depending on whether they were male or female. Female chicks were given antibiotics and made to lay eggs for as long as their bodies allowed, while male chicks were raised to be slaughtered or else sold as playthings to children near schools. I was the cold-blooded arbiter of the chicks' fates.

Chicken sexing required me to go on business trips all over the country. I would usually stay in one region for two or three days, and I would always slip a few pairs of chopsticks into my travel bag. On the last day of my work, while the other sexers went out for drinks or sightseeing, I would go on a quiet walk, waiting for a target to appear. Drunkards who could barely hold themselves upright, weak elderly people. When I got home from these trips, the first thing I did was boil some water in a pot and sterilize the chopsticks. And then I'd use those same chopsticks to eat.

But the man still didn't show up.

When work was busy, I would go on as many as three or four trips a month. When I wasn't away, I spent the days shut in with the tangled mass the two kids had become.

'You've been abandoned,' they would say. 'He's forgotten about you. Look, you're not even getting the payments to your bank account any more.'

'You're wrong. He's busy. Too busy to take a day off to come and scold me.'

'It's because you're so lazy. Do you know how much you could get done around here? There's an old lady with dementia who lives in Apartment 607 – did you know that?'

'What would I do if I got caught targeting one of my neighbours?'

'You haven't been caught once yet. What would make this time any different?'

By now, the two kids could only speak as one. They got me to get up by making noises with both their mouths at the same time.

I cooked in the dark. I made a thin batter from flour and sliced potatoes, chives, and zucchini. I turned on the gas,

MRS SHIM IS A KILLER

drizzled oil in a frying pan, and ladled in the batter. I didn't need to make it taste especially good. The old lady wouldn't be eating it anyway.

I put a single vegetable pancake on a plate, which I set on a tray beside a set of chopsticks. With so many people gone for the end-of-the-year holidays, the apartment building was quiet. I put on my trainers with the soft soles and took the stairs, careful not to make any noise. Like me, the old woman didn't leave her house much, but she was famous in the building for the loud commotions that sometimes broke out in her apartment. She thought she was being surveilled by someone and was afraid of other people. No one believed her, but it might have been true. I knew because I had no doubt no one would believe me, either, if I told them I spent all day chatting with the two dead kids who followed me around. It was impossible to know whether some white-gowned arbiters of fate had seen me and the old woman, identified us by the markings underneath our armpits, and shoved us on to a conveyor belt of distinctly cruel hardships. When I got to her apartment, I tried the door handle. It was locked.

'Are you all back again?' the old woman shouted from inside. Fortunately, she wasn't asleep.

'Grandmother, I came to help you. Please open the door.'

If she would just open the door, I'd have no problem achieving my goal.

'There's no grandmother here! Go away!'

I knew I had to calm her down.

'I came to take you somewhere no one can monitor you. I mean it.'

I set down the tray of food and picked up the chopsticks.

After a brief silence, the door opened. The old woman stood there in her pyjamas, looking up at me with cloudy grey eyes.

'Lower your voice,' she said. 'They'll hear you.'

She pressed a finger to her lips, signalling to me to be quiet.

I followed her inside.

'Honey, we have a guest,' she whispered in the direction of her empty bed. She still seemed to be on edge as she took a cardigan off its hook. When she put it on, she looked even smaller. She sat down at a low table in her living room and looked me up and down.

'Who are those two poor children? They look sick.'

Her eyes had stopped near the hem of my skirt. The two kids looked startled and hid behind me. It was the first time someone else had seen them. The old woman regarded them with concern, squinting to get a better look at them.

'Physically, they're not feeling all that well, but they're all right,' I said.

The old woman shuddered slightly at the sight of them.

'Honey, she says the kids aren't feeling well. What a shame, isn't it?'

This time, she touched the back of an empty chair as she spoke.

'Please close your eyes,' I said to her. 'If you pretend to be unconscious, I can take you away from here. No one will suspect a thing.'

The old woman looked back and forth between the empty chair and me, then lay down on the floor and closed her eyes. Now was the time to use the chopsticks I had hidden behind my back. I brought them up and drove them down, fast. But weirdly enough, my aim was off. The chopsticks glanced down the side of the old woman's face and struck the peeling plastic of the floorboard with a thunk. This had never happened before, and now I was anxious. The chopsticks had left only a deep wound near the old woman's temple. A groan escaped from the woman's lips. She couldn't open her eyes, she was in so much pain. I forced my hand to be still as I debated whether to run or whether to try stabbing her again. Either way, I knew an old woman with dementia wouldn't be able to find me. But I didn't want to ruin the track record I had built up to now.

'Is someone here? What's this pancake for?'

I heard a voice. Someone outside jiggled the door handle. Slowly, the door opened. A short, stout middle-aged woman I could have come across anywhere stood in the doorway staring blankly at me. She dropped the shopping bag she'd been holding. Kimchi juice spilled out on to the floor.

The old woman looked up and squinted. 'Mrs Shim, who's this?' she croaked.

The woman at the door, Mrs Shim, looked between me and the old woman whose face was covered in blood. Her mouth hung open in shock. Then she reached into her shopping bag and pulled something out. Was she grabbing her phone to call the police? I lunged at her with the chopsticks, but the woman's reflexes were surprisingly quick. And the thing she'd taken out of her bag wasn't a phone but a long, sleek knife. Without a second's hesitation, she plunged the knife into my gut.

'So it was you.'

I fell to the ground, and she expertly pulled the knife out. At first, I felt a coolness where the knife had been removed, but it was soon replaced by a scalding heat. The woman moved towards the sink and carefully rinsed the knife.

She made a call. 'It's me,' she said. 'I think you need to come here now. There's been an incident. I'll have to clean it up, but it'll be hard to handle on my own. And about the knife you gave me – I just used it. I know you told me to only use it when I needed to, but it was an urgent situation. I know how much you cherished it, since it was a gift from someone precious to you.'

On the flickering edges of consciousness, I looked over at the handle of the knife. It was engraved with the Chinese character 吳. It was a familiar character; the same one had been engraved on my third mum's knife, too. How I'd coveted that knife. Whenever the man left the house, I would sneak over and open the drawer where he kept it, staring at it until I felt my senses leaving my body. The knife was as sharp as a razor blade, and it cut through the air with a faint but distinct whistle like a woman wailing. Sometimes I would take his knife and go out to the Han River, where I would stab a pigeon missing a leg or a cat I found lapping up vomit. After, I would clean the knife and return it to its proper place so that the man would never know it had been gone.

He'd promised me that if I disobeyed him, he wouldn't forgive me and would come find me. But it was an empty promise. I was dying. I was gasping for breath, unable to speak, just like the people I had killed.

'Now you can become one with us. We've been so bored waiting for you.'

My vision was slowly darkening. But I still had my hearing.

Soon, I heard unfamiliar footsteps approaching, then a man's voice.

'Mrs Shim, were you hurt?'

'I'm fine, but this granny has a slight injury. She'll need some stitches, but we should deal with this woman first. Would the mountains do? Or the river?'

It wasn't my decision to make, but I preferred the river. Even from that dugout of a house my aunt and I had lived in, there was a view of a river. A tiny creek.

'Auntie, can I call you Mum when no one is around?' I used to ask her. 'You little brat, didn't I tell you if you asked me that again, I'd chuck you in the creek?' she would say. Sometimes she would take out my shrivelled-up umbilical cord from one of her vanity drawers and sniff it. Then she would fix her smudged mascara and wait for a phone call. Did my aunt still have my umbilical cord in that drawer? What had it smelled like that it used to make her cry?

As the pain faded, I began to feel weightless. My vision returned to me. The two children were standing beside me now. They were no longer a mess of blood, their arms and legs horribly mangled. The boy was neatly dressed in a white button-down shirt and navy trousers, while the girl wore a pink velour dress. I was wearing a white lace dress with a red beret. I tossed the chopstick I'd been holding to the floor, and my body became more feathery than air. I felt far removed from that body, the one gasping desperately for breath.

The plain-looking man who'd come into the apartment shoved that body into a plastic bag.

'It'll be hard to get to the mountains on account of the snow. We should do the river,' he said, hoisting the plastic bag over his shoulder. The same way I had decided on the fates of those baby chicks, this man had decided on the fate of my dead body.

And so I went, carried on his shoulder.

And so I went.

To the river.

To the river.

7

The Confidant

My grandmother had three mixed children. My aunt who spent all day murmuring to herself and plucking out strands of her kinky, curly hair was half Black. My mum, whose nickname was Red, was half white. And I wasn't fully sure about my uncle, but I would guess that he was half Vietnamese. They were family, but not by blood. My grandmother had married at eighteen, and when she still hadn't had any children by twenty-five, she split with her awful husband and settled down in a place called Boku Town, where she lived to this day. She had taken the time to explain the history of the town to me, even though I never asked.

My grandmother sometimes used English she'd learned from American soldiers in her youth, but because most of that English had to do with genitalia or sex, I was embarrassed about the little English I knew and went red in the face at the thought of having to speak it aloud. In fact, I knew that the *boku* in Boku Town came from the sound of the English word *fuck* to Korean ears. Since the 1950s and all the way to the present day,

Boku Town had been designated the country's premier adult entertainment district, making the city where it was located the second-wealthiest in the nation. Nowadays, Boku Town was a place anyone with money and balls sought out, but just thirty years ago, it had been known as a place crawling with foreigners – especially American soldiers.

Around the time my grandmother was abandoned by her husband and disowned by her own family, Boku Town was nothing but a small side street where twelve sex workers lived, paid rent, and did business out of three tile-roofed houses. According to my grandmother, the business owner offered the women who worked there the price of a whole cow, a sum that was nothing to sneeze at even by today's standards. My grandmother had no family besides her father to rely on, but when he kept getting bogged down in debt and suffering massive losses from buying cattle, he sent my grandmother to Boku Town. At first, no one would rent her a room. She stood no taller than a pack frame, her complexion was perpetually ruddy like a drunk's, and she had what they called slits for eyes and a pug nose. In the end, she found work as a kitchen maid instead. She planted her roots in Boku Town by washing the young women's underwear and clothing them, mopping the floors, and polishing combat boots. The same women who would howl like she-cats in bed every night would also, like cats, give birth quietly to babies they would then abandon as they fled Boku Town. That was how my grandmother came to take in my aunt, my mum, and my uncle, and she'd been watching over Boku Town in much the same way ever since.

Aside from me, my family has lived in Boku Town for more than forty years. They tore down the tile-roofed houses and put up new buildings, and my grandmother opened a shop there called the Rosemary Meal House. It wasn't the kind of place where young women received guests, but a comfort food shop that sold ramen and kimbap to guests who happened to pass through. We would sell overpriced soup broth and cheap rice balls to men who staggered in drunk at dawn. Of course, not everyone was hard at work in the shop. My aunt, quite heavyset at 120 kilograms, would lie down in a corner of the shop watching reruns of *Sex and the City*. My uncle was a taxi driver, so he would sit near bus stops and subway stations, waiting to bring wandering tourists to Boku Town. And the best-looking sibling – really, the best-looking person in town – was my mother, who rolled kimbap at the Rosemary. She had dark hair and eyes, but her paper-white complexion, red lips, and deep and plaintive expression earned her the reputation of a Madonna among the men who frequented Boku Town. And what captivated them most was my mother's, erm, *voluptuous* figure.

She wore T-shirts with low-cut necklines and sat in the shop entrance rolling kimbap, her breasts bouncing almost comically as she worked. If the weather was even slightly hot, her skin would redden in the sun, earning her the nickname Red. But no one ever hit on her or asked her out on dates, and that was because of my mum's sharp tongue.

'You're the kind of asshole who'd chase lightning and get struck once for every year of your pathetic life! Did you think that staring like that would make my nipples stand up in my bra and give three cheers for you and your viewing pleasure? You filthy dog. Go fuck yourself in a wood-burning stove.'

Clearly, she was something of a girl crush.

Every time Mr Kim came by with side dishes for us, my mum

would give him an earful, but it was all in vain. Everyone else in the family, including my grandmother, liked Mr Kim. That was because he'd put together my grandmother's seventieth birthday feast. And it wasn't dinner at some cheap buffet, either, but a full-course meal at a fairly nice restaurant. My mother immediately trashed Mr Kim's meddling, saying he was being as ridiculous as 'a horse's dick in a rat's cunt'. But on the day of the feast, she got more dolled up than usual and played the perfect hostess, greeting and shaking hands with all the young women who frequented the Rosemary as well as the thick-necked men accompanying them. It was a shame, of course, that she would soon get ahead of herself and drink too much, revealing her true colours.

My mother cursed at everyone who came by after she'd had too many drinks, calling them loose women and the bastards who sold those women to buy themselves gold underwear, and in the end the guests began to clear out before the allotted three hours was over, leaving my mum looking miserable as she sang Sim Soobong's songs to an audience of none. Then, after continuing to chug alcohol for the remaining two hours, she climbed on Mr Kim's back and threw up the tangsuyuk and japchae she'd eaten on to his bald head.

My grandmother often said that my life would be easier if my mum and Mr Kim moved in together. Honestly, it was because of my mum that I only had a middle school education. That winter, two months before my graduation, my mum disappeared, along with her chestnut-coloured cardigan that once hung on the hook year-round. According to my aunt, who shared a room with her, my mum had been tossing and turning one night, unable to sleep, when she suddenly asked my aunt around three in the morning what she would do if she came into three billion won. Would she split it with her family? Instead of answering, my aunt had merely snorted. My uncle was convinced that my mum had won the lottery and decided to skip town before more people found out and suddenly all her money was tied up in the Rosemary's expansion, my uncle's personal taxi business, and my aunt's liposuction.

They waited for a week, but my mum didn't come back. When I went with my uncle to file a missing person report, that was when I found out that she had been missing in the first place. Cho Boonja. Born 1970. The police didn't seem too concerned about the disappearance of a middle-aged woman who wasn't exactly steadily employed. Over time, the same family that had prayed so hard for her safe return grew to resent my mum and would become angry and jealous at the mere thought of her having pocketed billions of won and run off somewhere to bask in all her riches. When Mr Kim heard that my mum had run away, he burst into tears and confessed that he'd bought her the lottery tickets, only a few of them, but still. In the end, my grandmother's arthritis became so bad that she had to temporarily close down the Rosemary, and my aunt's weight, which she had been keeping down with disordered eating and purging, began to balloon once again. My uncle said he was going to look for my mum and took off in one of his company's taxis, only to end up being booked on carjacking charges.

Eventually, as my mother's only blood relative, I decided to go searching for her – the root cause of all this mess – myself. I had zero hobbies and no interest or aptitude for studying anyway, so I took the hundred and fifty thousand won I had hidden under the floorboards and bought a ticket to Seoul.

About three days after I got there, my emergency money ran out. In my hometown, finding somewhere to stay for a day or two would have been no problem, but Seoul was different. It was a city where people didn't trust other people, and only belatedly did I realize that it was no place for a country bumpkin like me to stay for the long term. As soon as I got off the train at Seoul Station, I lent a girl around my age ten thousand won as cab fare and took down her contact information, only for a street vendor to point at her and tell me she was a crook and a repeat offender. I spent the first night at a motel and the second night at an inn, then from the third day on, I stayed at a smaller inn, but it was like my pockets just continued to bleed money.

I had no idea what to do once I ran out. I fell asleep from the sheer exhaustion and hunger. When darkness came, I sat on a bench near the station and spread some newspaper over me to try to sleep when a drunk homeless man wearing rags sat on the bench beside me. He kindly informed me that there were plenty of jerks who would snatch up young boys like me, cut off their legs, and force them into panhandling, and with that, he took away my newspaper. I didn't want to become a beggar. If I could just find my mum, we could go home, figure out what to do about my grandma's arthritis, get my aunt's sack of a stomach snipped away so she could have a slim figure, and pay my uncle's settlement money. But first I had to sort out the basics of food and shelter. I decided to go towards the motel where I had stayed my first night, because I remembered that I had seen a boy around my age whose father was dragging him out of there by his ear and I realized what it had meant.

'Sir, you need workers, don't you?'

I couldn't tell whether the guy was the motel owner or maybe the owner's brother-in-law or nephew. He looked me up and down in all my shabbiness.

'Look, kid. Did you run away from home?'

'No, sir. I came to Seoul to find my mum. If you just provide room and board, I'll work really hard, I swear.'

My offer must have appealed to him because the guy stroked his chin for a moment before nodding. 'Let's do that, then,' he said. 'We'll provide meals and a place for you to sleep. Don't try to change your tune later. If you go to the police or the community centre spewing some nonsense, I'll bury you. I mean it.'

From that day on, I was an employee – what they called a hireling – at the Nimbora Motel.

'We mainly allow day-use bookings until eleven p.m. Any time after that, the customers have to stay overnight. We charge a thousand won for a toiletries kit, and condoms are free the first time, but if they ask for more, that's another a thousand won. When the guests leave, empty the wastebasket and put on new bedsheets, then mop the floor. Oh, and don't forget to stock the fridge with a fibre drink and a canned coffee. If someone asks, tell them you're twenty years old. Sometimes inspectors come around, so make sure you remember this ID number to tell them. Well, that's all. I'll be in the sauna.'

The guy I thought was the owner or else a relative of the owner turned out to be the owner's husband. When his wife wasn't around, he spent most of his time in the adult game room or else at the sauna. Sometimes drunk guests made a fuss, but most of the time my job only entailed sitting at the damp and run-down counter and waiting for guests to come. One day a week in my spare time, I went out looking for my mum.

'Money is the most rotten-smelling thing in the world. No matter where it's hiding, if you follow that smell, you'll find it.'

The boss told me there were several spots throughout Seoul where rich women were known to hang out. I carried around photos of my mum and handed them out to employees at different businesses who were doing more or less the same job as I was, only with a bit more class and a sense of refinement.

One day the boss's husband, who smelled heavily of lotion and must have just come from the sauna, gave me a tip. 'Instead of handing out those photos, what about hiring a private detective agency to help you?'

'A private detective agency? What's that?'

Still looking sleepy, he threw himself on to the cot next to the counter.

'It's a place that'll do anything you need done. They can find people for you, get back money you've been swindled out of.'

I rushed over and began massaging his fat thighs, begging to know where in the world I could find one of these private detective agencies and how much it might cost for them to find my mum.

'This motel used to be a sashimi centre,' he said. 'They added two storeys and revamped it as a motel. Around the time the remodelling was complete, some guy showed up out of the blue and booked a room on the fifth floor for a long-term stay. That would have been the rooftop of the old building, if I had to guess. Anyway, the guy asked me if the people who ran the sashimi centre had left us any items. I told him we had the broken scales the daughter had used in storage. His eyes lit up. As he walked off with those scales, he handed me his business card and told me to contact him if we found any other items like that. His card said he worked for the Smile Detective Agency. If you open that last drawer there, it's probably still inside. But why did he take those broken scales anyway? Maybe there were drugs or something stashed in them.'

He kept chattering on as I made my way over to the last drawer beneath the counter, opened it, and rummaged through all sorts of odds and ends until I found the business card. It was stuck to some flypaper. Fortunately, the flypaper hadn't peeled off the phone number. But where the name should have been, the dust-coated flypaper was stuck over, making it impossible to read. I decided to call first. I hoped the same guy who'd disappeared with those scales was still working there. I called about twenty times, but no one picked up. A couple of days later, and then a couple of days after that, I called again and again, but the man never picked up. And then, in the early morning before the sun had even come up, I told myself this would be the last time I tried and called the number once more.

'Smile Detective Agency.'

A low, gruff voice answered. A man. Suddenly I was at a loss for words. I didn't have a name for the guy I was looking for, and it was way too early in the morning to enquire about business. More than anything, I hadn't expected anyone to answer, so I was thrown off.

'This is the Nimbora Motel,' I finally managed to say. The man I was looking for probably wouldn't even remember the motel, though.

'Have you found any other objects?' he asked.

My heart was pounding.

'No,' I said. 'But I have a favour to ask. I need you to find someone for me.'

The man was slow to answer. Finally, he said, 'Take the number 3 bus and get off at the intersection with the gingko trees. We're on the third floor of the five-storey building. See you soon.'

At long last, I'd found someone who could help me find my mum and her lottery winnings. All day I mopped the room floors like a madman, stocked the drinks in the fridges, and swiped cards through the card reader without feeling the least bit tired.

Behind my sweat-drenched back, I could hear the boss's husband snoring, sound asleep. He only woke up at noon and gave me his enthusiastic permission to go and meet up with the man at the detective agency. The days I got permission to go out were usually the same days the boss came by the motel to inspect the accounting. The boss's husband took some of the cash from the front desk and stuffed it in my pocket with a little wink.

We hadn't agreed on a time, but I figured it would be polite to wait until after lunch, so I bought some undercooked bungeoppang from a cart on the street in front of the building and snacked on the fish-shaped pastries while I waited. I looked at my watch, and when it was a little past one o'clock, I went up to the third floor where the man had said to find him. There were two offices, and one of them had a sign up that said SMILE DETECTIVE AGENCY. As I opened the door, the cheery sound of chimes rang out. A man stood up and approached me, backlit by the sun. He wasn't that tall, but he looked strong as he stood before me.

'So you're from the Nimbora Motel,' he said. He led me to the sofa, where I sat with my knees pressed together. 'You said you were looking for someone, is that right?'

Tears welled up in my eyes all of a sudden. It might have been because this man was the first person I'd encountered in Seoul who had spoken to me politely, or because the coffee he had made for me was so hot. The man listened to my situation, all the while nodding and running a finger along the scar on the palm of his hand.

Once I finished telling him everything, he said, 'I can find your mother, but it'll be hard to do it for free.'

'How much will it cost? I don't have any money now, but if I get in touch with my family back home, I can probably scrape together a good amount.'

'The retainer fee, the costs to carry out the search, and the compensation for successfully finding your mother are all collected separately. It varies depending on how long it takes, but it's not an amount of money that would be easy for a student to obtain,' the man said.

I understood this to mean that he was turning me down. But I wasn't there to give in. And I didn't dare try to find my mum using my own strength alone.

'I have another item from the old sashimi centre. If you find my mother, I'll bring it to you to cover the compensation. I promise.'

It was a lie. I had no such thing. But it was the only way I could move this man who seemed as solid as a rock when I had nothing at all to my name. And I saw the payoff right away. His indifferent eyes lit up.

'Could you tell me what sort of item it is?' he asked.

'It's a letter. I found it in storage by accident. I can get it to you straight away if you can find my mother. And if you give me a job here, I could get it to you even sooner.'

I was negotiating with him now in a bold manner that didn't at all match my true country bumpkin nature. His sunken eyes sparkled, and he nodded once, vigorously. He was accepting my proposal. And I'd even come away with the promise of a job. I didn't even have any belongings I needed to go back for. Starting from that day, I threw in the towel as a hireling at the Nimbora Motel and started as an employee at the Smile Detective Agency.

A couple of days later, the man from the agency – Park Taesang – went on a business trip down to my hometown to try retracing my mum's steps. I felt uneasy thinking about what I'd do if he ended up finding her sooner than expected and I had to come up with that letter. Money was the most rotten-smelling thing in the world, so it would probably be easy for someone as experienced as Mr Park to find my mum and drag her back to me by the scruff of her neck.

Sure enough, when Mr Park returned from his business trip, he handed me his phone.

'Try giving the Rosemary Meal House a call,' he said.

At some point, he'd started speaking casually to me. It might have been because he was a bit angry. Confused, I dialled the number to my old home. My grandmother picked up.

'Grandma,' I said. 'It's me, Joongi.'

'You little punk. Do you have any idea how hard your mum's been looking for you?'

'Mum? She came back? Really?'

I couldn't believe it. My mum had returned. Like in a silly fairy tale, the bluebird I had been wandering around in search of had been at home the entire time. My mother had been at the Rosemary all along.

'The day after you left, she came home looking like a beggar. She'd taken her three million won in lottery winnings, gone to Seoul, and blown it all. Came back with nothing but a bag of mandarins.'

Mr Park took his phone from me and ended the call.

'Now give me the letter and go home,' he said.

If I went back, all that would be waiting for me was my grandma and her worsening arthritis, my aunt who'd put on even more weight in the meantime, my mum who would spew swear words so potent they made the sides of the kimbap rolls burst, and my uncle who may or may not have still been in prison. Maybe I'd never really wanted to go home from the start.

'No,' I said.

'You have to keep your word.'

'If we go on what was promised, then since you weren't the one who found my mum, the agreement is null and void. I can't give you the letter yet. I can't go back until I've worked and earned enough to pay for my grandmother's joint surgery. And when I'm done here, I'll give you the letter. But if you rush me out, I'll burn it.'

Looking like he had a headache, Mr Park took a seat and kept his eyes cast down for what felt like hours.

I still think about it. What kind of person would I be today if I'd been driven out of Mr Park's office and ended up back in my hometown? I might have gone to a specialized high school and graduated at the bottom of a class of thirty-seven students, then spent the rest of my youth making ramen at the Rosemary. But now, I was the ace at the Smile Detective Agency.

Or I was, before Mrs Shim came along.

Still, I didn't hate her. I wasn't jealous of her, either. Rather, I admired her. She never made mistakes. Whenever she came into the office, a tiny woman with her lips pursed like a general returning victorious from battle, her knife was always stained with blood. If my eyes were full of awe at the sight of her, then Mr Park's eyes held traces of fear and anxiety.

'Can I see you for a second?' Mr Park called to me. He hardly ever called for a meeting with me alone. I stopped mopping and followed him into the conference room.

'Do you have something to tell me?' I asked.

We sat at the table without turning on the lights. His eyes looked cold. I liked that. Unlike his gentle voice and demeanour when we'd first met, his true expression had a faint glow like the eyes of an animal with night vision.

'It's already been five years since we started working together, hasn't it?'

Five years. In that time, some strands of grey had begun to crop up in Mr Park's hair. Instead of making him look pitiful, though, they made him look trustworthy.

'I guess it has. Seeing as I'm twenty-one already.'

'Right. So we're family. Which means there should be no secrets between us.'

'I wouldn't deceive you, sir. Swear on my mum.'

'I'm not talking about you deceiving me,' he said. 'I'm talking about a secret I haven't told you before.'

Mr Park looked quite sincere. I moved to turn on the lights, but he held up a hand to stop me. I sat back down awkwardly across from him. I was terrified that he'd figured out the truth about the letter. And that I'd just lied to him about how I wouldn't deceive him.

Then he said, out of nowhere, 'I don't trust Mrs Shim.'

He didn't trust Mrs Shim?

The same highly lauded Mrs Shim who was ranked first in what we called sales? Had some sort of conflict arisen between the two of them that I didn't know about?

'Do you remember my birthday? When the police suddenly stormed in?'

'Of course I remember. We all had to make a bunch of trips to the police station. It was definitely unexpected, wasn't it?'

Mr Park's eyelids were slightly twitching.

'That day, if it hadn't been for the police, I might have died. Think about Mrs Shim's skill. It wouldn't be hard for her at all. And even though she knows I don't drink, the first thing she did when we got to the restaurant was order soju. Like she was planning to catch me off guard while I was drunk.'

Did Mrs Shim have a reason to kill Mr Park? Had he maybe swiped some of her compensation money? No. There was no way. The Mr Park I knew wasn't that sort of person. He was the one who'd secretly set aside part of my monthly cheque to send to my grandmother for her surgery fees last autumn.

'I was certain I saw Mrs Shim's knife drop to the floor at the restaurant. At first, I thought she was hiding the knife she always carried around with her when the police showed up so as not to draw suspicion. But while Mrs Shim was being questioned at the police station, I went back to the restaurant and searched under the chair, and the knife on the floor wasn't one of Mrs Shim's.'

'Then whose knife was it?'

'It had the Happy Detective Agency seal on it. Do you know about them? That's the agency Na Hancheol runs. I put that knife back under the chair and left. I couldn't figure out why Mrs Shim would have a knife of theirs. This field is small. Too small for the two of us. Mr Na can't possibly see me in a good light. But I still want to believe in Mrs Shim. Which is why I have a favour to ask of you.'

Was Mr Park saying that Mrs Shim must be a spy sent by Mr Na? I was confused. Then again, it didn't make sense to say that a human butcher seemed like a good person.

'What kind of favour?' I asked.

'You have to get into Mrs Shim's house. Tell her that you had a problem with your rent deposit and need a place to stay while you look for another apartment. As long as you're staying there, I'll be safe because you'll be able to keep an eye on her for me. Of course, I'm not sending you there to save myself the trouble of killing her. I may have vowed never to pick up a knife again, but that doesn't mean I want you to have one, either. First, just keep your eyes open and try to dig up anything you can find on Mrs Shim. I'll give you a month. If it turns out that she is in cahoots with the Happy Detective Agency, she won't want to wait too long to kill me if she's already failed once. If we can't find out the truth, and quickly, my life may be in danger.'

Mr Park stood up and walked back out into the main office. I sat there in the dark conference room, my head buried in my arms, thinking. For five years, all I'd been doing at the Smile Detective Agency was answering the phone, mopping the floors, and handing over materials I'd gathered from clients or taking pictures at the scenes of the affairs.

This was the first time I'd been officially tasked with doing something that could save someone's life. I couldn't let Mr Park down. I was a bit embarrassed to say so, but I figured this was the sort of emotion that naturally arose in a father–son type of relationship.

Luckily, after some deliberation, Mrs Shim took pity on me and ended up letting me stay with her.

'We only have two bedrooms,' she explained, 'so I'll use the main one with my daughter Jina, and you and my son will have to share the other room, cramped as it may be.'

'That's fine. It's only for a month. Though I'm sorry to your son for the inconvenience.'

I loaded my belongings into a taxi, and as the cab made its way to Mrs Shim's house, I felt myself growing excited. I wondered if this was how a killer heading into a big job might have felt.

'My son just started a new part-time job, so he really only comes home to sleep,' Mrs Shim explained. 'You two are about the same age, so I hope you'll get along.'

Her house was small but clean. Crochet lace patterns decorated the kimchi fridge and the table, as well as the cupboards.

'Oh, those two are so careless. Sorry.'

Only then did I notice the pantyhose strewn across the bed. In front of the wall mirror hung a neatly ironed school uniform blouse fluttering in the wind from the fan.

'My daughter usually gets home after ten o'clock once her evening study hall ends, and my son only comes back after midnight, so make yourself comfortable until then. How does spicy croaker stew sound for dinner?'

No matter how often I heard it, Mrs Shim's voice was always like music to my ears.

That evening, Mrs Shim and I sat across from each other and ate from the pot of spicy croaker stew in the centre of the table.

We watched the eight o'clock news together, and the whole time, no one came by or called. I was exhausted from how full I was. All my pent-up tension had dulled, too. I could feel myself about to fall into a long, deep sleep.

'Ugh, it smells all fishy in here. Is that why the window's open?'

The front door swung open and in walked a small girl who took off her flats in the entryway. Her voice wasn't loud, but her enunciation was clear and precise. The lights in the doorway came on, illuminating her face. She was as short as a middle school student, but her shrewd expression gave away the fact that she was a bit older. At a glance, she resembled Mrs Shim, only with fairer skin and thicker, more shapely eyebrows. She reminded me of someone else, too. Was it a K-pop idol? Or an actress?

'Jina, say hello,' said Mrs Shim. 'This young man will be living with us for the next month.'

The girl nodded to me in greeting. Her hair was long, and her plaid green uniform skirt looked a little loose on her.

'Oh, is this the live-in tutor? Nice to meet you. I'm Kim Jina.' She smiled, revealing her perfectly even teeth. Dark eyes, fair skin, sheer confidence. Then it hit me. She didn't remind me of an idol or an actress, but of my mum.

But hold on – live-in tutor?

'Get changed and come to the living room,' Mrs Shim said.

When Jina disappeared, Mrs Shim gave me a helpless look and leaned in to whisper, 'Sorry. I told her that when I didn't know how else to introduce you. Of course, I couldn't tell her the truth. You said you were a good student when you were in school. You can just pretend to teach her for a month.'

I couldn't remember when exactly I'd said that, but it seemed my latest problem stemmed from a lie I'd told at some point about being a prodigy, ranked first schoolwide. I couldn't believe she'd tasked someone who'd actually been ranked dead last in school with being a tutor. Seriously. It was too funny. If my mum were here, she would have screeched with laughter. *Him? A good student?*

If Jina was also ranked last like me, maybe I stood a chance. I could just pretend to know things that neither of us understood.

'She's ranked in the top ten schoolwide,' said Mrs Shim.

I was absolutely screwed.

I nibbled on a wedge of an apple Mrs Shim had peeled and sneaked a glance at Jina as she sat down next to me.

'So which university did you graduate from, Mr Choi?'

I nearly choked.

'Jina, what does that matter? Let Mr Choi rest for today.'

Even after her mother's scolding, though, the girl kept staring at my mouth with her dark, piercing eyes.

'I went to university overseas, so you probably wouldn't recognize the name,' I said. It seemed like a decent cover.

'You must speak pretty fluent English, then, right? That's amazing. I was just wanting to test out my English listening skills.'

'It wasn't in the US,' I said. 'It was in, er, Guatemala. You know where that is, don't you? Guatemala.'

'Oh, I see. Then you speak Spanish.'

Wait. They didn't speak Guatemalan in Guatemala?

While we talked, Mrs Shim slipped out to the balcony, where she was awkwardly pressing buttons on her phone.

'She must be location tracking,' Jina said, puffing out her

cheeks and pouting. 'My brother just started a new part-time job, and ever since, she's been fretting like that. There's no mum in the world who cares more about her kids than ours.'

I didn't know for sure that Mrs Shim was actually tracking her son's location. What was she so worried about a grown man for? Since I'd turned twenty, my own family had lost all interest in how I was doing aside from the small sum of money I sent them every month. Plus, since my mum and Mr Kim had gotten married earlier in the year, it had become hard to see her even during the holidays. Mrs Shim hurriedly put her phone in her pocket and returned to the living room, squeezing on to the couch between us. The front door opened again, and a tall young man stepped inside.

'I'm ho-ome!' he called. Without looking up, he took off his trainers and disappeared straight into the bathroom.

'You saw that, didn't you?' Jina whispered. 'She checked his location then rushed back in when she saw he was close to pretend like she didn't. Does she worry about him that much?'

Mrs Shim shot her a look when she heard her daughter whispering. 'Jina, go and finish your homework, then get to sleep. You must be tired.'

Mrs Shim then collected the plate that still had several apple slices on it and took it to the sink, looking like she was in a daze. Jina said goodnight to me, stretched a bit, then went to her room. Suddenly I had no reason to stay in the living room any more.

'Mrs Shim, I'll get going to bed, too,' I said. 'I'll introduce myself to your son later.'

Mrs Shim looked oddly anxious. Sort of like how Mr Park

had looked when he told me he was sending me here to keep an eye on her.

'Joongi. Please be good to my Jinseob,' she said.

To get to the bedroom, I had to pass by the bathroom with Jinseob inside. I heard a familiar clanging sound coming from the bathroom. The clang of metal. The sound made by thin but solid metal when it struck other metal.

Why would that sound be coming from a bathroom?

It was definitely different from the clang of a belt buckle. I was slowing my steps when I realized that might raise suspicion, so instead I quickly went inside the bedroom and pressed my ear against the wall adjoining the bathroom. That thin but solid metal could only be the blade of a knife – I'd heard it often enough since Mrs Shim joined the agency. Soon after, I heard the shower running. But even through the rush of water, I could hear the smooth sound of friction. The scrape of metal against something, the sound of the blade being worn down. A moment later, the water cut off, and I could hear him leaving the bathroom.

'Did you have dinner?' Mrs Shim asked quickly, almost as though she'd been waiting outside the bathroom to greet her son.

'I did,' he replied. 'You must be tired, Mum. You should get some sleep.'

'The guest I told you about this morning is here. Go on and say hello. I hope you two get along.'

I took my ear away from the wall and quickly moved to sit in the chair. When Jinseob came in, I greeted him as though I hadn't heard a thing. Like his sister, he had fair skin and elegant features. He carefully set the leather bag he'd been carrying down on the floor. It looked really heavy.

'I'm Kim Jinseob,' he said. 'I heard we're the same age. Please look after Jina and help her with her studies.'

He held out his hand. There were several red blisters on the skin between his thumb and forefinger.

'I'm Choi Joongi,' I said. 'I hope we'll get along for the next month. Please continue to use the bed. I'm comfortable sleeping on the floor.'

Jinseob took off his outside clothes and changed into a short-sleeved shirt.

'You don't have to be so formal with me,' he said. 'Since we're the same age.'

He rubbed some lotion with a musky fragrance on to his face and flashed me a good-natured smile. Just like Mrs Shim. Children inherited so much from their parents. If I were a girl, maybe I would have inherited my mum's beauty, but sadly I had the same nondescript face and short pug dog legs as my father, whose love for my mum burned hot for one night only before he'd flowed on elsewhere. As this young man sat hunched over, clipping his fingernails in front of me now, it occurred to me that his smile might not be the only thing he'd inherited from his mum.

Oh, Choi Joongi, I thought to myself. *You're well and truly fucked.*

8

The Daughter

The severe weather that summer had drastically increased the number of jellyfish in the waters, and it was now forbidden to go swimming at the beach. My brother and I wore inner tubes around our waists and stood watching the seafoam crash against the sandbar as we sadly licked at the strawberry ice cream melting and running all over our palms. It was our first summer vacation at the beach, but Mum had a giant rucksack with a tent and camping cookware on her back, face dripping sweat as she argued with the beach manager. She complained that it made no sense for them to charge a twenty thousand won entrance fee at a beach resort where we couldn't even use the beach. All the while, her sweat made trails through her caked-on foundation like winding ant tunnels. The manager, thoroughly browbeaten, agreed to lower the fee to ten thousand won and backed away from Mum.

As soon as he disappeared, Mum stuck some poles in the ground and pitched her tent, even making a sort of chamber pot by hollowing out a rotten watermelon someone had tossed on the ground, bustling about without a moment's rest under the glaring sun. At the same time, our dad was strumming the guitar and watching the sunset with three college girls who had invited him to their dinner party. Mum made us a stew out of canned tuna and vegetables with big chunks of kimchi. Then she found a discarded pole and stuck it to the top of a nearby tent, hanging my red swimsuit with the Miffy illustration on it as a kind of flag. She did this so our father could see and find us once he got back from wherever he had been. During the entire three days and four nights, our father wandered around half out of his mind, and our mum took me and my brother to the swimming pool instead of the beach to cool our reddened, sunburned backs. But the whole time, she never once lashed out at our father. It seemed she was satisfied that he'd come back to us in one piece.

When it came to our father, our mum was extremely lenient. Her only act of protest against him was to sit in the doorway for all to see, pour hot water into a scratched-up stainless brass bowl of cold rice, and chew and swallow the soggy grains. Tears would run like snot down her cheeks and nose to pool on her upper lip. Dad, of course, hardly batted an eye at Mum's silent demonstrations. At most, he might buy a mandarin or some crackers and come home perhaps an hour earlier than usual, and even then, he'd just watch TV in silence until he fell asleep. I always wondered what Mum loved about him.

My father had finished high school and was working in the alcohol delivery business when he inherited a small fortune from the sudden death of his father, with whom he'd always had a patchy relationship. Mum hoped he wouldn't rip through the little bit of money he'd gotten and would instead put it in the bank to use for me and my brother's schooling, all the while continuing to deliver alcohol. But our dad went and blew the entire fortune on setting up a butcher shop. It was a poorly thought-out decision, considering that nothing was as economically unviable as a food business.

The butcher shop was a small room with an even more crammed and shabby kitchen attached. If we wanted to use hot water, we had to work a lever to turn on the water heater like getting the fire going on a gas stove. Every morning, I would wake up to the sound of the water heater cranking to life and find Dad in the kitchen wearing a running shirt, panting as he washed his face. Mum would use the remaining warm and soapy water to wash the rags and socks right away, and when it was time to wash her own face or hair, the water heater would make a whizzing sound instead of its usual cranking, the sound of the water supply motor the only thing that could be heard.

The shop didn't even have a storefront sign, but the locals called our store the 'Half-Day Butcher Shop'. That was because of Dad. When he wasn't wearing his plastic apron and holding a butcher's knife, he looked tall and sturdy and handsome like the male lead from a soap opera. That was why so many diehard fans of his gathered at the shop every day just to see him. They were mostly bored housewives who would sit on the benches outside, lounging around and chatting. Women who would scoop puffed rice from a plastic bag into their mouths by the handful, scratching their thighs until their skin flaked with dandruff as they stared at my dad with longing in their eyes and then burst out laughing. They would spend half the day picking apart my mum's rough appearance and brusque personality, but then when it was time for their children to come home from school or their husbands who had been working since dawn to stop in for a nap, the women would buy some ingredients for a stew and rush out like the tide. For half the day, the shop was bustling with customers, and for the other half it sat as empty as a schoolyard on a Saturday, where only snack crumbs and forlorn tumbleweeds of hair remained. That was the Half-Day Butcher Shop.

Every Wednesday was slaughtering day. Of course, we didn't slaughter the cows in the shop itself. Wednesdays were the days the cows were slaughtered at the actual slaughterhouse, and the only days that raw meat, bible tripe, or raw liver could be served. Our mum would get up at dawn, do her makeup, and touch up her hair on Wednesdays – all to defend our dad from his many fans who were sure to stop by using the fresh meat as an excuse.

From early in the morning, Mum would section and cut the meat, sharpening dull knives on the whetstone. My brother and I would sluggishly stir awake from the noise, open the door to our room a crack and watch Mum work from behind. Her old red, plastic slippers that squeaked with every step. The clotted cow's blood that filled the eighteen-litre cooking oil tub. The crimson, fluorescent lights in the display window that blinked much like our mum's tired eyes. The printed calendar full of photos of Western beauties running on the sand in bright red bikinis. Everything outside our room was red. A blindingly red world. Our mum would have on red lipstick, too, as she turned to call to our father. He turned on the water heater to wash his face and hair while Mum sat crouched in the kitchen, setting dishes on the low dining table and scooping pats of freshly cooked rice into bowls.

'Sookhee said she saw you yesterday. Over at the railroad crossing.'

Dad's face hardened as he fished around his doenjang stew for some of the rare solid ingredients. He'd started growing out his moustache a few days earlier and now from the side looked like Clark Gable in *Gone With the Wind*. He left his spoon as though he were tossing it down, stood up looking flushed, and walked out of the shop. For a long time, the railroad crossing – which was a railroad crossing in name only now as the trains no longer ran through there – had been more famous as a red-light district full of pubs and motels, as well as two adult nightclubs. Because of that, being seen milling around there basically meant you were having an affair. Mum gathered up the food Dad hadn't taken more than a few bites of and followed after him. My brother and I sensed that something was off and hoped the rest of the day would pass without incident. We crawled back into our beds, under our blankets, tucked our cold hands under our armpits and fell back asleep.

Sookhee was a neighbour two years older than Mum who worked the bar at a place that served traditional liquor down at the railroad crossing. Mum, of course, would rather Sookhee went straight to work than stop by the butcher shop, but every day without fail Sookhee would open the door to the shop and call out, 'Good morning, Boss!'

Once the heated floor tiles had lost all their heat, my brother decided he couldn't stand the cold any more and needed to turn on the boiler. He left the room in his long johns. Through the gap in the open door, I saw Sookhee take a yoghurt out of her handbag and offer it to Dad, waving hello.

'Let's hear this eyewitness testimony,' Dad said.

Sookhee had a gap in her teeth as well as a flat face and nose, which made her look like a fool at first glance, but as expected of someone who handled money, she was quick-witted and knew how to protect her own interests. She gave Mum a look, but Mum shook her head, looking like she was on the verge of tears.

'Let's not do this today,' said Sookhee. 'I'm on my way to work, too, and—'

'It won't take long. Just confirm one thing for me. Are you certain it was me you saw at the railroad crossing yesterday?'

Sookhee took a moment to catch her breath, then looked at Mum apologetically before she said, 'What business would you have over at the railroad crossing? Mrs Shim, tell him you misunderstood. When did I ever say such a thing?'

Sookhee was sly. She must have noticed Mum's passiveness and thought she could easily get over on her and save herself by lying. My brother had been at school the previous afternoon, so he hadn't heard, but I was at home doing colouring exercises when I clearly overheard Sookhee tattling to my mum. Now, she ran out of the shop like she'd been doused in hot water, while Mum stood frozen in place with her head bowed as though *she* had been submerged in water full of ice.

'I've known about your delusional belief that I'm cheating on you for a long time now, but I never once dreamed you would make up a lie over it.'

Around lunchtime that day, the neighbourhood women ordered spicy seafood noodle soup for Dad and called him over to eat at one of the low benches, while Mum sat in the doorway wolfing down wet rice.

Mum was later proven innocent. The other neighbourhood

women had often seen Dad frequenting motels at the railroad crossing. Feeling as disappointed by Dad's behaviour as Mum had been, the other women began to turn on him one by one, saying they would rather eat vegetables that were cheap and good for them and prepared by a true bachelor than high-cholesterol meat. Like that, the Half-Day Butcher Shop became the All-Day Butcher Shop, and Mum's worries deepened by the day. But Dad's behaviour turned out not to be the typical affair that Mum and the neighbourhood ladies imagined. It would be a long time before the truth of it was revealed.

Even my father, who had seemed like he would perpetually be a beautiful young Adonis, couldn't win against the passage of time. As his diabetes – another thing passed down to him by his father – worsened, he grew noticeably emaciated and withered in appearance, and he soon aged into a mousy middle-aged man with none of the neat features of his youth. Just when Mum's hatred and resentment of him began to lessen, the notice arrived via registered mail that we had to put the butcher shop up for auction. Mum handed Dad the envelope with the red warning that it should only be opened by the addressee, her hands trembling as though she were handing a notice to the king. Dad turned his back to Mum and drank his lukewarm soju with a drained look on his face.

The reason he'd been visiting the motels at the railroad crossing almost every day was because of hwatu. His debt had snowballed after he'd gambled away the money he'd borrowed from the women who'd once been his fans, and now even the sarcastically renamed All-Day Butcher Shop that had been helping him by bringing in at least a little bit of money was gone overnight.

The day before the foreclosure auction, Dad poured himself a cup of soju and gulped it down, got into the old run-down car that was the last asset our family had, and crashed into a pub at the railroad crossing, killing himself. Mum took out the insurance policy and savings she had secretly kept for him. She used the money from the savings bond, which had been a month away from reaching maturity, to pay for the damage to the pub and the funeral expenses. With the little bit she received as condolence money, she paid back Dad's debts to the neighbours. Then she moved us into a smaller, two-bedroom apartment. The last thing our teary-eyed mum took from the butcher shop after she had run her hands over all the other worn appliances and furniture were three butcher's knives. We had to walk out into the jungle that was the world, our shoulders hunched and our footsteps timed to match the sound of knives chopping.

I never told this to my mum or my brother, but I was the one who'd bought Dad the soju. It was Parents' Day, and our teacher had told us to make sure we prepared a gift our parents would really love. On my way home, I took the loose change in my pocket that amounted to five hundred won and shook it around in my hand. I mindlessly went into a supermarket, but nothing that could be bought for five hundred won caught my eye. Right then, a tall man came in carrying a box of soju on his back like my dad once had in his youth. He set the box on the floor in front of the display shelves, filled it with the empty soju bottles for recycling, and took them away. Seeing that, I thought up a way to scrape together some money. I ran home and grabbed all the empty soju bottles under the rusty meat slicer, put them in a basket and made four trips back to the supermarket to sell them. With that money, plus the five hundred won I'd already had, I had enough to buy a new bottle of soju and a chocolate bar for my mum.

I added a carnation to both the chocolate and the soju and put them on the middle shelf in the fridge with a note that read: 'Thank you for raising me. – Jina.' But that night, Dad fell straight asleep and didn't go to the fridge. Mum also passed out immediately upon coming home from spending the day collecting money owed to us, and so Parents' Day went by without anyone getting a gift they really loved.

The following evening, my father – with his dark, rough skin that had lost its lustre and the few tufts of grey hair that remained on his head – got up and staggered to the fridge. He sagged and limped like clothes that had been shed, weakly opened the refrigerator door, and felt around until he found the cold soju bottle, twisting off the lid and filling a glass with liquor without saying a word of thanks to me.

He downed his soju in one go and turned to the wall. 'Who's there?' he asked.

I let out a cry, biting my lip and sniffling.

'What, am I dying or something? What are you crying for? Don't cry. Get it together. You and your brother are all your mum has left. It's no help to her if you're crying all the time. Promise me you won't cry any more and I'll give you a little spending money, all right? Come here.'

Dad's voice sounded faraway, like the dripping of an icicle melting under the eaves in early winter. I rubbed my tear-stained face against his shirt, which smelled sweet, and snivelled like a little kid until I fell asleep. When I opened my eyes, Dad was gone, and in his place were eight folded-up thousand won bills and two five hundred won coins in my hand.

Time had passed, yet my mum, my brother, and I still lived in that two-bedroom rental. Mum was working all sorts of part-time jobs to support us. Some time ago, she'd started working at the butcher's corner in the mart, and more recently she said she'd started work cleaning at a jjimjilbang. But I didn't take anything at face value. If she was working for the minimum wage, she would be earning 9,620 won per hour, and if she worked 209 hours per month, her monthly salary would come out at 2,010,580 won. Even doubling that, there was no way she had the money to hire a live-in tutor.

Among the women my mum's age who took good care of themselves, there were still a few with slender waists and no deep wrinkles. But as my mum, Shim Eunok, sat listening to the radio in the living room while she peeled garlic, she reminded me of an ancient tree. She had no curves, her skin was peppered with dark freckles that had started coming in early, and the thick calluses on her fingers were like the knots on a dead tree.

But from that tree, flowers had blossomed. Each branch was bursting with green leaves, so dazzling it hurt to look, and from the flower buds, pale pink blossoms had exploded into full bloom. Like the rainy season that began with scattered showers and ended with downpours and floods, that was exactly what made me so anxious, and so sad. I didn't want to see that sort of transformation in my mum.

Seven years earlier or so, on my mum's birthday, my brother and I went to a cosmetics store together and bought her some foundation. She tried it on just once, out of sheer excitement, but after that, she quietly stored it in the bottom drawer of her vanity. That was the same woman who had recently started wearing makeup. She'd also gotten an illegal eyebrow tattoo procedure done at the jjimjilbang and started covering her face in foundation and wearing a hot pink lipstick.

It all began right after she had quit working at the mart. She still came across as gaudy, but she wore something different every day and started coming home very late at night. If I asked her what she was doing, she would say she worked the front desk at the jjimjilbang and sometimes cleaned. But she never smelled like the cheap lotion they gave you at the jjimjilbang, nor did she reek of the bleach used to rinse mops. On days when she wasn't home yet despite the late hour, I stood on the balcony watching the dark bus stop. It wasn't so much an issue nowadays, but it was a habit I had gotten into around the time that a drunk man was murdered with chopsticks in the apartment's playground, sending chills down all the local residents' spines.

One night, not long after my brother had started his part-time job, I was waiting for mum, my eyes scanning the bus stop outside the window. Even after midnight, once the last bus had stopped running, Mum still wasn't home. After a while, a silver Sonata pulled up in front of the apartment. In the dark, I could see Mum's white teeth. She was laughing. The man who got out of the car with her bowed towards her. He looked trustworthy, somehow. I quickly turned off the lights and got under the blankets to pretend I was sleeping. A moment later, I heard

Mum's familiar footsteps stop outside the apartment, then the front door unlocking. Inside, too, Mum's steps felt quiet and careful. The next day, she paid for three months of my cram school classes at once.

There were always a few children of divorce or other kids who had lost a parent in my friend circles. The single parents often dated each other, believing their children wouldn't suspect a thing. Those relationships didn't always end well. Sometimes one would make off with the entire contents of the savings they had built up together over several years, or else one would come back from a training or retreat to find stained tissues or contraception in the wastebasket. Not wanting to face the other out of shame, they would simply pretend they hadn't noticed. It was clear that my mum wasn't loaning this man money or bringing him into the house. On the contrary, her bank account seemed fuller than ever, and more often lately it seemed that she was neglecting chores and having a hard time finding things around the house, her mind in a state of disarray. But no money in the world comes without a price. Even as a high school student, I knew that much. If I presumed the money in Mum's bank account had come from that man, then maybe their relationship wasn't merely one of dating.

'Mr Choi, when are we going to start our classes?'

My tutor, who'd been engrossed in the TV as he ate dinner, cast Mum a sideways glance at my question, cleared his throat, and stood up. It had been more than a week since he'd moved in, yet he still hadn't told me what textbooks we would be using, and every time I came home, he was fast asleep.

'Jina, Mr Choi works part-time during the day, so he's very

tired. What about the weekends? I think that'd be best, don't you?'

Mr Choi quietly slipped off to his room, and within seconds, I could hear him snoring. Something was clearly suspicious about how Mum and Mr Choi were acting. Sometimes when I was in the bathroom, I could hear the two of them talking, and it always seemed like they knew each other well, whispering in secret but friendly tones. But then when they heard me come out of the bathroom, their conversation would end abruptly. Another time, Mr Choi said that the capital of Russia was Putin, and yesterday he sent me a message that read:

Have a niec day at school. It's dangerous out there, so come straight home when your done, kk?

At first, I thought this was merely his cheesy sense of humour. But today's incident, I really couldn't make head or tail of.

Since Mum had suggested tutoring sessions at the weekends, I wrote down a bunch of questions I had in a notepad and went to knock on Mr Choi's door.

'Count to ten and then come in, all right?' he called from the other side.

I heard him moving around and urgently tidying up. After obediently counting to ten, I announced, 'I'm coming in,' and opened the door. Mr Choi was kicking a stack of magazines underneath the bed and smiling awkwardly.

'What is it, Jina?' he asked.

It was early evening. Mum had gone to the mart, and my brother still hadn't come back from his part-time job. I was secretly nervous, but I hesitated only a moment before handing Mr Choi my notebook, where I had written down a sequencing problem, a permutation problem, and an exponents problem that needed solving.

'I'm having trouble with A, B, and C. I understand them in theory, but not so much in practice.'

For a moment, Mr Choi stared at me, stroking his chin as though he were deep in thought. Then he suddenly got up and turned off the lights. The already awkward situation was even more awkward in the dark.

'So you're at that age where you have these kinds of worries, too,' said Mr Choi. 'Here, have a seat.'

Suddenly, I felt afraid, but seeing no reason not to listen, I stiffly sat on the edge of the bed.

'A, B, and C, you said?'

'Yes.'

'I wonder if my guess is right. Here for A, you wrote "SOOYEOL". And for B, you wrote "SOONYEOL". These two sound like they could be brothers. Maybe even twins. One is a cute little munchkin who's great at school and sports and is super popular with the ladies, while the other is a bit of a rebel, an outsider who cuts class a lot, gets into fights, and has only his bike to call his friend. The brothers are fighting over C, or "JISU", as you wrote here. Jisu's not the most beautiful girl out there, and she doesn't come from a ton of money, but she's tough and cheerful and bold. It seems your concern is that you can't figure out what's going on with these three. In that case, I wonder if this book I borrowed might be helpful. It's due back at the library today, but take your time reading it. I'll pay the late fees.'

Mr Choi handed me a manga book that had been sitting on his bedside table titled *My Heart-Pounding First Love Trigonometry*.

On the cover were twin boys who looked like corncobs with eyes and, of course, a girl who looked no different save for her long hair, with her arms around each boy's shoulders.

'Mr Choi, are you kidding me? Do you know how hard my mum and brother work to earn money and support me? None of your jokes are the least bit funny! From now on, I don't want you tutoring me ever again!'

Mr Choi looked confused. I stood to leave, but he reached out and grabbed my wrist.

'Have you figured it out?' he said.

With that, I found myself frozen, unable to move.

'Mr Choi,' I said. 'Do you know something about my mum? Tell me now.'

He let out a small sigh. Just then, the front door opened.

'Jina, could you help me carry some things?'

It was Mum. I left Mr Choi silently scratching his head and went to help her.

'What did you buy so much for?' I asked.

Mum brought in a box containing three heads of cabbage in a green mesh bag, one bag of onions, twenty kilograms of fresh garlic, a black bag of something that smelled fishy, milk, and all sorts of daily essentials.

'I won the pool of gye money this month, so the day after tomorrow, I'm going on a three-night trip with some friends to the hot springs to celebrate. I need to make kimchi and some other side dishes.'

I wasn't sure why, but the whole time Mum salted the cabbage and boiled down the mackerel and braised the quail eggs in soy sauce, Mr Choi didn't step foot out of his room.

'Of course, I trust you and Joongi, but I wouldn't dare leave a young man and woman alone in the house for several days with no grown-ups around,' Mum said. 'So starting the day I leave, you two should study together at a reading room until your brother comes home. Understood?'

I gave a half-hearted answer, pretending to be reading my maths textbook even as my eyes glazed over the information. Was Mum really going on a trip to the hot springs? And was she really going with her friends? I tried to erase the memory of it, but I couldn't stop picturing the dark silhouette of the man I'd secretly gotten a glimpse of the other night.

The next day when I got home around midnight, Mum was cooking. The kitchen looked nice and tidy.

'Mum, are you making beef bone soup?'

She poured the finished broth into glass food storage containers. There was so much of it that I couldn't even count how many servings it would make.

'What'd you make so much for? I don't even like this soup,' I said.

Mr Choi and my brother weren't home. For the first time in a while, I made myself comfortable, plopping down on the bed.

'Jina, do you know how to make kimchi?'

'Nope. But later, I'll have someone to do it for me, so don't worry.'

Mum's expression looked colder and harder than usual. She set down several sheets of paper with teensy print at my feet. I sat up and started scanning the papers – they were recipes for kimchi and other side dishes.

'Mum, I'm in my last year of high school. What use is any of this to me?'

'Don't throw those out. Keep them right by your desk. I'll do an inspection later.'

Mum had always told me to just study hard, and that after I got married, she would take care of all the housework. I felt sad all of a sudden, but I avoided my mum's eyes so as not to show it.

'Seems like the world could be yours if you only study hard, hm? But that's not true. Women have to get married to be seen as adults, and they have to give birth to be seen as people. So don't treat this as a joke!'

What in the world was going on with my mother? I had the sudden fear that she wasn't going on a trip to the hot springs but was planning to run away to some far-flung place with that man, never to return.

'Sorry. I'm sorry,' Mum said, rushing over to my side. Her nose was bright red.

That night, for the first time in a long time, Mum lent me her arm as a pillow while I slept. We shared a blanket as we lay there in silence, emanating only breaths and body heat. Deep in the night, I felt a warm, wet stream running down my forehead, and the same stream ran down my face on to my mother's arm.

Starting from the hazy hours of dawn, Mum busied herself packing her bags for her trip.

'You're going to school?' my brother asked me.

He was looking much gaunter these days. Because he'd gone to work part-time right after finishing his military service, it was rare that I saw him around the house any more. Growing up, we'd always wanted what the other had and were constantly arguing, but just three years or so ago, our relationship wasn't nearly as awkward as this. My brother started talking less and less, and even when we were all together, he would often avoid eye contact.

'Can I use the bathroom first?' he asked, and didn't wait for my answer before he slung a towel around his neck and went inside. Mr Choi, meanwhile, had left the evening before saying he had something to do and still hadn't come back. Now that I thought about it, I felt like the fact that Mum even knew a private tutor was weird. And that she spoke so casually to him when she wasn't the type to be overly familiar with strangers.

But even weirder than my mum was my brother. Lately he would spend half an hour or more in the bathroom. I tiptoed into the room across the hall. The blankets were neatly folded, the desk had been tidied up, and a thin navy-blue jacket hung from a hanger. Because I hadn't properly seen my brother in a while, I didn't know whether the jacket was his or Mr Choi's, but I decided to treat it as an object of suspicion. I stuck my hand in the pockets and felt around until my fingers brushed a small leather wallet. When I opened it, I saw my brother's official and student ID cards inside. The ID photo he'd taken before he enrolled had faded a little now. I closed the wallet and was tucking it back inside the jacket when I felt a crumpled-up piece of paper and pulled it out. It was a business card with HAPPY AGENCY written on it. It was my first time seeing a business card with no other information besides the company name and phone number printed on it. It occurred to me that I didn't know whether HAPPY AGENCY was where my brother worked part-time.

That evening, as Mum had asked, I went by the reading room to study. I wasn't really reading the words and was instead playing games on my phone to kill time when I sent my brother a text asking when he was going to be home. Just then, I sensed something behind me. I turned around and there was my brother. He mouthed, 'Let's go,' and I picked up my bag and followed after him.

'Do you remember the day that Dad died?' my brother asked.

It was twenty minutes on foot to our house. My brother and I were trying to match our paces to the other's, so one of us was walking more hurriedly and the other more slowly than usual.

'Do you remember?' I returned the question to him.

'It was right in the middle of midterms, so I was at school until late, and I remember my homeroom teacher was the one who took me home. Until then, I thought something bad had happened to Mum. Because I'd secretly seen her go into the fridge the night before and take out some soju and chocolate to go with it. She emptied the bottle, refilled it with plain water, put it back, and went to bed looking exhausted. It was the first time I'd seen Mum drinking alcohol. So I was worried the whole time, thinking something bad had happened to her, only to get to the hospital and see that Mum was fine, and the bad thing had happened to Dad instead.'

This was news to me. Until now, I had believed that Dad drank the soju I bought him and ended up dying in a drunk driving accident.

'Then, he wasn't drunk driving?' I asked.

'He had diabetes. He was losing his vision. A blind person behind the wheel *not* ending up in an accident would have been a miracle. Dad's death was a suicide.'

I had guessed that Dad had intentionally set out to die from the money he had left in my hand that day, but I had never imagined that losing his vision to diabetes would have been what caused the accident. An intense sorrow for the little girl who had sniffled as she stood watching her father rummage around for the soju moved me to tears.

Under the faint light of the streetlamps, I could see that my brother seriously took after our father. He was probably extremely popular with girls, but because of his tendency not to show his emotions, I imagined he was probably a bit of a loner, too.

'You were so young back then. I didn't want to go into detail about everything with you. But now, you're about to go to uni, and you're a good student, so you should get to live the life you want. If only money weren't an issue.'

The resoluteness in my brother's voice made me nervous.

'When I go to uni, I'm going to work part-time, too, so I can pay my share. You don't have to worry about that,' I told him curtly.

He grabbed my wrist as I moved to keep walking ahead.

'I know you'll be great at whatever you do,' he said. 'But to live, you at least need enough money to cover the basics. Housing, food, clothes, transportation. Even those basics would be a huge burden on Mum, though. She can't take on all that alone. So from now on, I've decided I'm going to earn money for us. Your bank account has all the money the three of us will need for the essentials.'

My brother reached into the pocket of the same navy jacket I had searched that morning and pulled out the bank book for my educational savings account. We'd all had to open one in middle school, but after making only a few deposits, I stopped keeping up with it and shoved the bank book deep into a drawer, pretending the account didn't exist. Somehow, that bank book had found its way into my brother's pocket. I opened it and checked the total amount in the account. Not counting the fifty-two thousand won I had put into it all those years ago, the balance was exactly thirty million won.

'Jinseob, what is this? You're scaring me.'

My brother's eyes reminded me of my father's the last time I saw him, when he promised to give me money if I stopped crying. My hands felt clammy, and I started to wheeze.

'Don't worry,' he said. 'I'm not doing anything so dangerous that you need to be scared. It's easier work than what Mum was doing, chopping meat and mopping floors under those hot, red lights all day. Honestly, my job is pretty much like cleaning, too. This is just a downpayment. I'll get even more money soon. But until then, you have to keep this bank book and my job a secret from Mum. I'll work there for another month at the most and then quit. Until I come back, you have to keep this safe. You're a smart kid, so I trust you'll under- stand what I'm saying.'

His phone buzzed from inside his pocket.

'When you get home, lock the doors,' he said. 'I already con- tacted Choi Joongi and set him up with somewhere else to stay for tonight and tomorrow. Get home safe.'

And with that, he disappeared across the street. It was early winter, and seeing my brother in only a thin jacket made my heart ache. What kind of cleaning gig would pay a twenty- one-year-old in the army reserves thirty million won in cash? A vague sense of fear tightened around my throat. I imagined my brother walking around the red-light district with a mas- sive dragon tattoo coiled up on his back, trading profanities with men built like bears. But I couldn't believe my brother, a lanky dweeb despite his height, would take the plunge into that lifestyle.

'It's dangerous for a young girl to be walking around by herself this late at night.'

I had been staring at the spot where my brother had disappeared when I was startled to hear someone speaking to me. It was Mr Choi.

'Put that away and follow me.'

He was looking at the bank book in my hands. I shoved it deep inside my bag as though I'd been caught holding a physical wad of cash in my hands. Mr Choi started walking towards the house as usual.

'Mr Choi, my brother said he found somewhere else for you to stay tonight and tomorrow, so I'll head home on my own,' I said.

I was firm, but he didn't seem to be slowing down at all.

'I know,' he said. 'Your mum went on her trip and your brother will be working. And you must have a huge amount of money, tens of millions of won, in that bank book. Do you think I'd follow you home knowing all that and how it would look if something happened? I'm just walking you there.'

This was the most mature and reliable I had seen him all week since he'd moved in. But I still couldn't quite let my guard down.

'How do you know all that, Mr Choi?'

I started to feel more at ease as we neared the apartment.

'Because your brother and I have the same type of job.'

When we finally came to the entrance, Mr Choi turned to me with a hard look on his face and stared me straight in the eyes. In a very low voice, he said, 'I haven't confirmed anything yet. But if what I'm thinking is correct, your family might be in serious danger. If your mum's trip to the hot springs lasts longer than expected, the money in that account of yours could double. If she comes back the day she said she would, your brother may quit his part-time job and never come back. You probably won't understand everything I'm saying, but you should be careful, too.'

Under the light of the streetlamps, Mr Choi's eyes flashed hot.

'Hurry and head inside. Make sure to lock the doors and hide that bank book somewhere only you would know to look for it. If anything happens, contact me. And . . .'

'And?'

'And even if nothing happens but you're just scared to be alone at night, call me.'

Mr Choi left me no room to reply before he was walking off, his face furiously red. I cupped my hands around my mouth and called after him.

'Mr Choi!'

He stopped and turned around. 'Yeah?'

I shouted back as loud as I could. 'You're not a real tutor, are you?'

He hesitated for a moment, then shouted back, 'That's right! I'm not!'

'So I don't have to call you Mr Choi any more, right?'

He hurried off without answering. I watched him get smaller and farther away, until I was left in the eerie darkness.

I had just gotten off the elevator and taken a few hesitant steps towards the empty apartment when I got a message.

Kim Jina! You got this! Forget what happened 2nite & sweet dreams.

The contact name was saved as 'Joongi oppa'.

9

The Rival

I cut my fingernails once a week. Have my hair cut once every two weeks, trim my nose hair once every ten days. I loathe it when taps don't run or when streetlamps come on before it is even fully dark out. Strands of hair clinging to my clothes, a chilli flake between the teeth, crooked frames and dust sitting under furniture – there are so many things in the world that I can't tolerate. And yet, to my dismay, I was born in a bathroom.

Even after ten months of carrying me, my mum wasn't having any contractions. Looking at my mum's belly, all swollen round like a toad's, everyone agreed that it seemed like the baby inside her was dead. And rumour had it that my mum believed them and thought she might have to live the rest of her life with an unborn baby in her big toad belly.

I was born at exactly eleven months.

One morning when the rest of the family had gone out to the rice paddies and fields, my mum clutched her stomach when it started to ache and waddled to the bathroom. What gushed out of her was different from the typical watery stool.

Her stomach still hurt, and she could still hear something gushing, which frightened her. She didn't dare look down. Her lower body kept clenching, and the baby was coiling itself up beneath the thin skin of her belly. My mum grabbed the doorknob in surprise and tried to stand. Her legs trembled as though they were about to give out from the pain. When she finally managed to lift herself up, she felt something warm writhing between her thighs. Terrified, she kicked open the bathroom door and ran out, stopping short when she heard a baby crying behind her. The fresh, wailing little beast was on the verge of slipping into the toilet. Even now, my mum told this story. Of how the jaundice-yellow baby that I was grabbed hold of my own umbilical cord to keep from falling into her shit.

Those bloodied hands that gripped that umbilical cord were still stained with blood to this day. I lived in a world of men now. It had been that way ever since I came of age. I chugged alcohol with men all night long, then stripped down with the same men and enjoyed a day at the sauna. *Enjoyed* was the wrong word. It was a break from the battlefield, a strategy planning session. In a world where the hierarchy between the higher-ups and those on the lower rungs was sharply carved out, it was a relatively easy chance to catch the attention of the top gun. I cut the old men's toenails, massaged their tattooed shoulders and backs, and tried squeezing my way into the bullet-less war they would be fighting again the next day. I never gained weight no matter how much I ate, so in order not to feel intimidated in that world, I bulked up on high-calorie dog food in secret. I once used my teeth to scrape the calluses off the top gun's feet, swollen inside his leather shoes. Though I didn't have as much energy or drive as other people, I managed to survive on my own.

I had forty-one younger siblings. Not counting the ones who had to go away for minor crimes, I always kept about thirty of them by my side. They managed the businesses by dividing up the work. They didn't go around threatening the business owners with clubs and jackknives or tussling with folks over petty cash like people did in movies. They split the businesses into three divisions, formed three merchant's associations, and set up three reliable men among them as the heads of each. Every month, the business owners just had to pay a fixed amount in dues. If they didn't pay, it wasn't like they had their things destroyed or faced any economic disadvantages. We simply worked according to what we were paid. Part of the dues went towards promotional costs. We hired assistants to help out at newly opened businesses and paid them a bonus to make coupons and flyers to drum up excitement about these places. We were basically entrepreneurs. It was the Happy Detective Agency that controlled the three merchant's associations. And the agency's CEO was none other than me, Na Hancheol.

'Boss, we just got a call from Nosé Nosé Karaoke. They said they worked with Smile last time to resolve the issue. They're sending over a bottle of liquor as an apology.'

The owner of the Nosé Nosé Karaoke Bar was a local who had run the same place for seventeen years. The bar had outlived its old names of the Black Rose Stand Bar and the World Beauty Karaoke Bar. It was rare in this field to hire hostesses from direct interviews instead of through sex trafficking rings. Some time ago, five of the girls on staff there had been scammed out of a huge sum by the same man at the same time. He'd lured them in with sweet nothings about how he could help them live completely different lives by falsifying their educational backgrounds and résumés. The girls were too naive to know real from fake, and they all dreamed of meeting a handsome man and living a normal life. But the conman, quite obviously in hindsight, turned out to be a fraud. One of the girls hanged herself in an empty room in the building. The owner arranged the funeral herself and came to see me. She said she had offered the girls some of the money from her cut as consolation, but they wouldn't accept it. So she decided to hire me to catch the man who'd conned the girls and put a hole in his stomach. But I'd had a lot on my plate, and she must have gotten tired of waiting around in the meantime and taken her request over to the Smile Detective Agency instead.

'Boss, should we impose a penalty this month?'

We had penalties in place to prevent solicitation. The use of sly tactics to draw away business was directly linked to sales, which was what business owners feared most. I shook my head. This was my fault for acting rashly and treating Smile's CEO, Park Taesang, like some has-been. It seemed he'd gotten his hands on a new weapon recently. His agency was the reason our agency's workload had decreased and we kept getting our clients snatched away. But I knew there was no way Park himself would return and pick up a knife yet again.

If he was a legitimate killer and knifeman, I was a dashing ruffian. Though our paths had been wildly different, we lived in the same area and had an unspoken rule not to encroach on each other's territory. I was the one who'd broken that rule first. Even though I'd sworn I wouldn't get mixed up with contract killings, I made an exception for a very big deal and a matter of loyalty.

It all began when I got a request to kill the stepfather of

someone I had at one point considered like an older brother. When he was younger, his stepfather would get drunk and beat this kid mercilessly. The worst of the abuse began two years after his mum had married the man, when she'd lost her mind and started making a ruckus around their neighbourhood. His stepfather would scrub him so hard with a coarse towel that he bled, all because the kid resembled his biological father with his darker skin and fierce eyes. He would unbuckle his belt and start using it to whip the boy, complaining about how he should have been out in the world making money by now like the kids in other families were. He would force the kid's mouth open and fill it with disgustingly salty soy sauce, saying that the reason he was so picky about food was because he wasn't hungry enough, clearly. It got to the point where the kid couldn't take it any more, and he dropped out of middle school and ran away to Seoul. He started off panhandling, then moved on to pickpocketing, and once he came of age he was initiated into a gang, taking the blows the way he had learned to from his stepfather. He earned the nickname 'Punch' from getting into so many fistfights and brawls that he ended up with nine assault charges on his record.

Punch thought that if he could take a few more beatings and rack up a couple more convictions, he could leave the gang and open up his own shop. He would go back for his mother who was probably still in the countryside living like a punching bag the way he had been, and he would get her some treatment for her mental illness, and once she was better, he would set her up at the front counter in his shop and watch her happily count money all morning and all evening long. His mother had stripped naked, thrown herself into the path of a speeding train, and broken her body to the point where she couldn't even apply makeup any more. Punch came to see me looking absolutely determined.

I couldn't turn him down. If it hadn't been for him, I might have become homeless, or else a petty criminal who couldn't stay out of jail. I told Punch to buy a good knife. Not even a day later, he brought me a dagger called a tsuge. A rippled pattern ran along the gunmetal blade, its weight was nice and balanced, and even its sleek yet sturdy tip was beautiful.

I accepted the knife and boarded the train alone. When you wounded someone in a fight, there was a chance the wound could become infected and kill them slowly over time, but this was back when I had never once gone into a fight determined to take a person's life from the beginning. The air conditioning on the train was strong, and I shivered from the cold and the even colder feeling of the knife against my chest, sleeping near my heart.

The train had departed around dawn, but it was past noon when it arrived at the station. I hailed a cab and headed to the address Punch had given me. And then, there it was: a run-down house with chipped slate tiles on the roof. One side of the rusted gate was completely missing, and in the middle of the yard was a water pump, a rare sight nowadays. An old man in his seventies was washing his feet at the tap. He was extremely short and seemed to have asthma, as his breathing was uneven. I heard what sounded like air deflating from his back, and now and then he would spit up wads of phlegm the colour of egg yolks. Maybe he was hard of hearing, because he didn't seem to notice I was there and took his time washing his legs and feet, the sparse hair on them. I had the opportunity to kill this old man with a single thrust of my knife. But at that moment, I realized. My reflection was clearly visible in the ripples on the surface of the water in the basin. The old man knew I was there. He simply wasn't looking back.

'Did Woongman send you?'

He removed his feet from the basin and poured the rest of the water into the flowerbed before he put on his old, tattered slippers. I could see the bones of his spine through his yellowed T-shirt, and watching him from behind as he stooped over and walked, I couldn't help but notice his bony hips.

'I made some barley rice,' he said. 'At least have some before you get to your business.'

He opened the sliding door that led into what seemed to be the kitchen and took something out with all sorts of banging and commotion. I gripped the bag with the knife in my hand and waited to see what the old man would do next. A moment later, he was struggling to carry out a serving table with vegetables and soybean paste on it and set it down on the narrow wooden deck outside. He took a seat across from me.

'Mix it all together and have a spoonful of everything at once,' he said. 'I know why you're here, so don't worry. I won't run away.'

My face burned red from having been found out. The old man dumped the bowl of rice into an empty, bigger brass bowl. Atop the rice, which resembled a burial mound, he added the soybean paste and several of the vegetables, then mixed them and offered the bowl to me. It smelled of grass and something more pungent. I dug in.

'Since I'm an old man about to die, I hope you'll just hear me out.'

As I was shovelling the flavourless barley rice into my mouth, the old man began to tell a story as though he were talking to himself.

'Woongman's father was the biggest gangster within a twenty-five-kilometre radius. He was a playboy and a con man. Once women came of age around here, they would run off to Seoul and find work there to avoid the man, which about says it all. I met Woongman's mum when I was assigned to this neighbourhood as a police officer. She was young and awfully pretty. Even her family treated me like a son-in-law. Those were the days. That was around the time Woongman's father did something downright vile to a young girl around nine years of age, and I had no choice but to slap handcuffs on the bastard and take him in. But as soon as that jerk got out of prison, he kidnapped Woongman's mum and ran off with her. I quit my job and went off searching every corner of the country for him. After five years, by the time I managed to find Woongman's mum, his dad had become a junkie. I reported him. But within a month, maybe a little longer, the jerk was dead. I remember how pitch-black little Woongman's eyes were back then. I knew right away he was my son. But I never once revealed the truth to him. I hated the fact that I hadn't been able to keep my woman and my kid safe. Like a damned fool. As Woongman got older, he started going down the wrong path. The minute he had some whiskers on his chin, he left home. And I didn't dare leave my woman alone when she wasn't in her right mind to go off somewhere looking for my kid.'

He took out a cheap leaf tobacco cigarette and lit it. From the side, I could see the resemblance to Punch – the one who'd asked me to kill him.

'He told me you did terrible things to him,' I said. 'His word's the only word I trust.'

The old man poured more water from the kettle and handed me a cup.

'He'll resent me for the rest of his life. Because he sees me as the one who threw his real dad in prison. It was a huge mistake on my part to have kept the truth from him. I deserve to die. With his mum gone now, too, what do I even have to live for? Maybe if I hadn't showed up, Woongman would never have gone down that path. Last week, I sold off a bit of my farmland and a few rice paddies and put the money on top of my wardrobe. That's the price for my life. Don't bother Woongman about the fees and just take that. And I pulled up the mallow and lettuce I'd planted in the flowerbed this morning. You can bury me there. Don't tell Woongman anything. To live and die a fool – it's what I deserve.'

I couldn't kill the old man. I got an upset stomach from eating the barley rice in such a hurry. I belched, excused myself, and took the train back up to Seoul. The news of my failure had made it to the city before I did, and Punch had already destroyed the office by the time I got back. I searched all over until I found a small sewing kit. Taking out the thinnest needle I could find, I pricked the skin under my thumbnail, drawing blood to quell the indigestion. I let out another long, sorrowful belch like the cry of a wild beast.

Some days later, I heard a rumour that the job had been reassigned to Park Taesang. Park was the best knifeman around, a professional who wouldn't sit on his hands and let the mark go free like I had. I drove back down to the old man's house. I didn't want to allow something so depraved as a son killing his father, even by proxy. When I pulled up outside the house, as old as that old man, I ran to the yard, where Park was already tamping down the flowerbed soil.

'You made a mistake,' he said, his expression never changing like a plaster cast. 'You broke the one rule we vowed to keep.'

At the edge of the flowerbed, one of the old man's fingers sprung up out of the soil like a sprout. Park seemed to notice it only then and covered it with another mound of dirt.

'That old man is Punch's real father,' I said. And then I stood there and rambled for a while, like a kid from the countryside competing in the national speech contest. I was gasping for breath when I raised my head and looked at Park Taesang. He glared at me in sheer disbelief, his knife still gleaming with the old man's blood.

'Goodbye,' he said, looking drained as he left through the front gate. I didn't see him again for a long time after that. The son who had ordered his own father killed took the money his father had left behind and squandered it playing slot machines. Soon enough, he was penniless. Park Taesang returned several years later with the air of a real estate agency owner. And then he set up the Smile Detective Agency and became its CEO.

'Boss, I don't think it's just a rumour that Smile's got themselves a new knifeman.'

My hands went clammy. If there was a new killer who'd inherited Park's skills, they were sure to dominate the industry soon. There was no way we wouldn't lose clients to them.

'Have you figured out who it is?' I asked.

The employee hesitated. 'Well, we know one new person joined Smile last year. An ajumma called Shim Eunok. But it can't be her – right?'

Shim Eunok. My breath hitched at the sound of that name.

The Shim Eunok I knew would be fifty-one years old now. The woman whose teeth looked like perfect rows of corn kernels when she smiled. The one who'd ended up becoming my friend's wife. Shim Eunok. My first love.

I met Dalho when I first entered into the world of men. He was a handsome guy, with fair skin and exotic features. This was around the time we were both just starting out. Dalho's sturdy shoulders were nicely tanned from carrying crates of beer on his back.

'Only one side's tanned. When I drive, I have a habit of keeping my left arm out of the window,' he would say.

Around dawn when he finished his beer deliveries for the day, he would hand me a bottle of liquor he had hidden away, then flip a coin and make me call out heads or tails. If I guessed right, he'd give me a lift to work in his truck. Soon enough, I was hanging out with him at his rooftop apartment. That was where I first met Shim Eunok. She made Dalho, a guy who had nothing going for him besides his looks, shine like the happiest guy in the world. When I came over, she would make warm egg soup and parboiled squid for us, shyly keeping her head bowed and hiding her smile as she stayed by Dalho's side.

Eunok had dark hair that she wore in a bob. She was two years older than me. But she was so shy and had such a baby face, she could have been years younger. On weekends, I would pick up the two of them, and we'd go on drives out to Wolmido or along the Han River. When I bought fruits that were in season or other snacks and went by Dalho's, I would be disappointed if Eunok wasn't there. I really only went there to see her. One such day when she wasn't around, Dalho declared that he was going to marry Eunok.

'She says once she gets back the deposit on her apartment, she'll have enough for a small jeonse lease. Come on, man, congratulate me.'

I clasped Dalho's outstretched hand and forced a smile. Then I stayed up all night drinking, feeling miserable, and around daybreak, I went down to the textile factory where Eunok worked. She was walking quickly towards the bus stop, a scarf around her head. Using my drunkenness as a shield, I stepped out to block her path.

'Hancheol, is that you?'

'It is,' I said. 'It's me.'

She looked both happy and surprised to see me. 'What are you doing here?' she asked.

'Eunok. If you don't like gangsters, I'll stop being a gangster. If you don't like my name, I'll change that, too. What does Dalho have that I don't? I'll do anything, so I'm asking you to give me a chance.'

That day, Eunok didn't slap me across the face, but instead took me to a restaurant nearby and fed me some warm soup. She even carefully wiped the dirt off the back of my hands with a wet wipe.

'I've always thought I had terrible luck, but now I know that's not entirely true. Still, Dalho and I have already made a promise to each other. I hope you'll stay a good friend to us. One who'll come to our housewarming party, and our children's first birthdays. And we'll do the same for you.'

I snatched my hand back and bolted out of the restaurant, on to the streets where sleet was falling. Dalho sent me a wedding invite, but I didn't go. Not long after, he stopped delivering beer and vanished without a trace. When I thought about Dalho and Eunok living somewhere in Seoul, having children, buying a house, arguing, I felt jealousy shoot up inside me like a flame, but that was all. I was neither brave nor capable enough to track them down and try to win her over. I was still a novice. A rookie.

Once I hit my thirties, I got married. To the stylist at the only beauty salon in the area. She was twenty-two, with wild curls and a snaggletooth. She didn't resemble Shim Eunok in the slightest. If she hadn't become a stylist, she said she would have been a dancer, and the first time we met she danced the tango for me. I'd heard all sorts of rumours about her, but I took no notice of them. Aside from Eunok, women were all the same to me. Three months after the stylist and I met, we rented out a grilled pork belly restaurant and casually tied the knot. Neither of us had any guests, so we used the money we would have spent on a wedding on that simple get-together. As she smelled the meat cooking, my wife – Hong Misook – began to cry. Her mascara smeared and made her eyes look ringed like a panda's.

My wife said I should shut down the detective agency and help her gain footing with her beauty salon. She was tired of washing my bloodstained shirts and packing up and moving somewhere new every year. But I couldn't heed her request. This line of work was how I practised a sort of self-denial that started when I couldn't control the sorrow I had felt at losing Dalho and Eunok at the same time. It was an ill-advised form of self-punishment, like stubbornly sewing new buttons on to a shirt whose existing buttons were all out of alignment. But now I was scared. Scared that once this all was over, the shirt with tens of thousands of buttons would wrap itself around me and strangle me to death. It was too late now to do what my wife was suggesting.

I made my way over to the Smile Detective Agency. I was curious to see this Shim Eunok, but more than that, I wanted to know whether she was indeed the same Shim Eunok I once knew. I drove to the intersection with the ginkgo trees where I knew the Smile Detective Agency building was located. I parked across the street and rolled down my window. I spotted the security booth first. The old guard who had been nodding off inside suddenly raised his binoculars to his face and looked up and down the street. Then he picked up the phone and had a short conversation. A moment later, the lights on the third floor where the Smile offices were cut out. I doubted the guard reported exclusively to Smile, so he probably hadn't paged them about something so minor as an unfamiliar car parked across the street.

I looked at my wristwatch and saw that it was past five-thirty p.m. They were probably getting ready to head home for the day. I waited for half an hour, then an hour, yet no one came out of the building. Then Park Taesang's car came into view at the end of the intersection, where traffic was stopped at a red light. He must have gone out through the back door. And what about Shim Eunok? I was about to move my car across the street when the security guard stood up, causing me to hesitate. A woman in a miniskirt, her face caked in makeup, waved at the guard. She looked to be in her late thirties or early forties. She couldn't be the Shim Eunok I knew. A moment later, a short woman came out holding a shopping bag, and the guard again saluted her as she left. I got out of the car and crossed the street.

'Mrs Shim, you're not fleeing out the back door?'

Eunok looked taken aback by the question and glared at the security guard.

'And why do you leave through the back door when the front door works perfectly fine? Seriously.'

He'd called this woman Mrs Shim – this must be Shim Eunok. But she seemed far different from the Shim Eunok I'd been searching for. From the glasses perched on her nose and the way she was squinting, it seemed she was already far-sighted, and her thick neck, freckled face, and hard expression didn't resemble my Eunok's at all. What was more, the plum dress draped over her like a curtain was something the Eunok I knew would never have chosen to wear. But even if she wasn't the woman I knew, there was a chance she could be the agency's new killer, in which case I needed to follow her.

Mrs Shim caught the bus. I carefully tailed it all the way to the apartment complex where she got off. She stopped at a street cart for a summer squash, some enoki mushrooms, and peas as I secretly watched. When she entered the apartment building, she caught the elevator. I looked up and checked which apartments had their lights on. It was rare for a person to live alone at that age, so her kids or her husband may have already been home. But it was always good to leave room for the possibilities. In the third room on the sixth floor the lights flicked on and off several times. Watching her faint shadow folding clothes, then opening the door to the balcony and stepping out to hang the laundry to dry, I could now be certain that this was Shim Eunok's apartment.

'Mum, should I buy some milk?'

From somewhere beside me, a young man as skinny as a cottonwood tree cupped his hands around his mouth and shouted up at the apartment.

Mrs Shim shouted back, 'We have milk. Just come on up, son.'

So this was Mrs Shim's son. She shut the balcony door, and the young man went inside the building. I rushed to follow him.

'Excuse me, but how old are you?' I asked.

He eyed me suspiciously. 'Why are you asking me that?'

I had to find an excuse. I'd been so quick to blurt out the question but hadn't thought at all about how the conversation would go after.

'I'm looking for someone to work part-time, and I was wondering if you were in university,' I said.

He immediately perked up. His hair was cropped short as though he'd just finished his military service. He looked gentle, with an intelligent glint in his eyes. I may have just been talking out of my ass, but I could see now that the kid might actually end up being useful.

'I'm twenty-one,' he said. 'I work part-time at a convenience store, but if the offer's good, I'd consider making the switch. What sort of work would I be doing?'

What an innocent guy. He should have been on alert, being offered a job by a stranger. Traps could be set for anyone, not only women or kids. I found myself worrying for him.

'There's some office work, and occasionally times where you'll need to work away from the office,' I said. 'If you give me your contact information, I'll give you a call.'

He pulled out a memo pad and a pen from his bag and wrote down his number. Then he bowed goodbye, and I got back in my car. If I could just get my hands on this guy, I would easily be able to dig up more dirt on his mother, this Mrs Shim woman.

Instead of going straight home, I stopped by the PC cafe. I made sure to pick one in a neighbourhood outside of the one where I did business. I rolled down my sleeves and buttoned my shirt. There was a hideous red scar on my forearm where the tattoo I'd gotten at twenty used to be. I'd had it lasered off at forty, and now I was nearly fifty with what looked like an awful burn.

In the PC cafe, I found the seat farthest from the others, put on the headset, and booted up the computer. Then I closed my eyes and willed myself to sleep. I listened to the computer's strange noises, like the whistle of a train in the distance. The other people there were busy looking at their own screens, tapping away at their keyboards, not one of them looking at me. Such were the moments when I felt the most at ease. In this space and time in which no one was paying me any attention. People only ever looked at me one of two ways – with a blend of reverence and contempt, or else with eyes that pleaded for mercy, just this once. I hated both. I longed for more moments like this one, where no one was looking at me. Where no one wanted anything from me at all.

I couldn't afford to waste any time, so I called the young man a few days later. Within two hours, he was at the Happy Detective Agency office. His expression was dark, clouded over with fear.

'Just because we're a detective agency doesn't mean we only sniff out people's dirty secrets and snap photos,' I explained.

The guy looked around the office and took a sip of coffee.

'We can give you the full tour if you want, but in short, we need someone to answer the phone, keep the office clean, and handle scheduling. We can pay twice what you're making now.'

The guy's name was Kim Jinseob. I guessed that it hadn't been much more than two months or so since he'd gotten back from the military, and that he was working part-time as he prepared to re-enrol in university. He chewed on his lip for a while before finally accepting the offer.

'I'd like to keep this a secret from my family,' he said.

I nodded.

The next day, Kim Jinseob was registered with the company and started clocking in for work. On his registration papers, I noticed only three names listed for his household – Shim Eunok, Kim Jinseob, and Kim Jina.

'Is your father deceased?' I asked.

His face darkened. It must not have been from something simple like an illness.

'Yes,' said Jinseob. 'I'm essentially the head of the household, though my mum is still alive and takes care of our living expenses.'

If I assumed that Mrs Shim was a killer, perhaps I could also assume that her husband's death had been her doing. That after she'd slain him in a fit of anger, she had joined the big, flashy world of a killer.

'I hope you don't mind my asking, but how did he die?'

Jinseob let out an empty, startled laugh and started picking at the hangnail on his thumb.

'Well, he had diabetes for a long time. I heard he used to deliver cases of alcohol when he was younger, so he was in good shape before. But then, in his thirties, he was diagnosed with a chronic illness. And soon enough my mum was running the family's butcher shop on her own and raising me and my sister.'

So Mrs Shim's husband used to do alcohol deliveries. Suddenly Jinseob's face seemed familiar.

'What was your father's name?'

My arms and legs ached as I asked him, as though blood were pooling all over again in all the countless wounds that knives had ever made on my body.

'Kim Dalho,' he said.

My friend. My friend Kim Dalho was dead. Pretty Shim Eunok with her short hair was a killer. And their son Kim Jinseob was now my employee. What to do? I wondered. Should I send Jinseob packing right then and there?

Suddenly I could picture the day me, Dalho, and Eunok had gone to the Yeouido Cherry Blossom Festival as if it were a movie. We walked around with fried snacks wearing paper hats and tried not to let go of each other as we made our way through the crowd. Dalho walked ahead, trying to get a better look at the music programme being broadcast live by the riverside, and

I followed. Eunok was too slow, though, and soon disappeared in the crowd.

I searched for her, pushing against the current, my clothes and hair getting dishevelled. Right then a popular singer took the stage for the music programme. Cheers erupted from the crowd as all the festival-goers who had been preoccupied with the flowers suddenly surged towards the stage like a wave. Only then did I spot Eunok. She was standing beneath a cherry tree that had been handled by so many people, not one of its leaves or blossoms remained. When she saw me, she ran over and took my hands in hers. Her teary eyes brightened. I shouldn't have let go of her hands then. I shouldn't have let go out of embarrassment and run off into the crowd. It was a clear error in judgement, a mistake. And now I was paying the price for it.

My resentment towards Park Taesang, who had Eunok bound to him, burned hot like a spark and drove itself into my chest. I gave Jinseob the desk near the window. He was good with his hands. Not just fast, but neat and precise as he organized his space.

'Do you resent your father,' I asked him, 'for passing away so early?'

'Well, it's not like I'm advocating for suicide,' Jinseob said. 'But everyone has the right to do what they want with their own bodies.'

'Oh, sorry. I didn't realize – I'm sorry to have brought it up.'

So Kim Dalho had died by suicide.

'It's fine. I like talking about my dad. Sometimes my mum will tell me stories from a long time ago. She said one of my dad's friends from before they got married had a crush on her. He tried not to make it obvious, but apparently, my mum and dad both knew. One day, my dad said to her, "If you like him, go and be with him." Mum gave him a good smack for that. Asked him if he couldn't tell the difference between love and sympathy. Even after they were married, they were never all that affectionate, but my mum didn't once regret choosing my dad. After he died, she told me that he pretended to be cold and standoffish, but that he'd lived his whole life worried Mum would leave him, and only once they were older and there was no one around to steal her away did he ease up and leave her himself. She said she'd done well in choosing him. Compared to growing old taking care of a gangster's son, a prisoner, she thought wielding knives in a butcher shop was better.'

Love and sympathy. Had Eunok and Dalho loved me? Or had they felt sorry for me? It had probably been that I'd wanted their love but had gotten their sympathy instead. And maybe the reason I didn't have any kids was because I was a gangster. I thought my heart had cooled down, but the fire in my chest surged up again. It wasn't like I'd believed Eunok shared my feelings, but I was disappointed to know that she'd introduced me to her son as some dirty gangster with a crush.

Neither Dalho nor Eunok had forgotten about me in all that time. Instead, they'd probably had a good laugh at my expense every time they watched a mob movie or drama. They might have just been waiting to see the life of lowdown rascal Na Hancheol shrivel up like dog leather. I didn't know whether she had killed Dalho, or whether he had indeed killed himself, but what I did know was that Eunok had planted herself in an even filthier cesspool than I ever had. She must have known that I was Happy's CEO. And that meant she wasn't the Shim Eunok I had once known.

I could hear my own teeth grinding, loud and clear.

On his first payday, I made Jinseob another proposal.

'With a little effort, you could make a lot of money. You could let your mum retire, move into a new house, and live out the rest of your days in luxury. You have to choose between a life of poverty and ordinariness, and a life of high intensity and colour. Make the choice you won't regret in twenty years.'

The confused look on his face made his resemblance to both Dalho and Eunok blatantly clear. His lips moved, but I didn't catch what he said. I told him to speak up. He flushed and repeated what he'd said. I had hoped he would choose the former option, but he had gone with the latter. Everyone had the right to do what they wanted with their own body. What he'd said had turned out to be true.

PART TWO

PART TWO

10

The Matchmaker

The Kim Sangho Marriage Research Institute was founded in 1988, the year of the Seoul Olympics, near Dapsimni Intersection by me, then thirty-eight-year-old bachelor Kim Sangho, and Han Byungpal, my friend of the same age who shamelessly loved to meddle in other people's business. I started researching marriage in the early winter one year soon after I turned thirty. At the time, I was getting a thousand won allowance each day from my mum who ran a boarding house near the university area to carry out the highly important task of changing out the charcoal briquettes in the boarders' rooms. Some would say, Is changing out the briquettes so hard that you have to take money from your own flesh and blood to do it? But those people have clearly never experienced the fierce world of changing out charcoal briquettes. Once a briquette goes out, you need another kind of briquette called a fire starter to save it. I had to change out the briquettes five times a day, meaning I had to get up at dawn to the sound of my mum's yelling and keep making trips to the shed where we kept them. If I overslept by even half an hour, all twelve rooms in the boarding house would turn to ice rinks. So I needed a total of twelve fire starters, but before I could get all of them ready, the boarders who had fallen sound asleep after staying up most of the night reading manga and porn magazines would start shuffling out of their rooms one at a time, unable to bear the cold.

'Hey, is the fire out again? This happens every couple of days. You get more heat using the fire starters than the plain charcoal briquettes.'

These sorts of admonishments were on the gentler side, as opposed to the complaints that went more like:

'Damn it, now I see why this place was twenty thousand won cheaper than the others. It's because you've got the air conditioning running year-round here. You have no sense of professionalism. No sense of professionalism at all.'

Actually, if they looked closely, they would find that one or two rooms usually had briquettes that were still burning, so if it came down to it, they could take a lit one from a neighbouring room, but that would leave the room freezing for a couple of hours. In the end, you realize that instead of replacing one briquette with another, it would have been better to just use the fire starter first thing in the morning to begin with.

The boarders, who hadn't been able to get much sleep because of the cold and the sunlight streaming in through the windows, started coming out on to the deck, scratching their bellies under their running shirts or else kneading their groins. Shameless as I was, I acted indifferent to their resentful glares. I could feel twelve pairs of eyes watching my every move, but I was after all the great traitor who had let the fires in their rooms go out. There was nothing I could say to that. I picked up a fire starter with the tongs, lit it, and stood there waving it underneath the eaves until my nose started tingling. I couldn't tell whether it was because of the acrid smoke from the fire starter or from the cigarettes every boarder had already been smoking when they gave me that morning's wake-up call.

My mum, who had to make fourteen servings of rice and soup, always came to the kitchen in her pyjamas with her hair tied up in a white cotton cloth. She could be as ferocious as an Inwangsan tiger, and when she was angry, her small eyes would turn triangular, and she would grind her molars. Even the boarders who loved to complain would notice Mum's eyes changing and duck into their rooms, lie down on the lukewarm floor, and cover themselves with a blanket, praying for my safe return. Mum would watch me tear up as I lit the fires from room to room, then dump the cloudy water left over from making rice on me and shout, 'Damn it, you little punk, you're going to die with your nose in a pile of shit.' I could handle being doused in the cold rice water, but when the last fire starter's flame snuffed itself out, that was when I lost it. That was the last fire starter I had. I'd have to wait two hours for the stores to open to buy more, and unlike the other rooms whose fire starters would be beginning to heat up the charcoal briquettes soon, the last room had two or three hours to go before it warmed up.

I wiped off the rice water with a hand towel and knocked on the door of the twelfth room. It belonged to a taciturn guy in the reserve forces who had moved into the boarding house the month before. He'd never said he was in the reserve forces, but considering his short-cropped hair and the fact that he still hadn't gone back to uni and just stayed holed up inside, it seemed like a reasonable guess.

'May I come in for a moment?' I asked when the guy opened the door. We had a rule that forbade smoking in the rooms, but he was sucking on the filter of a cigarette as though he'd just lit it and had to snuff it out.

'Come on in. The room's cold, though,' he said.

I hesitated before carefully stepping foot inside. When he'd moved in, he and another young guy who must have been his brother had hauled in several cardboard boxes. It seemed those boxes had been full of books. There was no bookcase in the room, but there were books stacked from the floor to the ceiling. Aside from the spot where he slept, his small dining table, and a space no bigger than his hand where he kept his ashtray, every available inch of his room was crammed with books. The titles were all written in Chinese characters, so I couldn't understand most of them.

'I'm really sorry, sir. I was lighting the charcoal for the rooms in order, but I'm down one fire starter. I really hope you can understand.'

Looking at his face, the guy seemed five or six years younger than me, but I knew I should speak to him politely nonetheless, as I was the boarding house owner's son. My mother's dignity and my position as someone preparing to take the state exam also demanded it. The guy looked up, blowing a doughnut-shaped ring of smoke at me.

'For the right price, I could forgive anything,' he said.

He wrapped himself in his blanket and farted.

'What would the right price be?' I asked.

He crushed the butt of his cigarette in his full ashtray and grinned.

'In just an hour or two, everyone else's rooms will be boiling, while I'll be here in this cold. I'm telling you not to let me be cold.'

'If you want, you can use my room.'

He yanked a dangling piece of thread from the blanket and ran it between his teeth like floss, scraping out some gunk.

'I don't want to,' he said. 'I like this room here. What I want is some body heat. A warm body to get inside this blanket and heat me up to 36.5 degrees Celsius.'

Thinking he was kidding, I burst out laughing. I laughed for a while before I looked him in the eyes again and saw them gleaming like the morning star.

That dawn, until Mum called us down with a roar of 'Come and eat, you rascals!', the reserve forces guy held me in his arms as we traded body heat. Now, don't get any weird ideas. We didn't fondle each other or get into any odd conversations. We ruminated deeply on women as he stared at the back of my head and I stared at his ashtray.

'Hey. What is a woman to you?'

His warm breath on my hair tickled.

'An animal that becomes a philosopher for three to seven days every month,' I answered. Those were my honest thoughts. Back in uni, whenever a woman suddenly fell into hysterics, all the guys in her year would whisper to each other behind her back, 'Is it her time of the month or what?' The women would commemorate *that day* themselves, circling it in red in their diaries, then disappear somewhere with a tiny pouch like they had a secret rendezvous only to return looking grouchy. If you asked them, 'Want to go bowling?' our female colleagues would reply with nothing but a vague question like, 'What's the point of anything?' before storming off with the other girls.

Men didn't ponder the point of life for any one of the 365 days of the year. And we didn't have handbags or pouches with little diaries in them where we could circle the date with a red pen. Who should we play pool with today? Should we go out to Myeongdong tomorrow and try picking up girls? Should we just knock back some drinks? This was the extent of our worries as men. Or at least that was the case in my uni days.

'For me, I think women are animals you can't trust,' said the guy. 'Socrates once said, "Trust not a woman when she weeps, for it is her nature to weep when she wants her will." Do you trust a woman when she weeps?'

Had I ever seen a woman weep? I thought for a moment but couldn't remember a single time I had. I'd only ever dated one girl, another student in our department a year older than me, and that had only lasted two months, but I remembered her as a heavy drinker and an oddball who would pass out from laughing non-stop when she was drunk. Once after she blacked out, I took her to an inn to recover, but when she came to a little while later, she made me do military drills that left my knees shredded as punishment before kicking me out to the streets wearing nothing but my underwear. The rumours made their rounds at uni, and I was effectively disqualified from ever seriously pursuing any other girls again.

'Have you ever been dumped by a girl?' the guy asked.

Every question he posed had to do with women's fake tears and their never-ending coyness, and research findings that claimed a woman's affection for a man was commensurate with the man's financial power. Considering all this, I thought without a doubt he'd recently had his heart broken. So maybe he longed for the soft touch of a woman and had dragged me, a guy so pale I looked like I had never seen the sun, in as a substitute.

'Love is the one emotion that humans should rid ourselves of. Even now, aren't there murders and fights between friends and siblings because of love? We can reproduce without love, so why waste our time on such an unnecessary emotion?'

I didn't think he was completely wrong. In fact, if love were to disappear, it seemed like genuine world peace would be possible. Without love, marriage would also die out, and without marriage, I would no longer have to hear my mum lashing out at me, saying, 'What girl with birds for brains would want a stupid punk like you? Goddamn blockhead. You'd burn your balls off in a bonfire.'

'It sounds like you're saying that without things like love or marriage, we might all be better off.'

'I said love is an unnecessary emotion, sure, but I never invalidated marriage. We have to get rid of the stereotype that marriages must happen between people who love each other. Marriage is a system by which incomplete people are made complete. They earn together and accomplish shared goals, they have children and allow the world to continue on, but falling in love is the one thing they shouldn't do. A marriage without love is the most genuinely beautiful union there is.'

His voice resonated throughout the room like he was a professional public speaker. As his leg hairs and the sleeves of his shirt brushed against my lower back, I felt as though our whole conversation had been a dream.

'Come and eat!'

We awkwardly untangled ourselves from the blanket wrapped around us like a cocoon and made our way to the dining room.

I didn't smoke, but I had the feeling I also reeked of sour, musty cigarettes. I kept thinking about what the reserves guy had said. His words were like tender wild rose shoots – the more I chewed on them, the sweeter their taste and fragrance grew. I decided then that I was going to research women, love, and marriage. I felt myself going mad with excitement, like an astronomer who had discovered a new planet in the vast cosmos. Now I had a purpose greater than changing out the briquettes. Maybe I would finally have the courage to stand up to my mother, who used to hit me on the back multiple times a day for the crime of growing old while doing nothing. But then – nothing happened. I still changed out the briquettes five times a day, started the fires anew once every other day, and whenever I had some spare time, I would stop by the reserves guy's room and have long, drawn-out philosophy sessions or debates that were like word association games.

One day, we got into a heated discussion about the correlation between the size of a woman's breasts and her maternal instincts. I argued that the bigger the breasts, the deeper the affection, while he insisted that if you looked at it that way, wouldn't Western women have superior maternal instincts?

Then someone started shouting from the yard.

'Han Byungpal! I know you're in there, you piece of shit! Are you really not going to come out?'

I opened the door and went to see who it was. There was a guy about my age kicking around the flowerpots that held desiccated plants outside. He looked irritated and like he'd been day drinking.

'Tell him you don't know anyone named Han Byungpal,'

the reserves guy whispered, begging. 'Or tell him . . . I moved. Yeah, tell him I moved out.'

So his name was Han Byungpal. I couldn't reject such a heartfelt plea. I smoothed out my clothes, put on my slippers, and went out to talk directly to the guy who was still shouting, 'Han Byungpal, come outside!'

'Looks like you overdid it on the drinking,' I said. 'Han Byungpal moved out more than two weeks ago. So quit making all this fuss and leave.'

The man looked me up and down with slightly unfocused eyes and reached out with his giant hands to grab me by the collar of my tracksuit. Having a man a head taller than me suddenly lunge at me like that, I had no idea what to do. He tossed me around like a sack of straw, and I fell backwards, right into a basin near the tap in the middle of the yard.

'Oh ho, so you're Han Byungpal, are you? The fake uni student who got tangled up with my innocent little sister. I found you. You're screwed, asshole.'

The sour stench of makgeolli wafted from his mouth as he shouted. *Huh.* The reserves guy *wasn't* actually a student at uni? So a guy who wasn't even in school had rented a room in a boarding house near campus to chat up bumbling girls and score with them.

'Sir, I'm just the son of this boarding house's owner,' I said. 'I barely know this Han Byungpal guy.'

It was a flimsy excuse, but what else could I do? If I lay there and did nothing, I'd end up taking all the blows meant for Byungpal, who'd sweet-talked this guy's sister and run off. For our quiet boarding house, where most of the boarders were in classes, this man's shouting was no different from throwing stones.

'My little sister Okja shaved her head and locked herself up in her room. All day, she lies there, wailing, "Han Byungpal, Han Byungpal." If you mess with a woman like that, shouldn't you take responsibility?'

I was sitting with my ass in a steel basin, covering my face with both hands, as this guy made to kick me. Right when I looked up, I saw my mum returning home, watching the scene from the front gate. It was the first time in my life my mum looked so happy to see me. Not even noticing how drenched I was, I shot up and ran to her. She was staring at the guy, and I could see her eyes taking on that triangular shape.

'Well, what do we have here? If you were in *The Tale of Chunhyang*, I bet you'd brush your teeth with Governor Byun's sperm. Do you know where you are and that you look like you're about to burst a blood vessel? Open your eyes and take a good look at this kid here. Does he look like some muscleman who could knock around a woman? When that day comes, I'll embroider this useless punk's name on a towel and throw a feast for the neighbourhood. Forget the governor's sperm, asshole – a jerk like you would wash your face with Chunhyang's discharge!'

Mum tossed aside the onions, bean sprouts, and other vegetables whose names I didn't know and grabbed the guy by the belt, giving him a good shake. His mind must have gone blank because he went limp in her clutches and ended up falling into the steel basin like I had.

'Han Byungpal, you dog, get out here!'

My mum started calling for Byungpal to come down. The door slid open very slightly, and in the crack, Byungpal's dark eyes appeared, blinking fast. The drunk guy, seeming to be feeling all that alcohol coming back up, was retching as he observed the situation. In the end, Byungpal's door swung open all the way. He slicked down his hair, dishevelled as a magpie's nest, with spit and hesitantly walked out.

'Ma'am, you're back,' he said to my mum, getting down on his knees to bow.

My mum flung a head of winter cabbage at him.

'I heard you were out here screwing around. You'd better fess up before I hack you into pieces.'

The boarders began to open their doors and come out on to the deck to watch the exciting events unfold.

'We dated briefly and then broke up,' Byungpal said. 'As you know, I'm in no position to be married, and I let her go and told her to find a better guy. You know what they say, don't you? About breaking up with someone *because* you love them? That's what I did.'

The drunk guy whose ass was now drenched suddenly shot up and rushed towards Byungpal.

'What? You said you were in medical school? I found out that not only did you fail the college entrance exam the dreaded three times, you decided that wasn't enough and went on to fail it two more times for good measure. Looks like your parents got fed up with your shit and forced you to go into the military, but what was it you said to my sister? That you were studying to be a public health doctor?'

Come to think of it, I had never heard Byungpal mention his age. In fact, I hadn't known his name until today, and we'd always simply addressed one another with a 'hey'. It turned out he was the same age as me. And on top of that, I'd incorrectly guessed he was majoring in philosophy because he kept name-dropping philosophers, but that had turned out to be wrong, too. That day, Byungpal let the drunk guy into his room and put him to bed. The drunk guy, who woke up only after dusk, soothed his stomach with the bean sprout hangover soup my mum had made, beat Byungpal up, and left.

Byungpal ended up marrying Lee Okja, a girl who looked like she had never missed a meal in her life. Being the lowlife scum that he was, he'd packed his bags and fled from the boarding house near the national university to our boarding house in the dead of night when he found out that Lee Okja was pregnant. And now he'd successfully found himself in the sort of loveless marriage he'd believed in. But our original research goal of getting married without being in love for the sake of world peace fizzled out into nothing. And it was all because of another woman named Park Sohwa.

There were no women at our boarding house. Most students aiming for the university famous for its engineering department were men, and the female nursing students preferred living in the dorms or at an all-girls boarding house rather than a boarding house swarming with shady guys. But when Byungpal left, Sohwa showed up looking to move into his old room.

'The room is very small. Plus, there's dust raining from the ceiling and an awful draught in here. It's absurd to charge eighty thousand won for a room like this. I'll pay seventy thousand.'

My mum, who almost never had a room open in the middle of the semester and who was shocked to see a female student at the boarding house for the first time, absentmindedly accepted her offer. Of course, the other boarders couldn't know she was getting a lower price. I stayed close to Sohwa, rushing over to carry in her bags and wiping down the floor of her room. I still remember how my mum had watched me, quietly clicking her tongue and turning away.

'I'll take care of the clothes,' Sohwa said. 'You can put these textbooks over there.'

The textbooks she pulled out of her bag were mostly related to the fashion industry, with titles like *Studies on Costume Culture* and *Defining Fashion*. It was my first time meeting a fashion design major.

'Look, if you're not going to help me, could you get out?'

I put the textbooks back in her bag and hurried out of the room. There was a power in her voice that made it so I couldn't refuse her.

Deep in the night, Byungpal knocked on my door. He'd moved into a rooftop apartment about a ten-minute walk away, and during the day he would sit out on the boarding house deck, drinking coffee and eating fruit prepared by Okja, just like he had when he was a boarder.

'There's no need to knock,' I said. 'Come on in.'

We had gotten to the point where we called each other by name and spoke informally. I didn't know what he was doing to make his living, but around that time of year he always came by with two bottles of beer and some fish jerky. After cracking his tooth trying to open the bottle cap with his mouth, he'd tied a bottle opener with a black rubber band around the leg of my desk. Drinking beer every day, it got tiring to keep going to the kitchen to get a new cup, so I kept the old cup and put a tissue over it after we were done drinking for the night. Now, Byungpal blew the tissue off my cup and poured me some beer.

'I told you,' he said. 'Marriage shouldn't be between two

people who love each other. That right there is the seed of unhappiness. You've been studying for months and you still don't know that? Look at me. I get to be such a free spirit now because I married a woman I don't love.'

His words still hadn't lost their persuasiveness, but how was love something I could control? As I drank my beer and tore off pieces of my jerky to eat, I thought of Sohwa's face, beautiful and elegant in a plain sort of way.

'Looks like you've lost your mind all because a woman came to stay here. It's just because you were starved for so long. The world is vast and full of women. I'm telling you, don't go falling in love with them, and just enjoy them with no strings attached.'

'I'm not a snob like you. I'm a romantic. I'm going to ask her out sincerely.'

Byungpal didn't respond, simply downed the rest of his beer in one go and went home. I pushed the empty beer bottles on the desk aside and sat up straight. I decided to write out all the feelings burning inside me as a letter to give to her. I was terrible at writing letters and always had been, and I kept writing about half of it before crumpling it up and tossing it away, only to start again. More so than the content, the issue was my awful handwriting. First, I started writing out how I felt, plain and simple, with no flowery language. Like I was writing in my diary, I praised her outfits, her hairstyle, the distinct fragrance she emanated despite using the same soap as everyone else. I struggled like that for a few days until I had a rough but sincere letter completed. Then I picked it up and brought it to the room of the boarder who had been with us the longest – a bespectacled literature major.

'What brings you here?' he asked.

I held out the money I had made from changing out the charcoal briquettes twice that day and said, 'I need a favour. I heard you have really good handwriting.'

The glasses-wearing guy counted the money I had handed him and, seeing no other choice, accepted my offer. Two hours later, he handed me a copy of my letter that was so neatly written, any woman was sure to fall for the sender at a glance. Now all I needed was the chance and the courage to give it to her. But I couldn't just go straight to her room, and her class schedule varied all the time, so I couldn't just pace outside the gate waiting for her to come back. Several days went by, and that letter was still clasped in my hands.

'A guy who gets excited by love gets ruined by love.'

Byungpal seemed to be losing his spark slowly but surely after having gotten married. What did those words have to do with this situation? Someone who had never been excited by love could be ruined by it – where in the world would someone have heard such an awful thing? Still, Byungpal gave me an excellent idea. While Sohwa was in class, I would stick the letter between the gap in the door, and when she came back that evening, I would ask her out on a date.

I left the letter wedged in the crack of her door and ran off to the laundromat right after. I planned on borrowing a nice suit instead of my usual tracksuit that I wore every day like a uniform. At the laundromat, there were several nice-looking suits that the owners hadn't yet come by to pick up. I paid a small rental fee to borrow one, which the owner loaned me with a pleased but sly look. The suit was a little too big on me, but it was a stylish Buckingham with silver stripes on black. In order to make sure our first date went well, as soon as I got home I called up my old classmates who were rumoured to be playboys. They told me everything I needed to know, like how there was a superstition that two people who went for a stroll along the stone wall trail at Deoksugung were bound to break up, and about the Western-style restaurant famous for its delicious donkatsu, cafes with a nice atmosphere that also sold beer and cocktails, and a taxi company that didn't charge a call fee for trips that came out to more than three thousand won on the meter. After I had gathered this intel, I eagerly waited for Sohwa to come back.

Dinner was served at seven p.m. in our boarding house, and boarders who didn't get home within the hour weren't served. That day, Sohwa still wasn't home after eight p.m. I stood in front of the mirror in my suit, reciting the famous slogan 'The answer is Buckingham' over and over.

She came staggering in after ten that night. She looked nowhere near as put-together as she normally did, and she was laughing heartily as she tottered to her room. I hid behind a wooden pillar and watched to see if she'd find my letter. When she flung open the door, the letter fell to the floor. She picked it up with her pale, beautiful hand. Then she looked around before disappearing into her room. It was already late, but thinking the date could be postponed, I went back to my room, too. Han Byungpal was there waiting for me.

'An ill-fated match is still a fated match,' he said, giggling as he offered me a seat where he'd been drinking a beer on his own.

'Socrates is rolling in his grave.'

I took off the suit and put it on a hanger. Byungpal kept

chuckling, saying nonsense like, 'I date, therefore I'm scammed' and 'Love is the father of misfortune'.

'Sohwa just picked up my letter and went into her room,' I said, pouring some tepid beer into a cup and downing it. I had been waiting for her all day on an empty stomach, so even that one drink made my head start to spin.

'So tonight, the choice between fortune and misfortune will be made. I'm wishing misfortune on you, my friend.'

I heard someone walking around on the deck. I opened my door, hoping that it might be Sohwa, but it was Glasses Guy. Sometimes, when he felt so compelled, he would step out on to the deck and, in a truly pretentious fashion, recite the poems of Byron or Yates.

'"But once I dared to lift my eyes— / To lift my eyes to thee; / And since that day, beneath the skies, / No other sight they see."'

His sonorous voice broke through the stillness of the night. I wanted to run out there and clamp a hand over his mouth, wondering why on earth he would stand outside of Sohwa's room, reciting a poem that would make even a man melt.

'"Can I cease to love thee? No! / Zoë mou, sas agapo!"'

Once his poetry recital was over, Glasses Guy shut his eyes tight and took a deep breath, as though still reeling emotionally. I wasn't the only one watching him. Sohwa, my beautiful muse, was also looking out at him. She opened her door and stepped outside, stopping in front of him. He slowly opened his eyes and met hers.

'This letter,' said Sohwa. 'You wrote it, didn't you? I've seen your handwriting before. You're the one who wrote the "Complaints to the Boarders" bulletin in the dining room.'

The letter clearly had Glasses Guy's penmanship all over it. But the earnest feelings expressed therein – those had all come from me, Kim Sangho. I decided to put my trust in Glasses Guy. In my heart, I was shouting for him to tell her, 'This letter is actually from Kim Sangho, the boarding house owner's son. He asked me to write it out as a favour.' Quick, I thought. Tell her!

'So you found out,' he said. 'I'm a little embarrassed.'

He reached out and put his hand on her shoulder. At that moment, Byungpal's hand came to rest on my shoulder, too.

'Love is bitter,' he said, 'as is its fruit.'

That night, I beat up Byungpal, stopping just short of killing him, and then let him beat me up just short of killing me. Early in the morning, as I was going to the laundromat with a black eye, I happened to see Sohwa opening her door and Glasses Guy slinking out. I rushed over and stepped in front of him.

'You despicable little shit.'

He looked startled and lost his balance, falling on his ass on the deck.

'Let's – let's talk this out with our words, yeah?' he said.

I hawked a lug of spit right on his glasses and left him there, walking away without thinking about where I was going. Suddenly it started to rain, and the suit I was carrying became stained with muddy water. The laundromat owner charged me an additional two thousand won cleaning fee.

'You used to spout all that bull about how you were going to do research, so why are you out here nowadays running around in thunderstorms like a dog? Are you dating someone?' my mum asked, not knowing her son had quietly had his heart broken.

When Sohwa and Glasses Guy officially became a couple,

I had no choice but to leave the boarding house. The two of them kept spoon feeding each other the side dishes at meals and going in and coming out of each other's rooms in the middle of the night.

In the meantime, Byungpal's wife gave birth to a boy. The reason he could afford to continue idling his life away was because his wife came from money. Her older brother, who had come by and raised such a fuss in the yard that time, took pity on his poor sister who had gotten involved with the wrong man and gave her money for her living expenses and rice and meat he'd bought for them each month. Byungpal had become a father, yet he still hadn't gotten himself together and would roam the streets with me to kill time. He couldn't even remember his own son's name and would teasingly call the baby Han No-Name.

Around the time the baby began to take his first steps, Byungpal's wife moved back in with her family. She even took the security deposit on the rooftop apartment, leaving Byungpal to pack his things into a single bundle and move back into the boarding house. By then, my wounds were slowly starting to heal. With Byungpal back, we decided in earnest to pursue genuine marriage research that would save humanity.

'Sangho, I need you to go to the post office and send a telegram,' I heard my mum say outside my room door. Strangely, not a single swear word had been tossed in. Her request sounded urgent, so I knew it must be serious and got up right away.

'Where to and what should it say?' I asked.

She handed me a paper that looked like it had been torn out of a phone book. The address was in Haenam, South Jeolla Province, and the recipient was named Park Cheolgon.

'Sohwa passed away,' my mum said. 'Last night at dinner, she was complaining of a stomach ache, and on her way home from classes, her appendix burst. Her boyfriend took her to the hospital, and they said it was peritonitis and moved her to the university hospital for surgery. But before she could even be seen, she was dead. Sad, isn't it?'

The old wound I had believed to be healed and sealed over burst open again like her appendix, filling me with pain. The funeral was held at the university hospital near our boarding house. Sohwa's father was a fisherman. He hadn't introduced himself as such, but his deeply tanned skin and gnarled hands told us everything, and even the tears streaming down his face smelled of the sea.

After the funeral, Glasses Guy suddenly came up to me at the crematorium.

'Hyung,' he said. 'I'm in trouble.'

'As hard as it is now, things will get better in time,' I said, keeping my consolations as short as possible.

'It's not that,' he said. 'Sohwa's dad wants to have a ghost wedding, and I can't just turn him down. What do I do?'

With tears and snot running down his face, he was really asking me for advice. In that moment, I finally knew the path I had to take. Living people could marry without love to promote the development of humankind, and then after they died, they could find their true match and spend their afterlives together in harmony.

'Are you going to do it?' I asked Glasses Guy.

'No! How can I marry a ghost? When I'm alive and perfectly well, at that? Just thinking about it is terrible.'

I could understand his point. But if Glasses Guy were to

die, that would be an entirely different story. Two dead people would make for a fair and harmonious union.

A month later, when Glasses Guy was heading back to his hometown to share the good news that he'd landed a job, he threw himself off the train. Of course, he'd needed my and Byungpal's active support for the sake of his harmonious marriage. We told him we wanted to see the Seomjin River, so we'd accompany him, and he seemed happy to have us along for the ride. On the train, Byungpal offered Glasses Guy a cigarette and invited him into the connecting car to smoke. Back then, passengers could open the windows and even the doors on the train themselves. Anyway, Glasses Guy's body split into thousands of pieces. Some people dressed in white came out to collect bits of his flesh with tweezers and put them in plastic

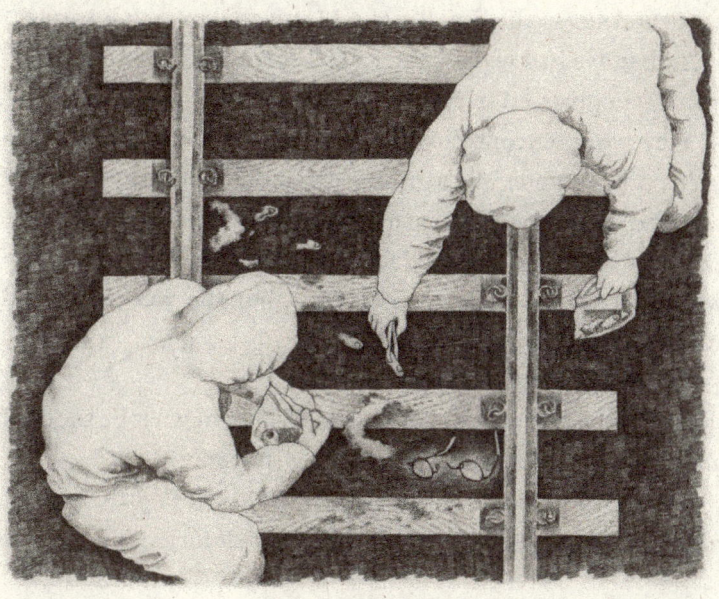

bags, handing the largest chunk they could recover to his parents and asking, 'Is this your son's armpit?' Before the year was over, Glasses Guy and Sohwa were able to make their eternal vows at a quiet Buddhist temple. It was a truly sad yet beautiful happy ending.

Although they had been accidents, the deaths of two young boarders led to the boarding house's steady decline. It was around that time that Mum's knees grew worse, too, and students began to prefer living alone, which caused the popularity of boarding houses to plummet. I begged my mum to sell off the place and give me some of the money from the sale to start my business. It was the summer of '88, when the long-awaited Olympic Games were taking place in Seoul. The sale of the boarding house brought in more money than I'd expected. With that cash, I found a small but new apartment in Wangsimni and set up the Kim Sangho Marriage Research Institute.

At first, we had no customers, so I spent all day sitting across from Byungpal and staring at the phone.

'Hey, we're in trouble. I talked this up as a great business idea to Misook, but now she's grilling me about it non-stop.'

In the meantime, Byungpal had gotten hitched a second time. Or, to be more specific, he'd found another woman to shack up with. She wasn't as rich as Lee Okja, but she was pretty and twelve years younger.

'Should we try advertising?'

Our budget was tight, but I asked Byungpal what he thought about taking out a small ad in the newspaper.

'Dude, what would we advertise? "We will find the perfect match for your dearly departed child. Is their former life partner refusing to listen? Here at the Kim Sangho Marriage Research Institute, we'll settle the matter without so much as the mice or the birds hearing a peep." Like that?'

'What's wrong with that?'

'What's wrong with it? That's not an ad for a marriage research institute, it's an ad for a murder-for-hire business. Are you trying to get hauled out of here in handcuffs?'

We ordered jjajangmyeon to eat, took a nap, ordered jjajangmyeon again and went home in silence. I felt frustrated not having anything to tell my mum, either, when I got back and she asked me if I'd made any matches that day. If she found out that her son was a matchmaker for the dead, not the living, I knew she would chuck a rice paddle at me, shouting that all the stupid shit I'd done up to now wasn't enough and I had to go and tarnish the family legacy.

Byungpal, apparently the head of our PR, doubled back and said, 'Man-to-man marketing. That's the only way to go.'

'What do we do for that?'

'Funeral homes are so crowded, it's hard to meet the bereaved families. Which is why we should look for them at the charnel house. Usually, when someone dies young, they don't get a burial. So we can meet the parents there, face to face. We tell them that if we send their child off like this, they'll become a vengeful ghost, and if we don't relieve them of their resentment, they'll be vengeful for all of eternity. We'll say it just like that.'

Starting the next day, Byungpal and I, along with his live-in girlfriend Misook, started going around to charnel houses. If we just started spouting nonsense about helping these parents find matches for their dead children, we knew we'd be treated as crazies, so we would first offer some incense, then subtly slip over one of our business cards.

'If you just let us know the name and address of your child's lover, we will take care of the matter within forty-nine days, before your child's soul has fully passed on from this life.'

Fortunately, the parents of deceased children could keep a secret. They shared only hints with each other. And the process was clean. That was because Misook had talked a gangster named Na Hancheol into helping us out. Misook was an assistant at a beauty salon, and she'd heard rumours that the guy, who claimed the neighbourhood where she worked was his territory, was quite good with a knife. In no time at all, Misook had Hancheol put up a storefront sign for the Happy Detective Agency and form a partnership with the Kim Sangho Marriage Research Institute.

Byungpal started getting worked up about Misook's close relationship with Hancheol and was planning to hire a different private detective agency to look into it, but what did it even matter if business was going well for us? Byungpal needed to realize as soon as possible that things like love were a necessary evil. Most of the cases he handled were treated as accidents, but on rare occasions, they escalated into murders. But don't worry. The trustworthy Happy Detective Agency will provide you, the bereaved parents, with an airtight alibi, so you can go on and look for a temple with a nice view for the ceremony.

You were so worried, so I told you all about my silly past, and now all that's left for you to do is have some faith and leave it to me. You don't want to? Oh, well, what to do? If you refuse, I don't think we'll be able to keep your secret. One second, let me make a quick call. Yes, is this Mr Na? It's me, Sangho. I think you'll need to come by for a bit. Ha, I told you I'd cover your transportation costs separately. Oh, never mind. No need to come. I think the customer's had a change of heart. Give my regards to Misook, will you? Then I'll place the order shortly. Sure, sure. Thank you.

11

The Wife

Laundry was a job for the washing machine, and dishwashing was a job for the dishwasher. I could call someone once every few days to come and do the cleaning, but I felt more comfortable running the little robot vacuum cleaner that looked like a horseshoe crab. I preferred machines that couldn't think for themselves to human beings and all their complexity. Not only did machines lack the mouths needed to blab about their owner's private lives, they knew how to finish their work without needless chatter and how to fall silent with the push of a button. But this time, there was a task I absolutely needed the help of a human being to carry out.

I had decided to murder my husband.

My husband didn't want kids. He was always busy, and even when he did come home, he was always on edge like someone being followed. He worked as a contract killer. Because of that, he had no designated weekends or holidays off, and we could never stay put anywhere for too long. In the seventeen years I had been living with him, I'd had to move twenty-two times and take out twelve different life insurance policies. To me, a child meant hope. If we just had a child, I believed I would never have to wash another one of my husband's bloody shirts again.

'Once you have a child, you'll have to sacrifice your own body in every aspect. And if you sacrifice yourself to live, you only end up dying.'

What made a person choose the path my husband had chosen? I ran a well-established beauty salon and had enough money saved up to live on for the rest of our lives if we didn't spend too lavishly. I tried appealing to him to visit the clinic with me. But my pleas were met with silence.

Then one day, he came home from a business trip and handed me a business card from his jacket pocket. 'I made an appointment for next Tuesday,' he said.

On the business card was the name of a fertility clinic and a picture of the clinic's director. My husband's tone betrayed nothing out of the ordinary. It was as though he were leafing through a newspaper or flipping through channels on the TV.

'What made you change your mind?'

He chewed the inside of his cheek. 'I met a guy who's looking for his wife. She ran away from home two years ago. But he wasn't looking for her because he missed her. He was just curious why she'd run away without powering off the vacuum cleaner. Today, I found the man's wife down in Gimhae. She was five months pregnant and pushing another baby no more than a year or so old around in a stroller. She looked so happy. When I asked her why she'd run away, she said it was because of her husband's infertility. She wanted a child, and so she went into hiding with the poor sap who got her pregnant.'

So my husband's business trip hadn't been a waste.

KANG JIYOUNG

'So did you kill anybody?'

'Nope.'

'Why not?'

'Because the client didn't want me to.'

'So you returned his money?'

My husband frowned and took a can of beer with him as he made his way to the bathroom.

'Let's not talk about work,' he said. 'I'm done for the day.'

I was so happy he'd agreed to have the baby, whatever the reason. The next day, we went together to the fertility clinic. Then a week later, when I got the results from my primary doctor, she looked so stern that I started to think maybe she'd gone her entire life without ever getting laid herself.

'The test results show that you have polycystic ovary syndrome, and your husband has issues with his sperm count and motility. There are many ways forward, but we'll start with artificial insemination. It doesn't guarantee a one hundred per cent chance of pregnancy. The success rate of the first procedure is somewhere between ten and twenty per cent, and the more procedures you undergo, the higher the success rate. But that's not to say there are never cases where the insemination fails in the end.'

Hearing the doctor's explanation, my husband subtly lowered his head and wrapped his hands around mine. The results were about what I'd expected from reading countless posts from mommy bloggers online.

On the third day of taking medication to induce ovulation, the doctor confirmed that I was ovulating and went ahead with the first round of the procedure. It involved inserting a small device with a thin straw-like piece attached into my uterus to inject my husband's specially treated sperm. This was so that the sperm, few in number and not very speedy, could more easily reach the egg. There was a painful pressure and discomfort stiffening my lower belly and thighs, and I was so anxious thinking about what I would do if all this effort didn't result in a pregnancy that I felt like I was going to be sick.

As soon as the procedure was over, I vomited yellow stomach acid on to the nurse's white uniform and went into the recovery room, where I silently cried. In the end, it was a failure. After the next two attempts also ended in failure, the doctor suggested changing methods. I took the medication I was prescribed for eight days, and then the nurse administered a shot with a hypodermic needle that looked like a small ballpoint pen. The shot was meant to induce superovulation. Once the injection was done, a number of the ovulated eggs were fertilized with my husband's sperm in vitro to make a test-tube baby.

The doctor told me in the end she had managed to collect a total of eleven healthy eggs. We would take the best three of those to inject into the uterus and wait for one of them to take. After nine ultrasounds, I learned that two of the eggs had taken without issue, and I was now pregnant with twins. I put my face into my hands and wept. Because I had no doubt that a child would be the thing to make me and my husband normal.

I made some traditional Korean swaddling clothes from organic, pure cotton fabric, and my husband ordered a sturdy, spacious twin bassinet made from black walnut wood. The twins were growing well. At first, they started off as two tiny specks, but soon enough they had heartbeats, bones, muscles, flesh, and blood. My husband tried his best not to miss my regular checkups, but sometimes when it couldn't be avoided, he would send along one of his coworkers to accompany me. This coworker was a middle-aged man with a face as pale as a steamed bun who was always smiling. I couldn't believe someone with such a kind face could kill people. He introduced himself to me as Lee Hyunseung, sat me not in the passenger seat but in the backseat of the car, and moved up the driver's seat so that I could spread out my legs. I insisted several times that he didn't have to, but he told me my husband had asked him to do this favour, so he went with me into the treatment room and studied the small, delicate life on the ultrasound screen in amazement.

'Who do they look like?'

Lee Hyunseung placed the ultrasound photo in his palm and ran a finger over it. The babies in the photo didn't look so much like humans as like newborn chicks with all their feathers plucked off.

'Their foreheads are wide. Most times, babies are born with the most distinctive features from their parents. The wide forehead, that's all him.'

I imagined babies with my husband's wide forehead and my thin lips, wailing like an old-fashioned telephone ringing.

'Can I have the ultrasound photo?' Hyunseung asked as he started the car.

'No way,' I said. 'If you have something like this on you, your wife could misunderstand.'

I took the photo from him, and he looked sheepish. Though I didn't especially like the guy, when he came by the house with baby supplies he had bought with my husband, I felt grateful that my husband, who'd lived so far away from his family for so long, had someone who was like a brother to him at his job. Still, it was too much for him to ask for an ultrasound photo.

'I saw a huge tree in my dream,' he told me. 'When I went closer to see what was dangling from the tree, I found that there were enormous chestnuts and peaches on the branches, growing on the same tree. I think it means the twins growing in your belly are a girl and a boy.'

Just as Hyunseung had predicted, when I was twenty-one weeks pregnant, the doctor hinted that I should make both a blue and a pink set of the swaddling clothes.

On my way home from receiving my last treatment, my husband and I went to take anniversary photos at the studio across from the hospital. The photo of me and my husband embracing as I proudly showed off my enormous belly arrived in the mail a week later.

I opened the photo album I had picked out and tucked that photo into the sleeve of the very first page. As I slipped the album into a spot on the bookshelf and turned around, a slight pain started up in my lower stomach. It was too subtle to call an ache, so I went out on to the balcony where the washing machine was to wash the carriers and swaddling blankets as well as their little caps and socks. My belly felt cold again, and my womb, swollen taut, felt like it was being pressed into a single lump. Because I was thirty-six weeks pregnant, with twins at that, I could have given birth at any time and it wouldn't have been out of the ordinary.

I hobbled into the living room and called my husband. The clenching pain throughout my entire stomach and my lower back was steadily growing more intense.

'Come quick,' I begged. 'Our babies are coming.'

Instead of answering, my husband let out a long sigh and ended the call. It took at least an hour to get home from his office. When the contractions subsided, I tried to put on my coat, and that was when the front of my dress got soaked as a red liquid gushed out of me.

My childbirth manual had clearly told me that the amniotic fluid could be clear or yellowish in colour, but nowhere did it say that the fluid might be blood red. As I took my phone out of my pocket and dialled the emergency number, the red fluid continued to stream down my legs. By the time three men in orange uniforms arrived, not even five minutes later, my stomach was half emptied out. As I explained to the paramedics how to get to the hospital I was supposed to give birth in, I kept having to bite down on my lower lip hard enough to draw blood to keep from losing consciousness. The pain was so intense that I felt like my internal organs were being dragged out of me – it felt like it would never end.

I had a stillbirth. Caused by placenta previa. I was told that the placenta was blocking the exit of the womb when the birth was imminent, which had led to a haemorrhage. I was moved to a hospital room where someone had placed a bouquet of white chrysanthemums on the bed. At the time, I thought it was my husband who'd left them for me. But as the night wore on, he didn't show up again.

The antibiotics and painkillers tasted bitter. The seaweed soup provided by the hospital was bland, and flies swarmed around the now-withered flowers. The next day and the day after that, too, my husband still didn't come.

Maybe he'd died. But the most likely scenario seemed to be that as he was attempting to finish off a dangerous target, they'd got into a tussle that ended with my husband's own knife being driven into his chest.

'Flower delivery.'

My husband was absent, but this was the fourth bouquet delivered to my hospital room in as many days.

'Do you know who sent them?'

The delivery guy, now a familiar face, took out a memo pad and looked through it.

'They're from someone named Lee Hyunseung.'

I scrolled through my contacts on my phone and tapped on his name to call him.

'Hello?' he answered quietly.

'Where's my husband?'

I heard Hyunseung take a steady breath.

'Is he dead?' I asked.

A long sigh.

'No, he's not,' he said. 'But he can't contact you.'

'Why not?'

Another long sigh.

'He thinks the babies were born.'

'*What?* If he thinks they were born, why is he hiding?'

This meant he'd never been at the hospital at all, not even during my surgery. I hadn't remembered signing a consent form as I went into the operating room, so I'd thought all along that he had signed it on my behalf.

'I can't tell you,' said Hyunseung.

I ended the call and sought out my doctor to ask to look at the surgery consent form. I saw his name signed in an unfamiliar hand. I called Hyunseung back.

'Was it you? The one who signed the consent form. Tell me! Why did you do it?'

My husband didn't want children. He didn't want to be shackled to anyone as an irresponsible man who could have died or ended up in prison at any time. I understood that.

'Mr Na found my wife after she ran away from home. But my wife had already become another person entirely. If I wanted to, I could have had her and the man who stole her from me killed on the spot. But when he told me of the happiness on my wife's face, I had a change of heart. I wondered, if I had a child, too, would I be as happy as she was? Mr Na told me that he'd gotten a vasectomy a long time ago. He said that you didn't know anything about it and that you wanted a baby. You and I wanted the same thing. So Mr Na used my sperm, not his, to give you the twins. Even if I couldn't raise them, I thought just becoming a father to them would make me as happy as my wife seemed to be—'

I ended the call. I didn't want to hear more.

Then I threw out the chrysanthemums whose smell reminded me of a jesa ceremony to remember the dead. My husband was nothing but a cold-blooded animal who'd pocketed Lee Hyun-seung's money and used it to impregnate his wife with another man's sperm.

The more I thought about it, the more it seemed that my husband had thought of me as an implant. Something inserted out of necessity, yet forever out of place, like someone else's skin – so fake and uncomfortable that it made his tongue curl up every time he touched me. I filled that position with an air of indifference, but inside, I was slowly festering.

It wasn't affection or loyalty to my husband that made me keep up this awful marriage. My goal was to start off as a small blister, then to become a deep-rooted boil that threatened his very life. I could forgive him for being a bad husband, but I couldn't forgive him for being a bad father. At some point, my husband's face had begun to resemble my father's twenty-two years ago.

Twenty-two years ago, I was dumped at an underpass crawling with beggars like maggots. All because of my father. In just a day and a half, he had gambled away the family burial grounds and our vineyard that was ready for harvest. Even though he pissed himself with every round of a game, my father couldn't get up from the betting table, greedy to win back his principal. Soon, he had to sell off several acres of his remaining land, the house, and his two daughters in the prime of their youth. He had fallen right into the trap that had been set for him.

'Now that I think about it, I'm sure those bastards planned to scam me from the start. And I had no idea.'

It all happened so fast. The man who'd won against my father at the gambling den tailed him home in case our family tried to make a nighttime getaway. The man woke me and my sister up and put us in a dusty jeep. Our mum ran out barefoot, wailing. And our father, who'd been standing there trembling, fell to his knees. The man, in his hunting hat with a furry animal tail, chuckled.

'All right, that's enough, old man. You look like shit. Quit all that blubbering and wire the twenty million won to the account I wrote down earlier. Then I'll return your girls, no problem. If you keep clinging like this, I'll get fed up fast, and we can't have that. Come on. By acting like this in front of the girls, you're making it look like *I* committed a crime.'

We were taken to a motel downtown. Two men who looked like they were in a gang chugged beer as they counted the cash they must have gotten from our father. My older sister and I knelt on the mats laid out by the men for us, barefoot and in our nightgowns. The gambler who'd dragged us there looked to be around our father's age, which would make him the oldest in the group, while the other men looked to be in their early forties. The three of them chuckled and ordered Chinese food and more beer, and got another game going that lasted all night. Stacks of cash and curse words moved back and forth across the table. The men didn't care if we cried as they shouted words like *seryuk*, *jangsa*, *gabo* during each round of hwatu.

The next day, our parents hanged themselves.

My father, who had lost his fortune in a hwatu game and put up his daughters as collateral, and my mother, who had realized the truth too late – they no longer had any reason to live. The gambler went back to our house, looking to collect on the money he was owed, and when he stumbled upon our parents dangling from the rafters like strings of dried persimmons hanging from the eaves in autumn, he got startled and ran away. One of his henchmen, in charge of keeping an eye on me and my sister, told us something bad had happened, let out a barrage of swear words, and then packed our dyed military rucksacks and loaded us into the car.

'You little bitches have been hollering and making all that noise. Cut it out. If you keep crying, I'll get angry. Do you know how scary I can be when I'm angry?'

As the man drove, my sister and I buried our faces in our sleeves and quietly swallowed our sobs, all the while cursing our parents who had given us up so irresponsibly and then were so quick to kick the bucket. The car drove along winding roads, and around noon, the man pulled over in front of a secluded shop and went inside to buy some snacks. I felt my head spinning and nausea in my stomach after a whole day of not eating and crying so hard. As I watched the man pay and then stand in the doorway of the shop merrily eating some kind of bready snack, I leaned my head against my sister's shoulder. I could hear gurgling. There was nothing to drink inside the car, yet my sister seemed to be gulping something at regular intervals. I rubbed my eyes and looked up at her. Bright red blood pooled in the corners of her pale lips.

'Unni, what are you eating? You had something to eat without telling me? Have you lost your mind?'

My sister's pale hands moved very slowly up my arms, came to rest for a moment on my shoulders and then found my cheeks with some difficulty. Her hands were cold to the touch. Her lidded eyes lingered on my face for a second. I shook her by the shoulders and screamed. The man, who had been calmly alternating between bites of his bread and sips of his milk, belatedly realized something was happening and ran out to the car, yanking the door open. But the light had already gone out of my sister's eyes. Inside her open mouth, I could see her tongue was shredded. At some point, my sister had chewed up her own tongue and swallowed the blood. The man looked clearly taken aback. He tossed the remaining half of his bread and milk, tried to catch his breath, and climbed into the driver's seat. He anxiously tapped on the steering wheel before starting the car and pulling off on to the road.

'Guess you and me are the boring ones,' he said.

I lay my sister down, resting her head on my lap. Her body had already gone cold and begun to stiffen. She always smelled nice, being someone who especially liked to get dolled up.

'You, clothes off. Quick,' barked the man.

He pulled over on an empty road, got out of the car, and came around to the backseat. Then he grabbed my sister by the arm and yanked her off my lap. She fell to the ground with a thud like a log, and I let out a horrified shriek.

'I told you to get undressed!' he shouted, ripping open the buttons on my nightgown with one jerk of his rough hands. He took a shovel out of the trunk and started digging up the soil in the woods on the roadside. As he dug a hole large enough to fit my sister's body, the sun began to set. The man must have been worried I would try to make a run for it as he worked, which was why he'd forced me to undress. Only after nine o'clock did he finish making a hole he was satisfied with, and that was where he chucked my sister's body, by then as solid and pale as a mannequin. He tossed my torn clothing on top to cover her. He buried her, his body steaming faintly from the exertion, and when he was done, he let out a long sigh.

Now that I thought about it, he could have buried me and my sister both that day. But he climbed back into the car and drove off to Seoul instead. It was late at night, and he looked every bit as anxious as I felt.

He hesitated several times before pulling over at a payphone and counting coins. It seemed like he was planning to call for help, but because of what had happened that day, he might have already been abandoned by the rest of his gang. He went inside the phone booth and took out a piece of paper from his pocket, carefully dialling the number. We were in the heart of downtown, but at that late hour and with the sleet falling, the streets were empty.

The man must have gotten through to whoever he'd called because his eyes lit up. Some drops of blood had dried and hardened on the backseat where my sister had been sitting. I ran a finger over the blood, which was gummy like wheat paste and left an imprint like a wax seal underneath my fingerprint. I couldn't wait any longer. Keeping an eye on the man, I carefully opened the car door. I could feel the click of the lock unlocking in my fingertips. The man was banging his head against the wall of the phone booth, looking distraught. I put all my strength into throwing the door open and took off running towards an underpass nearby. The man, hunched up in the phone booth with a grave look on his face, belatedly noticed and came running after me, but I looked around at the beggars crouched around me and the occasional pedestrian walking by and let out scream.

I figured it wasn't every day that the beggars saw a naked girl because they rubbed their sleepy eyes and burrowed inside their sleeping mats made from Styrofoam and cardboard boxes. In the end, it was an older foreign clergyman who provided free meals to the homeless who ended up taking me in. Thinking that the bad man might be waiting somewhere for me, I didn't dare try to run up the stairs to get away. I rubbed some sheets of newspaper between my hands to warm them, then covered myself with the newspaper and was drifting off to sleep when I heard voices whispering and smelled food. I opened my eyes. A priest along with two nuns and a man who looked to be a disciple and was red in the face from exertion were ladling rice soup on to plastic trays. One of the beggars whose facial hair covered his lips took hold of the Father's arm and said something to him as he pointed at me.

The clergyman approached me where I lay under dozens of pages of newspaper. Once he was close enough, I could see the surprise and sympathy that filled his green eyes. He hurried to remove his robes and offered them to me. The nuns covered me in the robes, which still held the priest's warmth, and guided me up the stairs into the blaring sunlight of the world aboveground. The man wasn't there at the top of the stairs. Instead, a van with a huge illustration of a cross in each window sat purring like a cat, ready to greet me. The sensation of cold from the icy pavement slowly thawed out, and I began to feel so hungry that my stomach hurt. One of the nuns who had opened the door of the van for me let out a small gasp and wiped between my legs with a cotton cloth. The white of the cloth was soon stained with fresh blood. My first period had come at last.

I lived in the church until I was an adult. At first, I wanted to be a dancer. But when I heard that there was a dormitory offering free cosmetology classes, I started working at the beauty salon attached to the dorm. I call it a dorm, but it was actually a tiny living space meant for students who lived alone as they studied for their exams, where four assistant hairdressers who had come up to the city from the countryside all slept cramped together. I didn't have a licence, so I had to wash the towels and hang them to dry, rinse and dry the tools caked in perm chemicals, then organize them by size after the other women were done working for the day. After I'd wiped the mirrors, swept the floors, and washed the customers' hair, I was ready to collapse around the early evening. But when I returned to the dorm, the four women who had been splitting all my work among themselves just days earlier, would put their swollen legs up on pillows and make me cook them noodles or ramen.

In the morning, I was the first one to wake up, and I would fold and stack the towels that had dried overnight on the shelves, mix the perm solution that required a lot of work in advance, or prepare the owner's coffee to her taste. During the day, I trimmed the regular customers' cuticles and massaged their backs and necks. And so the exhausting and tedious days of sweeping up hair and washing coffee mugs to prepare for the customers who would come in the afternoon went on.

The customers really started coming in after five p.m. There were hostess bars lined up in all directions around the beauty salon, so the girls who worked in them would stop by to get their hair touched up and have dinner before clocking in. I couldn't give haircuts or do perms, but when we were short-staffed, I could help with simple tasks like setting or curling hair.

The young women who frequented the salon divided

themselves into groups according to their regions of origin and maintained those ties, so there was the Honam Group, the Yeongnam Group, the Chungcheong Group, the Gangwon Group, and less frequently overseas groups, too. They normally spoke in standard Korean, but when they were in the salon with people from their same region, they would suddenly switch into their hometown dialects with a frightening energy. There was only one girl among them who never showed her regional colours – she truly had a baby face, didn't speak much, and seemed extremely shy, so at a glance, she looked like she could be a uni student. I didn't know her real name, but the ledger we wrote up for the month had her name listed as Maria. That was also the baptismal name the priest had given me. Whenever this other Maria stepped foot in the salon, no matter how busy I was, even if I was brewing the coffee for the owner, I would stop what I was doing and look up to greet her silently.

Maria liked wearing form-fitting dresses, but she never looked sleazy or lewd. Her skirt fluttered elegantly as she sat in front of the mirror, and I walked towards her with a rice ball made from warm rice, soy sauce, and seaweed flakes. She watched me standing near the washing room, hurriedly eating the rice ball, and opened her lips, pink as garden zinnias, to ask me what it tasted like. Starting the next day, I began to give her rice balls so that she wouldn't have to converse with the other girls in their noisy dialects as they slurped up ramen noodles or hand-torn dumplings.

Maria wasn't chatty. She never requested a particular hairstyle, nor did she ever complain. Her eyes, always staring dreamily off into the distance, held a sense of melancholy. She looked like a young girl with many dreams. As I was blow-drying her thin, brown hair and giving her gentle curls with the cylindrical comb, she kept her eyes lowered, their lids as delicate and thin as dumpling skins, and focused on her knitting. That year, I wore an ivory muffler and mittens to take the hairdresser licensing exam.

'Misook, let me tell you a secret. I have the money I'm saving up in this knitting bag. One day, we'll open our own beauty salon with our names.'

But Maria never kept that promise. The summer I withdrew my instalment savings for the second time, Maria was found stuffed inside a travel bag in the freezer at the hostess bar where she worked. Her killer was none other than Maria herself. According to the salon owner, who was well versed in all the goings-on in that area, Maria had been a drug addict. And her main supplier was her own boss at the hostess bar. When I pictured Maria rolling around in bed with a man in his forties who was high on drugs and had too much facial hair covering his pointed chin, I fell to my knees on the floor of the beauty salon covered in strands of hair.

Her boss who'd been shooting up with her had been terrified to see Maria suddenly go into shock and die. He stuffed her small, skin-and-bones body into the travel bag and tossed her in the freezer crammed with chicken and ham well past its expiry date. She was found by the head chef two weeks later. The boss, who had gone golfing in the Philippines, was caught by the police but given a suspended sentence for simple drug offences. The person who incurred the most damage from the incident wasn't the hostess bar guy but the director of our beauty salon. Her American husband was a drug supplier, and she was only now realizing that what he'd been selling to the guy who ran the hostess bar along with perm solution wasn't mere cigars or coffee beans.

Maria's belongings were sent to me, as I had been her only friend. She had left behind only some size-S dresses and her knitting bag. Inside the knitting bag, aside from the colourful balls of yarn, was a bundle of white powder in saran wrap. I could guess what it was. I took it to Na Hancheol, whom I'd just started seeing around then. A few days later, he showed up with a huge amount of money that was enough to buy out the struggling beauty salon. It was Maria's last gift to me.

After I lost the twins, the doctor told me I would never be able to have a child again. I grew old, still washing bloodied shirts and moving house. What had changed was that, while my husband and I still lived in the same house, we stopped calling each other's names. And another important thing that happened was that my ex came to see me. No one at the beauty salon knew I was the wife of a contract killer. I had a lover named Han Byungpal who could take the place of my husband.

He had been a regular at the first beauty salon where I'd worked. He was a one-time divorcee and an eccentric who spouted nonsense about love and marriage, but he had a child-like way about him that made him easy to read. Back then, I'd been more attracted to Hancheol, who was cold and heavy like lead, compared to Byungpal, who was as light as helium. Byungpal was running a struggling matchmaking business for ghost marriages, and I felt bad enough for him that I introduced him to my now-husband, and the two became business partners. But after I married Hancheol, my relationship with Byungpal naturally came to an end. So many things changed during that time. More than anything, my trust in my husband disappeared, leaving only faint traces like old scars. After losing the twins, I became indifferent to everything, and as a kind of compensation for myself, I took Byungpal as a lover once again. And like a miracle, one of the children I had lost returned to me.

The doctor turned up the volume on the ultrasound machine to let me hear the baby's heartbeat. It was so powerful, like a fountain suddenly gushing up from a closed-off well, that it startled me. My nose stung as I felt tears coming on. As soon as I left the room, I called the person who would be the happiest to hear the news.

'I'm at the hospital,' I said.

Byungpal had been the one to recommend that I visit the hospital after I couldn't eat a proper meal for days on account of indigestion and acid reflux.

'What's the prognosis? Should I guess? Reflux esophagitis? Stomach ulcer?'

'No. They're saying I'm pregnant. My due date is next year. January seventh.'

He let out a long sigh without answering at first. 'What should we do?'

I knew he was worried about my husband.

'What do you mean, what should we do? We have to get rid of him.'

'You're getting an abortion?'

'No. I mean we have to get rid of Na Hancheol.'

I ended the call and went to find someone who could get rid of my husband. In the world of murders-for-hire, no one compared to Park Taesang at the Smile Detective Agency, but he'd washed his hands clean of the business a long time ago. I'd heard rumours instead about his new subordinate, the ajumma killer. She was good with knives, handled business cleanly, and was like a padlock when it came to keeping secrets. But I didn't know how I was

supposed to find her when I didn't know her name or what she looked like. I parked across the street from the Smile Detective Agency building and waited for someone to come out.

The lights on the third floor of the building still weren't out. The same way my husband never seemed to have a regular schedule for when he got off work, the people at the Smile Detective Agency must not have had a set time when they left the office, either. I took one of the capsules of folic acid the doctor had prescribed me. No matter what, I had to protect this delicate life growing inside me.

The old security guard sitting in the booth bolted up suddenly and saluted someone – a middle-aged man with a sturdy build. He must have been Park Taesang. Following behind him were two middle-aged women walking arm in arm. One was short, looked well over fifty, and wore a tacky nylon T-shirt and pants. The other looked to be in her forties and wore her long, permed hair out and a miniskirt.

Which one of them could be the real killer? My eyes kept returning to the younger one. The older woman got on the bus first. I made a U-turn and approached the bus stop where the younger woman was waiting for her own bus. She took out some gum from her handbag and popped a piece in her mouth. Her front teeth were stained with red lipstick. I parked in front of her and rolled down the window.

'If we're headed in the same direction, let's go together,' I called.

The woman looked around, as though to confirm that I was talking to her.

'I'm headed to the Hanaro Mart,' she said.

I nodded, and the woman opened the passenger side door with a smile. Surprisingly, she seemed to trust people easily. A killer would have been suspicious. Wary of everything. A pure headache to deal with. Like my husband.

'You work at Smile, don't you?'

She chomped on her gum and glanced at me in surprise.

'Who are you?' she asked.

Who should I tell her I was? A beautician? A pregnant lady? Na Hancheol's cheating wife?

'Let's just say I'm a client,' I said.

The woman's eyes searched my face.

'Oh, I see. You want to do some private investigation into your husband, is that right? If so, you should come by the office during the day.'

Had my husband ever had a private investigation done on me? If he had, there was no way he didn't know I was having an affair. And no way I would still be alive.

The words that had been sitting on my tongue for so long came out easier than I'd expected. 'Please kill my husband for me.'

The woman gripped the strap of her seat belt tight. 'Oh, we . . . don't do that sort of thing.'

'I heard the rumours and did everything I could to find you all. If you open the glove compartment, you'll see the retainer fee inside. If you manage to pull this off, the pay will be ten times that amount. Enough cash to buy a small apartment.'

Once I put together all the money I would get from the life

insurance policies I'd taken out for my husband, I would probably be able to move to a small island. There, I could give birth to lots and lots of lively little babies. And I wouldn't have to pack up and move again or take out more life insurance policies – I could be an easy-going, ordinary woman.

'But like I said, we don't do that sort of thing,' said the woman. Contrary to what she was telling me, though, she opened the glove compartment and took a peek inside the envelope.

'You said ten times what's in here?' she said, her mouth falling open. In the meantime, we had arrived in front of the Hanaro Mart.

'I don't have time to wait, so please – let's make this quick.'

I handed her a stack of papers detailing my husband's personal information. The woman put the papers and the envelope with the money in her bag and swallowed hard.

'I'm no pushover. If you fail, you and I will both be in danger.'

The woman hesitated, blinking.

'You'll really pay ten times this amount? Because I can be a very scary person, too. So if you're lying, you and I will both be dead, and . . .'

She let the threat trail off. As she got out of the car, she lost her balance, wobbling on her ankles. Then she disappeared into the crowd inside the mart. She had a somewhat ditzy side to her. But for now, I had no choice but to put my faith in her and wait.

My phone rang. It was Byungpal.

'Are you still far away?'

'I'm leaving now. I should be there in half an hour. Could you order some bossam in the meantime? I'm craving it.'

I watched a pregnant woman walk into the mart holding her husband's hand.

'Actually, strike that. Let's go to the mart,' I said.

If I could blend in among the crowd of strangers, would I also be able to look like an ordinary pregnant woman like her? I suddenly wondered: could a woman like me, who kept her lies behind tightly shut lips and a sharp blade hidden deep inside the neat collar of her shirts, ever look like a woman like that?

12

The Teacher

There was this movie whose English title was *The Killer*. Before I started middle school, I vaguely knew that the titular killer in the film was someone who was paid to kill other people, but I had no idea that *killer* in English meant the same thing as a murderer. Granted, I was a problem child who made terrible marks and found Korean hard enough, let alone a foreign language.

To a teacher, students were as easy to manage as a flock of sheep – all you needed were some strong words and some grass. Draped in their absurdly oversized school uniforms, the navy-blue flock spent all day reading, memorizing, and solving problems, or else stuffing cold fried snacks in their mouths whenever they had a spare second, and each of them was assigned a number. But no matter how good the teachers were, they were in the end only foolish shepherd dogs looking after their flocks. When the bell rang, they gathered on a bench and chugged instant coffee, and when the bell rang again, they returned to their rooms where their flocks were waiting, interested only in whether there were empty seats, whether some of the sheep were nodding off or else being cheeky and hiding something.

Not long after I started middle school, as soon as the homeroom teacher had finished the morning assembly, I would hoist my desk over my shoulder and carry it to the bathroom. Sadly, there were some teachers foolish enough to believe that if they didn't see an empty desk, that meant no one was absent.

On a day like any other, I shoved the desk and chair into the space where the cleaning supplies were stored and stood before the wall that connected us to the world, ready to make my escape. The wall was high enough that it was hard for me to jump over, having just graduated from primary school. It was built from grey bricks and stood about a metre tall, the barbed wire at the top coiled like a spring with shards from broken glass bottles stuck in places, which made the school look like a high-security prison. But I had reliable seniors who had conquered it before me. Of course, I had never spoken to these older students face to face or heard their bloody tales of bravery from them directly. But I knew they were reliable because of the passageway underneath the wall.

Every year, there were bound to be deviants like me. They would have known from an early age that they were unlike the rest of the flock, but they wouldn't have been able to shrug off the expectations of their parents, whose eyes were as pure and innocent as those of herbivores. So these deviants had no choice but to try wearing sheep's masks, letting out fake cries of *baa baa*, while they waited for the end of the day to yank off the masks and shout, *This damned thing just makes my neck hurt*. They would have dug under the school wall devotedly, one scoop of dirt at a time, for themselves, or for the fellow fake sheep like me who would find themselves in this same position all these years later.

I pushed through the cluster of royal azaleas just beginning to bloom a few steps from the back gate and came across a hole that someone had blocked off with a wooden board. I took off my backpack and shoved it in the hole first, then removed my uniform jacket and belt and held them against my chest. I slowly squeezed my body in, all to try breaking through to that world of alcohol and movies and girls sucking on cigarettes that awaited me out there. But unlike any other day, the hole wasn't connected to the outside world. The bag I thought I'd pushed through as hard as I could was suddenly pushed back from the other end, dropping squarely on my head. In the pitch darkness of the hole, I could taste the bitter dirt.

'Looks like I've caught a mole.'

From the voice alone, I knew it was my English teacher. I couldn't leave, and at the same time, I couldn't return to school and face that voice's owner. So I wavered for a while in that hole, pinned beneath the wall. I imagined how nice it would be if the wall just collapsed and crushed me in two, allowing at least one half of me to escape from this maddening reality. But the wall was too sturdy, in no danger of collapse. There was nothing I could do but turn back, the English teacher's rough hands pulling me out by my trousers.

'You've got the nerve to try this when it's only first period on Monday. Shut your mouth and bow your head.'

This was back when corporal punishment was a daily occurrence. Sunlight shone on the teacher's head, over which he'd combed the sides of his hair that he'd grown out to hide his baldness. His eyes, already as small as the eyes in a pig's head on a ceremonial table spread, narrowed even more ferociously. He was frothing at the mouth, his lips the colour of red beans. Now that my escape plot had been discovered, there was nothing more I could do. I bowed my head towards his feet and moved my hands behind my back. Thinking back on it now, I feel like the doghole wasn't a way out just for the fake sheep but for the English teacher, too. He must have long known about the hole near the back gate where troublemaking kids would hang out. And when his stress reached its limits, he must have been grateful for the hole, which provided him with a plush cushion to absorb the sound of the tyranny he unleashed upon his students.

'You little jerk, what did you just say? Are you calling your teacher an asshole?'

I just kept my mouth shut and quietly played the part of the cushion he took out his stress on. In my heart, I'd called him an asshole countless times, but all that came out of my mouth were hot, ragged breaths. He was looking for reasons to lash out at me, finding words I hadn't even said to justify kicking me in the ribs.

'No, I never said that.'

The rough stems of the moist azalea buds brushed against my face, and the spot they grazed soon swelled up and turned red.

'So you're saying I'm making things up? Just know that you've met your maker today.'

If I really had sworn at him, he would have beaten me to a pulp. He would have grabbed me by the collar, dragged me up to the teachers' lounge, flung me at my homeroom teacher's feet, and doled out an appropriate punishment according to the school guidelines. Even if the punishment were excessively harsh, no one would have felt the slightest bit of concern for a poor troublemaker who only brought down the school's averages. But the English teacher's behaviour was exaggerated, like the main character in a silent film.

He stepped out of the muddy flowerbed, removed his cheap acupressure slippers and slapped me in the face with them, his hair flapping about wildly, pathetically, in his anger. Suddenly, a thin stream of blood ran from his nose, and he fell backwards. His lips moved to the right and twitched regularly, and his eyes were wide open and bloodshot. The school security guard who had been sweeping the grounds in the distance rushed over and lifted the English teacher up. The guard was as lanky as the English teacher was heavy.

'He's had a stroke,' said the guard. 'What to do, what to do . . .'

The teachers' lounge was only a minute or so from the back gate, but time was running out as the guard's old knees buckled several times on the walk there. The whole time, the English teacher's body was experiencing spasms as aftershocks of the stroke and his muscles must have relaxed because pee ran down the legs of his trousers.

'Dad, I'll carry him,' I said.

The school guard was my father. His shoes were so worn they sounded like walnuts rubbing against each other with every step he took. He stopped walking.

'What were you doing that was so bad you gave this fine man a stroke?' he said. 'Hyunsuk, no matter what, you should admit when you've done something wrong.'

The English teacher died. Like my father had told me to do,

I'd apologized for what I'd done wrong, but he didn't accept it. His cause of death was an acute cerebral infarction, and in the ambulance, the last thing he said was slurred and aimed right at me: *Killer*.

The English teacher's wife didn't resent me. Since all this happened the day he'd failed to get promoted to vice principal, she'd weakly shook the principal who had come to pay his respects by the collar a few times before taking his condolence money and disappearing to the bathroom. The person who did the most work at the funeral, beating out the English teacher's relatives and students, both the young and the grey-haired, was my father. He was constantly carrying trays of spicy beef stew and skate salad and soju around, tidying up the shoes that the funeral-goers had carelessly kicked off at the entrance and picking up the plastic packaging for wooden chopsticks and the cigarette butts that were strewn about on the floor, back hunched even more than usual. My father's hands filled and emptied hundreds of bottles of beverages and alcohol, and I couldn't forget how, whenever he had a spare minute, he went over to the English teacher's wife with a look on his face that said he was at her service.

I was suspended for a week. It was called a suspension, so I thought that meant I didn't have to go to school and was excited, but I soon learned that I had to go to school for the entire suspension period and sit trapped in a tiny, run-down room called the 'Enlightenment Room', writing the same reflection essay over and over. It was thanks to my dad the punishment was lessened from a flat-out suspension to a kind of probation instead. My dad had been working at the school since the principal took office, and whenever he had time, he would wash the principal's car and polish his shoes. The clothes the principal's family got tired of wearing and the household objects they no longer wanted were all given to our family, so our house was always filled with the floral patterns that the principal's wife liked.

The principal was smart. He knew that I'd played a role in the English teacher's death, but he'd agreed to overlook that in exchange for my father offering to take a reduced salary for three months and to do some upkeep around the principal's parents' graves, which had long been neglected.

Aside from the time I spent in the bathroom and the time I spent eating from the lunchboxes my father packed me, I spent all my time in the Enlightenment Room writing reflection essays or getting my hair pulled by the teachers who occasionally stopped by. When I tried to solve the Spot the Difference puzzles in the newspapers that teachers sometimes left behind, someone would rush in as though they had sensed what I was up to and whack me on the back with a notebook or their attendance logs, chiding me to really reflect on my actions or at least read a book for once.

I was sick of writing reflection essays, so I scanned the spines of the books in the bookcase and pulled out a Korean dictionary. I decided to look up the word I had managed to forget about for a while: *killer*.

killer (n.) a player in volleyball who delivers an attack the opponent cannot return

Somehow I didn't think this was the last thing my English teacher said to me. I took down an English dictionary and looked for the word *killer*. There, I found the definition and read its three wonderful syllables aloud: *murderer*.

Kyungsoo, whose parents ran a small mom-and-pop shop, would get a free movie ticket every month. It was the money he earned for putting up posters in the shop's windows. Kyungsoo would sometimes sell the tickets for half price to make some pocket money, but around that time, despite not having any money, I was completely obsessed with the new movie that had started showing downtown – *The Killer*. The poster, which showed Chow Yun Fat wearing jet-black sunglasses and pointing a gun, lingered in my mind even when my eyes were closed. You had to be with someone who was at least eighteen years old to see the movie, but Kyungsoo's parents were busy swatting the flies that congregated in the shop all day, and his older brother wasn't yet eighteen. I was only thirteen. No matter how hard I tried, I couldn't get myself to look any older than a middle schooler, yet I had this strange belief that if I could just get a hold of a ticket, I would somehow be able to see the film. Eventually, this desire grew more and more fervent, and I felt like I would never be able to become an adult if I didn't see it, even though I'd been circumcised and had hair on my legs.

I made a bold move by filling a soju bottle with some of the ginseng wine my mum had hidden in the attic and replacing what I'd taken with water, then trading the alcohol with Kyungsoo for a movie ticket. I wore a blue striped tracksuit that was all the rage along with a pair of massive basketball shoes that Kyungsoo had secretly stolen from his brother. I thought about smudging some black paint on my upper lip since I hadn't started growing facial hair yet, but figuring that would be an even more embarrassing way to get caught, I decided it was enough to just wear a baseball cap. I didn't bring anything like a bag that would get in the way, just in case I ended up being chased out by the ticket seller or a security guard at the theatre. I mentally braced myself for all sorts of scenarios that might play out, only to show up at the theatre and have the ticket seller not care a single bit about my age. She sat behind the fan-shaped Plexiglass window, loudly chewing her gum as she exchanged my voucher for a movie ticket.

I sat in the back row of the theatre with only about ten people inside, my heart pounding as I watched *The Killer*. Chow Yun Fat was as cool as ever and Sally Yeh was pure and innocent. The scene where they were firing shots while riding a motorboat made my palms sweat, and when I saw the bad guys holding twin pistols and getting shot up like bullet bait as the statue of

the Virgin Mary looked down on them, I found myself letting out a cheer. When that mournful name I couldn't forget even now – *Ah Jong, Ah Jong* – rang out, and Chow Yun Fat's character drew his last breath, I found myself sobbing so hard that my shoulders rattled.

That winter, *A Better Tomorrow 3* came out, and some years later, *The Killer 2* was released, but I was still fixated on the original I had seen that summer when I was thirteen. As my facial hair started coming in, I started thinking that it might be nice to work as a contract killer when I grew up. In the years that followed, whenever I watched *The Killer* again on video, I even came to feel as though it were my life mission.

Before I went to work, I would talk to myself in the mirror.

'Do you believe in God?'

'No. But I like the peace in here.'

This was a conversation between the killer, Ah Jong, and his client. But in reality, no client ever asked this sort of question. They only griped about wanting someone dead. Maybe because of some grudge deep in the marrow of their bones or else an obstacle that seemed insurmountable for the client, but for the killer, it was merely routine. It was no different from hearing a customer's whining about some flaw they'd found in an item and how they wanted a refund. For a killer, there were no refunds. A killer had to accept these customers' complaints in silence and carry out the task with a thorough preliminary investigation and a perfect strategy. If he failed, he had no choice but to destroy all the evidence and hide out in a hole dug by one-time students at his school, or else opt to die. I would choose the latter before I ever burrowed my way into the hole again. After all, the price that the clients paid me included the price of my life.

I liked the rookie's vibe. He could tell exactly who was approaching him from behind just by the sound of their footsteps. Depending on who it was, he would reach out to take a steaming cup of coffee or to grab a coat. He had the clean-cut look of a lamb who had never roughed anyone up or tried to go through a hole under a wall.

'Take care of him. He'll come in handy soon.'

The boss, Na Hancheol, requested this of me. He had gotten much quieter recently. He hadn't even dyed his greying hair, and now half his head was grizzled. This behaviour didn't match his normally obsessive personality. The Smile Detective Agency's new killer must have played some part in this change. Aside from their CEO, Park Taesang, they had only a young guy and two middle-aged women working there, and since the oldest of them, Mrs Shim Eunok, had been hired, the Happy Detective Agency's jobs had plummeted.

Until recently, even quick-witted Mr Na hadn't realized that an ajumma killer was the reason for the decline in business. Rumour had it that Smile's newest killer was the second coming of Park Taesang, that his long-lost daughter had returned as a cold-blooded killer with Park's blood flowing through her veins. But the fact that their new killer was an ajumma only came to light thanks to tips from a couple of the younger guys on our staff and our one-eyed regular. That was also around the time when Mr Na's hair started greying in earnest.

The first thing I taught the rookie was how to choose a knife. Foldable knives were easy to carry, but if the target was especially resistant, the blade could fold at the wrong moment and ruin the whole job. So killers used fixed-blade knives, choosing reliability over convenience. Aside from kitchen knives, even when it came to knives used for hobbies or decoration, you couldn't purchase a knife larger than 15.2 centimetres without a sword-carrying permit. Because of that, if you wanted to buy a knife for a particular purpose, you had to look for Hwang at a certain time and place.

Hwang had completely lost his vision in one eye. He'd been captured by the Viet Cong during the Vietnam War and had his right eye gouged out with a survival knife. After the US military turned the tides of the war and saved his life, he was able to return home to Korea, where he sought out a famous blind acupuncturist and volunteered to study under him. Not long after that, he opened up an acupuncture clinic called Tào Lao that faced the front gates of his teacher's home and started bringing in money.

'I didn't know any words aside from *tào lao*. What does it mean? To go nuts. To be out of your damn mind.'

He lived with a woman thirty years younger than him. He owned several buildings and luxury cars, but what gave him the most joy were the knives gleaming inside his glass display. The survival knife that had taken his eye out had been the last thing that eye had seen of the world, and it was the only thing that shone fully in Hwang's world where everything was halved.

'His footsteps are very heavy. And he smells nice. Like fresh bamboo shoots. You've brought me a decent kid.'

Hwang was carefully cleaning the handles and blades of his knife, a jet-black dagger.

'He's a rookie. Please choose something suitable for him. Like a Burke or a Gerber.'

Both companies put out lots of popular daggers, and the quality wasn't incredible, but they were cheap and good to use. The knife Mr Na had taken to Hwang and had my name engraved on was also one of those.

'You have to make good friends first. What do you think of this one?'

Hwang held up a knife made by an expert American craftsman.

'Can I touch it?' asked the rookie. His eyes were wide with fear and wonder, like a kid just starting primary school, as he reached for the knife.

'He doesn't even know how to wield a knife yet,' I said. I couldn't entrust such a pricey knife to a novice.

'You sound just like a teacher. Mr Na told me to give it to him. So hurry up and take it. My head's pounding. The aftereffects of all that napalm, I guess.'

Hwang oiled the knife, slipped it into its leather holder and held it out to me, then rubbed his temple as he turned on the radio. We left Hwang's shop, driven out by the sound of the radio host's boisterous laugh.

'An incredible knife, isn't it?'

The rookie tapped the pocket he'd slipped the knife into. Even though the kid had somehow ended up with an expensive knife like this, I knew there was no way Mr Na would have given such a pricey, renowned knife to a rookie who still had his baby hair if there wasn't a secret plot being cooked up.

'To a novice who doesn't know how to wield them, what's the difference between that blade and a toy knife?'

Back at the detective agency's office, I taught the kid how to hold a knife.

'If you stick up your index finger like that, you could end up cutting off all four of your other fingers. When you hold the knife, loosen up your ring finger, as you stab, put all the strength into that index finger. Straighten your back muscles and your arms!'

For his first time, his posture was quite good. If he just adjusted the angles of his arms once he was in that state, he could dig into any organ on the body, no problem.

'When the knife gets stuck in the muscle, it won't be easy to pull it out. Open up some space with the knife and then yank it out the same way you drove it in.'

When I first learned how to use knives from Mr Na, we had a freshly slaughtered pig in front of us. Mr Na stood with his arms crossed and ordered me to take out the pig's heart. I was drenched in cold sweat. I stabbed into the flank of the pig, removed the hide and opened up the flesh to successfully pull out the destroyed liver and pancreas, but I couldn't find the heart. Mr Na took the knife from me, turned the pig's head to the side, cut it off, and made another cut from the front leg to the bottom. Then he rolled his sleeves up to the forearms and plunged his hand inside the flesh of the pig's front leg. Without digging through flesh or breaking bones like I had done, he pulled out the heart, as big as two fists, in one swift motion.

'Look, hyung. Look what you did to the pig. I told you to find the heart and you mutilated its entire body. If this were a person, you would be covered in his blood and surrounded by police.'

The rookie was dozing off under the sun. He hadn't gone home in several days, busy learning to walk without making a sound and disable CCTVs and alarms.

'Why are you putting so much effort into that kid?' I asked.

Mr Na was absently watching the rookie.

'Because that knife of his is aimed at Mr Park,' he said.

By Mr Park, I knew he meant Park Taesang. The legendary killer. If I'd met Mr Park before Mr Na, I might have gone to work for him instead. He was the object of my longtime admiration, an idol whose light never faded in my eyes.

'He's a beginner who just learned how to hold a knife,' I said.

'If you want to take the knife from your enemy's hand, don't you have to cut off his wrist? The kid's already accepted my offer. Let's wait and see how he does.'

Park Taesang had a good knife called Shim Eunok. Could it be that Mr Na was trying to get rid of Mr Park by taking away his prized weapon? Still, I couldn't understand why in the world Mr Na would entrust that task to a newbie.

'When the kid wakes up, tell him to start by digging up information on Park Taesang. Where he lives, who he lives with, where he eats, who he hangs out with, how he goes about his day, in detail.'

Once Mr Na had left the office, the rookie slowly woke up from his nap. The knife handle had left an impression on his cheek. I told him what Mr Na had said and gave him a transportation card. He wolfed down some clam noodle soup he'd had delivered and left to go and investigate Park Taesang. It was only after the sun began to set that he called the office to say it didn't look like he'd make it back that day. He didn't come back the next day either. On the morning of the fourth day, he finally came in carrying a stack of documents.

'I went down to the Labour Office and checked the business registration number used on the Smile Detective Agency's local ads and had a personal ID number come up. But for some reason, the business wasn't registered in his own name. The person listed was a man in his sixties named Oh Gilsoo.'

I didn't know who Oh Gilsoo was, but I could guess why Park hadn't used his own name to set up the agency. Most killers had cut ties with their families and thus were presumed dead, and in some cases, they would even have a dead homeless person buried in their name. Whatever the case, the intention was the same: to avoid being fingerprinted and to expand their range of movement. Maybe the name he was known by, Park Taesang, wasn't even his real name.

'Is that all?'

If Mr Na found out that this was all the investigation into Mr Park had yielded, he'd be sorely disappointed.

'I went through the trash at Smile, too. Most of it was useless, but I found some receipts. Have a look. It seems like they buy most of their groceries from the Durimoa Mart, and sometimes they buy fishing equipment and books. But there was one much bigger expense I found. I think Park Taesang has a child.'

A child? It was the first time I was hearing about this. Rumour had it that he'd been avoiding women and living alone ever since he'd experienced an awful heartbreak.

'What's your evidence?'

The rookie handed me a crumpled-up receipt. It was a lump sum credit card payment for 4,450,000 won.

'He must have paid a university registration fee. I'm on a leave of absence, but the cost for next semester's tuition is similar. He's old enough to have a child in uni, isn't he?'

All that was known about Park Taesang was that he'd worked in a sashimi centre kitchen for a little while when he was younger, which was where he'd learned his knife skills. No one knew his whereabouts during his twenties. If he had a child, he could have had a wife, too, but for a killer, a family was nothing but a set of shackles that hindered you. It was the same for Mr Na. He had a wife, Hong Misook, but they didn't have a child. Misook was a beautician who ran two salons on the city's main street, but she and Mr Na had long been estranged.

'Is there nothing else?'

'I tried to follow him, but I don't have a car, and I didn't think the transportation card would work for that. Also, I was scared he'd notice.'

There were dark shadows beneath the rookie's eyes. It seemed like he hadn't eaten or slept properly in days.

'You can head home early today,' I said. 'And when you come in tomorrow, make sure you have all your practice knives sharpened until they shine. If they can't cut through paper in a single stroke, you're going to have a hard time.'

The rookie stashed his knife holder in his bag and bowed before he left.

All afternoon, I couldn't stop thinking about Park Taesang's hidden child. Maybe it wasn't really his child, but some uni student, still wet behind the ears, that he'd hired as a killer like Mr Na had done, or else maybe Mr Park was paying some poor high school student's tuition fees.

'Still no word from the rookie today?' Mr Na asked when he clocked in around sundown.

'I sent him home for the day. But that kid – he said something interesting earlier.'

I shared the information the rookie had dug up.

'Well, it's not impossible,' said Mr Na. He didn't look at all surprised. He studied the receipt the kid had brought me with a bored expression. Then he sent me home and stayed behind in the office, alone with the lights out. I gave up on my plans to head home, order some Chinese food for delivery, and watch *The Killer*. Instead, I started walking towards the Smile Detective Agency. If I imagined someone as the main character in *The Killer*, Park Taesang was a better fit than Na Hancheol. Unlike other contract killers, Mr Park wouldn't simply kill anyone. Like how Ah Jong had said, 'I thought I'd only kill bad people, not good people, but it isn't that easy.' I wondered what Mr Park's secret was.

I decided to follow him. I wanted to know everything about him – whether he had a child who was in uni, and if he did, whether that meant he really had been married, whether he lived in an apartment or a single-family house, how much his monthly mortgage payment was and how many years were left until he paid it off.

Just as I got to the intersection with the gingko trees where Smile was located, I saw Mr Park leaving the building and getting into his car. Behind him were two middle-aged women and a young guy who politely bid them farewell before the women walked towards the bus stop.

I stayed close behind Mr Park. He drove through downtown and into the suburbs. He entered a satellite city crowded with apartments and stopped at a Durimoa Mart to pick up a few items before he got back in his car and started driving again. He drove on for a while, passing through the forest of apartment buildings. It was rare to see houses on the national highways, but there were plenty of low mountains and paths between the rice paddies. At some point, the road became unpaved dirt, and at the end of the dirt path was a low mountain blocking the way. Suddenly, Mr Park pulled over and put on his hazard lights. If he wanted to get out, there was no other way but to put the car in reverse. Too late, I realized I had fallen right into a trap. Mr Park got out of his car and approached me, gesturing with his hand. His hazard lights blinked in the darkness.

'Did Hancheol send you?'

I really wanted to tell him that wasn't the case. For a killer, murder never had a personal aim. A client's request was the only thing that would make him brandish his knife. Even though I worked for Mr Na, I would never become his personal weapon unless he requested it.

I got out of my car.

'No,' I told him. 'I came here for personal reasons. My name is Park Hyunsuk.'

In between the flashes of his hazard lights, I saw Mr Park's lips twitch.

'What are your reasons?' he asked. I could hear a trot song in four-four time playing from inside his car.

'I want to know more about you,' I said.

'Why?'

'Because I've been admiring you from afar.'

This was the truth. I did admire him. Like I admired Ah Jong, someone I could never meet. Mr Park moved closer to me, as if being pulled.

'Perfect. There's something I'm curious about, too. What do you want to know?'

I wanted to ask him where he lived and with whom, and why he had become a killer, but my lips wouldn't move. *If I hadn't met Na Hancheol, I would have wanted to learn to use knives from you* – the words crumbled in my mouth like grains of sand and just sat there, rough, on my tongue.

'I gave you an opportunity, but you have nothing to say,' Mr Park observed. 'So, can I ask *you* something?'

I nodded.

'Why does Na Hancheol want to kill me?'

Somehow, Mr Park had found out that he was Mr Na's target.

'Probably because he doesn't want to split his turf with you, no?'

I was sure that Mr Na had other reasons, but I didn't know exactly what they were.

'If that were the only reason, he would have asked to negotiate first. It wouldn't be the worst if we took on joint orders and allocated them. But instead he sent a killer. A killer who's considered the best in the industry.'

My vision began to grow blurry. I had just wanted to know more about Mr Park, but I wasn't qualified to be the spokesperson for the Happy Detective Agency.

'That kid is just a rookie,' I said. 'He's just now learning how to wield knives. He's never been in a real fight.'

Mr Park's face grew shadowed. He raised an eyebrow.

'A rookie, you said? At the Happy Detective Agency?'

I slipped a hand into my pocket. I found my jackknife and gripped it tight. But Mr Park was quicker. His strong arms were already around my neck, squeezing. I was flailing to get out of his grip, using all my strength just to breathe.

'Tell me his name!' Mr Park shouted.

I took out my knife and swung it, but Mr Park kept his grip tight around my throat as he expertly dodged the blade.

'Kim – Kim Jinseob,' I choked out.

He let out a low groan when I said the kid's name. He dragged me over to his car and rummaged through the bags of stuff he'd bought at the mart until he found a small awl. In the meantime, I'd wounded his left arm with my knife, but he didn't react at all.

'So it wasn't Mrs Shim, but her son . . .' he murmured.

What was he talking about? Had he thought the person sent to kill him all this time was Mrs Shim? And wait – Kim Jinseob was Mrs Shim's son? Which meant that Mr Na had known and still planned to use the kid to target Mr Park. My vision went black, and not just because it was dark out.

Mr Park had stabbed me below the collarbone with the awl.

He got inside my car and started up the engine, then opened up the fuel tank, inserted a thin piece of cloth and lit the end on fire. As I lay bleeding out on the dirt, I had a feeling that the car was about to blow up.

I realized then that in all the time I had been living as a killer, I hadn't once thought seriously about death.

My father thought I was a teacher in Seoul. Or more accurately, he was pretending to believe that. I never got into the uni I would have needed to attend, and I was always covered in wounds, big and small. My father never asked me what I really did for work. When I went down to spend a few months in my hometown, claiming school had let out for the break, he would pretend not to see the low table I had set out in front of my closed door and just push it aside, coming and going as he pleased.

The middle school I'd gone to had shuttered on account of corruption among its board. My father, who had bad knees and shoulders, was now making his living keeping the charcoal grills lit in the grilled duck restaurant the principal went on to run. He would brag to people about his teacher son with tears in his eyes, likely due to the smoke.

Now that my vision had gone completely black, I felt sorry that I couldn't buy my father new shoes to replace his old ones with the worn heels. But what could I do? My father wouldn't have had anywhere to go in his new shoes anyway.

I heard a voice in my head. *Whenever the sun rises and whenever it sets, countless people die, but today is our turn.*

It was a line from *The Killer*. I moved my lips, trying to say the lines, but no sound came out. Only a burst of red blood.

13

Shim Eunok

The Happy Detective Agency's veteran killer, Park Hyun-suk, drove out of the heart of the city and on to the national highway. He was tailing *our* agency's Mr Park, and me and Joongi were tailing *him*.

'This is how you tail people. You have to keep as much distance as possible so the other person doesn't notice you, but you also have to keep them in your line of sight. Usually when I'm doing some private investigation into cheating spouses, I'll tail them by car, so I'm used to it now,' Joongi said.

If my hunch was right, Mr Park would have already caught on to the fact that he was being followed. In other words, he was trapping Park Hyunsuk. He slowed down more than necessary to stay within Hyunsuk's line of sight as he turned down a road leading to a remote mountain. Joongi pulled over on the side of the road and rested his chin on the backs of his hands. A moment later, flames shot up from inside the shadows of the mountain where the two men had disappeared.

'That's not like Mr Park.'

Mr Park, who'd caught a big fish like the skilled Duke Tai of Qi, was walking calmly away from the scene. Some mountain birds, startled by the explosion, fluttered up and away.

My son Jinseob had an unusual habit. When he told a lie, he would hurry to give the person he'd lied to one of his prized possessions. One day, when I asked him where his eraser and pencil sharpener and game cartridge were, he wouldn't look up as he told me he'd given them to his friend as a birthday gift. At first, I thought he was being bullied at school or else had gotten his things taken from him by a stronger kid, and I was angry. But the next morning, when I saw Jinseob's piggy bank on the nightstand next to my bed, I realized – he hadn't given his things away as birthday presents. He'd given them away out of guilt. After I scolded him for it, Jinseob became an overly honest kid.

His homeroom teachers used that to their advantage. Because Jinseob only ever told the truth, whenever the teachers asked him about his classmates' misbehaviour, he would tell them everything. That was more or less why he had no friends, but he liked doing things on his own anyway, so he never seemed to be especially lonely.

As of late, though, he'd started acting suspiciously.

After he finished his military service, he stopped spending time at home and was always out roaming the streets. Once he started work at his new part-time job, his hours weren't fixed, and he spent more and more days out. On top of that, even when it wasn't a special occasion, he would give Jina his treasured smartband or gift vouchers that were still far from expiring.

I knew without a doubt that Kim Jinseob was hiding something from me. Seeing young people around his age all dressed up and hanging around the red-light districts made me realize that the world was a place where if you had a young body, you could easily make money. I was afraid that Jinseob, like those other young people, was off somewhere doing something he shouldn't be doing. But I didn't have any clear reason to scold him.

How could I tell someone else off when I was buying rice and making kimchi with the money I earned from committing murders?

Meanwhile, I'd carried out four contract killings.

I'd slit the throat of a man who'd abandoned his lover, a pure-hearted girl, and gotten married. I'd torn open the stomach of the head of a multi-level marketing scheme who'd bankrupted a family and driven them to suicide. A sex offender who'd been acquitted and a vicious loan shark had also died by my hands.

On those days, I would get home and wash my hands for a long time. Even when I knew there was no blood left on them, I would scrub my palms with an exfoliating towel and even brush my fingernails clean with an old toothbrush. And still, I would wear rubber gloves as I washed the rice. I didn't want to leave any traces of slaughter in the food I was going to feed my children.

Jinseob rarely ate at home now that he'd started his new part-time job. He came home at dawn and barely stayed for five hours before he was rushing out again. He must have been sleep-deprived, but he still made sure to shower twice a day. This led to him and Jina having more arguments over her needing to get ready for school in the morning, too, and what he was doing that it took him so long to shower anyway.

One Sunday morning when all three of us were home for the

first time in a while, Jina shouted at him, 'What the heck? Were you really showering? Your hair isn't even wet.'

Sure enough, Jinseob's hair was dry and matted. He brought up his towel to cover it, eyes wide in surprise. That was when I spotted a small leather pouch that had been hidden underneath the towel. And for a brief moment, I heard the quiet but familiar clang of metal on metal coming from inside that pouch. It was the same sound I made every morning in the bathroom to start the day as the kids headed out. Every time I looked at the gleaming blade of a sharpened knife, I felt a chill run through me at the thought that no matter how much time went by, I would never be able to bring myself to like the sight of it.

Jinseob hid the leather pouch behind his back and turned around. As I was staring at him, the three fried eggs I had on the stove started to burn, black smoke rising from the pan.

Jinseob had been a good kid and had never given me a hard time. He'd made me happy by getting into a prestigious university without having to retake the college entrance exam, and he'd been earning his own money working part-time since his first year. Though he wasn't especially affectionate, he would wait for me at the bus stop on days when I got home late from work and silently walk home with me as if he were my guardian. My suspicions about him felt like a punishment for all the murders I had carried out. I hoped it all turned out to be a misunderstanding, a mother's needless worrying. But Jinseob's behaviour was only making me more and more anxious.

He had tiny blisters on the inside of his index finger that made it hard for him to hold a spoon. The blisters that had already burst and begun to heal left little wounds that made my heart ache. This was a common symptom for someone learning to wield a knife for the first time. And that wasn't the only thing that made me suspicious. Ever since he'd started his latest job, Jinseob, who used to love the colour red, went around wearing only dark clothes all the time now. When he went outside in the hot, humid weather, he always brought leather gloves with him. I couldn't simply overlook this.

So I decided to follow Jinseob.

I got up before him and hid behind the recycling area in the apartment complex. Around the time the sun was coming up, Jinseob left the house wearing a baseball cap pulled low over his face. This kid seemed somehow like a stranger. His eyes, which I'd always seen as gentle, had a fierce glint to them, and he moved with force whereas I'd always thought he was gangly and lacking muscle. He was loitering around the entrance when a car with tinted windows pulled up. I had already started getting more far-sighted in my old age, so I needed my glasses to read the number on the licence plate. But by the time I found them in my bag and put them on, the car had already disappeared.

It wasn't often that you saw employers come to pick up their part-timers from home. If my suspicions were true, Jinseob was risking his life for this job. A job where he had to wager his life for the promise of a ton of money, where he had to sharpen knives every morning until they gleamed, where blisters formed on every inch of his hands.

Most private detective agencies didn't do murders-for-hire. They made their living doing errands of a sort, things people couldn't bring themselves to do but also couldn't leave alone to fester like an abscess. According to Mr Park, he could count on his fingers the number of people in the entire country who did the work we did. That was because when one of them got caught, the others followed one after another, like a game of hot potato, so even though there was plenty of work, there was no one brave enough to take it on. That was why, to become a killer, you had to work alone and know how to calculate in detail a number of different kinds of cases. Which meant that the only person who could be considered a rival of Mr Park's was the CEO of the Happy Detective Agency. I'd never seen him, but I knew that he was steadily growing his influence by directly competing with Smile at close range. One day, on my way back from working outside the office, I saw Mr Park's car stopped for a moment outside the Happy Detective Agency and Mr Park with a bitter smile on his face.

I stuck a few patches on my aching knee and went to the Happy Detective Agency. I had to transfer buses twice and

walk for a while under the blaring sun, and, parked outside, I found the same car with the tinted windows that I had seen pull up to the entrance of the apartment complex that morning. A cold sweat ran down my back. Even though I had vaguely pieced together what was going on, I couldn't just barge inside. I needed definitive proof. I bought some fishcakes from a snack cart nearby and sat eating them as I watched people come and go.

'Ma'am, does anyone from the Happy Detective Agency ever stop by here for fishcakes?'

The woman running the cart who looked to be about my age laughed so hard that her wrinkles deepened.

'They buy fishcakes, rice cakes, you name it. There's a young man in particular who comes by every morning for ddeokbokki.'

'What does he look like?' I asked.

The woman scooped up some seasoning from a box and ladled a generous amount into the ddeokbokki.

'He's a young kid. Handsome, too. But ma'am, did you come here to do some private investigating? A lot of those types come by. What does it matter about his looks? Is it easier to find someone if he's good-looking?'

I picked up another fishcake skewer.

'Oh, Happy's most eligible bachelor is here again today.'

The street cart owner grinned, stirring around the ddeokbokki. I looked over, and there was Jinseob, standing next to me like something out of a dream.

'What are you doing here?' I asked.

Jinseob looked at me in surprise. 'What are *you* doing here, Mum?'

At a loss for words, I stuffed a half-eaten fishcake in my

mouth. Tears even hotter than the fishcake broth were spilling down my face.

'I was thinking about running a food cart,' I said. 'I heard the fishcakes here were delicious, so I came to check it out.'

The owner glanced at me with a disapproving look.

'Well, I'm here to run an errand,' Jinseob said, 'since I work close by.'

His earlobes were bright red.

'You want three servings of ddeokbokki and five fishcake skewers to go, right? The Happy Detective Agency folks are regulars here, so I remember. And I'll throw in some soondae for free,' said the owner, slicing the soondae into pieces.

'You work at a private detective agency?' I asked.

Jinseob looked embarrassed. I kept chewing the fishcake, not even registering the flavour any more.

'I just do errands. That's it, I swear. It's not what you think, Mum.'

The black leather pouch I had seen him wearing at home was around his waist. It had to be a knife holder. The whetstone he'd been using to sharpen his knife every morning was the same one I had been using all along.

'Of course,' I said. 'You're my son. I know you wouldn't do anything bad. I'm about to get going. Will you be home late again?'

The food cart owner handed Jinseob a bag with all the food in it. He hesitated after counting his money.

'I won't be home tonight,' he said. 'I'm the youngest, so it can't be helped. But they have a night-duty room where I can sleep, so don't worry.'

Jinseob held out ten thousand won to me.

'I have money,' I told him, but he wouldn't take the money back until I forgave him for his lies. I silently took the money from his hand. He scratched the back of his head and chewed on his lip before disappearing inside the Happy Detective Agency building.

I needed to calm down. First, I had to find out what sort of work Jinseob was doing at the agency. I bought a broom and a rice sack at the hardware store, a mask and a head towel at the convenience store, and a work uniform at the clothing store. Then I sat outside the convenience store under an outdoor umbrella and waited until evening when there weren't many people left inside the building. If I disguised myself as a janitor and went inside, it would be easy enough to sniff out what they were up to.

Aside from the Happy Detective Agency, the building was mainly occupied by study rooms and cram schools, so it was easy to tell who among the people coming and going weren't students. After five o'clock, a sturdy-looking middle-aged man came out of the building. Even with my glasses on, it was hard to get a good look at his face, and since I didn't know what the CEO looked like, I could only guess it was him. Around seven-thirty p.m., another man in a suit came out. Judging from the car he got into, the one with the tinted windows, he must have been the one who'd picked up Jinseob that morning.

I waited until eight o'clock, but all I could see were crowds of students rushing into the study rooms after classes. The lights still hadn't gone out in the second-floor windows of the Happy Detective Agency. I changed into my janitor's uniform in the convenience store bathroom and put on the mask and head towel. Then I went inside the building, quieting my shaky steps.

After climbing the stairs littered with torn ice cream wrappers and scraps of tissue, I stood, heart pounding, before the detective agency office, which didn't have a sign.

I took a deep breath and opened the door. Heavy metal music was blasting. Jinseob, who'd been leaning back in a swivel chair with his feet up on the desk, suddenly sat up straight. A sharp dagger fell from his hands to the floor. He hurriedly picked up the knife and stashed it. I lowered my head and hunched over as much as I could to hide my face and called out, 'Cleaning!'

I went through the trash can near each desk and dumped its contents into my rice sack.

As I was emptying the second one, Jinseob came towards me. 'I'll empty the trash,' he said.

I turned around and left the office before Jinseob could take another step. He shouted something after me from inside, but he was drowned out by the sound of chatter coming from the students heading up to the study room on the third floor.

Maybe because of the shock, my bladder, which hadn't been giving me too much trouble lately, gave out on me all of a sudden. The bottoms of my uniform were soaked through. The back of my neck stiffened, and my face was hot. I leaned against the wall and made my way slowly down the stairs. Outside, I feebly held out my hand. A taxi pulled up beside me, but when the driver saw a janitor holding a sack of trash, he slammed down on the accelerator again and sped away. I had no choice but to drag myself to the Smile Detective Agency, as it was closer than my house. I had some of my blood pressure medication there, and that way, Jina wouldn't be suspicious.

I took the local bus to the intersection with the ginkgo trees and got off just as Mr Park must have been heading home, as

I spotted him accepting a salute from the security guard at the building's entrance. Mr Park hurried over and took the sack of trash I was holding.

'I was worried when I didn't hear from you,' he said. His voice was surprisingly gentle for a man who had once had the world in the palm of his hand.

'I was on a bit of a stakeout. Sorry for not being in touch. I have something to check on at the office, so you should get going first.'

I didn't want him to find out about Jinseob's job or to notice my sopping wet trousers. He carried the sack up to the office and put on the lights for me.

'You don't look so good,' he said. 'You should rest tomorrow.'

He bowed and left.

I opened my desk drawer and took out my blood pressure medication, swallowing the pills dry. I sat down in my chair and took deep breaths until my vertigo began to subside. I wiped away the cold sweat with my sleeves, then dragged over the sack of trash and dumped it out on the floor. Most of what was inside was regular old rubbish, but there were a few receipts and scribbled notes. One of them was a crumpled piece of paper that looked like it had been ripped out of a spiral notebook. 'Rules for Dealing with Park Taesang.' It was Jinseob's handwriting.

1. He's good with knives, so must drug him beforehand
2. Track his family members' and employees' movements
3. Have Russian arms ready just in case
4. Once handled, report to immediate supervisor (not by phone)

5. Check the schedule for the Ilshin Shopping Centre Co-op's summer outing

My head was spinning. It was clear from the memo that 'dealing with' Mr Park meant murdering him. How could a kid who'd never used anything sharper than a shaving razor take on a seasoned killer? On top of that, there was something crucial missing from this list of rules – what to do, how to keep himself safe, if the plan failed.

When a killer failed to carry out the task, they usually tried to run away. To ensure the safety of their family and colleagues, they would hide out on an island or in a temple where no one could find them. But when a killer failed to take down one of his own kind? That was a different story. Mr Park would surely track Jinseob down and make him pay for daring to aim a knife at him. But even knowing this, I didn't have the courage to stop my son. I was afraid that if I confessed to him who I was – what I was – and told him to wash his hands clean of me, I would be cast out of our family forever.

There was one way to stop my son from becoming a murderer or a fugitive, and that was to take out Mr Park before Jinseob could. At the thought of trading one life for a life more precious to me, I began to cry. I reached for a tissue on the desk, and my fingers brushed a piece of paper. It was a note from Mr Park. 'I didn't mean to see it, but I noticed your son's tuition bill and paid it last week.' At the bottom of the note was a receipt for the cost of my son's enrolment fee.

Not long after I started working here, Mr Park had asked me until when I wanted to do this. I told him that once my son had graduated from college, I wouldn't look back. Of course, my daughter would be in college by then, and afterwards, the two of them would have to find their own life partners, but in a few years, I figured I would be able to open up a small store without having any more debt. I said all this with a smile on my face, and Mr Park had looked at me with a calm expression, but he couldn't seem to hide how sorry he felt for me. He must have been cowed by the guilt of making someone else into a killer to avoid getting blood on his own hands. I was grateful to Mr Park, but there was no other way for me to protect my son.

I was an anxious mess. First, I went to the phone store and requested location tracking for Jinseob's phone. Then later at home, as Jinseob was showering after work, I opened his leather pouch and wrote down the kind of knife he had and the signature on it. It was clear as crystal that Jinseob was the one meant to deal with Mr Park. I bought the same knife online and had the Chinese characters for the Happy Detective Agency engraved on it. But there was still so much I didn't know about Mr Park. Where he lived and with whom, or even why he couldn't quit this line of work. The only thing I did know about him was his birthday, which may or may not have been real.

Mr Park didn't go out with friends or out to the red-light districts and such. That made it hard to find an opening to take advantage of. So I'd planned to get him drunk under the pretence of throwing him a birthday party, after which I would follow him home and take him out. I'd even raised the money by doing part-time work with my coworkers to avoid raising suspicion. But then we'd had an unexpected guest show up at dinner – the police. They barged into the restaurant with their weapons, having been tipped off somehow. I'd had to stash the knife under the chair at the restaurant in case they searched me.

Mr Park wasn't an easy adversary. Perhaps he was already aware of my intentions. I guessed that was why Joongi had asked to stay with me for a month out of the blue. If he needed somewhere to sleep, there was a couch in the office, or he could have rented one of the cheap rooms meant for students to live in while they studied for exams, but Joongi had insisted on staying at my place. If I'd turned him down, it would have seemed more suspicious, so I'd put him up in my son's room and decided to quietly observe his movements.

It was past midnight, and Jinseob still hadn't come home. I was on my way to the bathroom when Joongi's voice stopped me.

'Mrs Shim, you know everything, don't you?'

'My goodness, you scared me,' I said.

'You know what your son is up to,' Joongi pressed.

Joongi wanted to become a killer, but Mr Park never gave him a knife. No matter how much Joongi pestered him and acted coy, nothing changed. I'd vaguely thought the way Mr Park treated Joongi resembled a father's love towards his son. Though he couldn't be a killer, Joongi was hardworking and quick-witted as an investigator. As skilled as he was, it wouldn't have taken him much effort to figure out what Jinseob had been up to.

'I don't know what you're talking about, Joongi,' I said. 'It's late. You'd better get some sleep.'

'I heard that the Happy Detective Agency got a new killer recently. As you know, that killer is Jinseob. The problem is that his target is Mr Park.'

It was too exact to be a mere guess. I let out a startled sound without realizing.

'Does Mr Park know that, too?'

'Mr Park thinks *you're* the one targeting him.'

At least it seemed Jinseob's cover hadn't yet been blown.

'I'm begging you,' I said. 'Don't mention Jinseob to him!'

At some point I had gotten down on my knees and clasped my hands together.

'Mrs Shim, what are you doing? You'll wake up Jina.' Joongi came towards me, grasping both of my hands tightly in his. 'I have a plan I'm confident won't fail. A plan that will let us save both Mr Park and Jinseob.'

'What is it? Tell me!'

'You know Mr Baek, right? He's brought us a big case this time. It'll probably be announced tomorrow during the morning meeting, but it looks like he's planning to make Happy and Smile compete for it. We're leaving for an island under the guise of a company outing, and once we get there, we'll probably run into the Happy Detective Agency folks. We'll have to strike first. If you take out Mr Na, we can save Jinseob and Mr Park. Don't you think?'

Why hadn't I thought of that? If we only got rid of the Happy Detective Agency's CEO, we could protect both of the people most precious to us. I hugged Joongi. The kind-hearted boy who had forgiven me for planning to kill the man who was like a father to him, the boy who had supported me, gently patted me on the back.

We gathered in the conference room in the morning, same as any other day, and ate the breakfast I had brought along. The only thing that was different was that everyone mostly stared in silence at the empty bowls afterwards, our mouths pressed shut.

'We got a request from Mr Baek. The target is the chairman

of the Ilshin Shopping Centre Co-op, and he's leaving for Bodeok Island in a week for a company outing. We're in a bit of a difficult situation, as Mr Baek has hired both the Smile and Happy Detective Agencies for the job with the goal of having us compete. The first team to successfully take the chairman out gets the money, and the outcome can have a big impact on our business. We need to prove we are the best. Mrs Shim, will you be all right on such a long trip?'

Mr Park had finished his food first and now looked at me expectantly.

'It's fine with me. I'll get ready,' I said.

His face was deeply shadowed. Mr Park dabbed his mouth clean with a tissue and left the office. Hardly any calls came in that afternoon, and Ms Lee was starting to doze. Joongi and I exchanged looks, reaffirming our plans. Mr Park returned to the office after six o'clock, tidied up his desk, and handed Ms Lee some receipts.

'All right, let's head home,' said Mr Park, putting on his jacket.

'Wait!' said Ms Lee, raising a hand. 'Shouldn't I follow you out?'

Mr Park stopped in his tracks. 'I think you should watch over things here at the office, Ms Lee,' he said. 'You never know when there will be someone calling with an enquiry.'

Outside the building, Mr Park bowed his head in greeting before he got into his car. As Joongi and I walked towards the bus stop, he nudged me in my side.

'What?'

He was looking over at a car with dark, tinted windows.

'That's the killer from Happy Detective Agency. As soon as Mr Park got in his car, this one started up the engine. Looks like they're planning to tail him. We should follow after them.'

Joongi and I headed back towards the building, leaving Ms Lee, who'd been walking ahead of us and talking to someone on the phone, on her own. Joongi rushed up to the security booth and called out for Mr Kim.

'Mr Kim, can I borrow the OK Karaoke Bar owner's car for a bit?'

Mr Kim adjusted his glasses with a frown.

'If I let you do that, I'll never hear the end of it,' he said. 'That's outside my purview.'

Mr Park's car was slowly leaving the intersection. My heart was racing.

'You're on our special task force and you can't even do this one thing for us? We're tracking someone down!'

Kim Seokbong, the only one around who knew the Smile Detective Agency's true identity, had been assigned to a special task force by Mr Park a few months earlier after what could only be described as a tantrum that was very nearly a threat. He'd even been receiving a little bonus pay for his efforts.

'You should have said so sooner,' he said.

With a sudden air of duty, Mr Kim opened a drawer and took out the car keys, handing them over.

'It's the Equus. I'm sticking my neck out here for you, so be careful!'

Joongi and I rushed to get in the car. Mr Park's car had already disappeared, but the Happy Detective Agency killer's car still hadn't left the intersection. Joongi took out a pair of the karaoke bar owner's sunglasses from the glove compartment and put them on to cover his eyes.

Given all his years of experience, Joongi's tailing skills were excellent. Keeping the car hidden behind trucks and buses, we followed our targets. Then, about two hundred metres from the foot of the mountain, we watched the Happy Detective Agency killer's car blow up. Sparks flashed across Joongi's sunglasses.

'What's the CEO of the Happy Detective Agency like?' I asked out of curiosity.

Joongi turned back towards the road we'd come up. Sirens wailed in the distance. 'I have no idea,' he said. 'I hear he comes from a gangster background, but that he looks like pickled radish.'

'The killer – do you think Happy sent him?'

'I don't know, but what I do know is that Mr Park sensed there was something going on and started taking action.'

By the time we pulled up to the entrance of the apartment complex, it was already late at night. Joongi looked up at my apartment, which had its lights off, and let out a sigh. I saw him off and got into the elevator, exhausted. If our plan failed, this was a path I would never step foot on again.

With the outing to Bodeok Island drawing nearer, I became more diligent. I washed the blankets and curtains I had been putting off washing and wiped down the windowsills until there wasn't a speck of dust on them. The cleaner the house became, the messier my own emotions grew. And suddenly, everything was only one day away. Jina came back from tutoring after midnight. My poor daughter's shoulders were slumped from fatigue.

'Mum, are you making beef bone soup?'

The soup I'd made earlier was in several glass food storage containers. In total, there were twenty-eight portions, which meant there was enough for both kids to eat for nearly a month, even if they took some out to heat up for every meal. If things

KANG JIYOUNG

didn't go well, Jina would have to eat it alone, but I couldn't let that happen. I rubbed my burning eyes with my hands and stacked the containers of soup in the freezer.

'What'd you make so much for? I don't even like this soup.'

Jina took off her uniform blouse and tossed it in the laundry basket, then plopped down on the bed.

'Jina, do you know how to make kimchi?'

She peeled off her stockings and her headband, looking up at me with a pure expression on her face.

'Nope,' she said, 'but later on I'll have someone to do it for me, so don't worry.'

I gave her the instructions I'd written down for how to make kimchi, how to stir-fry anchovy, how to boil soybean soup, and other recipes.

'Mum, I'm in my last year of high school. What use is any of this to me?'

'Don't throw those out. Keep them right by your desk. I'll do an inspection later.'

Jina had been half-listening with a pout on her face. Now, she stretched. Her bony shoulders jutted out. I tried to picture her in a wedding dress, but it wasn't easy to imagine. Nowadays, it seemed life wasn't so bad for the unmarried, though.

'Seems like the world could be yours if you only study hard, hm?' I said. 'But that's not true. Women have to get married to be seen as adults, and they have to give birth to be seen as people. So don't treat this as a joke!'

What I'd wanted to say to her was that everything was fine as long as she was happy – I honestly didn't know why the words of such a stubborn old woman had sprung out of me. I had been married, and I'd given birth, yet I couldn't be sure whether

I was indeed an adult or a person. Jina's eyes reddened. I drew her in close, hugging her gaunt shoulders. She trembled in my arms like a little bird.

'Sorry. I'm sorry,' I said.

That night, for the first time in a long time, I let Jina sleep using my arm as a pillow. I thought about the moment Jinseob had taken his first steps, about the day Jina was elected student body president. At the time, I didn't know that was what happiness was. If I'd known, I would have savoured the feeling a little more. As my thoughts continued to go in circles, the day was breaking in the distance. The silhouettes of the furniture and appliances in the house that had been hidden in the darkness began to come into view again. I wanted to run away. I didn't want to aim my knife at anyone. But if I failed, I wouldn't be able to guarantee that Jinseob would make it out with his life. And even if I did manage to save him, I knew I shouldn't expect us to make it out in one piece.

I woke Jina up, made her breakfast, and cleaned up some more. I made some of the side dishes the kids liked, stored them in the fridge, and watered the plants. Before I changed clothes, I realized I should shower first. I wouldn't want whoever might do my autopsy to be uncomfortable. Then again, there was no reason for a butcher to be up in arms over some dirty meat. Still, I took my time in the shower. I wore the new underwear Jinseob had bought me for my birthday the year before and the grey two-piece outfit Jina had picked out. Then, as one last courtesy to myself, I took a cab.

PART THREE

14

The Son

Our killer, Park Hyunsuk, was dead. According to the news reports, his car had blown up at the foot of a mountain on the outskirts of the city. His body was nothing more than a lump of burnt, black coal, but his identity was confirmed by a note found in his glove compartment that read like a will. But because Park Hyunsuk wasn't a Happy Detective Agency employee on paper, the police investigation ended up stalling around his cramped studio apartment and his family back in his hometown before coming to a close.

'If there was a note, does that mean it was a suicide?' I asked.

I'd heard that people who were planning suicide left silent clues for the people around them. But aside from seeming a little more excited than usual, Hyunsuk hadn't been behaving strangely or saying anything all that weird in the days leading up to his death.

Mr Na set down his newspaper. His grey hairs now stood out in dense patches, like the sod laid out over graves in early spring. 'I wouldn't be surprised if he carried something like a will on him, since you never know when you could die in this line of work,' he said.

'Then do you think it's possible he was killed out of spite?'

Mr Na wasn't giving anything away, but judging from his red eyes and puffy face, I could guess what he was feeling.

'It's the police's job to look into that,' he said. 'But more importantly, Hyunsuk's absence leaves you with huge shoes to fill, so you have to be on alert. This Mr Baek case will be the stage where you make your big debut.'

Seeing how he avoided giving a direct answer, it was clear that Mr Na had an idea who had murdered Hyunsuk. If he was thinking the same thing as me, the culprit had to be the Smile Detective Agency's new killer. She was rumoured to be an ajumma in her fifties, but no one had told me anything more than that.

I had gone by the Smile Detective Agency at the intersection with the ginkgo trees several times while investigating Mr Park, but the only women in their fifties I'd seen had been a yoghurt seller, a janitor, and a hawker. Maybe one of them was the new killer, but being a rookie, I couldn't really tell. She may have been an ajumma, but I couldn't help imagining that a true killer would have eyes as frosty as Mr Na's or else a sturdy, strapping build. In the end, though, my image of an ajumma was that of a short woman with a helmet head full of curls. I couldn't picture anyone other than my mum.

My mum, Shim Eunok, who had to start each day with breakfast even if the sky split in two, who wore bathroom slippers out to the mart simply because they were comfortable, who believed that valuables were safest kept in the zipper pocket of her underwear. I pictured my mum lifting up her floral-patterned skirt and pulling out two pistols from holsters on her panties, and I burst out laughing.

'This is no laughing matter,' said Mr Na. 'If you make a mistake, there's no going back. Take this deposit.'

He opened his safe, took out a bank book and a wooden seal and handed them to me. The bank book contained thirty million won. The Mr Baek case was originally going to be handled by Park Hyunsuk. With his sudden death, he had left more than the will behind. He'd also left a bank account full of money. Like a loan where the collateral was my life.

'Is it really fine for me to have this much cash?'

Mr Na opened his newspaper again, glancing up at me where I stood, dumbfounded, before him.

'It's only natural to be scared,' he said.

Three months earlier, Mr Na had offered me a part-time job at a rate of fifty thousand won per day. I had no reason to refuse. It was generous pay for organizing documents and answering phone calls. The job was nowhere near as hard as lugging things around at the construction site or as tiring as standing on my feet all day being harassed by customers.

For the first month, I did nothing but answer phones and sort through a mess of documents as instructed. Mr Na and Hyunsuk used to head out right after clocking in most mornings, so the office was always basically empty. Two months ago I had decided to do the same work as they were doing, the Friday I got my first cheque.

I took my time punching holes in documents and threading them together as I listened to my favourite heavy metal music. Some days I got excited, imagining taking my mum and sister out to a grilled pork galbi restaurant when my first cheque came in. When Mr Na returned to the office after five o'clock, he had a second bag tucked under his arm. He asked me to make him some coffee, then opened the safe and stuffed the second bag inside. He glanced at the wall clock and drummed his fingers on his neat desk. He seemed anxious, like he was waiting for something. At exactly six o'clock, he leapt up and went to the door like he couldn't stand it any more. Right as he reached for the knob, the door swung open. It was Park Hyunsuk.

'You're late,' said Mr Na, sheepishly scratching his head.

'I had to load some things in the trunk,' said Hyunsuk.

I was getting antsy, waiting for Mr Na to hurry and pay us so I could go home. Mr Na opened the safe. I set down coffee for Hyunsuk and sat beside him on the couch. Mr Na came over, but didn't sit. He fumblingly opened his second bag and held out something that glinted in the light.

'The rookie is here . . .' Hyunsuk said, hesitating. He looked back and forth between Mr Na and me. In Mr Na's hands were two gold bars.

'So what? He's one of us now.'

Hyunsuk glanced at me, then took the gold bars and carefully stashed them in the leather bag he always carried around. I was surprised that Hyunsuk, who I'd thought only did background checks or tracked people down, was getting paid two gold bars for a month's work. My mouth hung open as I stared at his leather bag.

'And this is yours,' said Mr Na, taking out a wad of cash and handing it to me. Even without counting, I could tell it was around one million won. I bowed my head and reached out to accept the money.

'I hope you'll understand that your salary will vary depending on the work you do. But there's a little more here than what I promised you.'

I wondered what exactly Hyunsuk did. If it really was background checks and tracking, I could do it, too. Of course, I didn't expect to be paid in gold for that. I just wanted to make sure my family could eat without worrying about debt.

'Um, whatever Hyunsuk does – could I learn to do it, too?'

Mr Na, still standing, finished his coffee and paused, as if lost in thought. His throat quivered, like he was swallowing nothing. Then Mr Na made me an offer that was hard to refuse.

'I'm sure you could learn. Equal opportunity and all that. With a little effort, you could make a ton of money. You could let your mum retire, move into a new house, and live out the rest of your days in luxury. You have to choose between a life of poverty and ordinariness, and a life of high intensity and colour. Make the choice you won't regret in twenty years.'

Mr Na spoke in a friendly tone as he laid out my options. By the time I realized that the gold bars were meant to cover the price of a life, it was already too late to turn back. I sat before two seasoned killers, and in that instant, my life was seized as collateral.

The more I learned about the work of a killer, the more I slowly came to regret my choice. But when I thought about my mum, off somewhere working from early dawn until late at night, not even able to straighten her back, I got a grip on my wavering heart. According to Mr Na and Hyunsuk, most of the targets of these contract killings were people who deserved to die. We dealt with cowards who lived wild and free, committing misdeeds yet hiding inside the blind spots of the law, the ones who would live their entire lives mocking the people they had wronged unless someone took action. And tonight, I was going to do just that – I was going to become a killer.

Mr Baek was a leader in the local community. He owned fifteen buildings in the area, including the building where our agency was located. The Ilshin Shopping Centre, a shopping complex with fifty-nine stores, was the prized yolk at the centre of that area, and Mr Baek had been drooling over it as of late. However, Jung Ilsoo, the chairman of the shopping centre's co-op, famous for being a real fat cat, had goaded the business owners there into quoting absurd prices, effectively blocking Mr Baek's purchase. Mr Baek had invited the business owners from the buildings he did own along with those from the Ilshin Shopping Centre and the other members of the co-op to Bodeok Island for a business outing that morning. His idea was that if we could take out Mr Jung there, he would have a solid alibi when suspicion naturally fell on him, and with the business owners all rattled, he could easily snatch up the shopping centre at last.

'Mr Baek is a highly suspicious man. He made it clear that he would only pay the balance of the fee to the agency that managed to kill Mr Jung first – either us or Smile. Park Taesang and another killer on their side might work together. We may not be able to beat them. But we have a separate goal. The person we're aiming for isn't Mr Jung – it's Park Taesang. Got it?'

The whole reason Mr Na had accepted the request was for this – the chance to take out the Smile Detective Agency and Mr Park.

'If you don't mind my asking, why are we trying to kill Mr Park?'

Mr Na had told me that clients always explained why the target had to die. Of course, the reasoning wasn't what drove

the killer to act, but at least hearing it allowed the killer to protect their conscience and walk around in broad daylight without
hiding their eyes behind sunglasses out of shame.

'The reason he has to die . . . is because he turned an innocent woman into a killer.'

'Do you know who the ajumma killer he hired is?'

Mr Na's eyes were as cold and dark as bronze. 'Park Taesang
is a killer,' he said. 'And what's more is that he taught the art of
killing to a good person. Is that not enough of a reason for him
to die? In a field as small as this one, it's only fair that he who
strikes first survives. Besides, he has no family who will cry for
him, so there's no need to feel bad. If you pull this off, it'll be a
huge blow to the ajumma killer, too. She'll never be able to set
foot in this world, or any world, again.'

Mr Na spoke with such venom that it wasn't hard to imagine
that he was hurling these words at himself. He was a killer, too,
and he was teaching an innocent young person the same art. It
was sad. I even wondered if it wasn't Mr Park that he wanted to
exact his revenge on, but the ajumma killer herself.

'This may be a little off topic, but if her skills are as good as
you say, how about recruiting the ajumma killer yourself?'

'I don't work with people I can't trust.'

Mr Na was about to say something else, but he shut his mouth.

I went home to pack my bags. I found a savings account bank
book in Jina's desk drawer. It had a total of fifty-two thousand
won in it, and no deposits since two years earlier. I went to the
bank to move all the money Mr Na had paid me to Jina's savings. Just in case I didn't come back from Bodeok Island. Then
I shredded the bank book for my now-empty account and went
to find Jina at her usual study room.

Every time I felt her bank book moving around in my inner chest pocket, I flinched. It was the first time in my life I had that much money. Mum had left for the hot springs that morning. Only Jina and the tutor who was living with us for the month were home. The tutor had introduced himself as a student at a prestigious foreign university, but the way he spoke and his behaviour made him seem somehow stuck at Jina's age, and he was extremely awkward. Even worse, the way he looked at Jina struck me as off, so there was no way I was leaving him alone in the house with her without Mum there.

In the study room, Jina sat with her short hair tied up like a bell atop her head, looking down at her phone. When she turned and saw me, her eyes went round and her mouth fell open. 'Let's go,' I mouthed. For the first time in a long time, I walked home with my sister.

'Do you remember the day Dad died?' I asked.

He'd suddenly come to mind. Our father had been a man of legend, an impossibly handsome and irresponsible man who'd driven his family into debt and then left us as though it were no big deal.

'Do you remember?' Jina asked.

'It was right in the middle of midterms, so I was at school until late, and I remember my homeroom teacher was the one who brought me home. Until then, I thought something bad had happened to Mum. Because I'd secretly seen her go into the fridge the night before and take out some soju to drink and some chocolate to go with it. Then she filled the empty soju bottle with plain water, put it back, and went to bed. It was the first time I'd seen Mum drinking alcohol. So I was worried the whole time, thinking something bad had happened to her, only to get to the hospital and see that Mum was fine, and the bad thing had happened to Dad instead.'

Jina looked at me in surprise. She must have remembered Dad's death as a simple drunk driving accident. But now, she was old enough to know the truth. No – she *had* to know.

'Then, he wasn't drunk driving?' Jina asked.

'He had diabetes. He was losing his vision. A blind person behind the wheel *not* ending up in an accident would have been a miracle. Dad's death was a suicide.'

Every time we passed under a streetlamp, I could see tears streaming down Jina's face, tinged orange from the light above.

'You were so young, I didn't want to go into detail about everything with you. But now, you're about to go to uni, and you're a good student, so you should get to live the life you want. If only money weren't an issue.'

I couldn't find a way to tell her about the bank book. The words sat inside my mouth, pricking my tongue like the barbs of hangnails, refusing to come out.

'When I go to uni, I'm going to work part-time, too, so I can pay my share. You don't have to worry about that.'

I reached out and grabbed Jina's wrist as she wiped away her tears.

'I know you'll be great at whatever you do,' I said. 'But to live, you at least need enough money to cover the basics. Housing, food, clothes, transportation. Even those basics would be a huge burden on Mum, though. She can't take on all that alone. So from now on, I've decided I'm going to earn money for us.'

We came to a stop.

'Your bank account has all the money the three of us will need for the essentials.'

I handed her the bank book.

She opened it and checked the balance, the headlights of the passing cars flashing across her face.

'Jinseob, what is this?' she said. 'You're scaring me.'

'Don't worry,' I told her. 'I'm not doing anything so dangerous that you need to be scared. It's easier work than what Mum was doing, chopping meat and mopping floors under those hot, red lights all day. Honestly, my job is pretty much like cleaning, too. This is just a downpayment. I'll get even more money soon. But until then, you have to keep this bank book and my job a secret from Mum. I'll work there for another month at the most and then quit. Until I come back, you have to keep this safe. You're a smart kid, so I trust you'll understand what I'm saying.'

My phone buzzed. It must have been Mr Na. I let go of Jina's wrist. But then she reached for mine.

'When you get home, lock the doors,' I said. 'I already contacted Choi Joongi and set him up with somewhere else to stay for tonight and tomorrow. Get home safe.'

Then I shook my arm free from her grip and took off across the street. My nose stung. My phone started to ring again. But this time, to my surprise, it was my mum calling.

'It's me.'

'Yes, Mum,' I said.

'Have you been running?'

It seemed she could hear me panting even on the other end of the call.

'Did you get there safely?' I asked. I faintly heard someone singing a trot song in the background.

'Yep, we got here and had some raw fish and a bit of soju.' There was a slight tipsiness in her voice.

'Don't worry about us and have fun,' I said. Her breathing blended in with the sound of several people applauding in the background.

'Jinseob!'

'Yes?'

'I have a favour to ask.'

'What is it?' I asked.

'Can you quit your part-time job? Someone I'm really grateful to helped me out and paid your registration fee, and I was able to sort out the security deposit on the apartment. I've got money now. You can just do like the other kids and focus on school.'

My mum's voice choked up at the end.

'Okay,' I said. 'I'll work until the end of this month and then quit. I promise.'

'All right,' she said. 'I've never been able to talk you out of being stubborn before, either, I guess. Jinseob, you said you wanted to become an architect, didn't you? You have to now. You hear me? No matter what, you have to make it happen.'

Mum didn't wait for my reply before ending the call. Maybe she'd hung up because someone there had slid another glass of alcohol in front of her.

An empty taxi slowed to a stop, and the driver tapped the horn. I felt like my legs were going to give out, so I caught the cab to the office. If everything went according to plan, Mr Na and I would soon be leaving for Bodeok Island. My stomach lurched like I was on a roller coaster right before the drop.

A shadow loomed over the window at the Happy Detective Agency. It must have been Mr Na. I couldn't head up to the office just yet, so I looked through my phone for Choi Joongi's number. Before it had even rung one full time, he picked up.

'It's me. Kim Jinseob.'

'I knew you'd call.'

It was a bizarre thing to say in reply. Even more bizarre was the fact that his usually dopey way of speaking had been replaced by this cold, articulate tone.

'My mum's gone on a trip,' I said, 'and I have to leave for a work trip, too. I'm sorry, but I think you should look into other places to stay for the next few days.'

'I'm actually leaving Seoul for a couple of days as well. Have a safe trip. Hopefully I'll see you again soon.'

With nothing more to say to each other, we both ended the call. I trudged up the stairs to the office. When I opened the door, Mr Na stood up. He was wearing a neat suit and holding a worn, brown leather pouch.

'What are you waiting for? Let's go,' he said.

Since I didn't have my driver's licence, Mr Na got behind the wheel. If Hyunsuk were still alive, that would have been his job. I sat in the passenger's seat and stroked the leather bag in my lap. My fingertips tingled at the thought of the three knives resting inside.

'Tell me about your mum,' said Mr Na.

The highway at night stretched on endlessly, scattering sparse and lonely bits of light.

'She's an ordinary mum,' I said. 'She's good at cooking, and she doesn't know how to lie. She's just a nice, easy-going, middle-aged lady.'

As I thought of my mum, my eyes suddenly stung with tears. I shut my mouth, worried that if I said another word, they would start to spill in earnest.

'I know a woman who was born with clubbed thumbs. She

would be around your mum's age now. Her thumbs were noticeably short and stubby. But she was so good with her hands, there was nothing she couldn't use them to do. She was especially good at cooking. Even with everyday ingredients like tofu and bean sprouts, she would season and stir-fry them until they were transformed into meals that could rival the food at a fancy restaurant's. But that woman – she was a liar.'

I had clubbed thumbs, too. It was a genetic condition. My mum and I both had strong grips, but our thumbs were a segment shorter than most people's. It made holding pencils or picking up small objects uncomfortable, but it also made it surprisingly easy to wield a knife. When I gripped a knife handle, my clubbed thumb held it firmly in place while shielding the other four fingers and preventing the knife from slipping. I spread my fingers out now and held them up in the intermittent light from the streetlamps we were driving past.

'What lies did she tell?' I asked.

The shadow of my stubby thumb fell over Mr Na's right cheek.

'If she'd been honest, I would be doing something completely different now. Maybe selling twisted doughnuts, or washing windows, or even preparing murdered corpses for funerals.'

One by one, I imagined Mr Na frying twisted doughnuts in a vat of bubbling oil, hanging from wires on the face of a building, stuffing cotton balls soaked in alcohol into a pale corpse's nostrils. None of the images seemed to suit him. Of course, in the last two months I'd been working at the Happy Detective Agency, I'd never seen Mr Na wielding a knife or chatting about his turbulent youth. But all the proof of a rocky past was plainly evident in the spiderweb of scars that remained on his body.

Still, I thought more than a doughnut maker, a window washer, or an undertaker, being a killer suited Mr Na the best.

Mr Na didn't say another word. He stopped twice to use the bathroom and quench his thirst at rest stops, but mostly he stared silently into the distance before taking hold of the steering wheel again. As I sat beside him, I applied several coats of clear nail polish to the skin of my fingertips. As it dried, it smoothed over the grooves of my fingerprints. Once we had passed through several provinces and cleared the toll gates, signs indicating the direction to Bodeok Island appeared. It was one of the small islands in the South Sea that had become a tourist attraction after a bridge connecting it to the mainland opened last spring. When we came to the bridge, crudely painted with local specialties like yuzu and abalone, the clock showed that it was just past eleven p.m. We had the car windows rolled up, but the smell of the sea still managed to seep in. As we went on, my heart pounded harder and a cold sweat began to run down my spine.

'The ajumma killer will probably be in disguise and keeping close to Park Taesang. Be on the lookout for a woman in her fifties with clubbed thumbs. Someone's heart has to stop beating tonight – either yours or his. That being said, don't expect any help from me. If the mission fails, the responsibility falls entirely on the killer. That's the rule of this world.'

The car pulled up in front of the Bodeok Youth Hostel, where we were staying. Even at this late hour, the yard was bustling with raucous drunk people. Mr Na got out of the car and opened the trunk. He took out two cases of soju and dried snacks.

'Starting now, you're an employee here with his boss who's

soon to open up a business in the shopping centre. You'll quietly hand out soju and snacks. Then, once people get drunk and disperse, you'll pick an appropriate time to get moving. With a little bit of skill, you'll be able to lure him somewhere close by.'

Mr Na handed me a case of soju. He ground his teeth and marched ahead towards the yard. At that moment, Mr Baek, who was holding a microphone, looked pleased to see him and came over to shake Mr Na's hand.

'Oh ho, you're here,' said Mr Baek. 'You must be tired, having come from so far away.'

He introduced Mr Na to a big, burly man next to him who was shaking a box of chopsticks and spoons to the rhythm.

'Nice to meet you, Chairman,' said Mr Na.

So the big man must have been Chairman Jung. Mr Na gave me a look, and I set down the soju and snacks on the long table and took an empty seat. An old woman who reeked of cigarettes sat next to me, emptied her glass in one shot, and offered me a drink.

'I haven't seen you around here before,' she said. 'Where are you from?'

I figured a drink might not be a bad way to ease the tension I was feeling, so I accepted the soju, turned to the side, and took a sip. The lukewarm, slightly sweet taste lingered unpleasantly on my tongue. The old woman watched me closely, dipping a piece of raw fish into a gochujang vinegar sauce and popping it in her mouth.

'I'm here with my boss. We're currently doing business elsewhere, but we're looking to open a store in the Ilshin Shopping Centre soon. I'll look forward to working with you in the future, ma'am.'

The old woman must have been in her seventies. She smiled at being called 'ma'am', and filled my empty glass again.

Chairman Jung grabbed the microphone and spoke loudly into it. 'Well, I think everyone who's coming has arrived, so can I make an announcement?'

Mr Na stood beside him, glaring over at a tent where a game of hwatu was underway. The tent was drooping such that it was hard to see the faces of any of the people inside, but judging by Mr Na's expression, they must have been from the Smile Detective Agency.

'Let's give a huge round of applause to Mr Baek for organizing today's event,' said Chairman Jung. He clapped while holding the microphone, the pounding sound ringing out through the speakers. Some people who had been nodding off looked up at the noise and started clapping half-heartedly.

Mr Baek gave the crowd a friendly smile.

'Union President Park, come on up here. Quickly, please,' Chairman Jung called out to a middle-aged man in the crowd. He smiled awkwardly and went to stand next to the chairman, bowing to greet the crowd.

'Everyone, life really feels like it's not worth living these days, doesn't it? I feel the same way. Stocks are crashing, the dollar is skyrocketing, and companies are going bankrupt left and right. How are small business owners like us meant to survive? The only thing that's kept us going until now is this co-op that's gone all out making and distributing flyers, designing apps to promote our businesses, and negotiating for bulk discounts to help us save on costs. The one light at the end of the tunnel is that by the end of next year, a huge apartment complex will be standing across from our Ilshin Shopping Centre. Union President Park here is leading the redevelopment association right across the way, and he's promised to work with Ilshin towards a shared vision here today. It's time to do away with the big discount marts and reclaim Ilshin's dominant place in the market. There's no doubt that the one who really hit the jackpot here is Mr Baek. He's basically striking gold, buying up stock at market price with a twenty per cent premium. But hey, isn't a win for him a win for everyone?'

Chairman Jung's face shone brightly as he smirked. Someone called out, 'Congrats!' Mr Baek's face paled and hardened in an instant. It seemed a twenty per cent premium was no small amount. Chairman Jung toyed with the karaoke machine and put on some up-tempo music, then began to move, swaying his big body as he danced with Union President Park.

The old woman, seeing that I hadn't finished my drink, took it and downed it herself, then lit another cigarette. She stood up and made her way over to the chairman, waving her arms excitedly. I stood up, too, and went towards the tent where the hwatu game was going on. There were three people gathered around the table inside. And in their hands weren't hwatu cards, but paper bills of Monopoly money.

'Mrs Shim, don't just put a building there. You should build a hotel. While you're the richest one of us all.'

A guy with a crew cut was shouting at the middle-aged woman across the table from him, her face obscured by a fan of fake cash.

'I like buildings better than hotels,' she said. 'There can be a butcher shop on the first floor, a hospital where my daughter

can work once she becomes a doctor on the second, and an apartment for my son and his future wife on the third. Who needs a thirty-storey building when three will do?'

I noticed that the woman's thumbs were quite stubby. She set her money down to place a building marker on the game board. It was at that moment that my heart stopped, then plummeted.

'Mum!'

Her messy hair was losing the curls from her perm showing her wrinkled neck with not even a plain gold necklace around it.

'You're late,' she said. 'Want to join in?'

Her face was calm, as if she were welcoming me home after work. Shocked as I was to see her, there was another familiar person sitting next to her, now shimmying aside to make room for me at the table.

'You know how to play, right?'

Choi Joongi.

'Why are you wearing white trainers on a day like today? The bloodstains don't come out easily,' Mum said, her eyes falling on the leather pouch that could be seen where my T-shirt had ridden up. As I flinched and took a step back, the middle-aged man sitting on the ground quietly stood up and approached me.

'It's our first time meeting, isn't it?' he said. 'I'm Park Tae-sang. I work with your mum.'

Mr Park offered me a handshake. Behind him, my mum was watching me with an expression that seemed torn between crying and laughing. While my hand was caught in Mr Park's rough grip, the three buildings that stood on the game board loomed coldly over the night that seemed like it would never end.

15

The Secret Agent

Right now in my handbag is a 38-calibre revolver. It's fast and precise, and much better than a knife at giving off that cool, killer vibe. I hadn't initially planned on bringing a gun. I finished washing the dishes from dinner and was doing my makeup when my husband who was supposed to be out all night stormed in.

'How come you're acting all suspicious?' he said.

I shouldn't have changed the front door lock to a digital one. My husband, whose only way of showing affection was meddling, wiped his oily forehead with his hand and stood in the entryway.

'If someone comes in, shouldn't they make a sound?'

I'd been too relaxed thinking he wouldn't be home any time soon.

'So now you're saying I can't come into my own house? I was in the area, and it was so humid out that I wanted to stop by and change my socks, all right? But where are you going in the middle of the night all dressed up?'

Even if I left right then, it would be hard to get there by midnight.

'To pay respects to my friend's mum,' I said curtly.

'Hm – I smell a rat. In what world would somebody show up to mourn with a face caked in makeup?'

Such were the sorrows of a killer living with a detective. My husband slowly circled me, eyeing me with suspicion as his finger tapped his chin.

'Aigo, my stomach. Why now of all times? Look, don't go anywhere until I finish what I need to do. We'll talk when I get back.'

It was the first time in our marriage that I'd been grateful for his IBS. My husband took his gun out of its holster and set it down on the table, then rushed to the bathroom clutching his belly. I had an opportunity that would never come again. I put down my lipstick and tiptoed over to the table. Then I stashed the 38-calibre revolver, a necessity for a killer, in my bag and raced out the door as fast as I could.

I felt a little sorry for my husband, who would finish his business and come out to find his gun and his wife missing. But I couldn't disappoint my first client. And I had already bought a bunch of cryptocurrency with the thirty million won deposit, so I couldn't back out now.

Who said Shim Eunok was the only ajumma killer in the world? Now that I had entered the field, it was time to hand in my resignation from my old role as a civil servant's wife. But there was one thing weighing on me. The person that cheating woman Hong Misook wanted me to kill was Na Hancheol, the CEO of the Happy Detective Agency. Not an easy target. But there was no need to be afraid. Now I had a gun.

It was well past midnight when I arrived at the youth hostel where we were staying, and it seemed the merrymaking was over, an eerie darkness and the sour-sweet smell of alcohol lingering in the yard. Of the building's many windows, the light was on in only one. I tiptoed inside, trying to mask the sound of my footsteps. But I couldn't tell where Na Hancheol would be sleeping just from looking at the doors. I took the gun out of my bag, checked that it was loaded, and put my finger on the trigger. Loud snores rang out through the halls.

'Ms Lee?'

Someone reached out and grabbed my shoulder in the dark.

'Oh my god, Joongi!'

He looked back and forth between me and the gun, then held his finger to his lips and took my wrist, swiftly leading me towards a room where light was seeping out on to the hallway floor. It hadn't even begun in earnest, yet my mission was somehow already failing.

'Joongi, can you pretend you didn't see me? I'll get going soon. Just, um, let go of me, please . . .'

I tried to pull back, but Joongi's hand, wrapped tight around my wrist like a vine, didn't budge. He opened the door to the room. And in that moment, I had a feeling. That it was time to use the gun.

16

The Confidant

Once all the Smile Detective Agency employees had left the office for the day, it was just me and Mr Park. He closed the poetry collection he had been reading earlier, got up, and walked over to the sofa where I sat waiting. I couldn't help but notice his increasingly narrow shoulders and the faint stains on his dress shirt.

Mr Park sat on the sofa, his back ramrod straight. 'Can I see it now?' he said, holding out his hand.

'See what?' I said.

'The letter. I think it's time you kept your promise.'

The letter – how could I have forgotten about that until now? The first time I met Mr Park, I promised that if he helped me find my mum, I would give him the letter I had found in storage at the motel that used to be a sashimi centre.

Of course, that had been a lie.

'Now isn't the time to talk about the letter,' I said, my voice rising awkwardly. 'Sir, your life is in danger!'

'True. If what you told me is correct, Mrs Shim's son was hired by the Happy Detective Agency, and I'm his first target. Mrs Shim figured it out and tried to take on the job in her son's place, but you caught on to her. So your solution is for us to strike first and take out Na Hancheol. But . . . I don't agree with your plan. I'm not interested in that. After all, no matter how hard we try to fight it, we can only live according to our pre-determined fate. Right now, what matters to me is that letter.'

His voice was as cold and sharp as an ice pick.

'No,' I said. 'Please, just listen to me this once. Why on earth would you choose to die?'

'Give me the letter.'

'I don't have it. I think I lost it.'

'There was never any letter, was there?' Mr Park's voice was suddenly gentle. Comforting. He put his arms behind his head and leaned back. 'You kept it a secret for so long.'

'How did you know?'

The storefront sign on the karaoke bar across the street was flickering, casting faint letters on Mr Park's forehead.

'She wouldn't have left something like a letter,' he said.

It was the first time I'd ever heard him talk about women. It felt almost wrong for me to hear this.

'Some time ago, I saw her on TV. She moved to Greece and opened up a raw seafood restaurant. It looked fancy on the outside, but inside it was just like one of the raw fish restaurants you'd find here in Korea, where the locals dipped raw fish into a gochujang and vinegar sauce and ate it. At the end of the segment, she expertly scooped up a piece of raw mackerel and fed it to her Greek husband, giving him a big thumbs up. By the end of that programme, I decided to finally let her go. Honestly, I had been holding on to this vague idea that she was somewhere wasting her life away, tormented by guilt. But my illusions were shattered by what I saw. She looked so happy, living in a world I would never be able to reach no matter how hard I tried. I thought maybe it was time for me to lower the shutters on the Smile Detective Agency, too.'

Mr Park stood up. The cushion where the imprint of his body lingered slowly returned to its original shape.

'I'm sorry for lying,' I said. 'But . . .'

Mr Park looked at me from where he stood putting on his jacket.

'But I don't want you to die, sir. Where am I supposed to go now?'

Mr Park smiled. 'Who's going to die?' he said. 'I'm saying that the Smile Detective Agency will close down. And then *you* will have to take your GED exam, you little brat.'

He straightened out the jacket over his shoulders, then opened his desk drawer and took something out, which he tossed to me.

'Enrol in a GED prep class,' he said. 'When you go to college, until you graduate, you won't have to worry about tuition. Oh, and that's an empty bank book. I've already sent money to your mum, so you should go back home.'

Mr Park took out something else and quickly shoved it inside my briefcase.

'You don't need to come visit me for every holiday, so just focus on living without getting into any trouble. Let's say our goodbyes here.'

He held out his hand for me to shake.

'This is a violation of employment law,' I said. 'Do you know that? You're a fraud, an outright fraud!'

I swatted away his hand and ran out of the office. I ran for a while, and once I was far from the intersection with the ginkgo trees, my shoulders started shaking. Not because I was out of breath, but because I was crying – tears of complete and utter joy.

17

The Boss

Despite what I'd asked of him, Joongi showed up at the youth hostel late at night. Looking angry, he opened up the Monopoly board on the table inside the tent.

'At first glance, this may look like a game where the winner is decided by a dice roll, but in fact, it's a game of wits that can't be won no matter how lucky you are, if you don't have a careful strategy and tactics,' he said.

With that explanation, we started the game. But I was clinging to luck without any strategy, and sure enough, my debts were growing and I couldn't avoid going bankrupt. Mrs Shim and Jinseob sat next to each other, their eyes bloodshot. At some point, the people gathered in the yard outside all succumbed to their drunkenness and retired to their rooms for the night. Only us three and Jinseob, plus Na Hancheol who had been standing some way off with his arms crossed, remained.

'Mr Na. It's been a while,' I said, setting down the last of my bills of fake money and standing to greet him. He walked towards me. His hand was cold.

Long, long ago, I had put down my knife after leaving a huge stain as a killer. I'd stabbed an old man, nothing but skin and bones, in the back, all at the behest of a man who had paid me to kill his stepfather. It turned out the old man was in fact his biological father. By the time Na Hancheol could tell me the truth, the old man was already buried in that flowerbed. Hancheol was the only one who had ever directly witnessed the true nature of the elusive killer Park Taesang. If he hadn't shown up that day, I would still be somewhere brandishing my knife, wandering around in the darkness. We'd met as enemies today, but at one time, we'd been comrades.

'I got your call,' Hancheol said. 'Thank you for taking care of Hyunsuk.'

He must have been talking about Park Hyunsuk, who had also once been a killer.

By now, he must have gone back to his hometown and started training in coating technologies. The person burned to ashes in his car was the loan shark who'd been trapped in his trunk. I took Hyunsuk in my car and dropped him off at the intercity bus terminal. His wound wasn't too deep, so the bleeding had stopped by the time we got there. He came back from the ticket booth, snapped his own ID card in two and replaced it with the dead man's.

We all gathered in the room at the end of the hallway that had been assigned to the Smile Detective Agency. Blankets and pillows were piled up haphazardly, and the four of us silently watched each other's movements instead of the twenty-inch colour TV. Joongi went out into the hall and scoped out the surroundings, while Mrs Shim and I stood inside the room, face to face with Na Hancheol and Jinseob.

'Let's get down to business,' said Hancheol. He loosened the necktie that had been nearly choking him and stepped towards Mrs Shim.

'Hancheol, why are you doing this to us?' she asked.

It seemed like they were old friends.

'Were you happy with Dalho?' Hancheol replied. 'You must have been, since you chose him. Because you didn't want to marry a gangster and grow old in prison.'

Jinseob looked back and forth between them, seeming puzzled.

'Is that why you put a knife in the hands of a child with a bright future?' Mrs Shim asked, her voice wavering ever so slightly.

'He made the choice himself.'

'Am I supposed to believe you?' Mrs Shim snapped, lifting her skirt. She pulled out her knife, and lunged at Na Hancheol in a rage. Jinseob, not able to stand by and watch his mother murder someone, rushed towards me and pressed his own knife to my neck. The cold sensation ran through my body like electricity. I felt the same fear everyone who had died by my knife must have felt. But I quickly realized something. That the knife Jinseob was holding was a crudely made prop dagger. Perhaps even he wasn't aware of that. Right now, Hancheol was risking his own life to drag Mrs Shim out of this hell. Our goals were one and the same.

Mrs Shim's knife was a run-of-the-mill cast iron kitchen knife.

But because she sharpened and polished it every morning, the blade was razor-edged. The knife she was unsheathing now wasn't her usual one but an old, rusted knife that had pierced through the lungs of an old man murdered by his son a long time ago. Mrs Shim, realizing that the knife she was aiming at Na Hancheol's chest was an unfamiliar one, looked between the rusty blade and me in pure confusion.

18

Shim Eunok

J inseob pulled out his knife and pointed it below Mr Park's Adam's apple.

'Mum!' he shouted, his face crumpled with pain. 'Put the knife down! Please.'

His hands and lips had gone deathly pale with fear. But I couldn't do what my son had asked of me. If I backed down now, Jinseob's dreams would be shattered. As Na Hancheol shot a fierce look at Jinseob, I lifted my skirt and grabbed the cold knife at my waist.

But the knife I pulled out wasn't the kitchen knife I always used. I was holding instead an unfamiliar knife whose edges were chipped and whose blade was stained red with rust. This knife had the same Chinese character 吳 engraved on the handle as the blade Mr Park had given me. I aimed the strange weapon at Na Hancheol's chest. And as if it had been waiting for that moment, the knife broke and fell to the floor in pieces.

19

The Secret Agent

The two groups, not noticing that Joongi and I had opened the door, were glaring at each other in some sort of heated standoff. Mrs Shim was rushing towards the man in the photograph Hong Misook had given me, with a knife she'd pulled from her waist, and a tall, handsome young man had another knife aimed at Mr Park's throat. Just then, the knife in Mrs Shim's hands broke in two and fell to the floor.

'Mum!' the young man cried out.

Mum? Then was he Mrs Shim's son? Oh, well – that didn't matter. I had one target and one target only. Na Hancheol looked like he couldn't hide his bafflement as he bent over, as though reaching to pick up the broken pieces of the knife. I rushed towards him, then pulled the trigger. And again. *Bang! Bang!*

The two bullets rang out, and I staggered back from the recoil, falling into Joongi's arms. My ears were ringing, and I couldn't hear a thing. Not a shrill scream, nor the sound of heavy breathing as someone uttered their last words like in a movie scene. Once the bullets left the gun, I slowly opened my eyes.

Na Hancheol was hunched over on the floor. His eyes were wide, and he was clutching his right side, but I didn't see any blood. Mrs Shim pushed his hands away and searched for where the bullet might have gone in.

'Both shots were blanks. That must be a police officer's gun.'

Mr Park cautiously approached Na Hancheol and helped him up. Joongi snatched the gun out of my hand. Even though they were blanks, the sound of the gunshots must have woken up the people sleeping in the hostel. I could hear slippered feet shuffling towards us. If the first two rounds were blanks, though, that meant the third round had to be a real bullet. I shook Joongi off me and removed the safety on the gun.

20

The Client

I believe in the power of steel. Guns, knives, and money never betrayed a person. Since I had plenty of money, it wasn't hard for me to buy plenty of guns and knives. If you really think about it, money is more powerful than a gun or a knife. If Chairman Jung were to be taken down, even more money would come my way, and with that money I could buy more guns and more knives. To make that happen, I needed a sure investment.

Park Taesang and Na Hancheol were just the people for that. They were similar, yet very different. If Park was a tormented dreamer, then Na was a calculating realist. Park handled things dramatically, according to his instincts, while Na wasn't satisfied unless things went off without veering even an inch of the mark, like he'd measured everything out with a ruler.

That was why I'd hired them both.

Chairman Jung, who had come to Seoul with nothing but a grain of rice on his lip, had built himself and his fortune up from nothing and was meticulous in everything he did. He never acted alone and relied on money and sweet talk to get people on his side who could be his human shields. Even when I offered him cake boxes stuffed with cash, they were always returned by his aides. And when I asked why, I always heard some nonsense about how Chairman Jung had high cholesterol. Thinking that the amount of money maybe wasn't large enough, I sent two boxes, but as always, they were returned to me in the end. And today, I realized why he was constantly sending them back. There was a hidden set of calculations happening – he couldn't hand over the Ilshin Shopping Centre, which was soon to be part of a huge redevelopment project and turned into a gold mine, for mere pennies just to fill someone else's stomach.

Now, the only question that remained was whether the dreamer or the realist would be the one to sink a knife into the chairman's grease-lined belly. But it was deep into the night, past midnight, and Jung's shields must have been fast asleep because the hostel was quiet. The chairman had been snoring in the next room over for an hour straight. If that snoring didn't stop in the next five minutes, I was going to fire both the dreamer and the realist. It seemed better to start over at square one and propose a partnership instead. Just then, I heard a loud noise in the hallway. But even after that, Chairman Jung's snoring didn't let up.

I put on my slippers and left my room, hurrying towards the room at the end of the hallway where the Smile Detective Agency folks were staying. Noise was stirring inside the once quiet hostel, and an employee in a tracksuit was belatedly running down the stairs. One of the Smile employees stood outside the room, and next to him was a chubby woman in a tight-fitting dress. The woman pushed the young man away, and that was when I saw that she had a gun in her hand. And inside the room were Park Taesang and Na Hancheol, a fat lady who must have been the ajumma killer, and the young guy that Hancheol had brought along, all of them looking drained in the face. Seeing as no one was bleeding, it seemed like the gun was a fake.

I felt a rage begin to grow inside me. What an idiot I was to entrust the task to these fools. From then on, both of them were fired. I snatched the fake gun from the woman's hand.

'You fucking idiots!' I shouted, pulling the trigger as I aimed at the ajumma killer, who was so fat that a BB gun pellet was sure to bounce right off her fleshy folds. *Bang!*

The fake gun was pretty heavy for something that only fired pellets.

'Oh my god!' someone screamed.

Blood was spreading out under the ajumma killer's chest.

'Mr Baek shot someone! Police! Call the police!'

Someone who had run outside in their nightclothes started shrieking.

'The police are already here,' said a voice.

A man with broad shoulders pushed his way through the onlookers, snatched the gun from me, and snapped handcuffs around my wrists.

'Honey!'

The woman in the tight dress ran over to the man and fell into his arms.

'You make me crazy and crazy happy, woman, I swear. You didn't know I put a tracking app on your phone?'

Meanwhile, I didn't understand how a fake bullet from a fake gun could harm anyone.

'Ma'am, get a grip. This is a fake gun. Why are you causing such a scene?'

The woman didn't answer. Na Hancheol clenched his jaw and hoisted the ajumma killer on to his back.

'If anything happens to her, I'm not going to let it slide!' shouted the young man next to Hancheol. I could hear ambulance sirens in the distance.

'Is that little punk who's still wet behind the ears threatening me? Can't you see? The lady's putting on an act!'

Two paramedics came rushing in, carrying a stretcher.

'Hey, listen,' said the ajumma killer in a quiet voice, some of the life in her eyes already beginning to dull. 'How can you speak that way to someone else's son? Cut it out.'

She was lowered from Hancheol's back on to the stretcher, and I could now hear the police sirens loud and clear.

'You've been caught in the act. You're under arrest.'

I was shoved out towards the yard. Two guys with sharp gazes got out of a police car and firmly saluted the one walking me out.

'I haven't done anything wrong,' I said. 'Park Taesang! Na Hancheol! Say something! You fucking pricks. You knew this would happen, didn't you?'

I was put in the back of the police car. If I exposed Park's and Na's identities now, I would only be charged with conspiracy to commit murder on top of everything else. This was truly pissing me off.

'Hey, let me go! Don't you know who I am, you crazy sons of bitches?'

The man who'd handcuffed me sat down. 'Who you are? Well, you're a gun snatcher, of course! And if you're not careful,

I could have you charged with murder, too. The lady you shot just now is in critical condition.'

From afar, Chairman Jung had stopped snoring and woken up. He looked at me in the handcuffs, his cheeks twitching in spasms as he smiled.

21

The Rival

My wife handed me the divorce papers. Her bulging belly rose and fell slowly with each breath she took. I opened my always-locked drawer and took out my name seal. Inside the drawer was a photo of a younger Shim Eunok smiling shyly.

My wife laughed for the first time in a while. Seeing her laugh made me a little bit happier, too.

22

The Secret Agent

My husband, who hadn't come home in the two days since we'd gotten back from Bodeok Island, came home last night drunk and passed out on the bed. He slept for twenty-four hours. His face looked unfamiliar, covered in scruff. I packed my bags rather simply. If he told me to leave, I would leave, and if he told me to stay, I would stay.

My husband woke up looking pinched and asked me to make him some dried pollack soup. He could have asked me anything else, but he was silent the whole time, lifting the spoon to his lips again and again. He didn't even look at the rice on the side, just kept gulping down the broth until he emptied his bowl. Then he downed two glasses of cold water in quick succession.

'I quit,' he said. 'What good's a police officer who can't even keep track of a gun? Should we open up a hangover soup restaurant? You make a good hangover soup, did you know that?'

My husband let out a long belch, then winked at me.

'Ay, knock it off,' I said. 'What're you talking about, a hangover soup restaurant? You're so tacky.'

MRS SHIM IS A KILLER

'Whoa. Been a long time since I heard your accent come out. It's so sexy.'

He tossed down his spoon and scooped me around the waist. I could feel his scratchy beard through the thin fabric of my T-shirt as it tickled my belly. I couldn't stop laughing.

351

23

The Daughter

These days, I still have tutoring sessions. The only difference is that I'm not the one being tutored – I'm doing the tutoring.

'Mr Choi, how many times do I have to explain this to you? Didn't you learn functions in middle school?'

I still called him Mr Choi even though he was my student, and he still called me by my name even though I was technically his teacher.

'Kim Jina,' he said. 'Is going to Seoul National University everything? Quit acting like a know-it-all.'

He looked grumpy, but underneath the desk, his fingertips were lightly brushing the back of my hand.

'It's so hot. Why don't you leave the door open?'

My mum suddenly burst into my room. She was home after getting a perm at the beauty salon. The Chuseok holiday was the next day – what did she mean, it was hot? Mr Choi quickly brought his hand up and grabbed hold of a pen. It was upside down.

'Mrs Shim, don't worry about Jina. You just focus on your work.'

He was the only one who didn't know that it wasn't *me* that Mum was worried about, but *him*.

'Of course. I believe in you, Joongi. You'll pass the GED exam this time for sure. Good luck!' my mum said, but all the while she eyed him suspiciously and kept glancing around the room.

Last summer, Mum didn't come home for two months. No one would give me a clear answer as to why. But as I watched my brother make anxious phone calls to someone, I started to worry that Mum might never come home. Then, exactly two months later, she returned, supported by a middle-aged man with a crew cut and a solid build. I couldn't be sure that this was the same man I'd seen drop Mum off that night, but I decided not to ask. Because just the fact that my mum and my brother made it home safe and sound made me happy. Like I had everything I needed in the world.

Mum opened up a butcher shop with the crew cut guy at the intersection with the ginkgo trees. Outside the shop, which didn't even have a storefront sign yet, some helpers that Mr Choi had found somewhere were dancing and handing out flyers. The already cramped butcher shop had a ceremonial table set up and several flower wreaths inside, which left hardly any room for customers to enter.

'Mum, the Ilshin Shopping Centre Co-op sent a huge wreath. This one is from the Happy Detective Agency, and this one is from the Kim Sangho Marriage Research Institute. Geez, why are there so many?'

Mum was deftly sharpening her knife on a whetstone. Beside

her, the crew cut guy was chopping red meat into tiny bite-sized pieces.

'Ma'am, your sign is here.'

A man in a work uniform squeezed inside between the wreaths. Mum and the crew cut guy stopped what they were doing and rushed out to see it.

The sign was like my mum. It was new, but it didn't glitter or glow. It was just an ordinary, plain design.

'Smile Butchery. It's a nice name.'

A worker on a ladder shielded his eyes from the sun as he looked down at Mum and smiled. Mum's laugh lines crinkled as she smiled, too.

'It'd be a shame not to take a commemorative photo on a day

like this, wouldn't it?' Mr Choi said, taking out his phone and opening the camera app. 'Look over here!'

Mum and the crew cut guy stood in front of the still-crooked sign.

'OK, I'm taking it now. Smile!'

The two knife masters smiled brightly, showing their teeth.

Even after the camera was gone and the workers had left, they continued smiling, looking off into the distance. I turned my head to follow their gazes.

A man dressed for the totally wrong season in a Hawaiian shirt and sunglasses was watching Mum from across the street. He had a huge suitcase with him, like someone leaving for a long vacation. He turned to go and slowly made his way down the alleyway. His steps were light, as if the blue Mediterranean Sea itself was waiting for him at the end of the road.

Kang Jiyoung is an established Korean writer based in Paju, near Seoul. She is the author of the story collections *Goodbye Paradise*, *Time for Dogs to Eat* and *The Killer's Shopping List*. Her novels include *Quarantine Station of New Culture*, *Elza's Ha-yin*, *Circus in the Dark Forest*, *Frankenstein Family*, *Yawning is Delicious*, *Pheromone Boutique* and *The Shop for Killers*. *The Shop for Killers* was adapted for television by Disney+ and was aired globally in January 2024. *Mrs Shim Is a Killer* will be published in over twenty languages worldwide.

Paige Morris is a writer and translator from Jersey City, New Jersey, who divides her time between South Korea and the United States. She has translated fiction by Hyun-joo Park, Ji-min Lee, Soyeon Jeong, and many more. She would probably make an awful killer as she is painfully clumsy and terrible with knives.